UNSEEN EVIL

Social Media can be the death of you ...

DI Gus McGuire Book 6

BY

LIZ MISTRY

First Published in 2019

By MB Publications

PUBLICATIONS

Copyright © Liz Mistry

Print ISBN: 978- 1- 9161835-1-3

DEDICATION

For Nilesh, Ravi, Kasi, and Jimi,
as always you have my back and I love you!

DI GUS MCGUIRE BOOKS

Unquiet Souls
Uncoiled Lies
Untainted Blood
Uncommon Cruelty
Unspoken Truths

DS NIKKI PAREKH BOOKS

Last Request
Broken Silence

Praise for Liz Mistry

'I have great admiration for Mistry's skill,
this is one of the best crime thrillers I've read
in ages.'

'Absolutely fantastic read.'
'Simply unputdownable.'
'Devoured in two days.'

PROLOGUE

March 2018
The Zodiac Club

We had to have a headquarters. Somewhere we could meet. Somewhere we wouldn't be seen and just by luck, while I was exploring, I found it. An old grocer's store on a side road. No *For Sale* sign, no indication anyone was interested in it… Nothing. It was easy to get in.

The front of the property faced a busy side street, but the windows were covered by a metal shutter with *Bradford City* spray painted on in black. Some smart-ass had crossed out the 'C' of City with a black marker and replaced it with a 'T'. How droll. I knew there was no way in from the front, so I wandered around the back. It looked promising, so I waited until dark and came back. Sure enough, the back of the shop had an enclosed yard with a sturdy door which was hanging off its hinges. But, more importantly, the properties behind it were also lying empty… apart from the druggies and tramps that occupied them by night. It was easy to get the gate fixed and I knew just the person to help me. A sturdy lock and we were sorted. Our own private space.

I love it. It's well enough out of the way as to be discreet, but not too far out of the way as to be difficult to get to. The headquarters we call it… HQ. Nobody sees us coming and going because we're invisible. Today's important. Today is the day we extend our manifesto… make more plans… finalise things.

'Neck it! Neck it! Neck it!'

Their chants are like hooligans at a football match as they loll about on the carpet, sprawled over the cushions, intent on getting pissed. Leo, dark eyes all sparkly, cheeks

1

flushed, hands clapping in time with the chants, is the most drunk. Pisces is a little less so... nervous, maybe? Picking those oozing pussy spots and licking cracked lips – yuk, enough to make me want to barf, but I cover it up... for now. Instead, I move my phone, taking in our handiwork... all this will go down in history... saved for posterity. I smile a little. I remember when I used to muddle that word with posterior... but that was a long time ago.

The items pinned to the wall document the progress we've made. A timeline of charts, newspaper clippings, photos... Each one evidence. Each one a piece of the plan. Ambling round the room I zoom in on my favourites.

First there's the list:

~~Sumaira Begum~~
~~Shannon Oyando~~
~~Billy Clark-Thompson~~
~~Becky Easton~~
~~Imran Sajid~~
~~Suki Singh~~

It's so satisfying to see them all crossed out. Next there's the first lot of evidence... the photos. Sumaira Begum, when she found the bacon in her locker... that was brilliant. She was hysterical... crying and yelling as if someone was stuffing the rasher down her throat. It served her right telling Ms Copley about me smoking in the girls' toilets. The one of Shannon Oyando with her tits out – 'cept they weren't really hers – we'd photoshopped over hers, printed them out, and stuck them up in the lads' toilets.

The other two are still necking the voddie... Leo's really flushed now and Pisces, all bleeding pox and nervous eyes, is getting there too. I'll call the meeting to order in a bit, but for now, I record the last few items… the newspaper clippings… Fame! I love the way we've moved on… the way we've developed. Progress… you can't whack it.

November 2017

Local Teacher Convicted of Grooming Students

Craig Borthwick, a teacher at a local secondary school, pictured here entering court, today received a ten-year sentence after images showing him booking into a low budget hotel with a fourteen-year-old student were anonymously uploaded to the Internet.

We did that! We made that happen. That snooty little bitch got what she deserved when that picture of her snogging Mr Borthwick went viral. That taught her. The way she dumped Leo, like a sack of hot potatoes, all the time on her phone sexting that dirty old perv. Served her right… served him right too.

January 2018

An unnamed Bradford teenager has been found dead in his bedroom in a suspected suicide. The fifteen-year-old's parents claim their son was being

> bullied on social media... a police investigation is ongoing.

Stupid bloody Billy Clark-Tosser. Couldn't take it. *Facebook* shut his page down... it was so funny. We all got the dick pics I sent from his *Facebook* page. That taught him to make sure he'd logged out... couldn't believe that he did that though... topped himself... what sort of sick shit is that?

I end the recording and flop down on the cushions between the other two and grab the bottle. No point in letting them get too rat arsed. This is our tenth meeting and today's the day we'll up the stakes. Right at the start, I gave us all code names. I'm Zodiac, of course. The Zodiac Killer, one of the world's most famous killers, but, more importantly, one of the few who has never been identified. I chose well.

Then there's Leo after Nathan Leopold Jr. Poor little rich kid, working as a team with his mate and thinking he could escape justice... how did that work out, Leo? My Leo doesn't have the same mental capacity but, well, beggars can't be choosers. I admit I had to push it a bit with Pisces, but I got there in the end. Pisces equals fish; Albert Fish, a cannibal and grotesque serial killer. My Pisces doesn't carry the same panache, but again, it's only a name. It makes me laugh that they don't get it, though, the joke's on them... just like I planned. The joke will always be on them.

I look at them and wait. That's my strategy... let one of them take the lead for now. If either opens up the subject, it'll be easier. They don't get it... neither of them. That's why I chose these two... gormless... impressionable... the exact opposite from me because I do want to make an impression.

Pisces keeps looking at the floor, head bowed, leg jittering. I wish the idea of a shower was higher on Pisces' list of priorities... that's why the other kids are always teasing and taunting the dirty git. No one likes smelly kids with crappy clothes. I sidle a little further away, don't want to catch anything, do I?

The game was the easiest sell I had to make. Who doesn't love a game, after all? The beauty of it is... it wasn't my idea... or was it? Who knows? Will we ever know?

All I'm saying, is that planting seeds is the easiest part, nurturing them? Now that's hard. I want to press my fingernails into Pisces' knee. Make the jittering stop. It's getting on my nerves big time. I want to yell, '*I've arranged everything, brought all the equipment, taken all the risks. What more do you want?*'

But, I don't. I need to make this work. I need to play one of my blinders... one of my aces. Gotta keep the minions on-board... keep them in line. An image of that stupid game my mum used to watch springs to mind... *The Weakest Link*. No points for guessing who's the weakest link here. Not rocket science, is it?

I remember how it was when we upped the stakes last time and I take a sip of the vodka. Not enough to get me pissed, just enough to smooth my edges... and I remember.

We sat down, the three of us. We were all excited, but I kept my excitement hidden as I handed the envelopes to Leo. We'd played the game before, but this time it was going to be different. This time we were moving up a level... Only they didn't know it yet. 'Lay them out.'

Leo took a last swig of the fizzy plonk and handed the dregs to me. I passed it to Pisces. They'd already downed one bottle and were at that giddy phase where they'd do anything. I just needed to sow the seeds and let them take it from there. 'You finish it. I've had loads already.'

As Pisces downed the last mouthful, Leo made a big show of shuffling the envelopes before laying them in a circle with just a little space between each one.

Arms spread, Leo grinned, all lopsided and stupid. 'Ta dah'… and promptly burped, which of course set the two of them off giggling again. Give me strength!

There were five tonight. Five names… They'd chosen them, not me, but they didn't get that. They were so willing to let things blur.

'Leeeeet's get this party started.' Pisces sang out of tune and out of rhythm… Story of their lives really… and placed the empty bottle in the middle of the circle.

'Go on then, Leo. Your turn to spin.' Pisces leant forward, legs crossed, keen to discover who it would be.

Leo looked to me as if asking permission and I nodded. 'Go on, your turn. Make it a good one.'

Pisces, clearly three too many, started to chant, 'Spin it! Spin it! Spin it!'

The bottle spun and ended up dead between two envelopes. 'Oh, let me do it again. I didn't spin it hard enough.'

Again, with the, 'Spin it! Spin it! Spin it!'

Didn't matter to me how many times they spun it as long as, by the end of it, we had a name… and we did.

Still grinning, I look at them. Leo's buzzing, but Pisces looks all pukey and scared.

'Don't think we should do this anymore.' Pisces picks at the craters again, leg going nineteen to the dozen.

For fuck's sake! Time for a little brain mess!

'*You* came up with this idea. *You* told us how much you needed to do this. It was your idea… surely you don't regret it, do you? I mean you got what you wanted. Remember you wrote it down. You spun the bottle and it landed right there... *you* chose it. You made all the arrangements; all we did was be your friends...' I don't look at either of them. Keep my head angled down at the floor, don't want them to see the rage. I need to play this tight.

'Wasn't my idea... it wasn't!'

I look up, straight at Pisces. 'Well it sure as hell wasn't mine or Leo's. You wanted to punish them. You said so. That right, Leo?'

Always up for a bit of bullying, Leo grins. 'Yip. You can't wiggle out of it now.'

I love the way Pisces' head jerks back, like Leo's landed a punch or something. 'Didn't want him to die though.'

I snort. 'Yeah right, after all he did to you? Billy was a knob. And he was always picking on you.'

Leo chips in, 'Yeah, Pisces, he was. Billy was a dick to you... and to everyone else too.'

Still with the picking, slender fingers, scraping over little smears of blood, linking up the spots like a kid's dot to dot.

'What if someone else dies? What if it happens again?'

Leo glances at me, wanting to curry favour, be my bestie and in a gruff, *I'm the big I am* voice says, 'Well, maybe that's what will happen. They deserve it. Look at the names. Think what they've done to us.'

And simple as that, we're sorted... the stakes are raised... Game on!

CHAPTER 1

SUMMER 2018
SUNDAY

Gus rolled onto his back and stretched, enjoying the release of tension throughout his body. One of the many bonuses of being in a steady relationship was making love to the accompaniment of tweeting birds as the sun rose, followed by the prospect of a mug of fresh coffee… and time with Patti. Despite the early hour, the oppressive heat of the last few weeks was almost overwhelming. Even with the windows open, not a single breath of air wafted the curtains. The fan, whirring at the bottom of the bed, was the only reprieve from the blanket of heat that pressed down on him. Sprawled in bed, a thin cotton sheet pulled up to his waist and with the smell of their lovemaking still in the air, Gus' body tingled with a soft post-coital glow.

Through the open bedroom door, the sounds of her pottering about downstairs, talking to Bingo, and singing along to the radio made him smile. Patti was the worst singer imaginable – completely tone deaf, yet she was addicted to Karaoke. Gus loved watching her as she belted out classics like, 'I Will Survive', with more enthusiasm than skill. The contrast with her normal reserved, dependable, head teacher image was only one of the many things he was growing to love about her. *Hell, there it was; the 'L' word.* He expelled a long low breath. *Why would someone like her want to be with someone like me?* Gus did what he always did and shoved it away, ignoring the persistent thought that if Alice were around, she'd tell him to grow a pair and tell Patti how he felt, but he wasn't ready for that… not yet.

Positioning a pillow more comfortably behind his back, he sighed. He missed his detective sergeant's sass, her irreverent, bouncy, say-it-as-it-is attitude and, deep down, he acknowledged that the Alice he once knew, may be gone forever. Last time he'd seen her she'd looked...decimated... yep, that was the best way to describe her... decimated and damaged, but what had been worse was the emptiness in her eyes – as if all her vitality had been stripped from her soul, leaving a black hole in its place. With an effort he pushed the maudlin thoughts from his mind; those were best explored from the safety of his psychiatrist's couch.

The smell of freshly brewed coffee drifted upstairs accompanied by another aroma – croissants? Freshly warmed-up croissants? *Oh my God! How much more indulgence could one man take on his day off?* A whirlwind of white fur tornadoed through the door and dived onto the bed, all wagging tail and excited yelps, landing just south of Gus' groin. As he moved Bingo to a less dangerous position, Patti, wearing one of his old T-shirts, walked in, carrying a tray. Heading straight for Gus, she held it under his nose, just long enough for him to snatch a croissant and with a mischievous grin on her face she said, 'Miss me?'

Gus snorted through a mouthful of croissant. 'Didn't miss your singing. Could hear it all the way up the damn stairs. Surprised the windows are still intact. Justin Bieber would kill you if he heard the way you murdered that.'

Patti laughed. 'You're just jealous... and it wasn't bloody Bieber anyway, it was Paloma Faith's 'Make Your Own Kind of Music'.'

'Yeah, Patti, *music* being the operative word not a bloody racket.'

Putting the tray down next to the bed, she poked her elbow into his side. 'Cheeky.' She turned to the puppy, running her fingers through his fur, making his small body quiver in delight. 'Mummy's a good singer, isn't she, Bingo?'

Seemingly delighted with the attention, Bingo licked her face with the same enthusiasm he normally reserved for Gus' mum, which gave Gus *just* enough time to recover from the 'Mummy' reference. The implication that he and Patti were Bingo's parents made them seem like a family and Gus didn't know what to do with that idea. Somehow it gave him hope but, after Gabriella and then Sadia, he'd learned to be cautious.

He pulled Bingo away from her. 'Hmph, what's a man to do to get some coffee around here? Lick your face?'

Patti punched him none too lightly on the arm. 'Watch it! You're lucky I made breakfast in this heat, and, just so you know, any man worth his salt would be standing by the headboard wafting a massive fan over their lady love, not making unnecessary demands.' She turned and picked up something from the tray. 'Oh, nearly forgot, this was on the mat downstairs. Love letter?'

Gus looked at the envelope in her hand and some of the magic of the morning dissipated immediately. The letter looked identical to the others; same blue envelope, similar size, no postmark this time though. He'd thought… hoped, he'd seen the last of them. There had been four letters in all, starting soon after the Izzie Dimou murder earlier in the year, but none for a month. After the second one, he'd found himself at odd moments looking into the shadows for signs of being watched. Don't say they've started up again? A coil of unease formed in his stomach, spreading across his chest. He could do without this crap – just when things were beginning to feel more settled.

His eyes drifted to Patti and snippets from the previous letters crashed in, piercing him. '*Your girlfriend's pretty... very pretty*!'

He dragged his gaze away from Patti. Bingo rolled onto his back revealing an expanse of white belly. '*...and your dog's so sweet. Soooo tiny! I could squeeze and squeeze and squeeze him.*'

Seemingly sensing Gus' mood, Bingo whined, his eyes full of concern as he looked at his master. In one fluid movement, the dog rolled back onto his front and laid his head on Gus' thigh, following through with an enthusiastic lick. Gus exhaled and patted the dog's head. There had been nothing overtly threatening in the previous letters... still his 'fan mail' was now being delivered direct to his home – *hand-delivered* straight to his home.

A slight frown appeared on Patti's forehead as she thrust the letter closer to him. 'Go on, take it then. It won't bite.'

'Gimme a second...' He turned, pulled open the top drawer of his bedside cabinet and took out an evidence bag. He kept his voice steady. 'Pop it in there.'

Eyes wide, she did as he asked. 'You going to tell me what that's all about?' With a nervous laugh she added, 'Oh, and while you're at it, why the hell do you keep evidence bags in the bedroom?'

Smiling at her attempt to lighten the situation, Gus took the bag from her and sealed it. 'I've had a few of these letters over the past few months, but until now they've been delivered to The Fort. There's never been anything overtly threatening in them, however, the fact that this one landed on my doorstep on a Sunday without a postmark, ups the stakes.'

He risked a quick grin. 'As for the bags. I have them all over the house – copper's habit, I suppose.' He reached for her hand. 'I'm sorry, Patti. Sorry to drag you into work stuff, but I'm going to have to ask you to come down to The Fort to get printed – for elimination purposes.'

Patti tutted and pulled her hand away, a frown spreading across her forehead. It was like a slap in the face, but Gus couldn't blame her. Why should she have to put up with this sort of shit? The letters were addressed to him.

But she wasn't done. 'Humph, damned if I'm letting my coffee go cold because some idiot's fixated on you. 'Fingerprints'll have to wait. I'm having my breakfast first.' She poured two mugs of coffee and offered Gus another pastry. 'Eat up.' Holding her mug, she lowered her tone. 'You can tell me these things, you know? I don't need protecting. If we're together, then you need to start sharing the shit with me, not blocking me out like you did with all the Alice and Gabriella stuff.'

A weight settled in his chest and started to expand. This always happened when he thought about his last big case. He recognised the sensation and, taking a deep breath, he pulled his shoulders back forcing the feeling away. Patti was right. If they were to take things to the next level, then he had to share… the thing was, he wasn't very good at that. Raising his head, he looked at her face. She was smiling, her brown eyes reassuring and calm.

The lingering tingle in his chest dissipated. Gus grabbed a croissant and munched. Just when he thought he'd got her sussed, Patti did something that made him love her even more. This time he allowed the 'L' word to linger in his mind before grabbing his mug and drinking.

'What do they say?'

'Eh?'

Patti laughed. 'The letters, what else? What do they say?'

'I'll show you them when we get to The Fort. I'm not too worried about them, but they do mention you… and Bingo.' His hand trailed to the dog's head as he spoke.

'What do you mean, they mention me?'

'Well… in one he asks me to pass on his regards.' Gus paused. 'He mentions your dress in another…'

'And you didn't think to tell me, that some sicko is *watching* me? You should have told me.'

She was right. Of course, she was. Her lips were in a tight line. Now wasn't the time to say he didn't want to frighten her. Patti wasn't easily frightened and the mood she was in, she'd challenge him on sexism. Shit, shit, and double shit. Yet again he was messing up a relationship that was beginning to mean a lot to him.

'Sorry.' Too little too late?

Patti nibbled her croissant in silence, avoiding his gaze.

This was going to be it. She was going to tell him it was finished… that she couldn't put up with all the crap that came with being with him and he couldn't bloody blame her. He was an idiot. What had he been thinking, keeping this from her?

She wiped the crumbs off her fingers and turned to him. Here it was. The big knock back. The big, 'It's over, we can't go on like this.' He clenched his jaw, bracing himself for the body blow her words would deliver.

Yet… her eyes were sparkling, and a huge grin spread across her face. Gus thought she'd never looked more beautiful and his jaw unclenched as she spoke.

'Can't wait to be printed. Wait until I tell them at school tomorrow… they'll be so damn jealous.'

Gus could've hugged her. Instead, he smothered his grin, as she continued.

'I have to say, it's a bit of a shame you don't have the same security here as you do at your mum's house. If your admirer had delivered the letter there, they'd have been recorded. Here?' she wafted her hand in the air. '… not a damn thing.'

She was right. His lack of home security meant they were reliant on the odd bit of home CCTV in a domestically populated area to see who'd delivered the letter. Or perhaps a super vigilant neighbour… if they were really lucky. Gus glanced at the clock. Not even seven o'clock – they'd be lucky if anyone was out and about at that time on a Sunday morning. The most they could hope for was someone with an 'I'm a Stalker' sign entering Marriners Drive from either Emm Lane or from the snicket near the Sainsbury's, otherwise they'd little hope of identifying their unofficial postie. Wishing he didn't sound quite so defensive, he said, 'If I'd known I was going to be stalked I'd have got some security.'

'Hmph, right. You're the typical, *I'll do it tomorrow* sort of guy, until someone you love gets threatened and then whatever needs doing gets done yesterday. Remember, I saw how you were with Alice.'

She was right. His first thought on seeing the letter without its postmark was of Patti and Bingo, not himself. He made a promise there and then, that nothing would happen to them. He'd make sure of it. He thought for a moment and then, remembering who was on duty, he picked up his phone and hit speed dial. 'Taffy, I need your help.'

Gus had no trouble imagining the lad standing to attention, his expression excited, his face flushed. It was one Taffy wore at least twice most days. No doubt, he'd already be sitting in the incident room at The Fort, trawling through paperwork as if it was Origami day at school. Really must insist he take some time off. Taffy had been an eager beaver ever since he got promoted to the team on a permanent basis and being greeted by his over-zealous face every morning drained Gus' limited enthusiasm. Hell, he wasn't that much older than Taffy, so why did Gus always feel like the boy's grandad?

'I got another one of those letters, Taff. Delivered to the house this time. I'm coming in in a bit with Patti and I need you to print her.'

There was silence from the phone, then Taffy cleared his throat before speaking. 'You think Patti sent them?'

For fuck's sake! 'No, of *course* I don't think Patti sent them.' The words 'you idiot' hung in the air. 'She picked it up off the doormat.'

∞∞∞∞

Taffy and Compo's faces lit up when Gus and Patti walked through the incident room doors, and they were on their feet in seconds. *Good to be popular*! But, before he'd managed even two steps into the room, he was brought down to earth as Compo slapped Taffy on the back, 'That's a fiver you owe me, Taffy boy. Told you they'd be here before nine.'

Should have known better than to expect respect from my damn team. Too lenient with them, that's my trouble. 'Making bets on your boss? That's taking liberties, that is. Better be a pot of coffee on the go to make up for it.'

Compo, in khaki cargo trousers topped by a faded *Game of Thrones* T-shirt, with coffee stains on the front and sweat pools under his armpits grinned and gestured to Gus' desk like an usher at a wedding. 'Let's see it, Boss.'

Switching the desk fan off so as not to send anything flying while they dealt with the letter, Gus placed the bagged blue envelope with his name and title typed on the front onto the table. If the other letters were anything to go by, the font was Times New Roman, size fourteen... He put on a pair of gloves and opened the bag.

Compo sniffed and Gus nodded. 'Smells the same, doesn't it? Same weird perfume smell.'

Carrying two mugs of coffee, Taffy joined them and handed one to Patti. Gus nodded towards the desk and

Taffy deposited Gus' drink there. Gus had learned to take possession of his drink as soon as it appeared because more than once, the lad had made him a drink and then, forgetting it wasn't his, had drunk it himself.

Using his index and middle fingers, Gus teased the envelope out of the bag. The previous letters had each had different postmarks on them; Leeds, Bradford, Wakefield, Huddersfield... *Wonder what prompted the change?* Seemed like his anonymous fan was mobile. If you called being at most an hour's train ride from Bradford mobile... and seemingly more confident too. Forensics on the previous letters had revealed zilch of importance. The envelopes were self-sealing, ex-Hallmark stock that could be picked up at any car boot sale in the district. The paper was bog-standard A4 used by businesses all over. Nothing unusual about the ink either. There were fingerprints on both the paper and the envelopes. None, however, that were in the IDENT1 files and, according to the technician, they most likely belonged to innocent handlers at the factories, sorting offices, post office, etc. No fingerprints obtained from the envelope matched those found on the paper.

It was frustrating. The only real lead left for Gus to follow was the content of the letters themselves. Gus decided that with the 'home delivery', it was now time to consult the eccentric psychologist, Professor Sebastian Carlton, from Leeds Trinity University. With any luck he'd be able to point him in the right direction.

Using a wooden letter opener, gifted by his mother at Christmas... who the hell, bar his mum, would use a bloody letter opener these days...? he slit the envelope across the top fold. This would save any possible forensic evidence caught on the seal. He'd been reprimanded by Sid for ripping the first one open – like he'd known it was going to be a bloody anonymous note. The perfume smell was stronger now he'd opened the envelope… just like the others.

Patti moved forward and sniffed. 'Smells familiar. Give me a moment.'

She leaned down, holding her hair away from her face and sniffed again. 'Obsession! I'm almost sure it's Obsession perfume.'

Somehow the word 'Obsession' seemed ominous. The scent was too strong to have been co-incidental. *Not good*! *Not good at all*!

'Get the lab to test for that – we'll no doubt have some perfume data base. Maybe that'll narrow things down a bit.'

With a tutting sound, Patti shook her head. 'God's sake, Gus, you clearly don't buy perfume much. If it is Obsession, that's not going to narrow it down much. It's a really popular brand. Millions of women wear it.' She tilted her head to one side, her lips scrunched up. 'Maybe if it's a knock-off the recipe might be a little different. Maybe that'll throw something up, but I bet there's loads of knock-off brands doing the rounds in Bradford too.'

Taffy got up a picture of the scent bottle on his phone and showed it to Gus. 'My sister likes that brand. I bought her some for her birthday.'

Gus threw him a dirty look. Trust the kid to be more up on women's perfume than he was. Gus made a mental note to find out what perfume Patti preferred. *Maybe buy her some for her birthday* and shook the contents from the envelope. When the single sheet, folded in half landed on Gus' desk, the silence in the room was as oppressive as the building heat outside. Even Compo's computers seemed to be holding their breath. A quick glance at the other three told Gus they were on tenterhooks. Patti bit her lip, her eyes glued to the letter. Taffy was executing a rocking movement on his feet, his hands behind his back as if to prevent him from grabbing the letter and ripping it open.

Compo glared at the letter as if it had just eaten his bacon butty until, with a quick smile, he nodded. 'Come on, Gus. What'ya waiting for. It's already written... not like you can change owt, is it?'

Taffy rocked some more. 'Maybe the bastard'll have slipped up this time.'

Gus snorted. 'Yeah, maybe we'll be lucky, and he'll have typed his name and address in the top right-hand corner.'

Compo clicked his fingers, making Gus and Taffy jump. 'Good one, Gus. Open it up and see.'

Choosing to assume that Compo too, was being sarcastic, Gus flipped open the folded letter... and there it was...

My Dearest Detective Inspector Angus McGuire,

It's been a long time, hasn't it? Miss me?

Poor Bingo! This heat really doesn't agree with him, does it? Good job that tree in your garden gives him a little bit of shade in the afternoon. I've had to refill his water a couple of times when your mum's been late picking him up.

You really need to tell her to be on time, you know?

You must tell Patti that I love that blue dress she's been wearing. Stunning. And of course, I like your bandana – very cool and practical for this weather. You sure your bosses approve? Maybe a bit too casual for their liking?

Anyway, you're probably wondering why I'm writing and, much as I love to chat, there is a reason. I've been working hard on a little surprise for you. Just remember though, things are never quite what they seem.

Watch this space!

CHAPTER 2

Zodiac

'You all set for tonight? Excited? This will be so brill. Better than anything we could ever have imagined.' I'm buzzing. But…what the fuck? I expect a little more interest… you know…? like a bit of excitement, a bit of *enthusiasm*. Talking to Pisces is like trying to light a fucking firework in a snowstorm. Shit, wish we could have some snow. Get away from this damn heat, just for a minute. Shit, I'd take a second of snow. Me… naked outside. I laugh, at the thought of snowflakes landing on my skin… sizzling and evaporating soon as they touch. I lift a handful of ice cubes and ram them down the back of my T-shirt. Picking up my iPhone, I pout and take a selfie.

The voice on the other end of the throwaway phone's wittering on again. I stifle a yawn. *Yada yada yada… Boring as shit*! Dumbass, stupid, juvenile crap! Like I give a shit about emotions and family and stuff. All I want is to get the job done, like we agreed. I add some doggie ears and a lolling tongue to my selfie and post it to *Instagram* with the caption 'panting in the heat.'

'Look.' Sharp enough to slice through the stupidity spouting from the phone. 'It's decided. It's planned. It's happening. Now get with the action! We're *not* delaying. You're *not* putting this off. It's tonight. You *know* what you need to bring. *Don't* let me down.'

I switch off as more nonsense spews out, flick the phone onto speaker and lay it down on the table, letting the div's crap wash over me. I know what's coming– what all this shit is leading up to. Next, it'll be the moany tone… the pleading whinge… the *I'm not strong like you*… the *I don't know if I can do this…* the *Are you sure it'll be all right…?* the *We won't get caught, will we…?* and, sure enough… here we goooo… I lie back on the couch, feet up, happy to break the house rules regarding feet on furniture and roll my eyes. Talk about fucking drama. I fling my legs onto the couch and grab my drink. Half the ice is melted already and the vodka tastes like shit – cheap, warm vodka and coke – yuk. I drag long and hard on the straw, draining the glass before shoving it back on the table next to my phone. Lying back down, wishing I wasn't so hot, but too bloody lazy to get more ice cubes, I idly stretch out a finger and smudge the liquid that's soaking into the shiny wood, leaving a dark ring where my glass stood. *Oh goody, I've left a mark on the coffee table… oops… ah well…*

I raise my voice and break through the fucking neediness that crackles down the line. 'I'm relying on you. We've been through this time and time again.

It.

Is.

Necessary.

'It's the only way and you *know* this. They're all liars and hypocrites. They deserve this and it is our duty to show everyone… to expose this to the world.'

Dramatic Pause… This next part of my delivery is important… crucial even. This will seal the deal.

'Are you with me?'

The voice, when Pisces responds, is weak… shaky. 'Yes.'

Glad that I'm home alone, I raise my voice to almost a shout. 'Are You With Me?'

'Yes.'

I stand up and little shards of ice trickle down my back and fall out the bottom of my T-shirt, landing on the carpet.

I pull my shoulders back and stare at my reflection in the wall mirror opposite. My eyes are sparkling, my cheeks flushed. I pull myself to my full height and glare at my image. I pull my mouth into a sneer, chin up. 'ARE YOU WITH ME?'

For a nano-second there's silence. *Probably shitting it.* I swallow the urge to giggle and school my face into its stern expression once more. Just when I'm about to let rip again, the reply comes.

'Yes!'

'AGAIN!'

'YES!'

'All right then, text me when you've set off – use the throwaway. No selfies or anything on that phone yeah?'

I smile and slump back down on the couch just as I hear the front door opening. I hang up, slip the phone in my pocket and, grabbing my empty glass, I slip off to my room. Everything's in place.

Locking the door behind me, I throw myself on my bed and make bets on how long it'll take until I hear her calling my name up the stairs. Fucking does my head in! Why can't she leave me alone…? stop breathing down my neck? Sometimes, it makes my skin crawl… she makes my fucking skin crawl. I know she can't help being needy, but sometimes I just need a break from it. I swallow the urge to bellow, I HATE YOU, into the air and instead, I slip my earbuds in and crank up the music. Now, if the bitch calls, I won't hear her. I've got things to do, plans to finesse and I don't need her chewing my ear off. She can find something to do without me holding her hand.

In some ways, I'm still pinching myself. A year ago, who'd have thought I'd be here now? That was a close call… everything could've gone tits up… but, hey, it didn't. Like always, I got myself out of it – easy when you're as clever as me... even easier when they're so stupid.

That's all in the past and I've got new puppets to control. It's so damn easy...

The first thing I do, wherever I am, is identify the weakest... those with baggage or vulnerabilities. And of course, you got the losers...the lonely... the outcasts. This part of the process can be time consuming, but it's well worth the wait. One of my many skills is the ability to blend into the crowd and observe. What most people don't realise is that they carry their problems with them on their person. These may be invisible to most people, but I pride myself on my ability to see what others can't. Perhaps it's because I've been invisible all my life... or have I? Maybe that's just a lie to confuse things, to put you off the scent... whatever... you'll never know, will you? Not unless I choose to tell you, but even then, you'll be wondering... every word I utter might be a lie... then again, it might be the truth. Who was it said that the 'definition of stupid is knowing the truth, seeing the truth, but still believing the lies?' – amazing how they do that – believe the lies... believe my lies.

I think I've found myself a worthy adversary though. Nearly one hundred per cent sure... we'll see. So far, I've nothing to back that up, nothing except gut instinct and... let's face it I'm rarely wrong there... time will tell... time will tell.

My body is light... as if I'm floating. All the tension's gone and I snuggle further down in the bed. Relaxed... happy... confident that everything will go to plan... I think ahead and go through each and every little segment of the evening. Minute by minute, I dissect what will happen, anticipate every reaction, every response... There is nothing I haven't thought of… nothing I've not accounted for.

With delicious precision, I home in on the best bits… and my body starts to tingle… my heartbeat accelerates, my face flushes I can hardly wait… but first… I pull the zip of my shorts down just enough to insert my hand… something a bit more important to deal with.

CHAPTER 3

*Ice cream, splash pools, and picnics here at Ilkley Lido as
the weekend draws to a close. Capital Radio on the ground
in a record heatwave as temperatures reach highs of...*

Fucking unbearable sauna-like proportions...'

'Eh?' Taffy looked up, startled, as the words
exploded from Gus' mouth. 'Eh?' he repeated.

Gus tightened the bandana round his head and pulled the
fan closer to him. The anonymous letter had been sent off
to the lab and Patti had kissed Gus goodbye, waving off
suggestions that he get a uniformed officer to escort her to
her own home.

A combination of the heat and the thought that his
stalker had somehow gained access to his back garden had
left Gus angry and anxious. Bingo, with his dog flap
allowing him into the house when he needed it, was free to
roam while Gus was at work and Gus had always
considered him safe. Not anymore! The reference to the
three people he loved most in the world was an implied
threat and, regardless of how firmly Gus tried to clamp
down on thoughts of his mum being mugged on entering
his garden through the back door, or some sinister figure
slipping poison into Bingo's water, or some dangerous
monster stalking Patti, he found it hard to focus. Although
the perfume on the letter hinted at the sender being a
woman, Gus was keeping an open mind. It could be anyone
and over the years he'd made more friends than enemies...
of all sexes. He'd left Patti with strict instructions to keep
her doors locked, her home alarm set, and to keep in touch.
He'd also tasked her with making a list of the places and

times she'd worn the vibrant blue dress mentioned in the letter. It was fairly new, and she thought she'd only worn it a few times. It would be useful to be able to catalogue when and where she could have been seen wearing it.

Gus' next-door neighbours on either side had cameras front and back, so Gus had asked if Compo could have access to their most recent recordings, as both were motion-activated and covered some of his drive and part of the steps leading to his front door. Compo, to the sounds of Stevie Wonder's 'You Are the Sunshine of My Life', was doing his thing with them. Gus had asked his dad to collect Bingo and take him to his house for the foreseeable future. Security made his parents' house on Shay Lane almost impenetrable and Bingo would be safe there. In fact, it was his second home and the dog would see it as a holiday. It was Gus who'd miss returning home to his wagging tail and determined lick fest.

...Factor to minimise the risk of contracting skin cancer...

Reaching over, Gus switched the radio off. If today had panned out as planned, he and Patti would have taken Mo and Naila's four youngest daughters to the lido but now, because of this, he had to let them down. It wasn't just that the girls were gutted, he'd hoped that taking the kids off their hands would give them the chance to spend uninterrupted time with their eldest daughter. Zarqa was playing up big time and Gus hated to see his friend's family in such pain. They'd been through months of hell with Zarqa finding it hard to adjust to the fact that the man she'd always thought was her father was in fact not... more to the point, he had been responsible for her real father's death. Mo and Naila were really struggling.

'Results back in yet, Taff?'

Gus wasn't surprised when the younger man shook his head. It was a Sunday and it wasn't urgent. Still, Gus was left with an uneasy feeling in the pit of his stomach. Rather than petering out as he'd hoped, his stalker had become more audacious by turning up at his door. The thing was, much as he wanted to get to the bottom of it himself, Gus was aware that procedurally he had to pass it along to another investigative team. 'Okay, gather everything we've got, make copies for me, and then pass the originals along to C team.'

He could almost feel the relief rolling off Taffy at his words and he ignored the conspiratorial nod his two officers shared. They'd wanted to pass it along when the first letter arrived, but Gus had dug his heels in. Now, however, even he knew it was time. Not that he wouldn't keep an eye on things, but someone else would be in charge.

Before he could say anything, Compo spoke, 'I'll send them copies of this footage, Gus, but I'm gonna look at it myself. Things are quiet today.'

Lifting his phone to contact a home security company, Gus nodded. 'Thanks, Comp. Appreciated.'

Within seconds he was arranging for someone to come and give a quote. He'd have to pay through the nose for a Sunday consultation, but he was prepared to pay over the odds for expedited service – this wasn't just about him anymore. As he hung up, his phone rang; 'The Bitch is Back' blared out against the sound of the whirring desk fan. Both Taffy and Compo's heads jerked up at the same time. Gus took a deep breath and dismissed the call.

He was in no mood to deal with his argumentative ex-wife today.

CHAPTER 4

It's getting dark – gloaming, that's what Gus' old dad calls it. Last year, when we were at Robin Hood's Bay, he kept singing that stupid song about *roaming in the gloaming wi a lassie by his side*. Never mind, I do like him. At least he's not always on my case – not like Mo, anyway.

I have to get out of the house. Mum seems to think she can feed me out of all this. 'Zarqa have some food.' 'Zarqa, I made this for you, beti.' Phuh! If I smell another kebab or see another fucking samosa, I'll scream. Makes my hair stink. That's the trouble with long hair, any bit of frying sticks to it. Mo always stinks of oil. Fucking samosa man – must have been thick at school if that's the only job he can get. Don't know what she sees in him, I really don't. He's pure uggers. And that was another thing. The way he went on when I got my tattoo… at least that stopped them moaning as much when I got my hair dip-dyed. Still, you'd think I'd shaved it off and converted to Buddhism the way they went on. She's the social worker, does she *really* think food's the answer?

It's so hot and I can't ever get away from them. Mum and Mo are always there, looking at me like I'm gonna slit my wrists or swallow a handful of paracetamol. Can't they just leave me alone? Just leave me a-fuckin' lone?

Can't stand this place. Bradford – Bradistan – full of bloody Pakis with their thobes and prayer hats and hijabs and niqabs, thinking they're all that. Like wearing that sort of shit makes them better people, when we all know all it does is cover-up their nasty sins – the shit they get up to underneath it all. The stuff they cover-up and ignore, the stuff happening right under their noses.

I slam out of the house.

'Zarqa! Come back here, right this minute!'

Yeah right, watch me. Ignoring the twinge of guilt at the thought of my mum begging me to stay, to stop arguing, I head off down the path and as I open the gate, I see *he's* at the door, with my mum holding him back. She's crying again, but so what? I'm crying too – just not out front, like her. She's not the one that hears all the whispers. She's not the one The Young Jihadists laugh about – idiots the lot of them. But I'll show them – I'll show them, all right.

I turn left and head down to the park to meet Jo Jo. Hope he's got the goods. I start jogging along North Park Road. The last of the sun makes me warm and I want to take my hoodie off, but the first beep from a car full of Asian lads with the windows down and the smell of weed drifting out, has me putting the hood up over my hair, making sure it's all tucked in. I stick my elbows out, bulking myself out and walk like a lad. Mind you, with shorts on it's hard to look masculine. Bloody dickwads! You'd think I was walking about in the scud, the way they heckle and jeer. As they drive past, I glance in. I recognise three of them – they go to our mosque. Butter wouldn't melt and shit when they're doing namaz – telling their sisters to cover-up and then off they go kerb crawling round Manningham looking to hassle anybody not wearing a hijab. How's that right? If I had a knife, I'd slash their tyres. Maybe next time they're at mosque I'll do just that – hit the bastards where it hurts.

Ping!

Text! Can't she just leave me alone? I shove my phone back in my pocket and keep moving. Lister Park's still busy. Used to like coming here with my mum and the kids and Mo. Can't call him 'Dad' – not anymore. How can I call the man who killed my biological dad, Dad? A scorpion uncurls in my chest – ready to sting – ready to make me cry. I swallow and let the anger smother it. Then again, how can I call the man who raped my mum, 'Dad' either? Truth is they're right. All of them are fucking right. The leering old bastards at the mosque are right, the gossiping hijabis at school are right, the pious Darth Vaders in their burkas looking down at me in Kanna Peena are right, and the dirty little Pakistani boys, trying to cop a feel in the dinner queue at school, are right too – I'm nowt but a bastard – a dirty fucking bastard without a dad. A dirty fucking bastard with a mum who's got a whole load of other kids who're not bastards. A dirty fucking bastard who doesn't belong – who doesn't have real sisters and with grandparents who'd rather live in Pakistan than see her.

I'm running hard now, trying to dislodge the scorpion before it stings. I'm fed up of crying. Won't think about Mo playing bowls, or the time he capsized the pedalo in the lake because he stood up to do a Titanic impression. Or us all with ice creams, the kids' faces all sticky and smiling. I was always the outsider, just didn't know it then.

Like I told Jo Jo, I'm done crying, done being weak. From now on *I'm* taking things into my own hands. I don't fit in here… don't belong. They all know it. So, from now on, I'm going to be *me*. No more Mo's daughter, Zarqa. No more the girl from the samosa shop. No, from now on I'm just me and they'll soon know all about it.

When I get to the bandstand, the park's gone quiet. Just shadowy figures and cigarettes lighting up near the trees and bushes. It's not dark yet, but it won't be long. I check my phone – see if he's texted. Nothing. Kids have scooted, the ice cream van's gone – just the no-gooders left – the drug dealers, the pimps, and the doggers. *Where the hell is Jo Jo*? I told him not to be late! I sit on the bottom step and check my phone again. Still nowt. He'll come up from the bottom of the park, up from Manningham Lane 'cause that's where his bus'll stop. I see a figure walking up the hill towards Cartwright Hall, but I don't stand up yet. Not going to draw attention to myself until I know it's him.

The figure raises an arm and waves. 'Zarqa?'

He's got his hoodie on too... and jeans. Must be sweltering. Best not to look too much like a white boy in this neck of the woods. I jump to my feet and run towards him. Thank God! I was beginning to think he'd stood me up. When I reach him, I give him a hug. He's all tall and spindly, but he smells nice – Lynx or summat. 'You're bloody late.'

He just grins, and shrugs. 'Sunday service. Besides, you know my motto – treat 'em mean keep 'em keen.'

I swat his arm and tut. 'Yeah right, whatever.' We start to walk back to the bandstand. The silence is never awkward when I'm with Jo Jo. Maybe cos he's gay, I don't know. Just one of those things, I suppose. Never feel I have to pretend with him. I'm just me, Zarqa, and that's enough for both of us. He doesn't talk all the time, just when he's got summat to say. Wish the rest of the kids our age were like him, instead of being dicks – giggling and yelling and slagging off folk all the time. 'Got a cig?'

He sighs and pulls a pack from his jean's pocket. 'You never used to smoke. You don't have to, you know? You could just be your own person.' He nudges me and grins. 'I'd still like you, you know?'

But I can see he's looking at me with that serious face of his. That's the thing with Jo Jo. He always wants to fix you. Well, he needs to learn that you can't fix everything – some things are beyond repair. 'Just give me a fucking cig, yeah?'

We sit on the bottom step for a while, blowing smoke circles. I'm crap at it, but Jo Jo can do right big ones.

Finally, I put my hand in my pocket and pull out a tenner. 'You got the stuff?'

He looks at me, his eyes all serious like he's my big brother or summat. 'You sure?'

'Give us a break. Course I'm sure. Why wouldn't I be?'

He shrugs. 'Just it's not really you, is it?'

'Course it is. It's the new me.'

I can see he's still reluctant, so I nudge him again. 'You don't have to do it.'

'Yeah, right, and let you do it all on your own. Don't think so. Come on, if we're doing this, we're doing it together. That was the deal.' He rummages in his rucksack for a minute and then shows me the goods. 'Happy?'

A zing of adrenalin zaps through me. My heart's thumping like bongos, but I'm ready. I've never done owt like this before, still, I'm ready. I leap to my feet, eager to get going now and Jo Jo follows me. I link arms with him, and we walk up to North Park Road and out of the park. As we get closer our steps slow down. Now it's time, I'm a bit nervous.

'You okay?' Jo Jo's giving me a get-out clause. He never wanted to do this. He's only here because he's my friend.

I nearly say 'no let's just leave it.' But then everything I've been feeling for the past months wells up inside me. All the misery, all the hate, all the rage, and I nod.

'Someone's got to pay. Let's do it.'

CHAPTER 5

It was that time just before dreams faded into a deep sleep. The central heating was cooling and, barring the occasional vehicle rumbling past, or the random owl's hoot as it flew by, its eyes no doubt zeroing in on its unsuspecting prey, there was near silence. Haider was uncomfortable. It was so damn hot… nobody else in the whole of Bradford would have their heating on but they had relatives over from Pakistan and his auntie was shivering and moaning; *It's so cold, put the heating up a little! Don't know how you can live here in this cold*!

As a result, everyone else was sweltering. *And* he'd had to give up his bed to accommodate his aunt and uncle. For the past week, he'd been unable to settle in the top bunk in the attic box room. He hated sharing with his brother, Adil. He snored like a pig and smelled twice as bad. As far as Haider was concerned, the sooner his aunt and uncle moved on to the next set of relatives, the better. At least Adil's snoring had stopped. Maybe now he could get some rest. He'd a GCSE in the morning and maths wasn't his best subject.

Rolling his tall frame into a more comfortable position, Haider tried to ignore the lumps in the mattress and the faint aroma of dirty socks that hung in the air as if Adil had hung them across the room with the explicit purpose of annoying him. He was a repulsive little scrote. Feeling the bed wobble, Haider tried to punch a dent into his washboard-stiff pillow and, when he failed, he gave up with a sigh. Of course, the best bedding had gone to the relatives. He wouldn't mind, but he didn't even like them. Neither did his mum. They were his dad's brother and sister-in-law and they had *issues* with the fact that Haider's

mum was a Gujarati Muslim and they were Pakistani.
Bloody load of old rubbish as far as Haider was concerned.
His cousins were all right though. Two girls, just a little bit
younger than him. As long as nobody got it into their heads
that he'd be up for marrying either of them. No chance!
He'd find his own wife when it was time, and if he had owt
to do with it, that wouldn't be for at least a decade.

Flinging off his duvet, he hung his legs over the edge of
the bed. Why was it so hot in here? Course he knew why.
Bloody visitors. It felt that everything they'd done for the
past few weeks had been dictated by the sodding relatives
that nobody really liked. They'd not been able to have their
regular Friday night Raja's Pizza treat because his uncle
could only eat curry and chapattis. When he'd suggested
the kids have the pizza and the parents have the curry, his
boring old uncle had put the kibosh on that saying he didn't
want his daughters being 'tempted into the ways of the
West.' *Idiot*! Raja's pizzas were a Pakistani tradition in
Bradford… part of the culture, just like Chicken Cottage.

As his body temperature cooled, Haider's eyes became
heavy and he was on the point of dropping off when Adil's
snoring started up again. *Fuck's sake*! Pulling himself into
a half-sitting position, to avoid banging his head on the
room's sloping ceiling, Haider edged his bum closer to the
bedrail where his feet still dangled and was just about to
jump onto the floor, not caring if he woke his brother,
when his phone vibrated. *Who the hell was contacting him
at this hour*? Stretching his hand back, he groped under his
pillow for the phone. When his fingers grabbed it, he edged
his backside over the rail and lowered himself off the bed,
jumping the last foot and a half. Adil, snorted, flapped his
lips, and heaved himself onto his side. Haider glared at him
and kicked the edge of the bed with his bare foot, but Adil
just commenced a rhythmic purring snore.

The floor was cool under Haider's feet. The box room was a junk room and so had only a bit of tatty old lino with a threadbare rug covering the floor. Haider hopped onto the rug and looked around in the semi-darkness for his slippers and clothes. Adil, as usual, had left a trail of clothes in bundles all over the floor and it took Haider a minute to locate his single pile near the door. Cursing, he removed the pile of underwear Adil had dumped on top of his clothing and sniffed the T-shirt that was topmost. He gritted his teeth. *Little shit*! His T-shirt smelled of pissy underpants now. Rummaging under the bed, he pulled out a suitcase containing his clothes ration for the duration of his exile. Still no response from his brother who slept on regardless of the evil looks Haider flung his way at regular intervals. Unzipping the bag and extracting clean clothes, Haider breathed in the scent of fabric conditioner as he pulled a top over his head before sliding his feet into a pair of shorts. He'd go and sleep on the sofa. He stretched up, yanked his duvet down, and slung it over one shoulder and then, phone in pocket, he turned back. With clawed fingertips, he gripped his brother's skull and shook hard before leaving the room, ignoring the confused yelps that followed him.

Downstairs it was cooler, and the lingering aroma of incense made him quite lethargic as he snuggled under his duvet, positioning cushions beneath his head. He'd just got comfortable when he remembered the notification on his phone and groaned. Now he'd remembered it, he'd *have* to look. That's the thing with phones; somehow, they demanded an instant response... even in the middle of the night... even when you were dog fucking tired. Using his fingerprint, he activated his phone and saw he had a *Snapchat*. He opened it and stared at the image. *What the fuck*? It disappeared. Haider shook his head as if to clear the image from his thoughts. What the hell was the knob playing at? This was *so* not funny. Not funny at all.

He replayed the image. What the hell would make him send Haider an image of himself covered in blood with a fake knife sticking out his neck at this time of night? *Fucking gross*! With the duvet pulled over his shoulders, Haider's fingers flew over the phone and, just before he settled down for the night, he hit send.

TOSSER!!!!

CHAPTER 6

Half ten on a Sunday night and it was still fucking boiling. As he turned off Toller Lane onto Smith Lane behind Bradford Royal, Karim Mirza welcomed the occasional whoosh of air as cars passed by him. When he licked his lips, they tasted of salt and his hair was all limp across his forehead. *Hope I don't bump into any of the lads... or Zarqa. Don't want her to see me looking like a div*!

Why'd it have to be so hot? His hands were stuffed in his pockets, Trixie-Belle's leash hooked over his right wrist. And why did his mum have to sign him up for this? Bloody Lubna. 'Oh, Ami, I'm too busy – got my biology tomorrow – make Karim do it.'

It was *her* job, not his. His sister had been the one to agree to walking the dog for their neighbour, not him. Why did he have to get dragged into it? Bad enough that he had to deliver chapattis and curry lunchtime and teatime, every day. Stupid old bat kept chuntering on, 'Oh could you just make me a cold drink, Karim?' or 'Can you move the fan a bit closer, Karim?' Least she sometimes slipped him a note which he promptly spent on a tenners bag on Scotchman Road.

Strolling on, Trixie-Belle trotting ahead of him, he considered cutting their walk short. It was bloody humiliating. Imagine if his friends saw him with a pooper scooper bag? They'd slag him for weeks. Trixie-Belle doubled back on herself and looked up at him, her head tilted to one side, ears twitching as if to say 'can we get a move on?' *Poor sod's feeling the heat too.*

Karim mimicked her head movements and then, grinning, reached down and scratched the top of her head. Trixie-Belle liked that, her mouth fell open and her tongue lolled out from the side all pink and rough looking. He took his phone out, checked his notifications, and shrugged. Nowt important. 'Poor Mrs Brown's hip op this, poor Mrs Brown's hip op that,' said Karim in a baby voice to the dog. Trixie-Belle looked up at him as if she understood every word. Karim laughed. His mother's words made him think of hip hop and Drake. He couldn't imagine Mrs Brown getting down with a bit of Drake or 50 Cent for that matter. Specially not with her 'hip op'. He sniggered and tugged Trixie-Belle's leash. 'You get it, Trixie-B! Hip Hop, Hip op.' He was still laughing when he dropped her leash to the pavement so he could search his shorts' pocket for his Clipper.

He'd just shoved the bent spliff between his lips and flicked the lighter to light it when Trixie-Belle made her bid for freedom. She was off, lead dragging behind her, straight up Smith Lane, past the Maternity Unit car park, and then she disappeared to the left. Karim cursed and took off after her, the light from the street lamps casting a white glow as he went. His heart pounded, unlit joint hanging from his lips as he panted after the dog. All the while he ran, he repeated to himself, 'Please not the Haunted House, Trixie-B. Please not the Haunted House.'

When he reached the point where he'd last seen her, he stopped, ran his fingers through his sweaty hair and spun in a complete circle, before kicking a nearby lamp post. 'Aaaaaaargh!' He snatched the spliff from his lips, shoved it back in his tin case beside his grinder, and rammed it in his pocket.

The Haunted House was right there, and he bet that was where the stupid dog had gone. To his left, back from the road, behind a line of overgrown bushes, the upper floor of a dilapidated building was visible. Its smashed windows, covered on the inside by bits of wood hanging loose as if a ghostly figure had tried to break out, glinted in the headlights of cars rounding the bend. 'Fucking Haunted House.'

Two huge boulders were placed at each end of the hedges, restricting access to the premises. Karim looked along the street in both directions hoping for some human presence in the distance, but there was none. *What am I going to do?* No way could he leave the dog out here on her own. Hip op or not, Mrs Brown would skin him alive if owt happened to Trixie-Belle. The trouble was, he couldn't bring himself to go in after her. Brought up on a recipe of jinns, demons, and angels from his parents, and spooks, ghosts, and poltergeists from his friends, Karim was scared. He'd never admit it to his mates, but the stories of the Grey Lady who floated round the grounds of the Haunted House looking for naughty kids to eat, still, on occasion, gave him nightmares. Then there was Smiling Jack. *Aw no, why did I have to think of Smiling Jack right now?*

He approached the nearest boulder and peered into the darkness beyond. There were large looming shapes at the back – trees. 'Why does there have to be trees? Trees and fucking Smiling Jack.'

He peered into the distance and then, when that didn't help him see any clearer, he got out his mobile and used the torch function. Now the trees in the distance took on an even more ghostly appearance. Was that a body hanging in that tree? Had Smiling Jack grabbed Trixie-Belle, stapled her mouth into a smile and hung her from a branch? *Fuck I hope not!*

Karim bounced his torch over the ground, his hand shaking, his voice tremulous as he called into the darkness beyond, 'Trixie-B. Trixie-Belle? Come on, girl. Please, come on.'

An answering bark from beyond the rocks confirmed his fears. Trixie-Belle was in the grounds of the Haunted House, but at least she was alive. Smiling Jack hadn't got her. He shook himself. *Aw, come on, Karim, don't be such a pussy. Smiling Jack's a myth, not real.*

He took a deep breath and squeezed between the boulders, bouncing his torch around him as he went. Now he was onto the drive, the house looked even scarier. The broken gutters cast weird shadows over the weeds that sprouted from between the pebbles on the drive. A dark outline of a plant growing up the walls to the smashed windows made them look like they were crying blood. He directed his spotlight towards the side of the house where the trees were, and, taking baby steps, moved forward, glad of the sound of the occasional car passing on the road behind. 'Trixie-B, Trixie.' *Why the fuck am I whispering?* 'Trixie-Belle – come on girl. Come to Karim.' A little louder this time. Again, the same answering bark, but no sight nor sound of Trixie rushing back to him. He groaned. *Maybe she's injured? Oh, fuck no!* Mrs Brown would definitely have him for that. No more tenners for bud if the dog was hurt.

He drew level with the house and risked moving his phone over the walls, just making sure the Grey Lady wasn't there waiting to jump out on him. There was a door at the side, with a half porch. *Just the place for Smiling Jack to hide!* Giving the porch a wide berth, Karim edged forward, his trainers dislodging pebbles as he walked, making too much noise. He tried to walk on tiptoes and that was a little quieter, but awkward. If he had to run, he'd not bother about the noise. Drawing level with the porch, he risked a glance towards it. Apart from the dark shadows, nothing. *Thank fuck.*

Moving on, Karim reached the end of the house – a few more steps and he'd be in the grassy area near the trees at the back of the property. 'Trixie-Belle? Trixie-B, come on, girl.'

Again, the yelp of an excited dog, closer this time. Summoning up every ounce of courage and avoiding looking at the trees, Karim walked on, peering to his right where he'd heard the dog. Trixie-Belle wriggled on her haunches, the lead lying on the ground behind her. 'Thank God, Trixie, why didn't you come when I called?'

Trixie-Belle turned to greet him, her mouth wide in a canine grin, not a staple in sight, her tongue a Scooby Doo loll. Karim grinned and bent to pick up the lead, *No way are you getting away from me now*. As he straightened, his torch landed on something a few feet away on the grass. Karim, yelped. Fingers frantic, he grabbed the lead and, dragging Trixie-Belle behind him, legged it back round the Haunted House, between the boulders and onto Smith Lane before stopping. A quick glance behind him reassured him he hadn't been followed. Bending over, bracing his hands on his knees, he struggled to catch his breath. 'Fuck, oh fuck. What was that?' Tears streamed from his eyes, his heart thundered, and he thought he would have to slide down onto the pavement.

A low growl rumbled in Trixie-Belle's throat. Through the dark, something gripped his shoulder. He jumped and spun round, arms raised, shining the torch in the eyes of the person who'd grabbed him. His sudden movement dislodged his baccy tin from his pocket. It crashed to the ground and Karim groaned. He swung his torch to the tin. *Aw fuck*! There on the pavement was his tin, lid to one side, joint and weed grinder on the other. He met the eyes of the police officer who looked pointedly at the spliff.

Her partner, a big fucker, grinning like he'd won the lottery, rocked on his feet, a sarcy grin on his face. 'Been spending our pocket money on naughties, have we?'

CHAPTER 7

And tomorrow's set to be another scorcher throughout
Yorkshire, with temperatures reaching highs of 24 degrees.
Watch out for thundery showers over the Dales overnight
and increased humidity…

Detective Inspector Gus McGuire switched Capital
Radio off and got out of the police pool vehicle.
Taffy had picked him up from home and as soon
as he'd left the house, he'd started to sweat. A kid's body
wasn't his idea of a great way to end the weekend. Not for
the first time in the last five months, he wished it was Alice
with him. Taffy was a great lad and was beginning to show
the makings of a good officer. His main failing was that he
wasn't Alice. He'd heard nothing from her in those five
months. His DCI, Nancy Chalmers, was happy to give
Alice more time after all she'd been through. However,
their new Detective Chief Superintendent Gazala Bashir
wasn't being so patient. Now that she'd got her feet under
the table, she was beginning to flex her muscles and Gus
was concerned that Alice would be forced to make a
decision she might regret because of Bashir's thirst to
assert herself.

Even after eleven at night, it was still sweltering. The
build-up of heat and humidity throughout the day made it
difficult to breathe and now hung like stagnant piss in a
spit-and-sawdust pub's urinal. Gus, dressed in shorts and a
T-shirt, was sweating like a pig at a barbecue. He'd taken
to wearing a bandana to create a bit of air between his short
dreads and his neck and to stop the sweat from running into
his eyes. All day he'd been wishing for a thunderstorm to
clear the air and, now that one was imminent, he was

hoping it would hold off until they'd processed the crime scene. *Sod's bloody law*. The thought of scrambling into crime scene overalls in this heat made his skin prickle.

There were two entrances to the Haunted House, and both were cordoned off with yellow and black crime scene tape attached to the gateposts and stretched over the two boulders that had been deposited at each entrance years ago. *This takes me back*. Last time he'd passed the house, the hedge had been covered in snow and hadn't looked quite as unkempt. Now it seemed that it was making a bid to seal off the entire length of the property with elongated leafy shoots branching out in all directions. He couldn't remember a hedge at all when he'd been a kid living on Wheatland's Drive. He, Mo, and Greg had spent a lot of time playing here, building dens and having picnics and making up imaginary worlds.

Everything seemed less grand now. The windows were all shuttered off with planks of wood that were hanging on by a single nail by the look of it. They'd had bother a few years ago with rough sleepers and junkies taking over the building, but now, with special constables being detailed in the area, this had been sorted. Since then, they'd padlocked the building off with chains and heavy-duty bars across the downstairs windows. To Gus, vacant properties like this were a scandal. According to the statistics that occasionally landed on his desk, there were nearly three thousand homeless folk in Bradford, so why didn't they do something with some of these abandoned properties?

A uniformed officer stood guard by each of the entrances and Gus and Taffy approached the nearest, signed in and ducked under the tape. Gus ignored the officer's far too cheery, 'Hot tonight, sir.'

The crime scene investigators had set up spotlights which illuminated the entire property. Closer up, the house looked even sadder than it had from the road. Roof tiles missing, with triffids growing out of the gaps, as if the peripheral hedge had somehow sent roots into the basement with the express purpose of escaping from the roof. The once yellow sandstone, now pitted in places, was crying out for a good clean. Half the pebbles had disappeared from the swooping semi-circular drive, leaving potholes and bare patches where once more Mother Nature had erupted in the form of spindly wildflowers and less attractive weeds. The front area had become a refuge for empty beer cans, spent cigarette packets, and the detritus left behind by drug users – bent spoons, empty lighters, syringes, and a flurry of empty bud bags.

Gus turned to Taffy. 'Used to play here when we were kids. Me, Mo, and Greg.'

'I'd be shit scared to play here when I were a kid. It's too creepy, like it's haunted or summat. Like some sort of unseen evil's lurking in the shadows.' The younger officer looked nervously around him, hands stuffed into his short's pockets, his brow furrowed. Taffy had clearly spent a bit too much time in the sun as his brown face had become red across his nose and cheeks and was beginning to peel. 'It's not really haunted, is it?'

'Yeah, well, it's got a reputation.' Gus laughed. 'But then again – you *are* a bit of a wuss, Taff.'

'Damn right – hate ghost stories and stuff. Rather face a serial killer any day.'

Considering the lad, unlike Gus, had never had to face a serial killer, Gus reckoned that the lad's perceptions might have to change one day. Gus sincerely hoped not. Bradford had had too damn many serial killers for its own good. Christ, he'd heard that some bright spark was researching whether the Bradford water was a factor in the high ratio of serial killers in the district.

Gus surveyed the dilapidated grounds. 'Mo made up this story to frighten the other kids away.' He looked around. 'What was it now? Ah that's it – Smiling Jack. Mo told them Smiling Jack was a bogeyman who caught kids and stapled smiles on their faces before killing them and hanging them over there.' He pointed to where the corner of the crime scene tent was visible among the trees. 'It worked too. The other kids steered clear, and me, Greg, and Mo spent our summers being explorers and pirates and what not. It was an orchard then – full of pear and apple trees.'

He sighed. Reminiscing about Greg always stirred feelings he'd rather only face in the privacy of his own home. It might have been over two years since he'd stabbed Greg to death, but the emotions were as raw as if it had happened yesterday. He inhaled sharply and released his breath just like Dr Mahmood, his psychiatrist had taught him. Slapping Taffy on the back, he said, 'Well, that's one sicko we can cross off our suspect list.'

'Eh?'

'Whoever did this, it wasn't Smiling Jack, now, was it?'

The crime scene crew were still placing the metal treads that provided a direct pathway between the tent and the entrance, to avoid contaminating possible evidence. With the threat of thundery showers in the offing, they'd want to crack on. Gus, deciding to give them space, looked around to see which officers were at his disposal. Leaning against the boulder out of sight of the tent was a young Asian lad in shorts and a T-shirt, gripping a dog leash for grim life. *Must be the lad who found the body.* Someone had draped a blanket round his shoulders and Gus assumed the lad must have started to shake with the shock of it all – either that or he was a damn reptile, for Gus was sweating buckets and Taffy had a sheen of sweat across his forehead. A uniformed officer stood beside the lad – a big bloke with a baby face. His arms were crossed over his chest as if he was about to arrest the lad. Sometimes, these uniforms were a bit too damn officious. The lad would be in a sorry state. No need for heavy-handed tactics. As Gus and Taffy walked towards them, the incongruously cheery officer approached, eagerness rolling off him in spades.

'Too hot in't it, sir.'

Gus scowled and tutted. Course it was bloody hot. Especially for the uniforms with all the tactical shit they had to carry. No need to be so damn jovial about it though, was there?

The officer continued regardless. 'Before you speak to the lad, sir, you need to see this.' He rummaged in his pocket and came out with two evidence bags which he handed to Gus. Inside one was an unsmoked, rather amateurishly rolled spliff and the remnants of a weed bag and, in the other, a tin and a bud grinder. 'Took it from the lad while he was fleeing the scene.'

Taffy snorted and turned it into a cough, as Gus replied, 'You think this young lad is implicated in the murder, then?'

The bulky man frowned, his jowls wobbling slightly as he shook his head. 'No, no. Reckon he just discovered the body, like.'

'Okaaay.' Gus stretched the word out before continuing, 'So, he's actually just a witness – a traumatised witness?'

'Eh well, yes, s'pose so. Got all shaky and that when we brought him back here.'

'Look, Officer…?'

'Sayed, sir.'

'So, Officer Sayed. This lad's what, fifteen? Sixteen?'

'Sixteen, sir – Karim Mirza's his name.'

'Okay, so Karim is sixteen. He's just found a dead body and he's shitting it. Is that a pretty fair assessment of the situation?'

Sayed shifted on his feet. 'Yes, sir.'

'Okay, so perhaps, we could cut him a bit of slack on the weed front – not like he's carrying enough to supply the district is it? Maybe focus on getting his statement without traumatising him anymore, eh?'

Sayed nodded once, blinking rapidly, face red. Gus took pity on him. 'Look, you're new to the job, yeah?'

Again, the nod and blinking eyes.

'Well, learn from this. It's good to frighten the kids up if you catch them with stuff but you also need to look at the bigger picture – murder and finding a dead body trumps possession of weed for personal use, right?'

Sayed looked deflated and Gus felt like a dick. Just because he was overheated didn't mean he should take it out on the uniforms. 'Don't worry about it. Just go and check if any of the houses opposite have cameras. See if you can catch anything suspicious. I suspect they're too far away from here to have caught anything, but you never know. We've got Karim now.'

As Sayed walked away, Taffy muttered, 'Tosser,' under his breath. Gus nudged him.

'Don't be so damn hard on him. He's learning, that's all.'

Taffy shrugged. 'Wasn't talking about him, Boss.'

Gus threw his head back and laughed. 'Cheeky sod!' and, still laughing, he strode past Taffy and approached the young lad.

Mirza's eyes were swollen and red and, as Gus neared, his bottom lip began to tremble. The dog growled deep in its throat and Gus stopped a few feet away. 'I'm DI Gus McGuire – you can call me Gus. Nice dog, Karim. She yours?'

Shuffling his feet, Karim shushed the dog. 'Nah, Mrs Brown's – she's had a hip op.'

'What's her name?'

'Not sure – think she's called Felicity or summat.'

Gus risked a glance at Taffy, who was biting his lip to stop himself from laughing. 'I meant the dog's name, Karim. Not Mrs Brown's.'

'Oh, eh, right – Trixie-Belle.'

Gus stared at him. 'You kidding me? Trixie-Belle? She's a bloody Rottweiler, for God's sake! She must weigh a hundred pounds. I was expecting Titan or Rocky or something. Why the hell would anyone name her Trixie-Belle?'

As he spoke, Gus had moved closer, his hand out for the dog to sniff. All his instincts told him to run. The scars on his leg and arm from last time he'd encountered a Rottweiler began to itch. He swallowed his fear and tried not to flinch when the dog's mouth opened, revealing razor-sharp teeth and a pink tongue. *How ferocious could a Rottweiler called Trixie-Belle be?*

Karim grinned. 'I know. It's embarrassing when I take her out.' He looked down at his trainers and then met Gus' eye. 'Sometimes, if people ask her name, I lie and tell them it's Tyson.'

Gus laughed. 'Don't blame you.' He let the dog lick him for a bit longer, then brought his hand up to scratch Trixie-Belle's head. 'Now, about this bud.'

Rubbing the back of his hand over his nose, Karim glanced round as if someone might swoop in to rescue him. 'I…'

Gus held out a hand to stop him. 'Stop. No excuses. We're going to overlook it this time, okay? We're more interested in what you saw and how you discovered the body.'

The lad's shoulders relaxed, and a small grin twitched his lips. He stretched his hand out to retrieve the bags from Gus.

Gus snatched them back. 'Eh, said we'd overlook it this time. Didn't say you're getting it back. It'll be disposed of in the normal way back at The Fort.'

The smile faded from Karim's face, making Gus smile. *Dozy kid.* Maybe he'd learn a lesson from this, though Gus didn't really think so. He remembered too well what it was to be young. 'So, walk me through what happened.'

Kicking the ground, Karim, his voice little more than a whisper, explained about being forced to walk Trixie-Belle, stopping to light his cig, and the dog escaping. His voice shook when he described how he'd entered the grounds and heard Trixie-Belle's barks coming from the corner. 'When I saw the body, I freaked, like. Didn't stop – just ran.' He sniffed and shrugged, trying to look nonchalant, but Gus wasn't fooled.

He laid a hand on the lad's shoulder, squeezing lightly. 'I'd have done the same, Karim. Most folk would.'

Brushing the back of his hand across his eyes, Karim wiggled his nose, head ducked towards the ground. 'Thing is, I think I recognised him. He goes to City Academy. I'm sure of it. He's in my sister's year. She knows him, but I don't know his name.'

Fuck's sake! It was always harder when it was a kid, and Gus had seen too many dead kids over the years. The City Academy link meant that Patti would have to be involved. *Why the hell do our paths always have to cross professionally as well as romantically*? He turned to Taffy. 'Take the lad home, explain to his parents what's happened, minus the weed, and take a statement. See if you can get the dead boy's name from his sister, I'm going to see what Hissing Sid and his crew have for me in the tent.'

CHAPTER 8

The sweltering night air catches in my throat, all clammy and cloying. My breath's a series of short gasps keeping time to my feet pounding the damp pavement as I jog. Adrenalin's still pumping. Just want to get home now… need to think… get my head right.

What the fuck just happened? My stomach lurches, acid hits the back of my throat and I gob it out into the gutter. It's like that releases something and I stop, my soles slipping on the concrete. As I bend over the kerb, hands on knees, a spatter of bile surges up my throat and into my mouth before spurting out. It splatters onto the road where it lies, caught in the light from the nearby street lamp.

'Ho', Jo Jo. Can't hold your drink, eh? Ya pussy.'

Fuck's sake! Of all the little scrotes I could have bumped into, why did it have to be Hamid, fucking, Farooqi? Hammerhead to his friends and *Fucking* Hammerhead to his enemies. Reluctant to stand upright, just in case I'm sick again, I turn my head and see four pairs of identical trainers attached to four pairs of legs in skinny jeans. They're standing in a semi-circle, crowding me, ready to move in if they feel like it. Like a huge fucking upright spider with me in the web. Hamid and his sidekicks are as toxic as a fucking tarantula too – and as ugly. Last thing I need is to have a convo with these wankers, but I've no option. I straighten and take a step back. Always wise to keep your distance from Hamid the Hammerhead. The knob's always looking for trouble and I could do without any – especially right now. I send a quick glance to my left, to make sure I've got an escape route and brace my shoulders.

51

'What'd you want? Bit past your bedtime, innit?' My heart thuds, but I snarl the words at them. Best not to show any chinks. Best to put on a front. It's the only way.

Hamid takes a step towards me and I make sure I don't react. Show weakness and the bastard'll have me.

His drongos step forward too, flanking their chief, two to the right, one to the left. Beer cans in one hand, spliffs in the other, each of them has the glazed eyes of the stoner.

'You back-chatting me, Jo Jo?' Hammerhead grins like it's all a big joke. Head tilts to one side, displaying the love bite on his neck.

I hold my hands out, palms up. 'Course not, wouldn't dick you about or owt, would I? Just heading home now.'

He steps right up to me, his breath a combination of weed and beer with a side of KFC. His tone changes, all jokiness gone. 'You need to get wise, Jo Jo. You know? Like my boys here.' He gestures to his slack-faced zombies. 'Need to sign up with either us or Razor's lot. Make your choice. Can't keep sitting on the fence forever. After all, you want to keep your mum and sister safe, don't you?'

He reaches over and grips my head; pressing hard into my scalp. He shakes it, and then let's go before slapping my forehead with the heel of his hand. I'm still recovering from that when his knee hits me in the balls. The drongos laugh like idiots as I bend over, clutching my crotch. The vomit's out of my mouth before I can even groan. Thank fuck the weed and alcohol combo seems to have weakened him because I'm not seeing stars or owt like I did last time.

He's not finished yet though. He grabs my hair and yanks my head up. 'Decision soon, right?'

Then he's off, sauntering towards the park, zombies in tow, still laughing.

I take a moment to regroup, before straightening and making my way up the road towards home.

Ping!

> Zarqa: You all right?

Fucking hell! Leave me alone! I fire off a reply and hope she gets the message.

> Me: Yep. Speak tomorrow.

Can't think about Zarqa right now. Can't think about what we done, and I definitely can't think about Hammerhead either. Too much else to crack on with and it's too late now. I try to shove it out of my mind. Tomorrow will be soon enough to rake over everything I did tonight and Hammerhead's ultimatum.

When I reach my house, it's in darkness. The gate creaks when you open it, so, despite my shakiness, I climb over. When I land on the other side, the slap of my trainers on the concrete seems loud. The meeting with Hamid's gang on top of what happened earlier has me on edge. Even the sound of my key turning in the lock makes me cringe. I open the door and walk in and hesitate, listening.

Ping!

The sound startles me, and I jump, then look at the screen. Not again!

> Zarqa: We cool?
>
> Me: Yep! Tomorrow, okay?
>
> Zarqa: Laters!

Fucking laters? Her and her fucking stupid laters. I put my phone to silent and breathe a sigh of relief. At least I can forget about her for now. I tune in again, hoping for no signs of movement. The only sound is next door's telly on too loud again and the annoying buzz from the fridge. Sounds like it's on its way out. Another fucking expense to consider. Using my phone as a torch, I slip my trainers off at the bottom of the stairs. The beam lands on Jessie's school shoes. They're all tattered, the heel trodden down and the sole coming away at the front. I bite my lip and glance at the time on my phone. Fifteen minutes to go. Better be quick then. Got to get ready.

I pick my way upstairs avoiding every creak and manage to get to my bedroom door without hassle. I unlock the door and, stepping in, heave a huge sigh. Sanctuary. Striding across the room, avoiding the mishmash of wires that snake from my PC, I flick on the bedside light and fling myself on the bed. Need to get my head together before work. Get into the zone. Twelve minutes to go!

A voice drifts along the corridor. 'That you, Jo Jo? You're late tonight. Help me to the loo, son. There's a doll.'

Fuck! I pull the pillow around my ears, blocking out her repeated call. Then a pang contracts my chest. How can I be so fucking tight? She must be starving. I made her scrambled eggs this morning and divided my share between her and Jessie, but that's all she'll have had to eat today. Benefits cheque's not due until tomorrow. Wonder if she's had her meds?

I rise, every muscle protesting. All I want to do is have a few minutes to collect my thoughts, but she can't wait. I can't let her down. 'Coming, Mam.'

Her room smells of stale piss and roses. She looks so frail on the bed. Today's not been a good day for her. Lines trail out from the corners of her mouth and across her forehead, like those root diagrams on the biology classroom walls. Still, she smiles when she sees me, her eyes lighting up. I paste a smile on my face and move over to drop a kiss on her greasy hair. 'Home Help not help you shower today, Mam?'

'Cancelled again, Jo Jo. Jessie brought me a cup of tea and some toast earlier.' Her face flushes. 'She tried to empty the commode, bless her, but it was too much for her. She spilt a bit.'

I deal with the commode, making a mental note to get on the phone to the care agency. Don't want to complain too much though in case they decide to take Jessie away. Then, I go back and help her shuffle through to the main bathroom. I stand her next to the toilet and then wait outside, giving her privacy. When I hear the flush, I go back inside and help her do an all-over sponge-wash and brush her teeth. She hates it. Hates that I have to do it, but folk like us have no option. No fucking choice. Not like I enjoy it either. But I'm all she's got. When she's back in bed, I nip downstairs and make her a tea. Only then do I sneak a glance at the time. Running well late. Three minutes to go.

'Got to go, Mam. Got homework to do.'

She grips my hand and squeezes it. 'You're a good boy, Jo Jo. Don't know what I'd do without you.'

I shrug and hand her the TV controls and pretend not to notice the glimmer of tears, or the fact that her grip is less firm than usual. Tomorrow will be a better day. It couldn't be any effing worse.

I smile and kiss her forehead. 'Night, Mam.'

So much for getting in the zone. Just have to force myself... need the dosh. I push open my bedroom door and then stop.

Shit! Anger surges from my toes right up to my head in a red-hot flame. I close the door, so I don't disturb Mam and try to keep my voice calm. 'What you doing in here, Jessie? You know you're not allowed.'

Standing there in her too-short PJs, her ginger hair mussed, My Little Pony toy under her arm, nipple clamps in one hand and a butt plug in the other, she blinks at me. 'Couldn't sleep, Jo Jo. Wanted a cuddle.' Her bottom lip trembles as she shifts her weight from one foot to the other. 'What are these, Jo Jo?'

'They're nowt, Jessie. Just some stuff for my machines. You've not to touch them again, okay?' She's so little. Still, her PJs slide up her arm and barely cover her knees. *How the hell did I forget to lock the door*? I never forget and now she's standing there holding fucking sex toys.

'Oh for…' I stride across the room, remove the clamps and butt plug from her tiny hands and throw them on the bed. Swinging her onto my hip, I head for the door, wondering what else she's touched, what else she's seen. Fucking idiot, should've locked the damn door. Need to get a grip on things. Can't let what happened earlier distract me. Got to hold things together for Jessie and me mam.

'You cross, Jo Jo?'

Her scrunched up nose and the downward tip of her lips tells me she's near to tears. I nuzzle my forehead into her hair and force a smile. 'No, Jessie. Course not. Now back to bed for you. It's a school day tomorrow.'

As I carry her from the room, the insistent flashing light on my laptop taunts me, reminding me I've got work to do. Nearly show time and I'm still not oiled up. Just hope to God tonight's client dun't want owt too kinky. After everything that's happened this evening, I'm so *not* in the mood.

CHAPTER 9

Sweat pooled under Gus' armpits as he made his way towards the Haunted House which was lit by harsh white light blasting from the spotlights. Still eerie, the savage lighting lent an almost ethereal glow to proceedings, conjuring up images in his mind of elves and fairies and goblins rather than the much scarier Smiling Jack that Karim had spoken about earlier. The house still loomed, silent and brooding, but its edges looked smoother, less abrasively threatening. Gus smiled and shrugged off the lingering fear he'd experienced as a child when dusk had crept up on him and his friends unexpectedly.

Near the front door of the house, he stopped and turned around to judge both the distance and the view to the road. As expected, visibility was poor. There was no risk of a passer-by noticing anything out of the ordinary unless they actually entered the grounds. What had enticed this young lad into the shrubbery? A dare gone wrong? Drug deal? Illicit meeting with a girlfriend... or boyfriend... or prostitute?

Moving closer, Gus could hear the mumbled voices of the crime scene officers. He dreaded putting on his crime scene suit – never had the term 'boiler suit' seemed more apt. He admired the fortitude of the crime scene techs who, without complaint, worked in them despite the heat. Hissing Sid's team had already erected a crime scene tent around the body and Gus was keen to view it in situ before it was moved to the morgue. When he reached the inner crime scene cordon, Gus signed himself in, before struggling into the suit he'd grabbed from a plastic box, abandoned on the parched grass.

His father's voice drifted through from inside. For once, he couldn't summon up the energy to be irked that his dad was the pathologist on call. Keeping to the metal treads, he approached a cluster of CSIs in white coveralls who were busy processing the scene. Gus was happy that his dad insisted on seeing the body where it lay. It was part of the deal his old man had signed with himself years ago when he first became a pathologist. Gus himself had signed a similar deal with himself when he became a detective. The weight that had settled in the pit of his stomach made him expect the worst. There was no way a teenager would be lying dead in the shrubbery of this derelict house if it wasn't suspicious circumstances. Taffy's notion of unseen evil suddenly didn't seem so far-fetched. Gus shuddered and peered into the shadows, trying to dispel the feeling that just out of sight a monster was lurking. *Get a grip, Gus!* He thrust those thoughts away and concentrated on the death he had been called out to investigate. Suicide, murder, or a grotesque accident, it made no difference to Gus. There was still a family out there somewhere who would be woken in the middle of the night to learn that they were minus a loved one and it was Gus' job to get to the bottom of it for them.

The two officers who'd called it in had referred to it as a murder scene and, although he hadn't said so, the lad, Karim, clearly thought that too. Fully covered and with damp dreads tucked inside his hood to avoid cross contamination of the area, Gus popped his head through the flap. 'Okay to come in, Sid?'

A man of smaller stature turned and grinned at him. 'Well if it isn't Gussy boy, late to the party but welcome, nonetheless. Come on in. Your dad's just about finished doing his magic.'

Used to Hissing Sid's blasé humour, Gus ignored the other man's tone and stepped through the flap into a wall of heat that immediately made him want to strip down to his shorts and T-shirt. A quick glance at his dad told him he was suffering too. His round face, ruddier than usual, was dappled with droplets of sweat and his beard had become a cluster of tight curls in the humidity. If Gus was struggling, his dad would be nearly at the end of his tether – a big man who carried a sizeable amount of excess weight, this weather was torture to him, especially when wrapped in a crime scene suit in the narrow confines of a sweltering tent.

Deliberately, Gus cleared his mind of any thoughts and approached the body, which was hidden by his father's large frame. Dr McGuire moved to the side in silence. His gaze remained on the boy sprawled on his back on the brown weeds as he allowed his son time to take in the scene.

The lad looked younger than sixteen and if it hadn't been for the knife protruding from his neck and the pool of coagulating blood on the grass beneath him, he could have been enjoying a doze. From the position of the head, face upwards, eyes closed, Gus could tell that he'd been placed like that deliberately. If he'd fallen, his head would naturally have angled to the opposite side from the entry wound. This observation was corroborated by the way the lad's legs were stretched straight out like tram lines, his toes pointing to the sky. Skinny legs stuck out from his denim shorts with a pair of newish looking Nike trainers on his feet. His arms had been brought forward and his hands clasped together on his abdomen, rather like he was in a coffin. Loosely grasped in his fingers was an iPhone.

Gus' gaze trailed up to the lad's face. A spattering of acne across his forehead and faint stubble on his chin seemed to emphasise the waste of life. His clothes were fashionable although not ostentatiously so. If the phone belonged to the lad, which seemed likely, Gus was sure they'd get an ID soon enough. He turned to Sid. 'When you've done photographing here can you get that phone off to the lab? I want to ID the kid asap.' Bending down to get a closer look, Gus spoke to the uniformed officer who'd accompanied him into the tent. 'No missing person's reports tonight?'

'No, sir. I've asked them to alert us if any come in fitting the lad's description.'

Satisfied, Gus nodded. 'Right, Sid, if Dr McGuire has finished and you've done your bit, can we check for other ID?'

'Done it just before you arrived. The lad's got nothing on him – nowt in his pockets. Maybe whoever did this to him swiped it.'

The weapon looked like any bog-standard kitchen knife, but they'd be able to get a brand and so on after it had been removed at the post mortem. Gus leaned in closer to the lad and sniffed. Apart from the coppery blood smell which he was desperately trying to ignore, he could detect something else. 'Alcohol?'

Sid clapped his gloved hands, making a slappy seal type of sound. 'Well done. Yep. I thought there was some booze consumed, so I got them,' he gestured widely with his hands to incorporate his team, 'to bag up all the bottles they find for printing. Maybe we'll be lucky and find our killer's prints.' He kicked the ground. 'We're fortunate it's been so dry. Almost perfect crime scene for us. No deterioration of evidence. Hopefully we'll get summat.' He paused and an elongated squeaky sound rent the air.

For a second, Gus looked round to identify the source of the noise before jumping to his feet, gagging. 'For fuck's sake, Sid. As if it's not bad enough in here without your pollution. Get the fuck away from me if all you can contribute is toxic farts.'

Sid looked at him, his smile clear even behind his mask. 'Summat's got to lighten the atmosphere, Gus.'

A quick glance at his dad told Gus that he was unamused too. 'Not the time nor the place as you well know. Just get out of here and let me talk to the doc. You really need to quit this shit, Sid. Nobody is amused – nobody!'

A ripple of approval went around the tent and one of the CSIs who'd paused to observe the disagreement nodded. Sid looked at them, then at Gus, before leaving the tent.

Releasing a sigh, Gus looked at his dad, who slapped a hand on his son's shoulder. 'He needs to know, laddie. It's getting beyond a joke and he does it on purpose. You did right telling him.'

Gus wasn't so sure his pulling rank on the CSI officer wouldn't come back to bite him on the arse. He'd had a run in with Hissing Sid previously and things were only just beginning to mend and now he'd felt compelled to pull him up yet again for disrespectful behaviour. Truth was, Gus had been on edge, trying to control his reaction to the blood, otherwise he'd probably have pulled Sid to the side and admonished him privately rather than in public. On second thoughts, he'd given Sid ample warnings previously and he'd chosen to ignore them. Maybe a short sharp shock was necessary. He pulled his thoughts back to the boy lying before them and focussed. 'Jugular?'

Doc McGuire, with effort, lowered himself onto one knee and inspected the wound. 'Yes, a forceful, vicious stab wound delivered by a right-handed person standing in front of him. However,' he leaned forward and turned the boy's wrists, 'these striations indicate to me that the victim was tied up. These cuts are quite deep into the skin.'

Gus studied the cuts. 'Looks like cable tie marks to me.'

One of the CSIs stepped forward holding out a bag containing a cable tie that had been sliced open. 'Funny you should say that. Just found this over in the bush at the back. There's blood trace on this.'

Gus smiled a thank you before looking at an area to the side of the boy's head where his dad was pointing. A series of faint bruises at either side of his skull fanned out with five distinct pressure points ranging from his forehead down to his jawline.

'Fingerprints?'

Dr McGuire nodded. 'It looks to me like someone held his head steady with a vice-like grip.' He struggled back to his feet, indicated that Gus should turn around and then positioned his hands on Gus' head. His father's spread fingers touched Gus' forehead and temple and his thumb rested at his lower jaw an inch or so below his ear.

It was odd to be so close to his dad like this, especially at a crime scene. It took him back to the rough and tumble they'd enjoyed when he was a kid. It seemed like years ago and his dad had added a substantial amount of weight in the interim which was why he was breathing so hard in Gus' ear now. He'd maybe have a word with his mum about putting him on a diet. Last thing he wanted was for the old bugger to keel over from a heart attack. 'So, there were two of them?'

'Looks pretty much like it to me. As usual, I'll be able to tell you more after the PM, but I think the bruising on his head happened at around the same time... no I'm pretty certain of that.'

Gus bit his lip and took a few minutes to study the boy. Kids' deaths were hard. He wondered what this lad's aspirations had been. Did he play sports? Was he arty? Who were his friends? His relatives? It didn't matter to Gus whether he'd been clever or not, whether he'd been talented or not... he was a kid whose life had been snuffed out violently and that meant that Gus was committed to finding whoever had done it. He waited for his dad to give instructions about the removal of the body and together they left the tent, retracing their steps over the metal treads.

Gus' limbs felt heavy and trickles of sweat rolled down his back, soaking into the T-shirt he wore under the suit. A minuscule breeze had picked up. Not enough to cool the air but enough to send gentle wafts of his dad's body odour in Gus' direction. The oppressive heat combined with the wonky air conditioning at The Fort meant that the past few weeks had been filled with an array of BO, with top notes of different perfumes and deodorants designed to disguise the smell. The weather couldn't break soon enough for Gus, yet the forecast showed no signs of a change.

As they moved closer to the road, Gus' phone rang, startling him. It was a ringtone he rarely heard any more, 'The Bitch is Back', and yet this was the third time today. Seemingly his dad also recognised it. 'You and Gabriella speaking again?'

Gus and his ex-wife had been avoiding each other for the past few months. Partly because she blamed him for her brother's death and partly because Gus couldn't stand the conflict she inevitably brought to his life. He flicked the phone to dismiss her call and shrugged. 'I've spoken to Katie, but not Gabriella. She's phoned a few times today, but I just can't handle her.'

'You'll have to speak to her sometime, lad. She's living with your sister, you can't just pretend she doesn't exist forever, you know? Besides...'

Besides nothing. Gus had had enough of his ex-wife's machinations to last a lifetime. Cursing inside, Gus smiled a tight smile and remained silent. Trust Gabriella to ring when he was with his dad. He'd had enough of his parents trying to smooth things over between them 'for Katie's sake'. He had the grace to feel a little bad for his sister, but overall, he couldn't summon up the energy to give a shit about Gabriella. He had more important relationships to nurture – like the one with Patti and the one with his team… thinking of his team made him think of Alice and another wave of tiredness rolled over him.

'…maybe they need you right now.'

Really? Gus looked at his dad, hurt that he'd play the guilt card. Giving himself a mental shake, he ignored his dad's words, raised a hand in farewell and strode towards Taffy who was waiting for him by the car. 'I'll send Taffy to the PM tomorrow, Dad. Let me know when it is.'

He could feel his father's eyes on his back as he walked away, but he couldn't bring himself to look back. This was the first PM he had delegated to a subordinate officer, yet for once, he carried no guilt. Taffy enjoyed the PMs, while Gus struggled with them. The work with his psychiatrist on delegating stuff was paying off.

CHAPTER 10

Heart hammering, I run down past the BRI, past the Duckworth Lane Roundabout, down Lilycroft Road, past The Fort and onto Oak Lane. Downhill all the way. My throat's raw through breathing in the warm night air. My hoodie sticks to me, damp and uncomfortable. As I pass Mo's Samosas, I slow slightly, wishing for even a small gasp of air to cool me down. Fucking café. No way I'll be helping there ever again. On cue, my phone vibrates… him again… Mo. What can't he just leave me alone?

> Mo: You okay, Zarqa? It's late. Mum and I are worried about you. Let us know you're okay, love Dad xxx

I shove it back in my pocket, wishing I could throw it on the road and jump on it. Better still, I wish it was Mo's head. Then I'd *really* enjoy stamping on it. My hair's tangled and sweat pours down my face, dripping off my chin. Impatient, I wipe my face with the sleeve of my hoodie. Then, gasping for air, I fold forward, resting my hands on my knees and try to draw breath. Apart from my own raw pants, the night is filled with sounds. Cars slow down as they reach the traffic lights at Manningham Lane. Distant sirens compete with souped-up lad racers. Over by the bank, the two homeless blokes I often see in the park are having an argument. The sounds roll over me, soothing me, and at last my breathing slows and my lungs stop hurting quite so much.

What the fuck have we done, Jo Jo and me? What the fuck did we do? I pushed him into it… forced him, really. He wasn't keen, had his reservations… but I wouldn't let go. Wouldn't give up. My breath hitches in my throat and I snort back a sob. Too bloody late to be getting upset now. Way too late.

I notice the group of lads behind me. They're still a distance away, but I can hear their voices; loud and full of swag. They're probably all right, but I can't be arsed with the hassle, so I straighten up, flip my hood back over my head, tuck my hair inside, and bulk up my frame before turning into my street. When I reach my house, the lights are on behind the curtains. That's the last thing I need – another yelling match. I turn on my heels, ready to retrace my steps – I'd rather take my chances with the Oak Lane lads than face Mo and my mum right now. I take two steps and falter.

Ping!

> Mum: Zarqa, please come home. You need your sleep, beti. Remember you've got an exam tomorrow? We're not cross. Just come home, Love Mum, xxx

Aw shit! My knees buckle a little as a wave of exhaustion rolls over me. I've enough sense to realise it's because of the adrenalin rush… that and guilt. I close my eyes for a second and then hear the chirrup chirrup of a car lock further down the street. That makes my mind up for me. Instead of heading back, I turn and squeeze myself through the hedge that borders our property and practically fall in a heap on the grass in the corner of the garden. This little bit of ground is just out of reach of the security sensor, so unless a fox or something strolls across the middle of the garden or up the main path, I should remain undetected for now.

I pull my hoodie off, peeling it off my arms like shedding a layer of flesh. The warm air feels good on my skin. It doesn't cool me, but quickly dries my sweat. I scrunch forward and manage to spread the hoodie under my bum before pulling my knees up under my chin and hugging them close to my chest. For what seems like a long time, I watch the shadows cast by the street lighting and the moon flicker before me. Each one is familiar to me, yet right now, none of them seems real. It's as if they're dissociated from me – part of another life, another time. The garden shed where I used to play with my dolls, the playhouse that my sisters use now, the washing whirligig, permanently open now it's summer, the shed where we keep the logs for winter... it all seems alien... like it was never mine.

I roll my head, trying to ease the crick in my neck and exhale. Now, I'm here, the night closing in around me, the sounds from the road muted, I need to think. I really need to think. What Jo Jo and I did tonight was bad... really bad. My mind keeps flashing to the actual act – the final act, but I can't let it stay there. I've got to think smart. What is it my godfather, Gus, always says? Yep that's it: 'It's the forensics that let them down every time, Zarqa.'

Right, so, have we left forensic evidence behind, Jo Jo and me? We covered up; we wore gloves. Jo Jo made sure we weren't spotted. As near as I could make out, we're okay – in the clear. So why do I feel like crap?

It'll be all over the news tomorrow. They'll all be chatting shit about it at school – maybe I'll skip school – maybe get Jo Jo to bunk off too. Couldn't care less about my exams, couldn't care less about anything. Shit, Zarqa, don't be soft. Course you can't bunk off school with Jo Jo – that'd be a sure way of drawing attention to yourself. Get a fucking grip! Got to act normal. Like nowt's happened.

I pull my knees tighter under my chin and try to breathe slowly. There's nothing pointing to us. They'll put it down to another hate crime, that's all. All Jo Jo and I need to do is brazen it out and not crack. So what if it's on the news? So what if everybody's talking about it? It's nowt to do with us. We'll keep our heads down until it all blows over. I mean how long can it all last?

I begin to rock on my bum. My eyes start to fill with tears, and I open my mouth and bite my knee to stop the sobs that want to break out from escaping. What we did was bad… really bad, but it's done now. There's nothing we can do about it, except stay schtum.

CHAPTER 11

B y the time Gus and Taffy got back to The Fort from the crime scene, they knew the victim's identity. When he hadn't returned home by eleven, Pratab Patel's parents had turned up at The Fort to report him missing. It took only a quick glance at one of the photos on Mrs Patel's phone to wrench their fragile hope away.

Grieving parents shouldn't be interviewed in a police station, yet Gus had no choice. They needed as much information as they could extract, and grieving would have to come second to expediency for now. Although he hated it, this was one job Gus couldn't delegate, so he took Pratab's parents into the coolest, most comfortable room they had. Like it mattered which room you were in when your heart was broken into a trillion pieces. As if they'd ever be truly comfortable again.

Mrs Patel, hair bundled up in a loose top knot sat tearless, clasping and unclasping her hands while Gus made drinks which would remain untouched. By the time Gus sat opposite them, her hands were still, and she sat, straight shouldered, looking directly at him. She was the strong one, maintaining her composure, although her lips were tight and tell-tale lines furrowed her brow. On entering the room, Mr Patel had collapsed in a heap on the couch and remained scrunched in on himself, a low keening sound his only response to Gus' questions.

As his wife soothed him, speaking all the time in Gujarati, holding his head to her chest, patting his hair as he sobbed, Gus felt like an intruder. He sipped tea he didn't want and waited until Mr Patel's blinding grief turned to numbness before speaking. 'Where was Pratab supposed to be this evening?'

Mrs Patel, gripping her husband's hand so tightly that her knuckles turned white, spoke quietly, her voice shaking over every word. 'Pratab said he was going to study at his friend Haider's house because they have…' realising her mistake she inhaled sharply. 'I mean *had* a maths exam tomorrow. When he hadn't returned by nine, we phoned round, but he hadn't turned up at his friend's, had never had an arrangement to study there. He lied to us and now…'

Tears trickled down her face and releasing her husband's hand she brushed them away with the back of her own hand. Gus suspected that the knowledge of that lie would haunt her for a long time to come… that and the *what ifs* that always accompanied a violent death. There was nothing he could do to soothe her, but he wished that even just for a few seconds, Mr Patel would respond to his wife's grief instead of allowing his own to swallow him up.

As if sensing Gus' thoughts, Mrs Patel sniffed and gripped her husband's hand again. 'Manoj is unwell. He suffers from anxiety and depression. This is too difficult for him to deal with. I need to take him home. I need to tell my other children what has happened… how will I do that, Detective McGuire?'

Helpless and ineffectual, Gus spoke words that he realised offered little comfort. 'All you can do is tell them the truth and then be there for each other.'

He waited a few moments and then said, 'I need to ask a few more things. Will you be all right?'

A gentle smile crossed her lips and she nodded. 'I just want to find out who did this to my boy. Ask anything you like.'

'Has Pratab seemed different recently? Anything out of the ordinary? Behaving erratically? Worried, anxious… anything?'

'Maybe a little anxious. We put it down to the stress of his GCSEs. He's been a bit distant. Skipping meals and things… but nothing major. Nothing that made us feel he was at risk. He's a good boy is Pratab. Set to get A*s in his exams.'

'You have other children?'

'Yes. Kiran is seventeen, nearly eighteen, and Mita is fifteen. We wanted to have them close together. Wanted them to be close growing up.'

Those poor kids to lose a brother like that.

'I have to ask a few more things. Was Pratab happy at school? Any new friends? No staying out later than normal? Playing up? A girlfriend?'

As expected, those questions had Mrs Patel bristling. No parent likes the hint that their child might be misbehaving, and no grieving parent wants to address their dead child's imperfections. Her lips tightened and a pulse at the side of her face twitched.

'My son is dead and you're hinting that he's somehow to blame?'

It didn't matter how prepared he was for this reaction, Gus hated having to ask the questions. 'I'm not for one minute suggesting Pratab is to blame. The only person to blame is the one who did this to him… and we'll do our best to find out who that is. However, if there is anything, no matter how small or seemingly insignificant that sticks in your mind, it could help us find his killer. I know this is hard and you're doing so well. Think about it overnight and if you remember anything at all, just let us know.'

'Can we go, now? We really need to go… Kiran and Mita… you know?'

Gus nodded. 'I'll allocate a Family Liaison Officer. Her role will be to liaise between you and us, but I will come to see you tomorrow. I'll want to talk to your other children and get more of a sense of who Pratab was.'

She nodded and stood up, gently cajoling her husband to his feet. Mr Patel wobbled and looked like he might collapse. Gus stepped forward and took his other arm. 'Will you be okay getting home? I can get a patrol car to take you.'

'If you can help me to the car, Kiran will help us when we get home. It's not far. I can drive. I'd rather have the car with me… just in case.'

Escorting them to their vehicle, Gus walked slowly and with his hand under Mr Patel's elbow, Gus could feel the grief wracking the man's body. He swore that whoever had destroyed this family's happiness would be brought to justice.

CHAPTER 12

Monday

E very stride was like slicing through a brick wall with a butter knife and Gus wasn't entirely sure why he was putting himself through it. Not five minutes away from his front door, he had only just entered Lister Park through the Emm Lane entrance and already his face was oozing sweat, and his T-shirt was clinging to him. Even the traffic seemed lethargic along Bradford Road, as if it was waiting for a storm to break. Hell, they'd been waiting for one to break for days and nothing had materialised.

It had been a long route to recovery since he'd been stabbed in February and, even now, he felt an acute stab of pain when he jogged; a pulling sensation from his upper thigh to his groin as the scar tissue mended. Still, this was *his* time. The time for him to think and after the anonymous note and the dead boy who had been discovered yesterday, he had plenty to think about.

Of course, there was Gabriella too. What the hell was she playing at, phoning him after all this time? He'd nearly fired off a text to his sister telling her to make Gaby stop hassling him, but he'd reconsidered. Last thing he needed was to get drawn into their dramas… not when he'd just landed a murder case. He could ring Gaby's bloody neck for the way she'd behaved at her brother's funeral… the things she'd said to him. Did she really want him to turn a blind eye to her murdering brother's misdeeds? His pace increased making his chest tighten and his muscles pull. He was aware that it was because he was thinking about Gaby and so he deliberately slowed a little. Just a damn pity the oppressive heat made his jog so much harder. Determined not to let the heat beat him, he made an impulse decision to add an extra circuit of the boating lake before heading up and past Cartwright Hall to work.

He swerved right and, seconds later, groaned as he felt the slight incline pull his leg muscles again. Gritting his teeth, he pushed through the burn and soon he was on the level, heading past the ducks and swans that had gathered at the top end of the pond near the islands. Warmth filled the air with a mulchy smell which, combined with the ammonia from the generous deposits made by the geese, had Gus breathing shallowly through his mouth. Dodging the excrement was hazardous and he slipped a couple of times. The park was busy, although mainly with power walkers who had seemingly slowed their pace in deference to the heat. Most were going in the opposite direction from Gus, so he waved and nodded at the few regulars he encountered. A few school kids sauntered around or sat, phones in hand, on the benches, some in uniform and some, clearly on exam leave, wearing shorts and T-shirts.

He'd nearly completed his self-enforced circle of the pond, when he saw that one of the benches ahead was inhabited by two familiar forms, their sleeping bags rolled up and tied with string on the floor at their feet. Smiling, Gus slowed as he approached. He'd not seen Dave and Jerry for a few weeks and was keen to make sure they were all right. During the Beast from the East, things had hit crisis point for Dave and he'd ended up in Lynfield Mount for a while. Now, Gus was pleased to see that he looked chubbier and rosier than when he'd last seen him. 'Hi, you two. Sunbathing?'

Jerry chortled, deep and low, his eyes sparkling as he replied. 'Sun gods, that's what we are, in't we, Dave?'

Gus turned his attention to Dave who gave an abrupt nod. For Dave, that was positively gregarious, and Gus was happy to see it. The homeless man's eyes were clear today and it was fair to assume that Jerry was keeping on top of his mate's meds. Gus had enlisted Mo's help in ensuring that the two old men had a regular supply of food and hot drinks during the winter, but now that the weather was so hot, Gus was more concerned that they'd dehydrate. He slipped off the small backpack he carried when jogging and took out two bottles of water. Handing one to each man, he was pleased to see no hesitancy from Dave when he accepted it. 'Keep your fluids up, yeah?'

Jerry grinned, opened the bottle, and took a hearty swig. Dave, after a quick glance at his friend, did likewise. 'Wanted to talk to you, Gus.'

Jerry had lowered his voice and began kicking the ground in front of the bench. The toe of his plimsoll flapped as his foot moved, prompting Gus to make a mental note to check if his old man had any spare shoes. He reckoned Jerry's feet were about the same size as his dad's. 'Yeah? Is something up?'

Jerry exchanged a quick glance with Dave, who nodded once before folding his arms over his chest and staring into the distance.

This was odd. 'You two okay?'

Jerry sighed and raised his head to look at straight at Gus. 'It's a bit sensitive like, Gus.'

Sensitive? Okay. 'You can tell me anything, Jerry. You know that. We're mates, aren't we?'

'Well yeah, course I know that. You and Mo and me and Dave… we're all mates together. Thing is, I don't want to get her into bother.'

Now Gus was well puzzled. 'Get who into bother?'

'That young lass of his. His oldest one. The one who helps out in the café sometimes. Zarqa.'

'Zarqa?' *What the hell's she been up to now*? Had Jerry and Dave seen her with a lad or something? They were always a bit protective of Mo and Gus' families.

Jerry sniffed. 'Saw her last night, jogging down from Lilycroft Road like she was being chased by the hounds of hell. Not right that. Young lass like her should be home before it gets dark.'

Dave emitted a growl from the depths of his chest and judging by the succession of quick nods that accompanied the rumble of sound, he was in complete agreement with his friend.

Jerry continued, a worried frown creasing his tanned forehead, 'Looked frightened she did.'

That wasn't like Mo to let Zarqa stay out late on her own, but then that was before she'd decided to act out. 'You sure it was her?'

'Yep, that oldest lass of his. It was after dark and you know what Oak Lane's like after closing time.'

Dark? After closing time? What the hell had Zarqa been out so late for? Wasn't it GCSE time? And did Mo even know anything about it? 'Was it that late then?'

Jerry shrugged and, surprisingly, it was Dave who answered. 'After eleven... too late.'

Seeing that it was preying on the two men's minds, Gus smiled. 'Don't worry, I'll speak to Mo about it. Teenagers, huh? They're always playing up.'

'You talk to Mo today, Gus. He's worried about her. I can tell. She's not been in the café recently. I think summat's up.'

Jerry was right. Something was up and he was glad that Jerry had shared this information with him. 'I'm on it. Now, are you two managing to get beds in one of the hostels?'

A grin flashed across Jerry's face and he nudged his friend, giggling a little. 'Nope. Why would we do that?

Dave and I like to sleep with the stars above us and in this weather that's no hardship, is it?'

The man's smile was contagious, and Gus found himself responding with a grin of his own. 'No, I suppose not. Just be safe, won't you? You still got that phone?'

Jerry tapped his coat pocket. 'Yes, sir!' And he did a mock salute, before relenting and adding, 'Mo lets us charge it up in his café and I make sure I keep it on at least two bars.'

Gus had tried to keep moving while talking to the men, but he could feel his legs stiffening. 'All right then, I'm off. Got work to do. Don't want to get sacked now, do I?'

As he headed up through the Botanic Gardens and past the bandstand, he made a mental note to speak to Zarqa first. Time he took this godfather job a bit more seriously than he had in recent months. When it had all kicked off at Mo's house, he'd thought that things would sort themselves out. Mo and Naila had always had a close relationship with their kids… sometimes though, events could put an almost unbearable strain on them and so maybe now was the time for an intervention, before Zarqa did something really stupid.

CHAPTER 13

Zodiac

A drenalin kept me up most of the night. Kept going over and over it, reliving every second. Each time, I remembered something new, something more. I've covered my tracks, so I'm not worried about that. No clues left behind, I'm sure of it… don't know about the others though, but that's all part of the plan. What we did was so bad… but sooo good too. The heat… the excitement… the pressure… I thought I was going to explode. Well, I certainly did *that* when I got home… exploded that is… twice.

Teamwork, that's what it was… but every team needs a leader and thank fuck, I was up to the mark.

Feel a bit flat now… deflated. Never mind though. I know just the thing. It's easy to sneak out early. I creep downstairs while it's all quiet. Nobody will notice I'm gone… why would they? The only time I'm noticed is when I've done something wrong. With any luck, I'll be back before breakfast.

Ping!

> Pisces: You awake? Need to talk! Feel crap.

What a div! Can't be doing with Pisces' shit right now. Dumbass. Anyway, I've got stuff to do… lots of stuff! I check in my bag to make sure I've got everything. Shoes on, I grab a couple of croissants and an energy drink and, careful not to bang the door behind me, I step outside.

Fucking boiling again. Suits me though. I like the sun. Gives me an excuse to be outside… to loiter, so I can keep an eye on things.

Doesn't take long for me to get to where I need to be. The café's not open yet, but I've brought my own breakfast. I sit down on one of the benches and share my croissants with the ducks.

Ping!

> Pisces: Can you answer, Zodiac? I'm losing it. Like Bigtime. Need to talk to you. Talk to someone.

Fuck's sake! Can you believe this shit? I think about ignoring the text, then reconsider. What if the idiot falls apart?

> Me: Hold tight. You did so good last night. Really good. I'm so impressed. You were better than Leo. No doubt about it. You just gotta hang in there, okay? I'll see you at school, right?

Needy, dumbass, div. I grin. The one thing I enjoy more than anything else is setting them off against each other… playing favourites. They're both so needy but in different ways. That's why I chose them.

Headphones in, I check my social media. *Instagram* first. Boy, do I have some pictures I could share! I laugh. Even the thought of everyone's reaction makes me grin. But, no. I'm not going to indulge myself… not yet, anyway. I'll save that image and use it for maximum effect, when the time's right.

That's the thing, if you do something too early, you mess up. Timing is everything. You get the timing right and you've nailed it – maximum effect – maximum chaos – maximum satisfaction for me. I move over to *Facebook* and scroll down.

Shit… shit…

Like…

Crap…

Like…

Smiley Face…

Rubbish… shit… shit…

Love Heart…

Boring… tedious… shit!

Then it gets interesting. It's leaked on *Facebook* and the vacuous comments start. Love that word vacuous… it was the word of the day last week in school. Sums up this situation perfectly. Vacuous comments for a vacuous piece of shit!

> You'll be missed my bestest friend, from Declan
>
> RIP, Pratab. Love you, Meena and Kamal xx :-(:-(
>
> You're loving angels instead! Missing you already, Love Betsy Reavley xxxxxx

Really? I mean *really*? Barf!

Yuk… makes me sick. Some of them are even posting pictures with them and the dumbass. Ones with love hearts round them or with flower haloes. What the fuck. Maybe they deserve to join him. What are they like? It's getting hotter and I wonder how much longer I'll have to wait.

It's then I see him. He's jogging round the lake, so I snap a couple of photos on zoom. Then he stops, talking to some mucky old tramps and I fire off another couple. Before he heads round in my direction, I backtrack down to the lower path and circle back. I've got a job to do before I head back home and last thing I need is to be seen. Not here... not right now.

CHAPTER 14

Compo had been a bit liberal with the Lynx, to the point where on entering the open plan investigation room after his shower, Gus nearly choked. He got why Compo had done it… it was stifling in the room. The windows only opened a couple of inches, presumably in case Gus decided to throw one of the team out. The air conditioning was broken, and the few fans dotted around the room weren't strong enough to waft a crisp packet never mind have a cooling effect. In short, the amalgamation of busy, sweaty bodies, in a confined space for hours on end, in the middle of a heat wave, had resulted in a less than palatable undertone.

Taffy and Compo between them were setting up the new, all singing, all dancing crime board that linked all the computers in the room to a touch screen interactive board at the front. He was sure he'd seen a Tom Cruise film with something similar in it. Was it wrong to wish they'd spent the money on the air con rather than equipment Gus wasn't sure he'd ever be able to master without Compo's presence?

'Soooo, we're up and running with that, are we?' Gus could hear the petulance in his voice and wished he could take the words back. It wasn't Compo's fault he was a dinosaur and deep down; he was aware that he really should get to grips with this tech stuff. He relied far too heavily on Compo for even the most basic of things.

Seemingly oblivious to his boss' mood, Compo grinned, his shiny cheeks wobbling as he nodded. 'It's brilliant, Gus. Don't you worry though, I'll get you trained up in no time.'

Gus snorted. It wasn't that he was worried exactly, more irritated. He always had so much on his plate that finding time to update his knowledge of the new-fangled system that had been foisted on him was way down his list of priorities. Watching with grudging admiration as Compo and Taffy effortlessly operated the system, he sighed. 'We'll see. But for now, we've got a killer to catch, yeah?'

Seeing he had both officers' attention, Gus began. 'Right, Compo, you've got the victim's phone – do your magic with that. I want to know everything he was up to for the last six months, who he spoke to, who his friends were, where he went, what his social media can tell us... the lot.'

He turned to Taffy. 'Although Dr McGuire didn't detect any sexual activity on site, this won't be confirmed until the PM, so I want to know about any perverts, paedophiles etc. in the area. Get to grips with drug activity and see if you can establish some sort of link there.' All too often teen deaths were gang and/or drug related and although there was no indication this was the case here; Gus would ensure his team explored all avenues. 'Also, check for any like or similar crimes in the region.'

As he'd been speaking Compo had input his *actions* and they were now on the screen next to two images of Pratab Patel. Gus took a moment to look at the lad. In death he looked pitifully young. In life he had a big grin, sparkling eyes, and a handsome face... *what a damn waste*!

'Pratab's one of Patti's pupils at City Academy so we'll head up there later. I'll address the older kids... see if we can drum up some information from them.'

'Poor Patti.' Compo's tone was morose, and this was reflected in his doleful expression and heavy sigh.

'Eh, why poor Patti?'

'Well, City Academy's had more than its fair share of press attention recently, hasn't it?'

Gus groaned. *What an idiot*! Of course, this would be crap for Patti. She'd had journalists laying siege at the school gates off and on for months now. Jez Hopkins had been particularly persistent after one of her kids was arrested last year. Gus still hadn't forgiven him for his irresponsible reporting before that and then the man had compounded his idiocy by exploiting the parents of a boy who'd committed suicide after online bullying and argued that City Academy was responsible for not having tighter policies on digital usage. Like a school could monitor kids' social media activity twenty-four/seven. 'Nearly forgot about Jez Hopkins' Suicide Watch articles.'

'Not to mention the field day the prat had when that teacher was arrested,' added Taffy. 'Hope he's not a dick about this.'

Gus hoped so too, although he suspected not being a dick wasn't top of Hopkins' priority list. 'We'll just have to get this solved quickly before he can be a dick. That's all there is to it.'

He walked over to the screen and looked at Pratab's picture from the crime scene. Was he posed like that? His dad certainly seemed to think so and Gus tended to agree. The phone clasped in his hands like some sort of homage to 4G and technology. The equivalent of rosary beads or something? Why did it smack of ritual? He had no real indication that it was a ritualistic kill... just experience, and he'd had more than his fair share of experience of rituals and evil and death. Yep, he'd definitely speak to Nancy. No point in risking things spiralling out of control because he hadn't acted on his finely honed instincts. Not this time.

CHAPTER 15

You can cut the atmosphere with a knife. Mum's trying to do the whole 'everything's normal' thing... the special breakfast to mark a special event... spicy scrambled eggs and paratha. It's just a fucking exam. The important thing happened before I was even born. The thing they don't want to talk about. The thing they haven't wanted to talk about since I was conceived. My acne's flared up again and I have to stop myself picking at it, especially the big one right on my chin. Instead, I play with my cutlery, head down, aware that he's watching me, all sad eyed, trying to make me feel guilty. He's the one that should be feeling fucking guilty. The silence is too much for Mum, I reckon that's why she switches on the radio.

...the youth found dead in Heaton last night has been identified. A police spokesperson says that the boy found at a property on Smith Lane has been identified as sixteen-year-old Pratab Patel. They are treating his death as suspicious and ask anyone in the Bradford Royal Infirmary area last evening between nine and eleven p.m. to contact them on this number...

'Zarqa, that's my T-shirt you're wearing. Give it back... Mum?'
'Sssh, Sabah. I'm listening to the news.'

...paint attack on a Bradford mosque in Manningham has prompted representatives from the Muslim community to call for a full investigation...

And now on yet another scorching Monday morning, here at Capital Radio, we wish GCSE students all the best as they start their exams…

My heart starts hammering. It's out there… on the news. Police are involved. Fuck. I hadn't thought it would hit the news so soon and then she's there, frowning at me, her face full of concern. 'Did you know the young boy? Pratab?'

My knee starts to judder up and down and I think I'm going to pass out as she puts a plate in front of me. I feel sick. She rests her hand on my shoulder and I have a sudden urge to lean against her, let her hug me tight… but I can't do that. I shrug her hand off and pretend I don't hear her sigh.

'He might have been in my year at school – don't know.'

But goodie fucking two shoes, Sabah, is sticking her nose in. 'You did know him Zarqa. You sometimes hung out with him at lunchtime, I saw you.'

Why's her voice so sly? Why's she always stirring it? I open my mouth to reply, but Mo jumps in first, laying a hand on her arm and telling her to, 'Shush.'

I scowl at him. Don't need him jumping to my defence. Don't want him sticking up for me. Don't want him looking at me all sad and stupid. Picking up my fork, I start shuffling the egg around on my plate. My stomach's gurgling and I feel faint. The smell of the Masala chai makes me want to barf, but I make myself roll up my paratha and dip it in the tea. Forcing myself, I bite off a chunk and chew. Despite the tea, it's like cardboard in my mouth and all I want to do is throw the mug and the eggs at the wall, shout at the top of my voice and run from the kitchen. I need to think. I need to think about what we did last night and with this fucking family around I can't concentrate. It's only the presence of my sisters… no, correction… my *half*-sisters, round the table that stops me. Sabah's already finished her egg and slurped her chai, like the greedy little shit she is.

'Come on, Zarqa, don't want to be late and you better not be. You're the one with the exam.'

I take another sip of tea. It lands in my belly like a brick and I swallow hard to keep it there. My head's thumping as I stand up. When Mum comes over to give me a hug, I pull away from her. If she knew what I'd done, she'd cast me out, just like her parents did to her. I scowl as I pass him and don't acknowledge my mum's strained voice when she says, 'Good luck, Zarqa. You can only do your best.'

Tears spring to my eyes. No, I don't have to do my best… I can do my very, very worst.

CHAPTER 16

It was still early, yet Gus thought he'd find DCI Nancy Chalmers at her desk and he was right. Her door was open, so he walked straight in, noticing her sandals kicked off near the door and the lingering smell of her perfume that was a sharp contrast to the sour smell in the investigation room just two floors down.

She glanced up, saw it was him, and took her glasses off, flinging them on top of her paperwork as if his visit couldn't have come soon enough. 'Can't get on top of this damn inbox no matter how early I come in. And half of it's shite! So much for going paperless... seems I'm the only one got *that* damn memo.'

Well aware of how much she hated the admin side of her job, Gus just walked over and sat down, allowing her the time to vent. She looked tired – bags under her eyes, crows' feet at the side of her eyes, and her normally perfectly styled hair looked decidedly floppy, which Gus put down to the heat more than anything else. He noted that the air con on this floor was working perfectly and savoured the coolness as Nancy ranted. When she finally ground to a halt, ending with an abrupt, 'Update!' Gus leaned forward, resting his arms on his knees.

'You've read the preliminary report?'

When she nodded, he continued, 'We've got an ID and I spoke to the parents last night. Thing is, this was staged – quite elaborately – and the lad who found him couldn't have come along very much after the killers left the scene.'

'Killers?' Nancy stood up and walked over to her coffee machine, her floral dress catching the slight air con breeze as she went. 'You sure about that?'

Inconsequentially, Gus noticed her hem was half undone and one of the buttons near her neck was missing. Nancy loved her feminine clothes, and bought upmarket – the trouble was, she never could quite carry it off. He nodded when she held the coffee pot up, asking if he wanted a drink. 'We'll know more when the PM results come back but that's where the evidence points so far. Definitely wasn't suicide. Looks like he was held in place while the actual killer stabbed him.'

'So, what are you saying, Gus?'

He took his time before replying, mentally going over everything he'd seen at the crime scene, checking if his gut instincts from the previous night still remained. Nancy walked over, handed him his drink and leaned on her desk, gently sipping her own drink, bare feet crossed in front of her, toenails painted a startling red. She tilted her head to one side and waited.

'I think we need to call in Sebastian.' Gus held her gaze. This, he was sure was the right thing to do. Sebastian Carlton, the ex-FBI behavioural analyst, who now lectured as a Professor in the Forensic Psychology Department at Leeds Trinity University, had worked with them before on cases with multiple victims. This was the first time Gus had asked for him to be brought in after only one victim.

'We can't afford to be caught on the back foot with this one, Nancy. This kid's death isn't a one-off... no way.'

To give Nancy her due, she nodded her acceptance of his words. They'd worked together for a long time and Gus hoped she realised he wouldn't ask for Carlton's involvement unless he was certain it was necessary. 'Budget's well and truly fucked as it is, Gus, you know that.'

Gus waited, of course he knew their budget was tight – it was always spent almost before it came in. But this was a kid… and it wasn't long after the other kids had been killed at that house party the previous year. He lowered his tone. 'We can't afford the bad press for this, Nance. Not after those kids last year. They'd slaughter us.'

Nancy, none too gently set her mug on the table, ignoring the coffee which slopped all over her paperwork. Placing both hands on her face, she rubbed her fingers into her eyes and then exhaled. 'You get hold of Carlton and leave the budget with me.'

She stood up and began soaking up the spilled coffee with some tissues. 'Now piss off, looks like I've got some books to cook to keep She Who Must Be Obeyed off my back.'

Gus grinned. Nancy hadn't taken to their new Chief Superintendent, and he suspected she'd rather enjoy thwarting her boss.

CHAPTER 17

'That's it, Mam, just one more pill.' I've got my arm round her holding her up against the pillow until she swallows her meds. She's a dead weight in my arms this morning... lifeless. I hate pumping her full of meds and leaving her lying there, but I've no choice.

'Look, Mam, there's some beans here right next to the bed. You'll eat them, won't you? In half an hour, yeah?'

She looks up at me, her eyes glazed, and her hand shakes as she tries to touch my cheek. 'You're a good lad, Jo Jo.'

I sigh and lower her back onto the bed. The food will still be there when I get home tonight. She's getting weaker and weaker. I kiss her forehead, but her eyes are already closed, her chest heaving under her nightie. What the hell will we do if she dies? As I leave the room, I turn back and whisper, 'Bye, Mam, have a good day.'

Pelting down the stairs, I grab Jessie's book bag. 'Come on, Jessie. Get a wriggle on. We're gonna be late if you don't hurry.' My skull's pounding like some bastard's playing basketball in there, my shoulders ache, and I've got a crick in my neck. Last night was mad... totally mad. Fuck! What did we do? Haven't had a chance to think about that yet either. Shit! What am I gonna say to her today?

Yesterday was mental, what with me mam and then Jessie followed by the webcamming. Nah, that's not true... not really. I could've thought about it... just didn't want to. Can't get my head round that. That was some big fucking shit we did. Then, that other bloke wanted the usual... said he'd pay big time. I need the money. Need it right now, but I'll have to wait. Looks like I'll need to go to the food bank again after school. Jessie needs to eat and so does me mam. Where the hell is she?

'Come on, Jess.'

The gas and leccy are due this week and Mum's benefit check will only just cover it. Maybe I should just give in and choose a side. Not like I'd be able to leave my mum and Jess to go to university, anyway. Might as well resign myself to selling E to scrotes in clubs to keep the gangs off my back.

'Jessie! Right now.'

I open the front door and the sweltering heat hits me in the face nearly knocking me backwards. *Aw for fuck's sake, Jess, come on*! Today of all days, I can't be late. 'Jess, you're making me late and I've got my exam. You don't want me disqualified, do you?'

What the hell is she doing? I turn and march back through into the kitchen and stop. Jess stands there, her little red and white school dress smeared with tomato sauce, her hair knotty and tangled, her face streaming with tears. I take a deep breath and bundle her into my arms. 'Aw, Jessie babes. Don't cry. Look, I'll sort it.'

Poor kid. She's got two school dresses and the other one is in a pile near the washing machine because I had no detergent to wash it over the weekend. Lifting her onto a chair in front of the sink, I use a cloth to wipe off as much of the sauce as I can. Her dress is sodden now, but the sauce has gone. 'It'll dry by the time you get to school.'

After rinsing the cloth, I wipe away her tears, before lifting her back down to the floor. 'I'll do your hair. Won't be as good as Mum does it, but it'll be all right. But then we need to scoot, right?'

Her bottom lip still trembles, but she nods at me and my heart breaks a little as she obediently turns around so I can brush her hair. I hate doing this. How the hell can I make robots and drones and stuff, with all their little fiddly components, but put a hairbrush in my hands and they turn into big fat sausage fingers. Although I'm yanking her hair, pulling the tugs until they're smooth, Jess doesn't so much as yelp. I could kiss her. She's a tough kid and I'm right proud of her.

As I flip the band into her hair and inexpertly twist it over again, I hear a noise. As I glance up my fingers tighten momentarily on Jess' shoulders before she turns away with an, 'Ouch, Jo Jo that hurt.'

But I've seen who's come into the house.

'What d'you want?' My voice is level and calm, but inside my stomach's flipping like it's Pancake Tuesday.

Razor, as smooth and articulate as Hammerhead is dumb, looks at me, a knowing grin all over his face. He's holding a fag in one hand and, as if sensing my annoyance that he's smoking in my house, he takes a slow drag and blows the smoke towards me. Over his shoulder his two enforcers are there, waiting for him to direct them. What the hell is it with little men leading the gangs in Bradford? For a single second, I wish I'd slammed the door shut behind me when I came looking for Jess – no point in that though. This was going to happen sooner or later... just wish it was later. Time's cracking on and I really need to get to school – get to my exam.

'Hey, Jess.' Razor ignores my question and bends down to make eye contact with my sister. 'Did you forget to tell Jo Jo I called last night?'

He called last night? My stomach clenches. Please say... but before I get the chance to formulate the thought, he's speaking again.

'D'int you tell him you read your reading book to me? Watched a bit of telly together last night?'

Jessie's smiling as if Razor's her best friend in the whole world and right then, I want to sink a fist in his stomach. Although I'm about a foot and a half taller than the shit, I can't do it. Not with his thugs there. Who am I kidding? Not at all. As if he can read my mind, the larger of his two mates pushes himself away from the wall and bulks out his arms, like he's the Hulk or summat.

Although he's looking at me, Razor's hand extends to Jess, five, one-pound coins in the palm. It's her he speaks to. 'Treat yourself to some chocolate on your way to school, Jess... or an ice cream. You'd like that, wouldn't you?'

I can almost feel the excitement rolling off her. When's the last time she had a treat? She looks up at me, her tear-swollen eyes pleading, and I can't resist. I give a taut smile and nod. Her face breaks into a smile and my heart breaks a little more as Razor, holding my gaze, drops the coins into her small hands. I swallow the thought that I could buy milk and tea bags and bread with that. I don't grudge Jess her treat, I just know that nowt comes free in this world.

'Thanks, Razor.' Jess's voice is all sweet and innocent and something curdles in my gut.

Razor glances towards the ceiling and the smirk on his face widens. My heart's doing that pounding thing again... did it ever stop? He was in the house last night with only Jess, and for the life of me, I can't remember if I left my bedroom door unlocked *after* I came home last night or *before* I went out. Either way, Razor thinks he's got summat on me.

'You not thanking me, Jo Jo?'

His tone's all smooth and friendly, but I know that in a second it can turn and he'll slice off my hand if it suits him. I've heard the stories and that's why I've always steered clear of Razor McCarthy... until now.

The voice that leaves my mouth doesn't belong to me. 'Thanks, Razor. Jess likes ice cream.'

He turns sideways and beckons to his mates. For a long moment, as they approach, blocking the sunlight flooding through the door with their bulk, I wonder if this is it… if I'm going to die here in this room… if I won't get to sit my first exam… and worse… I can't decide if I'm bothered or not. As they squeeze past their boss, I notice they're both carrying Aldi bags.

'Unpack the stuff onto the table, let them see what we've got for them. Treats for you, Jess, eh?' Razor reaches out and ruffles Jess' hair and she all but dances towards the table where Razor's boys are unpacking Frosties and Cheerios and milk and stuff.

'Put the frozen and fridge stuff away, lads. Jo Jo can unpack everything else when he gets back from school.' He reaches over and punches me none too gently on the arm. 'Manners, lad?'

My gaze moves from Jessie to the ever-increasing pile of goodies on the table to Razor and, as I say 'Thanks,' I wonder just what the *real* cost of a few groceries will be.

CHAPTER 18

Leo

I'm leaning out my bedroom window smoking. Wishing I could be outside. Instead, I've got to keep an ear open for any of them coming near. I don't usually do this when there's anyone at home, but I deserve it, don't I? A ciggie to calm my nerves. I exhale, blowing a half-hearted smoke ring. Wish I had some bud, but even I can't risk that.

Shit! What did we do last night?

It was all planned. I brought the drugs; Zodiac brought the booze... Pisces brought fucking attitude... Moaning on, being a right bell end. We'd already decided... that was the rules... so there was no need for Pisces to be such an arsehole about everything. Spoiling it for us, that's what Zodiac told me, and I agree. Maybe it's the nicotine, I don't know, but my heart's clopping in my chest and it won't stop. I hadn't thought it'd be like that. Now it's sinking in and I'm scared shitless. What if they find out what we did? What will my parents say?

When we were hammered last night, it was like we were gods... nothing mattered... nothing except paying *him* back for all the shit. Just because he's dead doesn't stop him being a bell end, does it? Being dead doesn't make all the other shit go away, that's what Zodiac says.

Soon as I sneaked back in, I had to rush upstairs and throw my load. I barfed all over the floor and had to clean it up quick, before the parents started asking awkward questions. The barf stank of alcohol and they're not daft... mind you, they had other things on their minds, didn't even

CHAPTER 19

The lad's eyes flitted round the room, yet Gus thought he probably wasn't really taking in the décor. His mum kept trying to comfort him – putting her arms round him, but he kept pulling away from her. Gus got it. He had an over-effusive mother himself and he'd been the same at that age... hell, he still was! He'd lost count of the times his mother had embarrassed him. Now, though, he tended to give in gracefully to her hugs... you never knew when they could be taken away from you.

He'd no sooner left Nancy, when the duty officer grabbed him, telling him he had a witness who might have some bearing on Pratab Patel's death. When Gus had heard the officer's report, he agreed, particularly, when that witness was the lad who Pratab was supposed to have been with the previous evening.

Now, gesturing towards the sofa that Pratab Patel's parents had sat on a couple of hours earlier and failing to shift the image of Mrs Patel's measured stoicism or Mr Patel's complete breakdown from his mind, Gus swallowed hard. 'Sit down, Haider, Dr and Mrs Ayyub.'

Haider glared at the sofa and with an exaggerated sigh, side-stepped his mother and flung himself onto one of the two comfy chairs that sat opposite. Gus couldn't blame him. Mrs Ayyub's concern was understandable, yet even Gus was beginning to think it was too cloying. Mr Ayyub, on the other hand, looked stern and a little distant from the proceedings.

Taking the time to assess the family group as the parents settled themselves down, Gus saw a concerned mother and father, out of their depth and each trying to cope with an alien situation in the best way they could. The duty officer had taken an initial statement when they had turned up at The Fort and so Gus knew that Dr Ayyub was an anaesthetist at BRI, while Mrs Ayyub was in the process of setting up her own bespoke halal cakes business.

Dr Ayyub was the first to break the silence. 'We need to do this very quickly, Inspector. Haider has an exam soon and he can't afford to miss it. It's a GCSE.'

A quick glance at Haider told him the lad would be more than happy to miss the exam and he couldn't blame him. It wasn't every day you realised the 'hoax' *Snapchat* message you'd got, showing your best mate lying in a pool of blood with a knife sticking out of his jugular, was actually real.

'Look, Haider, I'm not going to keep you hanging around here. You gave a statement this morning to DC Singh and it covers most things. I just need to ask a couple of questions.'

He waited until Haider nodded before continuing. 'Who was Pratab meeting last night? He told his parents he was studying with you, but that wasn't true, was it?'

Haider's shrug was one Gus had seen a thousand times. The 'I'm buying myself time here' sort of shrug, the 'I don't know what to share with you' sort of shrug. He leaned towards Haider. 'Pratab's gone, Haider. Any secret you and Pratab shared might be the clue we need. If you have any idea at all who he was meeting or where he was going last night, you need to tell me. You know that, don't you?'

Looking away, Haider repeated the shrug and then took a moment before replying, 'I don't know who he was meeting. He *was* meeting someone – don't know who, though.' After a quick glance at his parents, whose hands were linked, the whiteness of their knuckles the only outward indication of how difficult this was for them,

Haider lowered his voice as if he thought they might not hear his words. 'He said I was too pussy to know.'

Gus let the words hang there for a moment until Haider continued.

'We'd fallen out recently. He were being a dick.' Again, a glance at his parents, 'Sorry, Mum...' then back to Gus. 'He was hanging out with another group.' He held up his hand as though to ward off Gus' next question, 'And before you ask, I've no idea who. None of his regular mates knew. We were all pissed off with him. Truth is, that *Snapchat* was the first I'd had from him in weeks.' *It'll be the last*, remained unsaid.

Compo had Pratab's phone now, so hopefully they'd be able to work out from there who exactly the lad had been hanging out with recently. Strange though that their killer had chosen to send a *Snapchat* message to Haider. Did that mean the killer didn't realise the friends were estranged? Or was it that they wanted to punish Haider? The whole idea of sending a photograph message of the person you'd just killed left Gus cold. This, he was becoming more and more convinced, was not your average killer.

Picking at an imaginary piece of fluff on his fingers, the lad continued, 'Reckon he was taking drugs too.' He glanced at Gus. 'Don't mean just bud either... coke... MDMA – who knows? But he were different, skiving school... cheeking the teachers... getting pissed, blazed, you name it, Pratab seemed to be doing it.'

Gus made a mental note to talk to Patti to see if she or her staff could shed any light on this new friendship group Pratab was a part of. He'd have to broach the subject with the lad's parents and siblings too. See if they'd noticed anything amiss. The trouble was, in situations like these, family sometimes tried to keep these sorts of things quiet, which was a real shame as it was very often the things they kept hidden that could move an investigation onwards. He'd speak to their Family Liaison Officer and see what she reckoned. The FLO usually managed to get a handle on the family dynamics pretty quickly. He'd see if she'd managed to build up enough of a relationship with any of them to ask.

'You remember the actual *Snapchat...* the one that came from Pratab's phone?'

Haider nodded, his lips tightening.

'Well, I want you to do something for me. I want you to close your eyes and really focus on it for a minute. I don't want you to talk – just try to remember it. I know this is hard for you and I wouldn't ask if it wasn't necessary... we really need to find who did this to your friend. The more you can tell us the more it'll help.'

Mrs Ayyub opened her mouth, but her husband shook his head and she bit her lip. All she wanted to do was protect her son, and Gus could sympathise, but this was important. He nodded his appreciation to Dr Ayyub who returned the gesture with a tight smile.

'You up for this, Haider?'

Haider looked anything but up for it. His foot was still jangling and now his fingers were clenched against his thighs.

'It's hard, I know it's hard, but please... for Pratab's sake.'

With an abrupt nod that was the carbon copy of his dad's earlier one, Haider inhaled, leaned back in the chair, and closed his eyes. Now that no one was talking, the clock ticking in the room seemed overly loud and ominous. The sound of traffic drifted up, muted but insistent in the near silence and, all the while, Haider's parents' gazes scoured their son's face. Frown lines furrowed Haider's brow, his eyes, although loosely shut, moved under his lids, his mouth was a thin line and his cheeks were flushed, whether because of the heat or anxiety Gus couldn't tell.

'Okay, Haider. Just think about the *Snapchat* image and tell me what you see. If you need to stop you can, it's your call.'

When he spoke, Haider's voice was steadier than Gus had expected. 'Pratab's lying on the ground – grass, I think. There's a knife sticking out of the side of his neck and blood all around his head. I thought it were fake. I thought he were winding me up.'

'You're doing good, Haider. Can you tell me how his head is positioned?'

Haider opened his eyes and blinked a few times. 'Look, I'll answer owt you want, but I'm not keeping my eyes shut.'

'That's fine, this is all your call – we stop whenever you've had enough, okay?'

Haider picked up a bottle of water from the table, unscrewed the lid and gulped half of it in one go. 'His head was to the side – that's why I could see the knife so clear. Blood were trickling down his neck.'

'What about his hands, can you remember anything about them?'

Haider drank some more water before replying, 'They were tied together in front of him… looked like plastic ties or something. It wasn't rope.'

So, the *Snapchat* had been taken before the killer had fully positioned the body and before the cable ties or the knife had been removed.

'What about the knife, Haider? What does it look like?'

The lad scowled in a 'what the fuck' sort of way. 'A knife's a knife, innit?'

Gus smothered his smile. It was good that Haider was showing a bit of attitude. It might be just what he needed to get himself through this traumatic experience. 'Just wondered about the handle, Haider. What did it look like?'

He scraped his fingers along his jawline, his slight stubble making a scratching sound as he did so. 'It were just a kitchen knife. A bit like that long thin one you use for cutting the chicken, Dad.'

Dr Ayyub nodded. 'A carving knife.'

'Yeah, a carving knife. I think the handle was black – not sure though.' Haider made to stand up. 'I've had enough now. I don't want to think about this anymore.'

Gus wasn't surprised, Haider had done better than he'd expected, and Gus was pleased. 'Only one more thing. I need to ask you for your phone, so we can try to retrieve the *Snapchat* image.'

Haider's eyes widened and his foot began tapping the floor. 'You can't take my phone. I need it. It's mine. Anyway, the Chat's gone... long gone. It deletes after you've seen it.'

Earlier, Compo had given Gus a crash course on how *Snapchat* operated and although he wasn't one hundred per cent up to speed, Gus was aware that the Chat had 'disappeared' after a few seconds from Haider's phone. However, Compo had also gone on about how things were never fully gone. 'We've got experts who can analyse your phone – digital forensic experts. You never know, the image you saw might provide additional information... crucial information... information that might help us find out who did this to Pratab.'

Haider swiped a hand over his face and sniffed, his tapping foot increased its tempo, but it wasn't until the lad cast a sideways glance at his parents that Gus realised the real reason behind his reluctance. The lad probably had pornography or some dodgy messages on his phone that he wanted to keep from his parents. The question was, how, without his parents realising, did Gus make it clear to the lad, that unless they found evidence of criminal activity on the phone, they were only interested in his communications with Pratab. Feeling like a piece of shit yet knowing that the lad had to hand over his phone and head straight to school if he was going to make his exam in time, Gus sharpened his tone. 'Hand over your phone right now, Haider.'

Haider, in a last-ditch attempt to buy some time, glanced at his parents and then, head down, mumbled, 'I'll drop it off later. In all the rush this morning, I left it at home.'

Not a bad deflection, Gus conceded, but it wasn't going to wash. Almost before the words were out of his mouth both parents turned to him. 'Haider!'

Mrs Ayyub muttered something in Urdu under her breath and tapped his knee while Dr Ayyub extended his hand. 'Don't lie, Haider. You were using the phone on the way over here. You've always got that phone in your hand. Hand it over. Like the inspector said, this is crucial evidence. Pratab was *murdered.*'

As if saying the words out loud had loosened something in his wife, Mrs Ayyub began to sob. 'Hand the phone over. I won't feel safe with you or your brother out of my sight until this monster is caught.'

While his dad's stern words had resulted only in a tightening of the boy's lips, his mother's tears had him sliding the phone from his pocket. He handed it to Gus before jumping to his feet and slinging his backpack over one shoulder. 'Right, gotta go, come on.'

Gus waited until Haider's mum and dad had left the room and then called the boy back with a, 'You need to sign this.'

Haider shuffled back to Gus and, despite his affected swag, he avoided meeting Gus' eyes as he grabbed the pen and bent over the table to sign the form.

Glancing to make sure his parents were out of earshot; Gus lowered his voice. 'As long as you have nothing illegal or incriminating on your phone, your parents will never learn of anything else we find. We're not looking for pornography – as long as it's legal, nor stupid texts about weed use – for example.'

Haider's head jerked up and for the first time since he'd handed over his phone, he met Gus' eyes and nodded. A small smile lifted his lips for a moment and then disappeared. 'Pratab won't be sitting in the hall doing his exam this morning.'

Gus put a hand on the lad's shoulder and squeezed. The empty desk would be a distraction for all of Pratab's friends. 'Just do your best, Haider. It's all you can do.'

Sniffing, Haider handed the pen and paper back to Gus. 'Just find the bastard who did this.'

Gus waited until the lad joined his parents and then said, 'You know the information you've shared is important?'

All three of them nodded.

'Well, you need to keep this to yourself, all right? You can't share it with anyone – not your friends, no one. You could get in bother if you do. It could be critical to finding out what happened to your friend.'

Dr Ayyub put an arm round his son's shoulder. 'We won't repeat this. The last thing we want is to interfere with your investigation.'

Gus hoped that was true. However, he suspected that once the initial shock had worn off, Haider might be tempted to share his knowledge with his friends and then it would, without doubt, grace the front pages of the tabloids.

CHAPTER 20

Pisces

I never slept a wink. How could I? How am I supposed to go to school after all this? Act normal? Zodiac will be there and the last thing I need is that. I can't get up. I need a shower, but I can't have another one, not so soon and I had to have one last night. It was like I had blood all over me. Like it was everywhere. It wasn't, really. I *knew* that, but I still needed to wash it off. I used the last of the shampoo and the water was freezing but I deserved it.

How can they not care? Specially Leo? We all just do what Zodiac says... but do we? *We're* the ones came up with the names. Came up with the game. *We're* the bad ones. It's all on us. Zodiac just keeps us to task. When we started, it was a laugh. Getting folk in trouble, getting our own back. We only chose the ones who deserved it. Then it got worse. Mr Borthwick ending up in prison was okay. He deserved it but posting the photos of Becky online... outing her as Mr Borthwick's tart, that wasn't nice. Yeah, she'd dumped Leo, said some bad things, done some worse things, but that was bad. She were off school for months after and then she only came back for a few weeks and then moved to another school.

Ping!

Ping!

Ping!

Fucking *Instagram*! They're all over it. Posting photos of Pratab with stupid love hearts round them.

> RIP Pratab you'll be missed! Tom :-(
>
> Best mate in the world. Miss you! Jamie
> Grieves :-(
>
> You'll always be in my heart,
> xxxxxxxxxx!
>
> Play with the Angles! Sally

Spelled *angles*… Twat can't even spell angels right.

Maybe I'll add her to the Zodiac Club hit list… Fuck, what am I thinking?

I'm a knobhead, I am. I'm not adding no one else to the list. Soon as these are done, so am I.

Billy though? Billy was *all* my fault. He'd made my life hell. Calling me names. I really wanted to hurt him. I wanted him dead, I really did… but then… he was dead and all I could think was that I wished he were back at school being a wanker. That would've been better than him being gone. I visit his grave sometimes after school. Hard to believe he's down there with all the worms and shit. There'll be nowt left of him. I looked it up one day in the library. Just his bones and a few scraps of skin and his hair.

I scroll through *Facebook*. Fuck's sake. They're all posting to his timeline too. Fucking tossers. Half of them don't even know him, I bet!

> Heaven will be a better place with you in it! Love Holly xxx
>
> Can't believe I'll never see your face again. Miss you forever! Love Sonal xxx :-(:-(
>
> Miss you mate, Haider :-(
>
> The Angels will protect you, Love Krishna and Trupti xxx

Could've done with the effing angels last night, couldn't you, Pratab? I realise I'm laughing at nothing and shove my fist in my mouth. Shut up! Get a grip! Get an effing grip!

What am I going to do? If I don't go to school, Zodiac will kill me... not literally. Well, maybe not literally. I keep having flashbacks. We put the pills in the voddie. Leo ground them up at home and we put them in before we got there. We gave him some weed, and the bottle and he was being a knobhead, as usual. I was shit scared... nervous. He was such a wanker though... such a dick!

Leo was jumping about like it was a bloody rave or summat. All hyped up like we were there to party... downed a couple of pills too, I reckon. When it was time, I thought one of us would say *no, stop*. I waited. I looked at Leo. I looked at Zodiac... but no.

When the knife went in, it hardly made a sound. Still can't believe it. The *Snapchat*... can't remember whose idea that was. Part of the plan... part of the fucking plan. Did I suggest that? Was it me? It could've been. I just can't remember now. Then it's spurting out, over the handle, over the hand... blood... fucking blood everywhere. And they're laughing... we're laughing. Pratab's dead... lying there dead, with his hands tied up and we're moving his body, cutting the ties off, making him just right and taking fucking *Snapchat*s on his phone.

I get up. I've got to get sorted. Got to get ready for school. Got to do it... it's all part of the plan and we can't deviate from the fucking plan.

CHAPTER 21

'Boss wants to see you, Gus – asap.' Gus paused, coffee pot mid-pour.

'Nancy?' His heart skipped a beat, maybe she had sorted out Professor Carlton. No, too soon. Some news on Alice, then? Perhaps Alice was coming back, but Compo's next words dashed those hopes.

'Nah, the DCS.'

It wasn't even half eight and she was on his case. Gus continued pouring his drink and moved over to sit behind his desk. He hadn't had breakfast after jogging up to work. He'd had a quick shower, met with Nancy, and immediately went into the interview with Haider. He was starving and now he had to go and see the DCS? Well, she can surely wait ten minutes, couldn't she? He grabbed a cereal bar from his drawer and ripped it open, just as his stomach growled. Leaning back in his chair, he balanced his feet on his desk and took a sip of his coffee. He needed a bit of time to absorb everything Haider had told him about Pratab. Changes in behaviour in teen boys was always something to watch out for, but in this particular instance suicide wasn't an option. It seemed like Pratab had fallen into the wrong crowd... maybe got in over his head? Or, maybe it was a chance encounter? A predator?

Gus shook his head and took a bite of his breakfast bar. No, that didn't sit right with him. The location, for one, seemed too out of the way to be a chance encounter and the CSIs hadn't seen anything to indicate Pratab had been dragged from the main road to the back of the house. Was it a drug deal gone wrong? Again, that didn't explain the way the body had been positioned after death and, according to Haider, after the *Snapchat* had been sent. That was another thing… why send a *Snapchat* at all? At that point, nobody even knew he was missing and surely sending the *Snapchat* to a family member would have been more effective if the aim was just to shock.

His desk phone rang, interrupting Gus' train of thought. He swung his legs off his desk and grabbed the receiver. 'DI Gus McGuire. How can I help?'

'Well, perhaps answering your mobile would be a start.'

Recognising the sarcastic tones, Gus glared at the phone. DCS Gazala Bashir didn't sound very happy. Not that that was unusual in itself… still, her snarky tone put Gus on edge. Truth was he'd switched his mobile on vibrate the previous evening after he left the crime scene because he was fed up listening to 'The Bitch is Back' blaring from it. He'd known the DCS was trying to contact him but had chosen to defer replying. 'I've been in an interview this morning. Seems that whoever killed Pratab Patel sent a *Snapchat* of the body to one of the mates of the victim last night.'

'Hmm, DS Compton mentioned that you were in interview…'

For a moment Gus wondered who the hell DS Compton was, then he realised… Compo. Why the hell couldn't she just call him Compo like everyone else did?

'…seems strange that the boy only came in this morning. Is he a suspect?'

'Well, clearly we can't rule him out completely, but he has an alibi – dinner with his extended family – and the reason he didn't report it last night is because he thought it was a prank. The thing is with *Snapchat*, the sender decides how long you view the live 'Snap' for, and you can only see it twice before it's deleted automatically. Lad says it was only on screen for a second and last thing he thought of was screenshotting it.'

'Well, that's as may be, but you need to double check his alibi. Can't have a young lad being killed and we're not on the ball...'

And there it was... The real reason for her call. Bashir was a micromanager like he'd never come across before and it rankled. Gus was used to being trusted to do his job. Nancy trusted his judgement and he had a track record to back it up. Yet ever since she'd arrived, DCS Bashir had been at great pains to second guess him, question his actions, and make him justify his decisions. That really pissed him off. He'd no time to be filling in reports, then heading up two floors to her office to repeat the written report verbally. Nancy had tried to have a word with her, but Bashir was insistent that she wanted to have her ear to the ground.

Sitting straighter, Gus rolled his chair further under his desk and shook his mouse to activate his screen. What he really wanted to do was respond with a breathy sort of '...OMG! I didn't think of that! God! I see why you're sat up there in the ivory tower and I'm boiling my arse off in an overheated, smelly investigation room with no air con.'

Instead, he took a deep breath before replying, every word sticking in his throat. 'Yes, Ma'am, I've actioned a check on that already. Uniforms are taking statements at Haider's home.'

'And you've kept him here, haven't you?'

Gus bristled and tried not to feel like he'd been caught out. 'Actually, no. I've allowed him to go into school so he can sit his maths GCSE. No point in him missing it.'

For a moment there was silence and he could imagine the wheels turning in Gazala Bashir's head before she said, her tone grudging, 'Right. Good call. You seem to have this under control and right now I've got my work cut out with public relations after the graffiti on the mosque last night.'

Gus took that as a dismissal and was about to hang up when…

'What I actually phoned for was, I want you to come to my office… there's something I need to discuss with you. Shall we say…' The sound of her shuffling papers on her desk drifted down the line… 'five minutes?' And without waiting for his reply she hung up.

'You all right, Boss – it's just, you've gone all red in the face.'

Gus frowned at his colleague. He didn't need Compo telling him how he looked, he could feel the steam coming from his ears. Seeing Compo's grin as the lad popped his ear buds back in, Gus relaxed. Cheeky sod was teasing him.

'Gotta go upstairs, Comps, you crack on with those phones, will you? And tell Taff you and I are going to head out to the Patel family and then City Academy. He can join us there before starting on the CCTV footage when he gets back from the PM.'

Draining his coffee mug, Gus stood and then hesitated for a moment. Should he remove his bandana before his meeting with the DCS? He snorted and strode to the door. When she got the damn air con working, then he'd take off his bandana, until then, tough shit.

He took the lift up to the DCS' floor and strode along the carpeted corridor to her office, noting as he went that there was a distinct waft of cool air along this corridor and an equally distinct lack of BO… the perks of being top brass, eh?

From outside her open door he could hear her speaking on the phone. He raised his hand ready to do a perfunctory rap on the door, when she glanced up and saw him. She waved him in with one hand and gestured to a chair on the opposite side of her desk.

Gus sat and allowed the conversation she was having, presumably with her daughter, to drift over him, as he surveyed her office. A familiar perfume filled the room.

'…well, where were you? All I ask is that you'll let me know…' She tapped her pen on the desk, head tilted to one side. '…I know you'll try your…'

Her desk was wood and covered with paperwork, folders piled up to one side and an in-tray that was overflowing… perhaps if she didn't spend so much time micromanaging him, she'd be on top of her paperwork.

'…I didn't say that and that's not what I meant. You know I think you'll do well… I just wish you'd maybe studied a bit more… you skipped breakfast.'

Gus' eyes drifted over various awards framed in silver that lined up symmetrically on the wall next to her bookshelf. He wondered if she'd deliberately hold off framing one if it would unbalance the display. Everything he'd gleaned about Gazala Bashir in the months since she'd joined Bradford Met spoke of a regimented personality.

'Mehmoona, I know you won't mess up again… why should you? We've moved on from that… It's in the past.'

There was one picture of her with her daughter on the bookshelf alongside various well-thumbed policing manuals. Gus recognised the girl from when she'd come into the office earlier in the year. He smirked, remembering how he'd shared a smile with the daughter when his mum's dogs had jumped up at her mum, leaving a dark wet patch on her skirt.

'Look, we'll talk tonight, and you can tell me all about your exam. Good luck, Meh—'

She shrugged and threw her phone onto the desk, before, with the first hint of a smile Gus had ever seen from her, saying, 'Kids, huh? Who'd have them?'

Hoping that his smile was sympathetic rather than gloating, Gus shook his head but remained silent.

Closing her eyes for a moment as if to gather her thoughts, Bashir tapped her fingers on the table. 'I hear you've been receiving anonymous letters and that the last one was delivered directly to your home?'

Shit! Someone had spilled the beans to her. This was the last thing he wanted. If he knew anything about DCS Bashir, it was that she was meticulous when it came to sticking to the rules. She was about to warn him off looking into it on his own. He opened his mouth to insist on his involvement, when she stuck a pin in his balloon. 'Do you think it's your ex-wife?'

Eh? Where had that come from? Gaby was a bitch, sure enough, but even she wouldn't stoop to sending him anonymous letters. No, if Gaby had something to say to him, then she wouldn't hang back... which, of course, was the main reason he was deflecting her calls. You never knew what you were going to get with her, and he just couldn't be arsed with her dramatics. 'No, no. It's not Gabriella. Not her style – Bitch, yes, anonymous stalker, most definitely no.'

Bashir steepled her hands at her mouth. 'You're sure?'

'Positive.'

She nodded. 'Okaaay... well, you've handed everything over to C team and DI Byrne is very capable... still – you need to be involved in a purely advisory role.'

To say Gus was surprised would have been an understatement. He'd expected to be warned off and yet here she was telling him to be involved.

'You must have crossed paths with this person and so you're best placed to know who it is. Another thought that *did* cross my mind was that it was something to do with the Russians or Syrians after you kyboshed their attempts to buy that bioweapon.'

Gus scratched his forehead. *Yeah right, I can really see the Russians and Syrians sending me scented letters.* 'Again, no, Ma'am. If they were pissed at me, they'd be a hell of a lot more direct and a hell of a lot more threatening. At the moment, these letters are more conversational with mildly threatening observations. It's someone local... not a terrorist organisation.'

'I won't take any sort of threat to one of my officers lightly. I've arranged for extra drive-bys at your home, your parents' home, and your girlfriend's home, until we find out who is doing this. I expect you to be extra vigilant in the meantime. Now, if you're happy to liaise with Byrne then—'

She abruptly turned to her paperwork without finishing her sentence and Gus realised he'd been dismissed. As he made his way back downstairs, he wondered what had just happened. A DCS taking an extra interest in his welfare was surprising... but very refreshing. Perhaps she wasn't as bad as he imagined. That warm fuzzy feeling lasted until he got back to find his desk phone ringing. He snatched up the receiver.

'Turn your damn mobile on, McGuire...' And once more she hung up before he had the chance to reply.

CHAPTER 22

Zodiac

They're all crowding past us. Some have come off the bus, the rest have grabbed their breakfast at Lidl and they're all laughing and joking. The thick smell of nicotine hangs in the air as they have their last fags before entering school property... banter, jokes, kids mucking around. Lynx, BO, perfume, weed...

I don't mind talking about 'it' as we walk. *It* being what we got up to last night, but the way Pisces is acting, you'd think I'm parading up and down outside the school with a loudhailer instead of whispering. After the texts earlier, I thought all we'd be doing is talking about it, but Pisces is scared people will hear. I keep saying, 'We're invisible, chillax.' But the div's too pussy.

Me? I'm desperate to chat, desperate to relive every awesome moment. You'd think I'd set off a firework on the pavement right in front of us with Pisces' furtive glances. Mumbling like an idiot, head swivelling from side to side to see who's nearby. I want to laugh, but I know that'll knock the dumbass right over the edge. Today is all about containment... holding the boat steady, steering us out of the storm. It's about me keeping up the charade.

I try again, keeping my tone reassuring. 'Nobody gives a toss... not about us, not about what we've done... not about Pratab.'

'That's not what they're saying on *Facebook* and *Instagram*. Everyone's talking about it. Sending RIP messages.'

That's true. It is all over social media and I love it. They're all talking about it, every one of them and none of them know it's me... us.

You look at me, your eye's all red, and I hope you're not going to give in. I grab your arm and you wince, cowering from me. 'Remember what I know? About Billy?' I'm still whispering, but there's an edge now.

Fear flicks across your eyes for a moment and I change tack, smile and let go your arm, rubbing it twice to tell you I don't mean to hurt you. You're not sure what you saw in my eyes. Not sure if it was a threat and I like that. I cup your chin in my hand and look right into your eyes, gentle and soothing I say, 'We got to stick together. Remember what they done... all of them... not just him... not just that dick, Pratab... but *all* of them.'

You smile back and then you glance round, scared that somebody will see us. I stroke my finger down your cheek and lean closer. 'We're invisible.'

Truth is, I've made us this way and the beauty of this is that you don't see it. Among the crowds, we are the invisibles, the ones nobody sees, the ones they only notice when they want to act big in front of their mates. We *are* the outsiders. But soon they'll wake up and take notice. The very thought of it excites me. My entire body is buzzing. It's like I'm on fire, like every synapse is firing double quick. It's like I'm on speed... that's it... speed! Every muscle, every thought, every movement is on speed. Yet, none of the rest of them can see that. Just me. I grin and nudge you. 'Now, stop being a wuss. We got away with it... and we can do it again.'

You shake your head, but I link arms with you and pull you on. You resist for a nano-second and then you're there with me, side by side we walk on, through the crowds... invisible.

You stare straight ahead, like I've taught you, your head high, but me, I keep my head down… I want to be more invisible than you… that's the plan.

CHAPTER 23

I see Zarqa in the distance and deliberately slow down. I don't want to see her right now. I can't get my head straight. Not with all that Razor shit this morning… and the other stuff.

Got another one of them weird texts last night, with a video attachment. I open it and it's me… in my room covered in baby oil, doing what I get paid to do. The message is the same as the others. *Do this or else.* I've no choice, so I'll do it. I'll collect what I need after school and do it tonight. Last thing I need though is for anyone else to have owt on me. If Razor saw my room, he'll know what I do… bad enough that I'm already paying someone off. Bad enough that I don't even know who they are or how they know this shit about me? Sometimes all I want to do is run… and if it was just me, that's what I'd do. But I can't leave Jessie. Zarqa's really pissing me off. She needs to grow up. She's got her parents and her sisters and enough money. What shit does she have to worry about?

Fuck, she's *Snapchatting* me. Stupid fucking Gif with a bear and a thought bubble with maths equations scratching his head and then flopping onto the desk in front of him. If I was in a better mood, I'd find it funny, but right now it's all so trivial. I ignore it. I can't be arsed adding to her story. I'd like to see her struggling on like I do… doing the shit I have to do just to survive.

I'm being tight and I know it. She's all right, really, is Zarqa. She's always had my back, but right now, she's doing my head in… and after what we did last night? Fuck!

Ping!

Ping!

Ping!

I don't need to look to see what those are. More of the fucking shit on *Facebook* about how wonderful Pratab was. Well, he wasn't so wonderful when he tricked me into giving him a blow job in the lad's toilets after school and posted it on *Instagram*. I'd thought he liked me... *really* liked me. Course he didn't admit he actually let me do it... made out he'd pushed me away before we got down and dirty... prick didn't admit he'd enjoyed it. Didn't tell them he did me too. Didn't stop him coming back for more a few weeks later. Did he really think he could just bat his long lashes at me, flash me a grin, and say sorry and that would be it? So, am I sorry he's dead? Am I fuck? He deserved it!

Ping!

Ping!

Ping!

I can't help myself; I look at the posts to his timeline.

> RIP Mate! Bash
>
> The Angels will look after you xx xx

Yeah right, so they will. I'm not sure he's up there. He might be finding it even hotter than we are right now. I shove my phone in my bag. No phones allowed in the exam.

She's looking around now, jumping up and down to see over everyone's heads. I crouch over, trying to make myself smaller. Can't believe we did that. Can't believe I helped her. What was I thinking? That was some heavy bad shit. What happens if we get caught? Shit, what would Jessie and my mam do if I went to jail? Jessie would end up in some bloody home or other and my mum...? Shit... she'd just give up and die.

She's seen me. I try to head off to the side, but she grabs my arm just as I'm heading through the door.

'Did you hear it on the news this morning?'

Fuck, it's on the news already? Course it is. They found out what we did. I glance round, half expecting to see two plods approaching, rattling their handcuffs. But it's only that Mehmoona and Claire. Couple of weirdos. I keep my head down. They're always trying to talk to me, but I can't be arsed.

Grabbing Zarqa by the arm, I pull her to the side. 'We can't do this again, Zarqa... we can't.' But there's something in her eye. True, she's a bit edgy. Got in a panic last night, but there's that look, and I can tell she wants to do it again.

'Jo Jo, last night was scary as shit... it really was. I ran all the way home, my heart thumping and I thought it would never stop... but, you know what?'

My heart sinks as she raises her chin and looks right at me. 'It was great. The first time in a long time I felt I did the right thing. Now they're taking notice. We're making a mark. Next time it'll be even better.'

I want to shake my head and say 'No', but I've got no fight left. It's not even half eight and I'm cream crackered. All I want to do is climb in a hole and cover myself up and come out when I'm fifty and all this crap behind me.

The buzzer goes, reminding me we've still got an exam to sit. 'Later, Zarqa. Come on. Don't want to be late.'

CHAPTER 24

Don't see why you couldn't have brought one of the uniformed officers, Gus.' Compo, arms crossed over his chest, slumped like a moody toddler in the passenger seat of Gus' car. 'You know I'm better in the office... nearly had summat on them phones, you know? Now you've dragged me away. We could be missing crucial evidence as we speak.'

Driving towards Clayton, where the Patel family lived, Capital Radio blasting out a Little Mix song, Gus hid his smile. Compo had told him it would take a good couple of hours to retrieve everything off both the victim's and Haider's phones. He'd been happy to leave whatever programme he had initiated running away quietly on its own, until Gus had suggested he accompany him. Much as Gus would have preferred to have his old DS, Alice Cooper, with him, he was determined to continue with Compo's training. He wanted to make sure the lad was a well-rounded officer and not just a computer nerd and for the past few months he'd been gradually taking him more and more out of his comfort zone. Yes, there were plenty of other good officers he could have enlisted, but Compo needed to be stretched. 'Stop griping, Comps. You'll be great. All I need is for you to take notes on your tablet, that's all... oh, and keep an eye out for anyone you think might be concealing information.'

Compo inhaled and Gus' smile again twitched his lips. 'Look on it as training. All of this looks good on your professional development record.'

'Hmmph.' Compo looked out the side window. He'd no need to expand on that single sound for Gus to understand that he really meant 'sod my professional development record', but Gus knew that they were looking to cut back and that every officer had to demonstrate versatility. He didn't want to lose one of his team. Nancy was having enough trouble keeping Alice's position open for now and there were at least three Detective Sergeants that he knew of with their eye on Alice's job. The last thing Gus wanted was for anyone to say Compo had limited skills.

...still no sign of a let-up in this weather and with temperatures soaring into the twenties, with highs of twenty-nine degrees in some areas, the Met office reports that this has been...

The vinyl seat was creating a humidity that soaked through the short-sleeved shirt Gus had changed into as a mark of respect for the family. Shifting his body away from the backrest, Gus felt a dribble of sweat roll down his back and realised that, in this weather, it was near impossible to look cool and collected. The pool car's air conditioning was no more effective than The Fort's.

He drove along Buckingham Crescent, past a row of newly built houses that would have looked out onto extensive farmland, had someone not bordered the road intermittently with hedges and trees. Gus wasn't surprised that this was where the Patels lived. A significant number of Bradford's Hindu community lived in this area and he'd visited families here before. The Patels' home was easily identifiable by the number of cars parked up outside, some spilling onto the neighbours' drives. He drove past the house, took the first available space, and parked up. He turned to address Compo. 'Right, this is the first house call to a grieving family you've made. This isn't going to be pleasant, but just remember that however unpleasant it is for us, the whole situation must be completely unbearable for Pratab's family.'

When he looked at Gus, Compo's normally cheerful face was lined with worry, his shoulders slumped as he glanced away and mumbled. 'Wish Alice were here.'

Gus took the key out of the ignition and opened the driver's door. 'So do I, Comps, so do I.'

There was no let-up as they left the car, the heat suffocated them as soon as they got out. A slight heat shimmer gurgled on the pavement like a stream on a summer's day. Gus took a moment to peer through the hedges to the dry-looking fields beyond. The trees which should have offered shade and reduced the temperature, looked starved of liquid and, not for the first time, Gus wished the sky would open up with a torrent of rain.

As they approached the house, Compo's pace got slower and he trailed behind Gus a little. Hot and sticky, Gus held onto his irritation by a very thin thread. 'For God's sake, Compo. Pull yourself together. It's your job.'

Compo glared at him but straightened his shoulders and increased his pace to match that of his boss. 'Won't let you down, Gus. I got this.'

Gus suspected that his last words were more for his own benefit than Gus', but he appreciated them, nonetheless.

In front of a large double garage stood two upmarket cars and below the front room window was a landscaped paved area dotted with several small, contained flowerpots. On raised decking in the bottom corner of the garden stood a wooden bench with a couple of empty glasses left there. The blinds were half shut with shapes passing the window every so often. The door was opened by the Family Liaison Officer, Amanjeet Kaur, who gestured them inside. As soon as he entered, Gus was impressed by the amount of support the family had. People of all ages moved in and out of the rooms, carrying tea, food, or flowers.

'The family are in there. The Brahmin will be coming to conduct prayers in about an hour, so you timed this nicely. If you want to go in to pay your respects, you need to remove your shoes.' Amanjeet, herself, was barefoot.

Gus slipped his shoes off, placing them in a pile of shoes that was near the door and waited for Compo to do the same. As he followed Amanjeet into the living room, Gus gave Compo an encouraging smile.

The room they entered was gently fragranced with incense and all the furniture had been moved to the sides of the room and the carpet covered by a cloth. Mrs Patel, wearing a sari as opposed to the jeans and T-shirt she'd worn the previous day, sat on a small pouffe next to a shrine. A large silver-framed photo of Pratab, hair spiked up with gel stood in the centre. The boy was smiling, his eyes sparkling and mischievous and it was difficult to imagine him dead. A red chandlo, the Hindu mark of respect, was on his forehead, as a blessing. The picture was surrounded by flowers and a diva candle was lit next to it.

Gus had been in Hindu homes before at such times and was familiar with the ceremonial rituals. A quick glance at Compo told him that his colleague was focussed on the photograph of the dead boy. Mrs Patel's eyes were swollen. The police presence was an intrusion into the family's grief, yet Gus had no choice. Following Amanjeet's lead, he approached first Mrs Patel and then her husband, who, with his blank gaze, seemed barely aware of their presence. Gus, once more, expressed his condolences over the death of their son. Rising to her feet, Mrs Patel, showing the same stoic composure she'd demonstrated at the police station, leaned over and helped her husband up. She gestured to a boy who looked older than Pratab and a bespectacled girl who looked younger. 'Come on, we'll talk to the detectives in the dining room.'

The boy, wan looking, moved to his mother's side and taking his father's arm began to guide him from the room. The girl approached Gus, her posture straight, despite her red-rimmed eyes. 'Couldn't you just leave us alone for a bit? We're grieving. My mum and dad need time.'

Seems like the Patel women are feistier than the Patel men. He wondered if Pratab had taken after his mum or his dad. 'If we could, we would, but right now we need to do everything we can to find out who did this to your brother. It's intrusive, I know, but we need to ask you some questions… and we need to look at Pratab's room.'

'Mita! It's fine. Let them ask their questions.' Mrs Patel smiled tightly. 'We can grieve when we know who did this to your brother.' She turned, sari swishing, and indicated they should follow.

The dining room was a large room that adjoined the kitchen. It held a table big enough to seat at least ten people. A woman who looked enough like Pratab's mum for Gus to work out she was his auntie, popped her head in. 'Chai? Tea? Soft drink?'

Gus inclined his head. 'Chai would be nice.'

Compo following Gus' lead nodded and smiled. 'Yes, chai please.'

Knowing better than to start the conversation until the chai had been served, Gus took the time to look round. A fan, in the corner of the room, sent a welcome breeze into the air and Gus savoured it each time the fan rotated in his direction. Apart from the oversized table, there was a sideboard that had a display of finest whiskies and brandies as well as a well-stocked wine rack. Otherwise, the room, painted in soothing pastel green shades, was minimalist with no ornaments or other furniture. A couple of family portraits decked the walls and Gus surmised they'd been taken at a studio. A family of five, reduced by one. In both the photos the entire family was laughing, and Gus wondered when they'd be able to do that again.

Mrs Patel moved to the sideboard and picked up a photo album. She handed it to Gus. 'These are of my son. This is the boy who has been taken away from us. I want you to look at them and remember him as you try to find the monster who did this.'

Gus took the album from her and positioned it between him and Compo. Taking his time, he studied each picture. Most were of the three siblings together; at a farm, at Harry Potter World, the seaside, Alton Towers. Some were of the whole family having barbecues, family gatherings. In each, the essence of life was poignant and clear. It wasn't until he sensed Mrs Patel moving over to hand Compo a tissue, that he realised his colleague was crying silently. A tear dropped onto the table in front of them and then Compo, making Gus proud, said, 'You have a lovely family, Mrs Patel. DI McGuire and I will not stop until we catch who took your beautiful son away.' And he wiped his eyes, blew his nose, and shoved the tissue in his pocket just as the chai arrived.

Mrs Patel studied Compo for a moment and then nodded. Gus looked at her husband, but he was still gazing blankly into space. 'Has Mr Patel seen a doctor?'

'Yes, he's been prescribed medication but, for now, Manoj is refusing to take it. He'll come around in his own time.' And she patted her husband's hand, before placing his tea in front of him. 'If we could get on with it. We have prayers to do soon and I don't want to miss those.'

Gus nodded, making a mental note to get Amanjeet to keep him updated on Mr Patel's condition. Though his condition would be worsened by grief and shock, Gus was experienced enough not to discount the possibility that Mr Patel had something to do with his son's death or knew something about it. Being well-off or grieving was no guarantee that something wasn't off in a family. Gus had learned that first-hand only the previous year. He waited until Compo got his tablet out before starting. 'Do any of you have any idea why Pratab would be over in the Bradford Nine area? It's quite a distance from here.'

As he waited for them to think about his question, Gus paid particular attention to Pratab's siblings. If anyone knew the boy's secrets it was more likely to be them than his parents.

While the brother, Kiran, shook his head, Gus thought he detected a slight hesitation from Pratab's sister, before she too shook her head. Another note for Amanjeet – get the sister on her own and see what secrets she was keeping. Surprisingly, it was Mr Patel who spoke, his voice shaky and raw as if he hadn't spoken for months. 'Pratab was being secretive recently. Not telling us where he was going, on occasion he'd be home late… he even shouted at us if we questioned him… he was being a typical teenager, rebelling against his parents… you know?' And then just as suddenly, he switched off again, as if the effort of answering that one question was too much for him.

Gus waited, but none of the other three added anything. 'What about his friends?'

Mrs Patel smiled. 'He was popular, lots of friends, but his best friend was Haider. The lad he was supposed to be studying with last night. He'll be devastated. He and Pratab were almost inseparable since they started secondary school.'

'Mrs Patel, we spoke to Haider this morning. He told us he and Pratab hadn't been friends for a few months now. He said Pratab seemed to have a new group of friends, do you perhaps know who?' Gus turned his gaze on Mita and Kiran. 'Do either of you two know who your brother was hanging out with these days?'

The siblings exchanged glances and then Mita sighed. 'He was being a dick recently.'

'Mita!' But Mrs Patel's tone was resigned, as if her daughter's language was way down her list of priorities right now, but that she felt she should make the effort. She caught Gus' eye and waved an apologetic hand as if to say, 'what can you do?'

'He was, Mum... wasn't he, Kiran? Pratab was being more of a di... idiot than usual.'

Kiran fidgeted in his chair, his cheeks flushing. He looked down but nodded.

'Kiran and I thought he might have a girlfriend... but if he did, he didn't tell us and I hope if he did, he treated her better than he treated us.'

'Mita!' This time it was Mr Patel. 'Your brother's dead. Show some respect.' His tone was like a bullet through the air and Mita flinched. Her eyes welled up and she jumped up and ran around the table to her father, hugging him tight. 'I'm sorry, Dad. So sorry. I'm just so angry with him. If he'd just stayed in and studied like he was supposed to, he'd be sitting his maths exam right now... with Haider and everyone.'

Mr Patel patted her hand, 'I know, beti, I know. It's hard, sssh, sssh.'

Gus gave them a moment before continuing. 'Just one last thing. Can we have a look at Pratab's room? Crime scene officers will come and take his computer and stuff, but I'd like to have a look right now. I want to get a sense of Pratab. Then we'll leave you to your prayers.'

Mrs Patel sighed and nodded. 'Whatever you need, Inspector. Kiran, take them upstairs.'

Kiran had been reluctant to leave them alone in his brother's room which was one of two attic rooms, but Gus gently insisted that he go down and look after his parents.

A sign on the opposite door told them that it belonged to Kiran. Despite the tasteful pastel blue paint on the walls, the room was like most teenage boys' rooms… if you ignored the fact that it had an en suite and was as big as the master bedroom in Gus' house. A double bed with a Bradford City duvet set combined with the burgundy and yellow scarf that was slung over the end of the bed declared Pratab's football allegiances. The duvet looked crumpled like someone had lain there but not got under the covers. A Bradford City T-shirt was scrunched up next to the pillow and a faint floral perfume in the air suggested that it had probably been Mrs Patel who, in her grief, had wanted to get as close to her dead son as she could.

Gus put on gloves and stood for a minute just inside the door. A huge pinboard, covered in revision notes with a study schedule pinned in the middle, hung above a computer desk with a state-of-the-art computer system that immediately attracted Compo's attention. Gus left Compo to ooh and aah like a nerd and focussed instead on the study schedule. Until Easter each study target had been marked off in fluorescent highlighter. From Easter onwards the list of study aims remained unhighlighted. What had made Pratab neglect his study schedule from Easter onwards? Gus took a photo of it.

'Can't wait to get this back to The Fort. If there's owt on there to help us, I'll find it.'

Gus prowled round the room, looking in Pratab's drawers and wardrobe. Apart from his school polo shirts, Pratab favoured brand names like Nike and Adidas. Two posters were on his walls; one of Wiz Khalifa and one of Eminem. His clothes hung neatly, ironed and new, each one in its place. There was a clothes' basket in the corner, but it was empty.

Gus moved over to the bed and, lifting the mattress slightly, inserted his hands and felt round the bed. The first thing he found was three pornographic magazines. He replaced them and continued his search. Within seconds he pulled a plastic bag out.

'Look, Compo. More than enough bud for home consumption... but not too much.'

Compo approached with an evidence bag and Gus put it in.

'Haider told me he thought Pratab was on coke and MDMA, do you think the weed under the mattress is just a distraction?'

Compo shrugged. 'Well, we know where most drugs are stored, don't we...?'

Gus moved to the bathroom and lifted the cistern at the back of the toilet. 'Right here for easy disposal if you get raided.'

And, sure enough, wrapped in three plastic bags and sealed with parcel tape were two packets. He wiped the bags dry on the pristine hand towel that hung near the sink and he and Compo took them into the bedroom.

Just about to drop the first bag into an evidence bag, Gus saw movement by the door.

Mita leaned against the frame, hands shoved into her jeans. 'You found his stash then?'

Gus finished bagging up the drugs before replying. 'You knew they were here?'

Taking a step into the room, the girl shrugged. 'Didn't *know*... suspected... I suppose.' She glanced towards the bathroom door that Gus had left a little ajar and plopped herself onto her brother's bed. 'Can you maybe just keep this from them... just for today... just until the first lot of prayers are over with at least?'

Gus knew that by 'them' she meant her parents and now it was his turn to shrug. He needed to ask them about it... thing was, would a twenty-four-hour delay matter? He suspected not. How many parents had he come across that had no idea that their kid was dealing or even taking drugs? He was saved from responding by his phone ringing that familiar tune again... Bloody Gaby. She chose her moments, didn't she?

CHAPTER 25

I write my name at the top of the paper, Zarqa Siddique. The air con hums away in the background sending an occasional waft of cool air round the room. It's sort of familiar and reassuring... what isn't familiar and reassuring is the awareness that the empty seat just down from me belonged to a dead boy. I'd never liked him. He'd been a knob. Don't know why Haider hung out with him. Pratab Patel thought he was all that, but he wasn't. He was just a big-headed rich kid who was so spoilt he thought everybody owed him summat. Dick! Still, that empty chair is a bit distracting.

Before I'd even got off the bus, I'd heard them talking. News travels fast and Karim was giving it all that at the back of the bus, bigging himself up, like he was some sort of hero because he'd found Pratab. At the back of my mind, I knew a lot of his swag was because of me. Karim made no secret of the fact that he liked me... and I made no secret of the fact that I wasn't into him. Still, it didn't seem to deter him, and he could be a laugh when he wanted to.

'Hey, Zarqa. You know I found that dead kid last night, don't you? Pratab Patel, he's in your year, in't he?'

Karim is a year older than me but, like most lads, acts like he's about twelve and he's one of the Young Jihadis too. I kept my head pointed toward the window and ignored him. I didn't want to be reminded of the friends I'd left behind in the Young Jihadis. It was still a bit raw. It wasn't that I didn't get what they were trying to do. I thought they were right to try to work out how Muslim kids could live in today's society. Shit, I got how hard it was to be Muslim and British. Sometimes it was like walking a tightrope between two cultures. I'd always thought I was lucky because my parents, well Mo and Mum, had always been quite liberal. Pushing me to make friends from all walks of life, no emphasis on arranged marriages. I'd always thought they were cool. I get it now, though. It was all because of the things they were keeping from me… the secrets… the lies. The problem was me. I was the one rebelling… couldn't stomach the self-righteous shit and the hypocrisy any longer. I was fed up with all the rubbish they spouted about challenging the cultural stuff that wasn't part of the religion. Didn't seem to me like it made any difference… they still looked down on anybody who wasn't what they called a 'true Muslim'.

'Hey, Zarqa? You ignoring me?'

Well, duh? You think so? I look round and see Claire Stevens in the seat behind. I roll my eyes at her, but she looks straight through me. Probably scared I'm going to pick on her. Always feel a bit sorry for her. She always seems to be the butt of someone's jokes. Was relieved to grab my backpack and hop off the bus before Karim and his loud-mouthed mates could catch-up. I looked around for Jo Jo wondering if he was thinking about what we'd done. I'd heard it on the morning news, so the shit had already started to hit the fan.

I shake my head and realise that I've been staring into space for the last fifteen minutes and glance round the room. Mehmoona's scribbling away like nobody's business. She's a smart-ass. She'll pass no sweat. Claire's three chairs down from me and she looks like she's struggling. Keeps fidgeting. Know how she feels. It's too damn hot to think. Jo Jo's sitting three rows along from me and two seats down. Doesn't look like he's doing much writing either. As I watch, I see him steal a look at Pratab's empty chair. I look round and notice that everyone's doing that... sneaking glances at Pratab's empty chair. Wonder how the dick would feel about being the elephant in the room. Seems like karma to me. He always was a bit of a bully.

The tip tap of the invigilator's heels on the floor behind me as she walks up and down the lines of students, makes me look at the paper on the desk in front of me. Well, I've managed my name and I think that's right. She slows as she nears Pratab's place and I wonder if she's thinking about him too. But she speeds up again, clip clopping down the aisle. Fuck, it's hard enough to focus without that racket. Why is she not forced to wear soft soles like the rest of us? Then she's off tap, tap, tapping up the next row. You'd think in this heat she'd plonk her chair right in front of a fan and watch us from there, but no, Mrs Husseini takes her job very seriously.

I put Pratab and Mrs Husseini to the back of my mind and try to focus, but my mind keeps going back to last night. At first it was all exciting, a big adventure. Yeah, my heart was pounding, but in a good way... not like it is now. Not like it's been doing off and on since then. I pull my ponytail over my shoulder and study the ends. Some are split. It'll be the bleach. She told me not to dye it, but no way was I listening to her.

Back to last night. At one point, the adrenalin kicked in so much, I thought my veins would burst, thought I'd explode. My head was light, and my legs shook, but no way was I going to let Jo Jo back out then.

Now, though. That's a different thing. On the one hand it's kind of cool to hear everyone talking about what we've done. Asking me my opinion and not knowing it was me... not suspecting that good little Zarqa Siddique could do something so shameful... so awful. Now that's a bit of a turn on. For the first time in ages I feel like I matter, like I can make a difference, that I'm important.

I glance at the clock on the wall; twenty minutes to go. I smile and open my paper…

I hate maths.

CHAPTER 26

Getting back into the car was like inflicting torture on himself. The leather seat was boiling against Gus' back and the steering wheel almost too hot to touch. He left the door open and switched on the engine, activating the faulty air conditioning immediately. When he felt the warmth from it on his face, he quickly turned it back off again.

'Windows down, Compo.'

As he drove off, he wondered about Pratab's sister. She'd known about the drugs in her brother's room, or at the very least wasn't surprised that they'd found them. However, what intrigued him more was the heated discussion he'd witnessed between Mita and Kiran round the side of the house as they were leaving. He'd not been able to hear anything, but Mita's anger was evident in the way she prodded her brother hard in the shoulder, before storming off, her, 'I'll speak to you laters, yeah?' ringing in the air. The look on Kiran's face had been a combination of anger… anger and fear? Gus wasn't sure but as soon as the lad had seen Gus, he strode off down the side of the house towards the back garden after his sister. He'd taken the time to text the FLO asking her to keep an eye on the two kids. If Gus wasn't mistaken, those two were keeping something secret. The big question was, had it anything to do with their investigation?

'What's your thoughts on it all, Comps?'

Wiping a trickle of sweat from his brow, Compo leaned his head closer to the open window. The draught, causing his wavy brown hair to waft about his round face, made Gus realise he'd never seen Compo without a beanie or a bobble hat on before. Presumably the heat was proving too much even for him.

'It's so sad… How will they get through it? I kept thinking how your mum would be if it were you, Gus… and your dad and Katie?'

His friend's words hit Gus in the solar plexus, not because they tugged his heart strings on his own behalf, but because they betrayed Compo's lack of family… his inability to believe that he himself would be missed.

'Shit, Comps. Do you think if you went, we'd miss you any less than we did Sampson? Don't be daft. My mum and dad and the whole team would be devastated. We're your family.'

Compo turned his head and looked out the window. Gus sensed he needed a moment, so he switched on the radio.

…in a Bradford village are keeping checks on the elderly and, with temperatures showing no sign of dropping, urge communities to drop in to ensure their neighbours are keeping hydrated. While in other news a dog owner has been charged with animal cruelty after leaving their Japanese Akita locked in an unventilated car. The dog is expected…

'The kids are hiding summat, Gus. The girl, despite all her attitude, is definitely covering up.' He paused for a moment and then added, 'I'd get the CSIs to focus on printing the inside of that cistern… I reckon the outside will be wiped clean, but they might have forgotten the ridge at the top.'

Gus was pleased. He'd been thinking along those lines himself and the fact that Compo had picked up on the way the girl kept glancing at her brother's en suite, reinforced it. He'd make an all-round detective out of his computer nerd yet. 'Contact Hissing Sid, Compo, and be sure to tell him to check the underside of the cistern lid... hopefully the Patel kids aren't fans of *CSI*.'

As Compo made the call, Gus considered his suspicion that either Mita knew only too well where her brother had kept his drug stash or she'd nosed around on her own when he was out and found it... either way, the biggest question was why she hadn't told her parents? Perhaps she'd told her other brother? Had her brother shared his secret? Confided in his younger sister?

When his phone rang again, Gus was relieved to see that it was Taffy rather than Gaby. He answered the hands-free with a, 'Whassup, Taff?''

'PM toxicity came back with a right cocktail of shit... MDMA, coke... even a bit of Rohypnol and that's before we consider the alcohol levels. The doc says the lad would have been well out of it. He reckons it would have barely been necessary to use the cable ties.'

So, if it was unnecessary, why then did the killers use them... and then remove them only to discard them so carelessly only feet away from the body? Clearly, they didn't need to use them. Maybe they just enjoyed cuffing the lad... but why not leave them on? Gus suspected it was to do with the posing afterwards... maybe the cable ties offended the killer's sense of how the crime scene should look when Pratab was discovered. 'I take it the blood on the cable ties belongs to our victim?'

'Yup. Cause of death was the knife wound to the jugular, but your da..., I mean the doc, reckons it would have been touch and go for the lad anyway, what with the drugs and alcohol combo. One other interesting thing about the ties though... the doc sees no evidence of a struggle. He says the ties didn't appear to have tightened around Pratab's wrist as he struggled... he says the wounds would have been wider if the lad had struggled. He reckons the killer pulled them that tight and Pratab was either unconscious or too drugged to fight back. He also says that that and the bruising along the head were done just pre-mortem and he suspects that unnecessary force was used then too. Pratab wouldn't have been able to struggle. Time of death was around ten o'clock. Dr McGuire will send the report over asap.'

'Has he had any luck lifting prints from the hand marks on his head?'

Gus could hear Taffy flicking over pages on his notebook. 'Oops, forgot that bit – yep. Doc says it looks like they wore gloves. We're still waiting for all the trace forensic analyses to come back.'

'Okay, Taff, thanks for that. Head up to City Academy. We'll meet you there.'

'Oh, wait a minute, Gus, your dad wants a word before you go.'

As his dad's booming voice filled the car, Gus scowled, ignoring Compo's, 'Hi, doc,' followed by his dad's 'Hi, Compo, Angus got you out and about today? Corrine always says he should make sure you get a bit more sunshine, you often look a bit peaky. It's good to keep your vitamin D topped up.'

The Dr lowered his tone conspiratorially before continuing, 'She's just dropped off some brownies here and I do believe she's heading up to The Fort to leave you some too.'

With Compo's, 'Brilliant, I love Mrs M's chocolate brownies,' ringing in his ears, Gus snorted. His mother's brownies would be inedible to all but Compo, but she didn't realise and continued to bring her burnt offerings into Gus' place of work for his team to share.

'I heard that, Angus.' Dr McGuire's tone was mildly disapproving.

Gus had a momentary pang of guilt which was dispelled when he saw a group of paparazzi gathered outside the school gates. 'Window's up, Compo. Don't want any microphones stuck in my face. Dad, give me a sec, there's a whole load of journalists outside the school and I'm just pulling into the car park.'

'Oh, I won't take a minute, laddie. Just think that maybe you need to speak to Gabriella. Poor thing's been trying to contact you for days now. You should take the time… she's not going away, you know… she's family after all.'

For a moment Gus was speechless. *Poor thing*? *Family*? Gus had a childish urge to say *What the fuck*! in the same tone he'd heard various teenagers using. Instead, he took a deep breath and glowered out his closed window at the journalists who were rapping their knuckles against the glass. His temptation to mouth the words 'eff off' to them was strong. 'I'm working, Dad. Now's not the time, as I thought you'd realise, bearing in mind the post mortem you've just done.'

Except for Compo's exaggerated intake of breath there was silence in the car. Compo looked at Gus, his mouth a perfect 'O', his forehead puckered, and Gus could almost feel the waves of disapproval adding to the temperature in the already overheated vehicle.

Showing his warrant card to the gate camera, Gus waited for the barrier to go up and drove past the media herd and into the nearest parking space before mumbling, 'Sorry.'

'I think you know fine and well that I haven't forgotten the wee dead laddie, Angus. I've just been up to my elbows in his innards. I'll not forget the waste of that young lad's life in a hurry. Which is why it's important that you patch up your differences with Gabriella. Life is too short… shorter than you know.'

Was his dad getting maudlin? Before he had a chance to ask what he was on about, Dr McGuire continued, back to its usual brusqueness, 'Besides she has something important to ask you.'

Gus bit down on the retort that sprung to his lips. No point in making things worse by saying that his ex-wife was always after something. 'I'm busy, Dad. Gotta go.'

As they exited the vehicle, Gus heard a familiar voice yell, 'Could you comment on this *Snapchat Killer*, DI McGuire?'

Shit! It had leaked already. He knew it would, but he'd expected to have a while longer before the likes of Jez Hopkins got his hand on that info and created a stupid tagline that glorified the killers. He turned and glared at Hopkins, who grinned at him from behind the gates. What Gus would give for that tosser to be behind bars for real.

'Come on, ignore them.'

But Compo, shoulders hunched, scowled at Gus. 'No need for that you know.'

For a moment Gus thought Compo was defending the journalist.

'No need at all. You should be thankful you got a lovely family. Your dad dun't deserve that.'

Ah, not the reporter, but his dad. Gus had the grace to admit, if only to himself, that Compo was right. 'Come on, we got other things to think about. Patti's got all the senior year groups together, so we can talk to them.'

CHAPTER 27

City Academy was a fairly new building, with an additional annex off to the side. Its cold concrete dazzled in the sunlight, little sparks of colour glistening from the slabs. Gus ran up the steps and entered the building by the visitors' entrance, to find Patti waiting for him there. It always made Gus feel a little awkward being with Patti in the school building. Here at her place of work she presented a calm yet efficient aura, that masked the bouts of giggles she was prone to in his company. He never quite knew how to greet her here either, so he took his cue from her as she said, 'Ah, DI McGuire and DC Compton, the students are waiting for you.'

Despite her smile, Gus recognised the tension in the way she held her body and the faint lines around her mouth. She would hold things together for her staff and students, but this would be difficult for her. No head teacher wanted to have to deal with the death of one of their students, yet Patti had had this experience before, and not so very long ago and now, once more, she had a team of journalists on the doorstep and her school was in the spotlight. He followed her along a corridor towards the theatre and was taken aback by a display table covered in a velvet drape with a large photograph of Pratab hanging behind it. Beneath it were small offerings of soft toys and flowers and in centre place was an ornate glass bowl with a simple sign containing the words, 'Our thoughts for Pratab'. A supply of pens and multicoloured Post-it notes were scattered in front and already the vase was more than half full of the students' messages and thoughts.

Patti gestured at the shrine. 'A group of students asked if they could do something to remember Pratab. It's all part of the grieving process.'

They passed the shrine and Patti opened the door leading into the theatre. At once the subdued tones of the waiting youngsters drifted into the corridor. Gus wished they were waiting for a normal assembly or a school play rather than to be asked for information about their deceased schoolmate. This was not going to be easy, but it was important that he represented the face of the investigation to these kids. They needed to see both him and his team as approachable despite the presence of four uniformed officers lining the edge of the auditorium. Taffy was already there, standing next to them. Gus made a mental note to remind the lad about speeding.

Patti introduced Gus and his team to the assembled year group.

From where he stood in front of the rows of students, a welcome breeze from the massive fan that hung from the ceiling cooled him down, drying the sweat on his body, but leaving him feeling sticky and uncomfortable. Gus took a moment to cast his eyes along the lines of students and realised he recognised a few. Zarqa was sitting halfway up and to the left. There were a couple of lads he'd interviewed the previous year when their friend had gone missing. Haider and Karim were sitting a few seats apart, a few of Zarqa's friends he'd met in passing at Mo's and another girl who nodded at him were in the third row. Belatedly, he realised she was the DCS's daughter.

Taking the time to make sure he engaged in eye contact with as many students as he could, Gus began. He projected his voice so it hit the back wall. 'I know this has been a difficult day for you. Exams, the unbearable heat, and most of all, the death of your school friend. I won't keep you here for long.' He paused and moved closer to the front row.

'It's never easy to come to terms with this sort of tragedy... but one thing that will help with that, is finding justice for Pratab. And in order to do that, we need to have as much information as we can about him. We need to know about his friends, the places he went, the things he liked to do, the people he knew inside and outside of school. I expect some of you might have shared secrets with Pratab – things he perhaps didn't tell his siblings or parents. These sorts of things might be what helps us catch his killer. These officers,' Gus pointed towards his uniformed colleagues, 'will be available in the school at lunchtime, and before and after school. If you know anything, no matter how insignificant, we'd like you to share it with them.'

A few students began to cry, muffled sobs that were probably a combination of grief and fear. 'I'm not going to keep you much longer. These officers will be interviewing those of you who were closest to Pratab. However, any one of you can arrange a meeting with one of my team by texting this number.' Gus pointed to a number on the screen behind him.

'These meetings will be confidential. We want you to feel comfortable coming forward with any information you may have. I want you all to take a moment to put that number into your phones.' He paused and waited.

A few of the kids took out their phones and began to input the number, others looked restlessly around them. Gus cleared his throat. 'I mean all of you... please... if all of you could take down this number.' He waited and more students took out their phones, some reluctantly, a few in resignation, and most apparently quite happily. There was no guarantee that all the students were actually taking the number down, or even that they'd bother to contact the police with information, but he was determined to make it as easy for them as possible to do so.

'The number will also be posted on walls around school. In my experience, sometimes things occur to people hours, even days after they've been asked for information. Please use this function. If you don't want to meet up, you could text the information to us. We will take every piece of information seriously. Thank you.'

Gus left the theatre with Patti, leaving Taffy, Compo, and the uniformed officers available to chat to the students. Together they went to Patti's office and Gus was glad to sit on a comfy seat right in front of a fan. Now that he'd conducted his 'official' police business for the day, he drew out his bandana and tied it round his hair, glad to feel coolness between his neck and his dreads.

'So, what can you tell me about Pratab Patel?'

Patti slid behind her desk, taking advantage of the desk fan that whirred in a desultory fashion. 'Pratab Patel? Well, obviously I knew you'd be asking, so I asked around. Seems he'd been a bit of an idiot over the past few months. Skiving school, his grades have gone down. He was a solid A and B student, but...' She shrugged and shook her head. 'None of that matters now. A couple of his teachers say he doesn't seem to be friends with the lads he was friends with before. They've seen him on his own at lunch and break times, on his phone mainly. We had his parents in a few times, but it didn't seem like things were improving. Before that though he'd been great – studious, pleasant.'

That tallied with what Haider had told him. 'What about the brother and sister? How have they been?'

'Ah, Mita and Kiran. Pratab was the middle child. Mita can be a handful. Spoilt, but bright.' She frowned. 'We had a few reports of Mita bullying one of the Polish girls and last year, she sent a couple of inappropriate texts to a girl she'd fallen out with. There was also talk that Mita shoved some ham in one of the Muslim girl's lockers, but that was never proven. She seems to be settling down now. Hope this doesn't spark her off again.'

Patti pursed her lips in a way that told Gus she had more to add but was weighing up her words. He waited. Patti would speak when she was ready.

'Hmm, Kiran? Well. Kiran is a bit of an enigma. He's smart, A*s all the way, but... and this is only my own personal feeling, he can be sly.'

'Sly?'

Patti got up, walked round her desk, and leaned on it and sighed. 'He's one of those kids you find hard to like.' She wafted her hands at Gus as if to ward off any criticism he might have of her words. 'I know, I know. It's a horrible thing to say... and it's just my opinion. It's not often I can't see something to like in a kid... but he's the exception.'

Okay, he hadn't expected that. Patti wasn't one to dislike her pupils for no good reason and the fact that she clearly was distressed at sharing this with him was an indication that she was conflicted. 'Patti, you can't love 'em all.'

Her glare was enough to tell him that she wished very much that she could.

'Any chance you could give me a bit more, Patti? If that's how you feel about the lad, then it must have some basis.'

Steepling her fingers in front of her lips, Patti gave his question due consideration before replying, 'He's always there, you know? On the periphery of things... other kids get dragged over the coals for something and he's... just there. Looking sly and a bit self-satisfied.'

Gus was surprised. This hadn't been the impression he'd got of Kiran, but then kids were often different at school than they were at home. Apart from that, today must be particularly difficult for the lad. However, he trusted Patti's judgement. If she thought there was something off with him, then he wouldn't dismiss it out of hand.

As if relieved she'd got that off her chest, Patti straightened. 'It's just a feeling, okay? Nothing more, nothing concrete, and it probably says more about me than him.'

Gus stood up and walked over to her. He put his arms round her and hugged her for a moment, breathing in the fresh smell of her perfume, glad it wasn't the one he'd come to associate with those wretched anonymous letters. Releasing her, he dropped a kiss on her cheek. 'You take care of yourself, Patti.' That thought reminded him of something. 'You'll never believe this, but DCS Bashir has ordered additional drive-bys on your street and mine. Who'd have thought it, eh?'

Patti raised a perfectly curved eyebrow. 'She thinks I need protection?'

'Hmm, perhaps not protection exactly. It's just a precaution. There's been no implied threat—'

'Other than that single little omission, you mean? That in itself is a threat, I'd say.'

'Omission?'

'Their name. People who don't sign off their letters are generally up to no good. You know that, Gus.'

He had to admit that was true.

As he went back to pick up his team, Gus wondered about Patti's assessment of Kiran Patel. Sly and smug? Well he couldn't arrest him for that, but it was strange that, out of the three Patel children, the dead kid was the one who'd only started to play up recently.

CHAPTER 28

Pisces

> Me: Need to talk!

Wish Zodiac would answer. Just want to know what's going on. That's all.

Ping!

Fucking notification. Gonna block them. They're getting on my tits, big time. Come on Zodiac, just reply.

Ping!

Why's the daft git not replying? I'll try Leo.

> Me: You all right? Heard from Zodiac?

Surely the loser will reply at least.

Ping!

> Leo: All right. Keeping my head down.
> So should you. Stop texting.

Arse! *Who the fuck do you think you are*? I nearly text back, but I hear someone outside the door, so I slip the phone in my school bag. I'll try again later. Just need to keep my cool and we'll be sorted.

CHAPTER 29

Heading for the school canteen, Gus kept an eye open for Zarqa. He'd seen her in the assembly, and he wanted to have a quick word with her if he could before he left. Jerry and Dave's words about her running down Oak Lane late the previous night had made him worried for her. Time he stood up to the mark and acted like her godfather. Zarqa was acting up. She had every right to, she'd suffered a tremendous shock. Everything she'd believed to be true had been upended and it wasn't surprising she was being a pain.

The situation was deteriorating. Mo was worried about Naila. Naila was worried about Mo. They were both worried about Zarqa and their other kids and Gus was worried about all of them. There was too damn much worry going around and something needed to be done. He'd taken a back seat, assuming things would level off, but hearing that Zarqa was out on her own after eleven at night, possibly near where a murder had taken place and especially on a school night, was worrying.

A crowd of kids gathered round the vending machines near the cafeteria and Gus cast his eye over them looking for Zarqa. Then he caught sight of her sitting on a silver chair, slightly away from the other kids, fingers speeding over her phone. In front of her was a pile of books and her bag. She'd done something to her hair. The bottom bit was a mucky yellow colour. It was probably the fashion, but he thought it looked horrid. She looked skinny and frail and, in that moment, when she didn't realise she was being observed, her eyes looked haunted. As he weaved through the milling pupils, she caught his eye. Her expression changed. Her mouth pulled down and a frown shot across her forehead. She jumped to her feet and began scurrying away from him towards a corridor leading to a maze of classrooms.

Gus frowned. What was she playing at? He only wanted to chat. 'Zarqa. Stop!'

As soon as the words left his mouth, he regretted them, for every one of the pupils turned to look at him. Their eyes following him as he headed along the corridor after his goddaughter who had sped up. For goodness's sake, what had he done? He was on her side. Zarqa was usually happy to chat to him, but her trying to avoid him worried him.

About ten steps in front of him, Zarqa banged into someone and the pile of books she was carrying scattered onto the floor. She glanced behind, her face contorted into a combination of frustration and anger. Gus was stricken by how desperate she seemed to escape him. He increased his stride and in two seconds was with her, helping her pick up her fallen books. He kept his voice light. 'You avoiding me, Zarqa?'

She shrugged as he handed the last of her belongings to her. 'Didn't notice you, that's all.'

They both knew that was a barefaced lie, but Gus chose to ignore that detail. 'Look, I wanted to have a quick chat with you.'

He hesitated, watching the way her eyes darted around as if looking for an escape route. This probably wasn't the best place to start this sort of dialogue, but he wasn't sure when he'd get another chance, now they were in the middle of a major investigation. Glancing around, he saw an area under the stairs that would afford them some privacy. 'Over here.'

With reluctance written all over her face, and dragging her heels, Zarqa joined him. 'I don't have time for this, you know, Gus. It's exam time and I need to study every minute I've got.' Her tone was insolent, each word an accusation, and Gus was momentarily thrown. Where had the sweet acquiescent kid he'd known since she was born gone?

'Oh, so that's why you're tearing down Oak Lane after eleven p.m. on the night before an important exam, is it?' Again, just too late, he realised he'd misspoken. Fuck's sake, he really needed to get better at this parenting lark.

Zarqa's lips thinned, her eyes, so similar to her mother's, sparked their fury... and something else? Gus couldn't decide before she was hissing at him. 'Now he's got someone *following* me? Really. Fuck's sake, Gus, just leave me alone.'

She tried to brush past him, but Gus moved so that his body blocked her escape. He too was now cross. Cross with Zarqa and cross with himself. He had no experience of this fatherhood carry-on and he was clearly out of his depth, but he loved Zarqa and was working on the theory that hurt was making her lash out.

'Don't be stupid, Zarqa. Course your dad's not got someone watching you. He trusts you not to do owt daft.'

Her, 'He's not my dad,' lashed him like a whip. This was Mo she was talking about. The man who'd been willing to give up everything, including his life, for the woman he loved... and for Zarqa. The man who'd loved her from the moment she was born. When he spoke, his words were sharp. 'So, what is he then? A piece of shit on your shoe?'

Zarqa lowered her head. Her shoulders were shaking, but Gus wasn't sure if it was in anger or tears. He lowered his tone, softened it, and tried again, wishing he was anywhere but here right now doing this. 'Mo is your dad, in all the ways that count, Zarqa, and I know that when you've had a chance to think it through, you'll realise that.'

Her head jerked up; her chin raised. 'Don't patronise me. He's a murderer. He's not my dad.'

Gus stepped back and raised his hands placatingly, palms up. 'Okay, okay. We can't talk about this here. All I wanted to do was ask you not to wander around the streets on your own after dark. It's not safe. Just last night a mosque was attacked, and then... well you already know about Pratab.'

Zarqa snorted and pushed her way past him. 'Pep talk delivered. You can chill now.' Gus grabbed her arm lightly, 'Don't go, Zarq. I want to try to help... I'm here for you.'

She yanked her arm away. 'If *that's* how you deal with kids, it's just as well you have none of your own. That's all I can say.'

Stunned, Gus watched her run around the corner and out of sight. Perhaps she was right. Perhaps parenthood wasn't for him.

CHAPTER 30

Last thing I needed was to see Uncle Gus. Bet my da... Mo's got him on the case. Spying on me, keeping an eye on me. I was sure he was going to ask where I'd been last night. Shit, don't know what I'd have said. It wouldn't have been the truth though – no way.

I scurry along to my locker and start to fill my bag. School's out for today. Can't stand being here. Everywhere I go they're talking about it and I want to just yell at the top of my voice... 'That was me! I did it and I don't regret a fucking thing!'

Imagine how that would go down. Imagine Ms Copley escorting me into her office, picking up the phone and phoning Gus... maybe my mum and Mo. She'd have that disappointed look on her face. The one where she frowns just a little... just enough to make you feel like shit. She'd sit me in the chair at the other side of her desk, like she did that time I was sick. But this time, she'd be scowling at me... bet she'd hardly know what to say. She'd wonder how her friend Naila's daughter could have done something so truly awful.

Thing is, I don't bloody care... before I found out about what Mo did to my real dad, I'd have been a nervous wreck, all jittery and nervous. Now, I don't know what's wrong with me, but I can't seem to feel anything. Most of the time I walk about like I'm in a trance. The conversations around me seem like they're filtered through water. Like at the swimming pool, when you bomb to the bottom and you can hear stuff, but you can't make sense of it all. Like you're in your own world and nobody else can reach you... that's how I feel. The only time I feel anywhere near normal is when I'm with Jo Jo. Only then do I feel… connected. Like I'm here… present in my own life.

No, that's not quite right. I *do* feel one thing… can't describe it, can't shake it off, can't forget about it. Everywhere I go, I carry this big concrete lump in my chest. It weighs me down so I can hardly breathe and when I see *him*, it gets bigger and bigger. Sometimes I think it's going to burst right out of my body and splatter the floor with my blood and my lungs and my ribs and… my heart.

A sob gulps up into my throat and I swallow it back down. It presses on top of the block and I can't catch my breath. I lean my forehead against my locker door, welcoming the cool metal against my skin and I take deep, slow breaths. The lump's still there, still dragging me down. Not caring who's around, I push myself upright and kick the bottom locker. The crash reverberates all around, but nobody hears. Everyone else is in class. I'm alone in my misery.

So, what would Gus do if Patti told him what I'd done? Hm, that's easy. He'd come dashing right over. Uncle Gus, knight in shining armour and dreads. I grin at the image, but it soon fades from my lips. He wouldn't be able to save me. Not now. Not after what I've done. But he'd still come. Wonder if he'd put the sirens on? Wonder if he'd stop to pick up Mum and Mo?

Wonder how long we'd get in prison, me and Jo Jo? No, not Jo Jo. He's got his mum and his sister to look after and I've heard if you're young and gay in prison it's not a good thing. Wouldn't do that to Jo Jo. He's got enough crap to deal with. No, I wouldn't dob Jo Jo in. It was my idea. He didn't really want to do it. He doesn't want to do the next one either. But I know he will. I'll be able to convince him.

I turn around and see Claire Stevens sitting there, phone in her hand. All quiet, watching me. *How long has she been there*? She smiles, one of those 'I'm sorry' kind of smiles. Sorry for spying on me? Sorry for seeing me lose control... sorry for being alive? I look at her more closely now. She's not there to spy on me... like me, she's hiding. I glance round. There's no one else around, just the two of us. I plonk myself down next to her and she moves away from me, like I've got something catching. Maybe she can sense the badness in me... maybe even this timid, little, spotty freak can smell the festering rot that's just waiting there to burst out. I don't blame her. Instead I jump to my feet and not making eye contact with her, I walk over to my locker. 'You haven't seen me, right?'

Her laugh drifts after me. 'Who's going to ask me, anyway? Go! I've not seen you.'

I sling my bag over my shoulder, slam my locker shut, and wander out of school, ignoring the receptionist at the front desk as she shouts after me to sign out.

Not signing out of school's not gonna get me in any more bother than I'm in already.

CHAPTER 31

Gus watched Compo with a slight smile on his face. The lad was delighted to find the huge box of brownies Gus' mum had left by the coffee machine. Despite having already devoured two bacon butties and a slice of lemon cake at The Lunch Monkey before returning to work, he immediately opened the container and stuffed a charred looking brownie in his mouth. The lad had a belly of iron.

Taffy winked at Gus as he sat down behind his desk. 'Good to see the heat's not affecting your appetite, Comps.'

Crumbs falling out of his mouth, Compo grinned and settled himself beside his own desk, where a range of PCs and different modems and so forth sat. He sparked open a can of Fanta, he'd taken from the mini fridge and took a long slurp before studying his screens. The radio played in the background as they worked...

...are looking for a suspect the media has dubbed The Snapchat Killer. The murderer of a teenage boy is reported to have sent an image of the dead boy to his friend using the social media app Snapchat. The police have dec...

Gus was on his feet in an instant. 'Switch that bloody thing off. What the hell are they playing at? I'll get Nancy on the case.'

He knew that it was too late though. The information was out there, and the name would stick. It really angered him that the press appeared to put more emphasis on sensationalising evil than in grieving with the victim's relatives. 'Please say you've got something to move this investigation forward, Comps.'

'Well, I've just got the info from Pratab's and Haider's phones. I'll put it on the main screen.'

Gus moved over so he could see the interactive screen and waited for Compo to talk them through his findings. 'Pratab first, if you don't mind.'

'Okay, here's his text history.'

A list of numbers with names and dates and times showed on the screen. Gus looked at it for a moment. '… And?'

'Well, looking at this, it seems that, from Easter until his death, Pratab only used this phone to contact his family. There are no other texts… only those sent to his parents and his siblings… But…' the screen scrolled down and Compo highlighted a date just before the school Easter holidays, 'before this date, his texts went to both his family and friends… granted, his texts to family are more than those to friends, but that's because he'd mainly use *Snapchat* or *Instagram* or *Messenger* to contact his mates. But from Easter he deleted all social media apps off this phone… strange.'

Gus studied the screen. There was a clear difference in Pratab's phone usage between the period after Easter and the period before. Gus had his own ideas why that might be. 'Like Haider said, he cut off contact with all his usual friends around that time – which tallies with his text usage, but where are the texts to his new friends? Why is he only ever texting family?'

Absentmindedly sipping the Irn Bru Compo had given him earlier, Gus studied the list. 'Can we have a look at his contact lists? Even if he's not sending texts to his new friends, he'll surely have them in his contacts.'

Compo pressed some keys and the screen displayed Pratab's contact list.

'I want you to contact everyone on that list and see when he last communicated with them. Also, what about call history? I can see that his parents and siblings texted him repeatedly on Sunday evening, did they call him? Did anyone else? Any unknown numbers?'

Again, Compo worked his magic and the screen changed. 'There's lots of voicemails and missed calls from his parents and Kiran. A few from Mita, but not as many. She's younger so she'd probably be out of the loop on that... he ignored them all.'

Gus looked at Compo. 'Can you get all of those communications triangulated? Just to be sure they all were where they said they were, you know?'

'On it, boss.'

'Also, can you access his emails and other social media accounts? We need to know who he's been communicating with apart from family and from which device. You're not telling me a sixteen-year-old lad's only communications were with his mum and dad... that's just not feasible. I suspect he had another phone. Get Amanjeet to have a poke around, see if she can find a second phone or ask about one and get Sid to be on the lookout for one when he's processing Pratab's room. Also get on the phone to one of the uniforms at the school and request access to Pratab's locker – although I think it's unlikely he would have left a phone there over the weekend – you never know though, we might find something else. Can you retrieve any of those *Snapchat* things you mentioned? Like the one that went to Haider?'

Compo grinned like he'd just won the lottery... or in his case, been presented with a big cream cake. 'I've shared access to both Pratab and Haider's email, *Facebook*, *Twitter*, and *Instagram* right now for you. *Snapchat* will take time. I should, at some point, be able to identify which device he used to access the different accounts too.'

Compo's eyes shone with the prospect of a computer challenge. And already he was putting his ear buds in and settling in for the task.

Gus looked at Taffy. 'Get a couple of uniforms in to go over the two lads' social media accounts. It's too time consuming for us.'

Gus had just moved back over to his own desk when his PC pinged and Compo yelled across the room. 'That's the CCTV footage from the cameras around your house, Gus. I've shared it with C team too.'

Gus had all but forgotten about his stalker and wished that they'd hurry up with his new home security system so that he could have Bingo back home. They'd told him a couple of days if they fast-tracked the order... and if he was prepared to pay through the nose for it. Which, of course, he was. He opened the file and began to fast forward through it. Compo had managed to isolate the times when his neighbour's motion-activated lights came on and then rolled it onto one thread from the time Gus and Patti had entered his house on Saturday night until the time Patti had picked up the envelope on the Sunday. Within fifteen minutes, Gus realised it would be a fruitless task as there was an area from the side street, right up his drive to his front door that was completely uncovered by any of the surrounding cameras. His stalker had a clear, unmonitored route to his door.

Deciding not to waste his time with that, Gus cursed himself for hoping that his stalker would turn up with another letter soon... but not until after his new system was up and running. If they caught the fucker, that would be one less thing to worry about.

'Oh, Gus, glad I caught you.'

Gus looked up smiling at Nancy who'd popped her head through the door.

'Sebastian Carlton will be thrilled to help out… seems he can't wait to catch-up with you and the team. Especially now the bastards have given him a name. The *Snapchat Killer* – who the hell leaked that?'

'We knew we wouldn't be able to keep that under wraps for long, Nance. The kid who received it wouldn't have been able to help himself sharing that with his mates.' He shrugged. 'That's life. Looks like you and Bashir will have to make some sort of statement though, but we've nothing much to give you. It's early days yet.'

'Yep.' She blew a kiss at Compo, who grinned although his face reddened a little. He was getting used to Nancy's teasing ways. 'Got to dash, Basher the Gnasher called.'

And she was off, leaving Gus smirking at the new name she'd coined for their DCS.

CHAPTER 32

Zodiac

...dubbed The Snapchat Killer because he used the social media app Snapchat to send an image to the victim's friend. Here on Capital Radio we have the weather. Over to John ... and it looks like the sun is here to stay for a few more weeks at least with highs of...

The *Snapchat Killer*! I like it. Sort of funky. All the best killers have a catchy nickname; The Zodiac Killer, The Boston Strangler, Bible John, The Yorkshire Ripper, The Crossbow Cannibal... and, now we have...

...Drum Roll...

...The *Snapchat Killer*!

Course the snaps were my idea... sort of. Gotta claim kudos when you can, don't you? I don't get any at home. Got a few surprises lined up and I can't wait. Be a surprise for Pisces and Leo too.

I'm glad to get out of the house. It really does my head in. Like I'm not good enough, like I'm failing... the constant glances letting me know how much of a disappointment I am.

I just want to escape into the freedom of the outdoors where I can breathe and be myself. I snag some bread for the ducks. Like they need it. Half the lake's clogged up with bread and chapattis and shit. Poor ducks – that'll kill them off. It passes the time though. Maybe I'll grab an ice cream before the café shuts. A Magnum. Then I'll have another walk round the lake. Those smelly old bastards are sitting there again. Nothing better to do with their time. They should be moved on. They make the place look like shit.

Park's heaving. Filled with families with screaming brats. Want a go on the rope swing, so I tell one of them to fuck off. They tell their dad and he gives me a mouthful. Stupid old bastard. I know I'm too old. Just wanted a quick go, that's all.

I go into the café and over to the freezer. No white chocolate Magnums and that pisses me off. In the end I settle for a nutty one. I sit down near the boats and get the burner phone out. Quick glance around me. Nobody there so I take a sneaky peak at the video... my guilty, or in my case, not so guilty pleasure.

Pratab's zonked out already. That was a joke. I'd expected him to be a div about it, but all he wanted to do was show off, so he swigged the voddie like it was going out of fashion – dumbass, didn't get that we'd spiked it. Ten minutes and he was all over the place. Didn't even notice when I put gloves on. Neither did the other two.

There's Pisces putting the cable ties round him. Out of focus for a bit. That'll be when I had to pull them tighter, so they'd dig right into his skin. That wuss Pisces was too squeamish. While my phone's down, I draw the line on the neck, so we get it right first time. You can hear them giggling in the background. *Idiots*!

Best bit coming up – Leo sticking the knife in. Stuck the vein first time. Got it just right. The blood spurting out. Selfie then, making sure I'm not in it I told the other two I'd delete them... and I will. Just not yet. Got to keep some insurance. Never know when I'll need it.

I nibble my Magnum. I prefer the white chocolate, but this is nice too. When I'm done, I chuck the stick in the lake, wipe my hands on a tissue, and get my phone out.

Selfie time! Nothing incriminating about being in Lister Park. Nothing at all, so I post it to *Instagram* and *Snapchat* it to Leo and Pisces on their real phones.

The park's emptying out. Only a couple of boats still bobbing about on the boating lake. Surely, it won't be much longer. I'm thirsty. Ice cream always makes me thirsty. Should've bought a can of Coke. Could walk to the Sainsburys. It'll be open, but then I might miss him. I've not waited all this time to miss him at the last minute. Besides, I'll have to come back later… that's the plan. Got to get everything sorted. I grin… that stupid tosser still hasn't worked out how I know. So much for being a geek. Can't even keep his room secure. Oh, I love storing little secrets… intelligence. That's what the pigs call it. That's wrong. The information itself isn't intelligence. No, it's what you do with it that uses intelligence and I know just how to use it.

Wish he'd hurry up. I flick through the photos on my iPhone, wondering which ones I'll use next time. Probably the one I took this morning. I like the one I used today though – it'll have him wondering how I got it… let him figure out just how inventive I can be. I like that thought. I want him to appreciate my brilliance. But I'm not using that trick again. Not just now anyway. I'll save that trick for my next big surprise.

My burner phone vibrates. Pisces! I dismiss the call. First rule of, well… of ruling, is to take control. Or, in other words, make everyone else feel out of control. It starts to vibrate again. Persistent! I switch it off and shove it in my pocket. No time for distractions.

It's dark, but I don't mind. I'm not scared. I think of this park as mine now. After all, I seem to spend half of my time here. I glance up and check in the distance. Sure enough, he's jogging down past the kid's playground. I slink off into the shadows, in the bushes and wait until he passes. Not long now. Not long at all!

CHAPTER 33

I close my bedroom door and go over to look out the window. Jessie and Mum are in bed. Mum looked a bit better tonight... still flushed, but the warm soup with buttered bread, followed by custard and jam roly poly brought a smile to her lips. She only ate half, but that was better than she'd managed earlier. The cold beans, sauce hardening on the plate, had remained uneaten during the day. Who could blame her? I'd half expected her to question where I'd got the money for butter from, but she didn't. Too grateful for something warm, I suspect. I refilled her bottles of water and left them in hands-reach as she drifted off to sleep. If she's still flushed like that tomorrow, I'll phone the doctor. I've not got an exam tomorrow, so I can wait in – maybe get some work done.

Got a special order in and I have to have it ready and at the drop off point by midnight tonight. It's a bespoke model and if it hadn't cost me an arm and a leg, I'd have been buzzing about it. As it is, I resent having to make it. Wonder what the fuck whoever it is wants it for.

Taking care to not move the curtain much, I peek through the gap between it and the window frame. Razor's henchman's still out there. Goyley, they call him. Big fucker, he is, with tattoos and fists that seem permanently clenched. He was there when I brought Jessie home from school. He was still there when I took her to the park, and he was still there when we got back. He never said owt, just stared at me, fag in one hand, a smirk on his ugly puss. He didn't need to say owt. I knew fine why he was there. Keeping an eye on me for Razor. If Razor's crew hadn't been banned from the school vicinity and given a restraining order, Razor would have had either Goyley or HP waiting for me at the gates. Mind you, it's a pretty safe bet that I'll come home at some point... can't leave Jessie and my mam and they know that. They're counting on that. He's sitting on old Mrs Udoka's wall with a can of Stella. She'll be furious, but she won't say owt. Nobody says owt on our estate... not to Razor's thugs. Not to Hammerhead's thugs.

I get a notification on my phone. It's an email and as usual the sender has bounced it round the world like a fucking kangaroo. No way even I can work out where it originates. This is crap. I know who it's from. What it's about. My finger hovers over the delete button. I'm tempted... really tempted, but instead I open it.

> Midnight. Bandstand. Come alone... or
> you know what'll happen, Cheeky Boy!

That's it.

But now I've got another problem. How the hell do I shake off Razor's crew? Last thing I need is for my activities as Cheeky Boy to end up viral. How the fuck did they find out? I want to throw my phone against the wall, stamp on it, flush it down the toilet... but none of that would make any difference. I've got no fucking choice. I'm trapped. So, I lie down on the floor and do twenty push-ups. *Focus, Jo Jo. Focus*!

When I'm done and my muscles are on fire, I glug a half bottle of water, double check I've locked my bedroom door and sit down at my worktable. All the components are spread out before me. I've only got the finishing touches to do now. I'll give myself an hour, hour and a half tops and then I'll try to sneak out the back. When I looked out mam's bedroom window earlier, I couldn't see anybody watching, but just in case, I won't go through the yard, instead I'll climb over the fences, until I reach the end garden and then I'll skip out and head through the back streets. With any luck, Goyley won't even realise I'm gone.

Plan in place, I settle down with my screwdriver, flick on the lamp, and crack on.

CHAPTER 34

It had got dark by the time Gus looked up from his desk. His neck was stiff, so he cricked it, grimacing when the bones grated together sending a sharp pain up to his skull. Compo was on the other side of the room, his head bobbing in time to whatever music he'd deemed appropriate for this investigation. Taffy had gone home hours earlier. Gus suspected that he had a date because he looked shifty as he headed to the shower rooms with a bag, only to return twenty minutes later red faced and smelling of something a bit more up market than the Lynx Compo favoured.

Gus logged out and got to his feet. With a stretch, he loosened as much of the tension as he could. There was no point in telling Compo it was time to go. The lad often stayed all night, fortifying himself with packets of crisps, chocolate bars, and an endless supply of full sugar fizzy drinks. A conversation Gus had had with Taffy a few months back illuminated the reason for Compo's unwillingness to leave The Fort, in short, this was his home and the team, with the addition of Gus' relatives, were Compo's family. Taffy had described Compo's flat and Gus had felt a pang of guilt that he hadn't been more tuned in to Compo's loneliness. He suspected Alice had been only too aware of it and that was one of the reasons she always planned outings and suchlike for them all to go on. He shrugged... his own mum had realised too. That's why she inundated Compo with home baking and invites to Sunday lunch.

Unsettled by these insights, Gus yawned, retied his bandana and went over to Compo, laying a hand on the computer nerd's shoulder.

'I'm off now, Comps. Don't stay too late, will you?'

Spinning round on his chair, Compo grinned. 'Nah, I'll just finish up here, then I'll head off home.'

Yeah right.

'If you get anything useful from the *Snapchat* stuff, let me know right away.' Remembering Compo's propensity to forget the time he added, 'Only if you think it's urgent like.' But Compo was already bopping away to his music.

Smiling, Gus headed towards the door, thinking about grabbing a Raja's Pizza on his way home. It'd been ages since he'd had one and he had a sudden craving for a spicy keema achar topping. As he exited the lift, his phone vibrated. Hoping it wasn't Gabriella, he reluctantly pulled it out of his pocket and groaned when he saw the caller ID. Heading out the door with a last wave to the duty officer, he paused on the steps before answering. 'Hi, Katie, you okay?'

There was a moment of silence from the phone and Gus realised that his sister hadn't expected him to reply. He glanced up to Lister Mills and saw that the lights were on in Katie's flat. He wondered if she was phoning from there or from work.

Not one to beat about the bush, Katie got straight to the point. 'She's phoned you loads of times, Gus, you should've answered.'

His sister was right, of course she was, he should have answered, but still it irked him that she called him out on it. 'Been busy, Katie... you've heard about the dead kid?'

Her indrawn breath was audible down the line and Gus smiled. Katie would have straightened her back and raised her chin. Her eyes would be closed, and she'd do that mental count to three before replying. He counted it with her, one banana... two bananas... three bananas...

'She phoned you before you caught that case, Gus. Look, you two need to make up and move on...' She paused and Gus frowned. Her voice had wobbled on the last word, like she was struggling to hold things together. 'It's important to me that you two bury the hatchet.'

Now there was an image. Yep, Gus could go with that one... the only thing was, he reckoned his interpretation of his sister's phrase was definitely very far from hers.

'She's the one carrying the hatchet...' His voice trailed away, as he heard a single sob over the line.

'You okay, Katie bear?' The childhood endearment fell from his lips naturally for the first time since he'd discovered his sister's relationship with his ex-wife.

She sniffed, and when she next spoke, all trace of emotion was removed from her voice. 'I'm fine. What I'm phoning for is to invite you to tea tomorrow night.'

Gus started to make excuses, but Katie spoke over him. 'This is important, Gus... I know you're in the middle of an investigation right now, but...' she paused '...I *need* to see you. I *need* to ask you something.'

Fuck. He hated it when she guilt-tripped him like that. She'd done it all through their childhood and she was still damn well doing it now. 'Okay, I'll check with Patti and get back to you.'

'Erm... can it just be you, Gus? No Patti this time.' And as if sensing Gus' annoyance that his girlfriend wasn't invited, she added a tortured, 'Please' to the end.

Well, this was going to be a meal to look forward to. Gabriella might be a great cook, but right then, Gus would prefer his mother's cooking any day. 'Right, I'll come whenever I can break off.'

'Thanks, Gus... I... we appreciate it.'

As Gus hung up, he decided that he'd have a single malt with his pizza… he certainly needed it. Fifteen minutes later, armed with a pizza box, Gus walked through the park. Some people didn't like to walk through it in the dark, but Gus had always liked it. The slight gurgle of the fountains in the Mogul Garden, the faint sounds of nature settling down for the night soothed him and gave him the space to think. He was sure he'd covered everything he could regarding the Pratab Patel case. His DCI, Nancy Chalmers, had released a short statement to the press asking for information from anyone in that area on Sunday night. Everything was in hand. He'd spent the evening checking out any interviews highlighted by the uniformed officers, but everything seemed to back-up the fact that, for some reason, Pratab Patel had gone off the rails a little since Easter.

He just hoped they'd have a break in the case tomorrow… because he was as sure as he could be, based on his experience, that the sort of killing they'd witnessed wasn't an isolated occurrence.

He crossed Emm Lane and turned into Marriners Drive, waving at the police car that was just pulling out of his street. He recognised both officers but couldn't remember their names. The one in the passenger's seat, leaned out his open window and said, 'Nowt to report, sir.'

Gus chatted to them for a few minutes and then continued along the street. Most curtains were closed now that it was proper dark and, Gus' only company was a scruffy cat, taking advantage of the dark to hunt. Humming to himself, Gus walked up the incline that was his drive and turned onto the path. As he raised his foot to climb the steps, he heard a sound behind him. Spinning round, fists up ready to take on the intruder, the pizza box landed on his steps, spilling its contents. The first thing he saw was a hooded figure, so he lunged at it. His foot landed on the squelchy pizza and slipping slightly, he executed a misaimed punch, catching his assailant on the shoulder. His hooded assailant fell backwards, with Gus landing on top.

Using his weight to pin his squirming adversary down, Gus grabbed their hood and yanked it off…

'You…?'

CHAPTER 35

Pisces

Should I leave a message? Will it look odd if I do…? odd if I don't? Fuuuuck! What'll I do? What'll I do? I need to stop pacing around, but I can't stop myself. Want to relax, chill!

Ping!

Ping!

Ping!

I'm gonna turn them off. Switch the notifications off. That's what I'll do. Just have a look first. Just a quick look, that's all.

Ping!

Ping!

Ping!

In my heart forever, Pratab, Love Chrissie xxxx

RIP. You will be missed, but the angels will look after you sweet boy, love always Teena Kaki and Suraj Kaka xxx

Be at peace. Taken too soon, love Mrs Johnston xxx

What the fuck? Like two crying emojis shows you'll miss him more than anyone else?

I start to type.

> Missing you...

I delete it... what can I say...?

> Sorry I killed you, RIP :-(

I start to laugh. RIP... RIP... RIP.
You were a fucking knobhead, Pratab... a fucking dick.
That's what I should write. Then I'm crying and I don't
know how to stop, so I punch the wall... once... twice.

CHAPTER 36

I t's been a shit day! Full of prayers and crying and relatives getting in my head. No space to think, no space to just be by myself and fucking think! They're always at me. 'Have some chai', 'You've got to eat', 'Come and see auntie fucking so and so.' I don't give a toss about auntie fucking so and so – don't know how she's related, and I don't care. Why did auntie fucking so and so not turn up when Pratab was alive? They're all fucking ghouls!

I sneak out the back door before anyone sees me. Got to take the chance while I can. Otherwise they'll be all over me, smothering me. It's still hot, but after the atmosphere in there I feel free. I shrug off the guilt and ignore the clawing in my stomach. I need to have some space. Darting across the road at an angle away from the house, in case someone's looking out the window, I breathe in deeply. It's so good. I squeeze through the bushes and onto the field beyond and throw myself onto the grass.

Can't believe he's not coming back. Can't believe he's gone. Everything's got out of hand... everything and I don't know what to do. It's beginning to get dark and out here, in the field with the moon where you can barely hear the traffic, it's like I'm on another planet. I wish I was! I lie back, arms behind my head, and watch the clouds. They're not moving, just hanging there like grey smoke. When I was little, I used to see pictures in the clouds; monsters, animals, other lands – islands far away, with aliens. Now, I wonder who the monsters really are... where they are.

I want to cry, but I can't. There's nothing there to come out. It's like everyone else has stolen my tears and I've none left. What if they never come back, what if I can never, ever cry again? Will my eyes always have grit scratching them every time I blink? Is that my punishment? And what about my stomach? Will it always feel raw? Will I ever be able to eat again? The very thought of food makes me jerk upright. I spin onto my knees and turn my head to the side, spewing up a trail of clear liquid that stings my throat and my nostrils. I've no tissue, so I grab a clump of grass and use it to wipe my mouth, then I throw it on top of the spot of bile. I flip back onto my bum and inspect the pinpricks of grass indented on my bare knees. I wish they'd drawn blood. I pick up a stone and start pressing it into the indents. It's not sharp enough. All it's doing is making my knees red, not piercing the skin. I throw it away, disgusted with it... disgusted with myself.

I shouldn't really do this, but I can't stop myself. Glad I'd retrieved it before the police visit, I pull the phone out of my pocket. The phone I need to keep hidden at all costs. I pull it out of its plastic bag and, not giving myself time to think, I dial.

Come on, come on! For God's sake pick up!

I try again... still no reply. What the hell am I going to do? If this all gets out, it'll be the end for me. I can't keep the phone on me, not with the police around, not with so many people going in and out the house. What can I do with it? The house isn't safe. My glance lands on the stone I tossed aside, and I pick it up again. 'At least you're useful for something.'

I dig up a little clump of grass and with the phone safely back in its protective bag, I put it in the space and cover it with the dirt and grass. No one will look here for it. No one will find it.

CHAPTER 37

Eyes narrowed, Gus glared at the figure on the ground until it began to wriggle. 'You gonna let me up then, Gus?'

His heart was pounding and right then he couldn't move. Anger bubbled up from his feet to his head and exploded. 'What the fuck, Alice? You've not been in touch for months and then you turn up on my doorstep like a fucking stalker or something.'

He glared at her for a full minute, trying to slow his heartbeat before easing himself off her skinny frame.

Alice snorted. 'Stalker? Who the hell would want to stalk someone as boring as you?'

Perhaps it was the tension still coming off his body in waves, or perhaps it was the tightness around his mouth, but whatever it was, Alice frowned as she pulled herself to her feet. 'You mean you do have a stalker?'

'No need to sound so surprised.' Gus was aware that his tone was petulant, but right then he didn't care. Alice had disappeared, leaving him alone with his guilt and now here she was acting like he wasn't worthy of a damn stalker. Cow!

Alice laughed and jumped to her feet much more agilely than Gus had. 'Well, you aren't exactly Olly Murs, are you?'

Something in the familiar tinkle of her laughter loosened his anger and, without even realising it, he was grinning at her. 'Thank fuck for that... I'm more Craig David, than Olly bloody Murs.'

For a second or two they stared at each other, then Gus turned, rescued what he could of his pizza and opened the door. 'Come on. I suppose you're...'

His words died on his lips as he looked down at the familiar blue envelope lying on the mat. As Alice moved past him to pick it up, he grabbed her arm. 'No, wait.'

He thrust the bashed pizza box in her arms and walked over to the small table at the bottom of the stairs that housed the home phone. Pulling open the drawer, he grabbed a pair of gloves and an evidence bag, before lifting the envelope and dropping it in.

'So, you do have a stalker... well I'll be damned. Tell me.' And like she'd never been gone, Alice marched through into the kitchen, leaving Gus to slam the door behind him and trail after her, mumbling under his breath. 'Sooner I get that security in the better.'

Once in the kitchen, pizza box open in front of them, and a glass of whisky each on the table, Gus took the time to study Alice. Last time he'd seen her she'd been skinny... almost wasted. Her eyes had been dead and at the time Gus had doubted they'd ever shine again. He was wrong. Her eyes were sparkling... okay, perhaps not as brightly as before... but they weren't emotionless. He felt a tear come to his eye and then Alice groaned.

'Oh, for God's sake, Gus, if you're going to cry like a damn wuss, then I'm out of here... right now. Just tell me all about that.' And she pointed to the letter in its sealed bag that Gus had shoved on the kitchen table.

Her words made him smile. His Alice was back... or nearly. She was still scrawny. Her once smooth face, had faint wrinkles fanning out across her forehead and from the sides of her mouth. Her cheeks were still a little sunken, her hair, although it had grown back in, was still shorter than before. 'My anonymous letter will keep until tomorrow. Nobody there to process it tonight. I'm more interested in you.'

She jumped to her feet. 'I'm skinnier, my body's damaged... but look at these beauties.' And she whipped off her hoodie, revealing a tight vest top and raised her arms like a weightlifter... 'I'm effing built, Gus.'

She was right, she might carry a little less weight, but Al had muscles that even Gus envied.

'I went back to Greece with my parents for a while... after... you know?' She picked a bit of grit from a slice of pizza before biting a bit off. Gus sipped his whisky, happy to let her tell her story at her own speed as she chewed.

'At first I was a wreck, but then slowly I realised, I couldn't let *him* beat me.'

She didn't need to say his name for Gus to know she meant Sean, the man who'd been responsible for nearly killing her and framing her, so she spent a hellish few months in prison.

'So, I joined a gym... like I did in prison and I worked like a dog and... Somewhere along the line, I reconnected with life and realised I was getting better.' She raised her hands palms up in a 'ta da' action. 'And here I am.'

'You coming back to work?'

Alice smiled. 'Yep. I've been back a few weeks. Nancy got me passed fit to work... I can start whenever as long as I keep seeing the psychiatrist.'

'Nancy knew you were back?' That nugget pissed him off. Nancy hadn't given him a head's up and that hurt. Not that he really thought he deserved it... not after the way he'd doubted his friend.

'Yeah, I've been in touch with her throughout.' She looked at Gus, 'Told her not to say anything to you. I didn't think I'd ever be back... didn't think I'd still be here... but...'

Her eyes darkened and Gus reached over and squeezed her arm. He had suffered dark thoughts in the past himself and he knew how hard it was to come back from the edge. 'We'll do this together, Al. We're a team, like we've always been.' For a nano-second, his thoughts flashed to the look on Compo's face when he'd challenged Gus for giving up on Alice. Compo had said it was forgotten and Gus believed that, in Compo's world, it was. However, in his world guilt was never quite so easy to assuage.

She grinned at him. 'Well, just as well, cause I don't fancy living in my own house right now, so if it's all the same to you, I'm moving into your spare room for a while.'

She jumped to her feet and headed into the hallway, yelling over her shoulder. 'I cleared it with Patti... just going to get my stuff, you helping or what?'

Hell! Patti had known she was back too?

CHAPTER 38

It's been ages since I climbed out the bathroom window. Way before mam got poorly. Last time I did she were furious. Grounded me for days and threatened to take away my computer. Went on and on and on... What if I'd slipped? What if I'd landed on the extension? What if I'd broken every bone in my body? She wouldn't have it that I was safe, that I knew what I were doing. I've been keeping an eye out through my bedroom curtains and it seems like Goyley and HP are taking turns to keep an eye on me. Thought they might go if I put my bedroom light off, but no, they're still there.

The window's a bit tighter than it used to be so I push my rucksack out and hook it onto a bit of sticking out brick. Hope it holds, for if it smashes to the ground, I'll be fucked. Somewhere in the back of my mind, I half wish it would just fall. Then, I wouldn't have to do the drop, wouldn't have to leave the house. I sigh. What's the point? If I don't go, everyone would know about me; me mam, Jessie, kids in school. A huge wave of relief comes over me... at least it'd be over. Then the guilt sets in. Fucking guilt, it's like a putrid spot oozing pus and shit. I could just throw myself off the roof... end it all... but knowing my luck I'd end up breaking a leg and everyone would still know about my secrets; *He's the one wiggles his willy at dirty old pervs for bitcoins. He's the one stick's dildos up his arse so pervs can get off. He's the one slathers oil over himself and wanks in front of a webcam.*

Who am I kidding? There's no way, I'm *not* gonna deliver the fucking thing. No way in hell.

It's a bit easier to push myself up from the bath onto the sill. I push my shoulders through first, angling them this way and that until they pop through... the rest's easy. I manoeuvre the bag back onto my back and then, hanging by my fingertips, I drop onto the roof and again, it's not such a big jump this time. I lie flat on the tiles, waiting to see if anybody's noticed and when there's nothing bar a dog barking in the distance, I crawl over to the pipe and I slide down until my feet touch the neighbour's fence. Now's the hard bit, making sure I don't waken anyone. I make it onto the ground and through the first two gardens without any hassle, but in the third one, the dog wakes up and starts throwing itself at the back door. There's nothing I can do, except dart across and launch myself at the next fence... up and over... and hope I'm hidden by the shadows.

'Shut the fuck up, Bruno.' The dog gives a few more half-hearted yelps and then it's quiet again.

I start to cross their bit of grass and trip on a toy that's been discarded in the middle of the yard. A light flicks on in the house and I turn and dart back to the bush by the fence. My breath's coming in short gasps and I try to swallow the noise. Fuck, that was close. When the light goes out again, I count to fifty... slowly. My legs are shaking now. Not used to this sort of exercise, not used to hiding from the estate's gangs.

Shit! I wish I hadn't thought of that. If Goyley or HP catch me, I'll be in big shit. How could I explain what I'm doing? What if they found the bag? Knowing that I've got to repeat this all in reverse later on, I edge my way round the garden. Two panels of wood are hanging off, so I squeeze myself through, praying they don't clatter to the floor and wake the household up. Once I'm through, I'm in the street. This is the hard bit... I need to head up towards

Heaton without being seen. It'll take me longer, but I've no option as I skip through the back alleys and down to the terraced houses at the top. Once I reach them, I'll be safer. Razor and that lot don't often head into Manningham. On the other hand, Manningham has its own gangs and that brings its own issues.

CHAPTER 39

Zodiac

It wasn't too bad sneaking out of the house. I'm invisible most of the time and that suits me fine. The night's warm and my only company are the few winos and tramps that seem to congregate with their bottles in the park after dark. They're too drunk to bother me and I don't bother them. When it gets close to midnight, I settle myself near Lister's Mansions. Their big wheelie bins give me all the cover I need.

It's funny watching him. He's shitting it. I can tell. Keeps looking around him, like he thinks someone's gonna jump him. Maybe he wants to be jumped. Maybe he's gonna dump the parcel and then try to hook up for a bit of dogging or something. I've nothing against gays. Doesn't bother me, but I know Jo Jo doesn't like people to know. Doesn't like to accept that he's gay. Ah well, that's his problem.

I wait until he crosses North Park Drive and goes in the side entrance to the park before I move. I head down towards Cartwright Hall and skip over the fence. I'll circle round and catch-up with him from the other side of the park. He's trying to act like he doesn't care... like he's not scared, but he is. He keeps glancing behind him and yanking the straps of his backpack further up his arms. He must be desperate to know who's been blackmailing him. I would be. Wonder what he'd say if he found out it was me... would he feel let down?

Well, that'd be his problem, not mine. I've found out the hard way that the only people you can truly rely on is yourself... time he found that out too. Well, not quite time... not yet. But soon. Maybe soon.

As he gets nearer to the bandstand, he speeds up, like he can't wait to get rid of what's in his bag… like he can't wait to get me off his back. Then he stops. Pretends to tie his shoelace. Again, looking behind, under his arm. It's so obvious it makes me smile. Why do people always think they're being watched from behind or to the side? He's never once really looked ahead of him. Not that he'd see me anyway, I'm too well hidden, too much in the shadows. His furtive glances to either side amuse me. As he approaches the bandstand, he slips his bag off his back, and begins to unzip it. He's getting close now, but then I hear a noise from the bushes to Jo Jo's right and two figures come out. The two tramps McGuire was talking to earlier. Where the hell did they come from?

I want to yell at them to piss off. But Jo Jo's walking past the bandstand, trying to look all casual now. Trouble is he's getting closer to my hiding place. Shit! I back away, merging into the dark, glad I'd changed into dark clothes. I avert my face in case he sees me and when I look back, he's spun on his heel and is heading back to the bandstand, the two homeless guys are walking down towards the lake. Phew. That was a close thing. All I want to do now is grab the packet and go home. It's been a long day and I'm fucking knackered. I just want him to dump it and go. All enjoyment in the whole escapade has gone.

He climbs up the stairs to the raised platform and he's out of sight for a couple of minutes. Then he's back on the footpath and heading past the bowling green. He's almost running now. I doubt he'll hang about to see me, but I make myself wait. Slumping down, leaning against a tree, I look up at the stars and wait.

CHAPTER 40

Tuesday

Gus had expected chaos when Alice turned up in the investigation room. She'd done this once before and he still remembered the uproar that day. He was right. He'd gone in ahead of her to break the news to Compo and Taffy, leaving her in the corridor outside, but in true Alice style she'd thwarted his plans for a controlled meeting by poking her head through the door and yelling in a mockery of Jack Nicholson, 'Honey, I'm home.'

Compo could hardly put down the pizza slice he was eating quick enough, and en route to greet his friend, he knocked over three drinks, upended two chairs, and all but fell on top of her. Alice took it all in her stride, allowing Compo to grip her for a full minute or more, all the while patting his back. At last he pulled away from her and made space for Taffy, who, not knowing Alice quite as well as Compo, settled for a quick hug and a mumbled, 'Good to see you back, Al.'

Keen to restore order in the room – they were in the middle of a major investigation after all, Gus cleared his throat. 'There's been a development, guys.'

When everyone's eyes were on him, he pulled from his bag, an evidence bag containing his most recent mail, a photocopy of the letter and another evidence bag.

'Another one? When did this arrive?' Compo's tone was full of indignant fury as he strode over to study it.

'No idea, sometime yesterday, but my new home security isn't being installed until today, so we've got nothing other than this letter.'

'You open it yet?'

'Yep.'

'Still stink of that perfume?'

'Yep. Same font and everything.' Gus scowled. He wanted to yell, but it wasn't his team he was angry with. 'Before I came here, I got it processed. Surprise, surprise there's nothing useful but I'm not passing it onto Byrne and C team until we've had a look.'

'It's accelerating, boss. Who knows what they might do? The letters haven't been delivered so closely together before, have they?' Compo tugged at his T-shirt, a sure sign he was nervous.

The reduction in time between the letters was something Gus had already considered, and it made him a little anxious, but that wasn't the only thing that had him on edge. 'That's not all… there's been a…' he glanced at Alice who finished his sentence for him

'…a fucking massive development…'

Laying one of the evidence bags on the desk, Gus indicated that they should look. Inside was a photograph. Taffy and Compo stared at it and as Gus watched them, he saw their expressions change from interest to horror. Compo spoke first. 'Is that you and Patti snogging, through your kitchen window?'

Tight lipped, Gus nodded. He could identify *exactly* when the image had been taken. Saturday. They'd been in the woods with Bingo and then nipped into Sainsburys for some ingredients. They were cooking their tea together.

Taffy frowned. 'Someone was in your garden?'

Exhaling, Gus shrugged. 'Don't know. You'd think we'd have spotted them. The fence at the back is too…'

'Nope!'

The single word exploded from Compo's mouth making everyone eyes move from the photograph to Compo. Just as he picked it up, the incident room door opened, and everyone's eyes swung towards it.

A girl stood there, her eyes, drawn to the images on the large screen, widened and Gus moved to stand in front of her, blocking her view. 'You can't be in here? Can I help?'

'Oh, sorry, of course not. It's just, I was looking for my mum'

Only then did it dawn on Gus that he recognised her. 'Of course, you're DCS Bahir's daughter. Moona isn't it?'

She smiled and looked down. 'Yes. Look I'm sorry for butting in. I didn't think. I'll go check her office again.' Mehmoona backed to the door and hesitated, biting her lip. 'You won't tell her I was here, will you? Could do without a telling off today.'

Gus remembered what it had been like visiting his own parents at work and how once or twice he'd ended up somewhere he shouldn't. 'No probs. Our lips are sealed.'

Compo waited until the door closed behind her before continuing. 'What I mean is, the angle's wrong. Look. If someone had been in your garden, the image would have been taken from this angle. Your garden is on a slope remember?' He placed his hand in front of him, palm down, fingers slanting upwards. 'It's clear it's been taken at a downward angle.'

The other three crowded round, studying the photo. 'So, you think they were on top of my fence… or maybe from one of the bordering neighbours' upstairs windows?' Despite attempting to keep his tone neutral, Gus' disbelief was clear. When he was with Patti, his attention was all hers, still, even in those circumstances he'd have noticed someone on top of the fence… and if he didn't Bingo would have. As for his neighbours. No way could he see them doing this sort of thing. For a start two of them were in their eighties and rarely made it to their upstairs rooms and the others had been to barbecues at his house in the past few weeks. Surely, he'd have spotted something off about them.

Comp sniffed and bit on a Rice Crispy cereal bar. 'Nah, your neighbours' windows don't look onto your house directly. I reckon, whoever did this was in the woods to the side of your house.'

'But...'

Compo cut Gus short. 'They probably controlled a drone from there and took a series of shots.'

Gus let that sit for a moment. The idea of some anonymous person lurking in the woods near his home, spying on him and Patti through his kitchen window was unthinkable. It was an invasion of privacy, all the worse because he had no idea of how long it had been going on. Images of him and Patti in his bedroom, which also looked out the back of the house, flashed through his head. The heat made it impossible to close the curtains as they were desperate for any meagre breeze. What sort of images did they have? And more to the point, what were they planning on doing with them? Those innocuous letters suddenly took on an entirely new and completely threatening overtone.

Bringing his attention back to the room, Taffy said, 'Any clues of their intentions in the letter?' Gus shrugged and drew out a photocopy of the original letter. Putting the original back in its envelope, he flattened the copy on his desk.

My Dearest Detective Inspector Angus McGuire,

It's good to keep in touch, isn't it? Are you enjoying my surprises, Angus?

Caught the mood perfectly, didn't I? You two make such a cute, loved-up couple. Both so attractive, so… sexy… yes, I think sexy's the word I'm looking for. Bet I'm not the only one that thinks so either. Bet there's loads of people who would just loooove to see how cute you two are. Do you and Patti use social media much? Maybe it's time to start.

Anyway, things to do and all that and I know you're busy too. You'll hear from me soon.

Watch this space!

'Shit.' Compo's face had turned red, as he stuffed the rest of his cereal bar in his mouth. 'This is too much, Gus. That fucker could've taken pictures of you and Patti.' He stopped abruptly and his face went even more red. 'What I mean is…'

'I get it, Comps. I'm taking that as a direct threat. I need you on the case to monitor all social media channels. I don't know what sort of images this person may have, but I sure as hell don't want any going viral. You need to liaise with C team on this.'

Pulling his bandana from his hair and retying it, Gus continued. 'I know this is a lot of pressure for you, with this ongoing investigation... truth is, Comps, you're the best we've got and I know that you'll catch anything that goes out there. I want this cut off at source.'

Taffy, voice hesitant, glanced at Gus. 'Maybe it's just bluster. Maybe it's an empty threat. Whoever took that photo didn't say they had more.'

Alice snorted. 'You know, Taffy. The first lesson you should have learned as a copper is this. Imagine the vilest thing you can and then...' her eyes clouded, 'expect it to be even worse.'

Her words had come out sharp and Gus recognised the momentary darkness in her eyes for what it was... despair. She looked up at him and just as quickly it was gone. Gus made a mental note to keep an eye on her. He didn't want Alice going under and he was certain that despite her cockiness, she wasn't as strong as she made out. He'd heard her pacing in her room the previous night. No, Alice was far from begin as 'sorted' as she made out.

In the middle of working his magic at the computer, Compo stopped and looked straight at Gus. 'You've alerted Patti, haven't you, boss?'

Shit! He *hadn't* spoken to Patti. Partly because he'd not had time, but being honest with himself, it was mainly avoidance. He didn't want to bring something so tawdry into their lives, but Compo was right. He didn't really have much of a choice. As soon as the briefing was over, he'd speak to her. 'I'll deal with that in a bit, but for now, let's focus on this investigation. We've got a murdered boy and no clue who did it. Taffy, you can bring Alice up to speed, Compo, any news on retrieving the *Snapchat* message?'

For a second, the lad looked stricken and then he pressed a button and a headshot of Pratab Patel lying on the ground, a knife sticking out of his neck and blood pooling under him, filled the screen. 'In the end, I didn't need to. This image hit the Internet not five minutes ago.'

The four of them looked at the image for a few seconds in stunned silence and then Gus yelled, 'Get that down asap. Don't care who you have to sell – but I want that image off the Internet right now. Taffy, contact the Patel's FLO and alert her. Compo, can you trace it?'

Fuck, he'd been worried about a few snaps of him and Patti being posted on some online platform, but this was infinitely worse. He only hoped it came down before the Patels saw it.

Compo shrugged, his fingers speeding over keys, his gaze flicking from one screen to another. 'I can try, but you know what it's like – it's already been bounced round the world from server to server. Whoever uploaded that had enough knowledge to hide their identity. I'll extend my alerts to make sure if anything else comes up we'll know right away.'

Gus turned to Alice. 'Baptism of fire for you, Al. You up for it?'

Her smile may have lacked her usual buoyancy, but she nodded, resolute. 'I was ready before, but that's just fired me up. I'm on it. Come on, Taffy, update me so I can be useful.'

After a perfunctory knock on the door, a familiar figure entered. 'Ah, DS Cooper. So pleased you're back. Last thing I wanted was to work with this one without you as a buffer.' Professor Sebastian Carlton glared at Gus from over the top of his specs which, today, sported a Barbie plaster across the nose bridge to hold them together.

Brilliant! Nancy had come through for him. Gus looked forward to hearing what the professor had to say about this case and, about his anonymous letter writer/stalker. True to form Carlton was straight over, at the screen, his nose, slightly peeling and a little red, twitched as he looked at the image. 'And this is?'

Gus explained about the *Snapchat* message Haider had received from the dead boy's phone and how this had just been posted.

Carlton listened attentively, rocking back and forth on the balls of his feet like some kid's wobbly toy. 'I'll need to see the crime scene photos. Compo, can you compare them to see how much the lad's position was moved? This is interesting, very interesting.'

Gus itched to ask if it was interesting enough to have brought the professor in on a professional basis, or just 'interesting'.

As if he sensed Gus' question, Carlton turned to him. 'You'll need me for this one, Gus. No doubt about it, this killer, or killers, are just getting started. The positioning of the body, the *Snapchat*, the posting the images online – all of it smacks of *look at me*. Shame really, that the media's added kudos to the killing with their stupid moniker. It'll only egg the killer on and of course make the public bay for blood.' He clapped his hands together and looked at Gus. 'Now, I've told Nancy, I'll waive my fee on one condition.'

Gus waited. Carlton was unpredictable at the best of times and he dreaded to hear what 'condition' Nancy had signed him up for.

'Doughnuts… Krispy Kreme ones, mind… none of those cheapo six for a quid from Tesco, eh?'

Gus would happily fork out for the cost of a few doughnuts if it gave them some insight into these killers. He nodded to Taffy who rushed off to get someone to go for them. They both knew they'd get little sense from Carlton until he had his doughnuts. It was purely an affectation from his doughnut eating FBI days, but Gus was happy to go with it.

Walking over to an empty desk, the professor, his neon orange T-shirt riding up revealing a portly belly, sat down. Gus, reeling from the brightness of the T-shirt over the equally neon lime green budgie-snuggling Lycra cycling shorts, averted his eyes. It wouldn't be half as bad if he thought for one moment that Sebastian Carlton had cycled to The Fort. Truth was, Carlton seemed to have a clashing-of-neon-colours fetish, which Gus was prepared to overlook on account of his ability to offer insights that might otherwise be missed. A sideways glance at Alice told him she was barely suppressing her laughter, while Compo's, 'Wow, love your T-shirt, Prof. where'd you get that?' had him wondering if the lad lived on planet earth.

Please don't let Compo gain access to replicas of those T-shirts. Gus had forgotten his computer geek and the professor had forged an unlikely friendship in previous cases. He hoped that alliance wouldn't extend to swopping wardrobe tips.

CHAPTER 41

It was after lunchtime before the images of Gus and Patti hit the Internet. Compo's, 'Shit, they're there. Don't worry, Gus, I'll get them down asap,' momentarily confused Gus.

He'd got involved in scouring interviews and reports for some glimmer of a clue into who could have killed Pratab Patel and had completely forgotten about the anonymous letter with its threatening photo. He'd shown them to Sebastian Carlton, who agreed that their tone and the fact that two had been delivered in such a short space of time combined with the added implied threat of photographing Gus in the privacy of his own home, was an escalation that would, more than likely, result in violence. Gus had cleared it with DCS Bashir to have an officer attached to Patti, until such time as they caught the letter sender.

Carlton wouldn't be pinned down on who would be on the receiving end of the violence, should it arise. 'It all depends on how things pan out. If they decide to punish you, it might be Patti… or your dog that they target. On the other hand, depending on their perceptions, they may turn on you. You need to be just as vigilant as Patti… oh, and I'd make sure your parents are vigilant too.'

That was all the hint Gus needed to get himself on the phone to his dad, telling him to be extra careful. He was relieved that his parents had such extensive security. He would never forgive himself if anything happened to them.

Pushing himself to his feet, Gus took a moment to register the images that Compo had routed to the main screen. The screen split into eight sections, each of which had an image of Gus and Patti being intimate in his bedroom. He couldn't drag his eyes away even as he snarled at Compo. 'Get them down.' It was at that point that he realised he hadn't actually contacted Patti. He'd got distracted and it had just slipped his mind. Fuck, fuck, fucking, fuck, shit, crap. She'd be livid. What the hell had he been thinking? Contacting Patti should have been his priority. What was wrong with him? Did he have some sort of masochistic desire to be dumped?

Compo, flustered, fumbling with his keyboard, typing furiously, and muttering under his breath, struggled to do so. In under a minute, the images were removed from the screen, but as Gus turned around, he saw that Carlton, Taffy, and Alice had all seen them. His face went hot, and a streak of cold flashed up his spine.

His colleagues averted their eyes and continued working, but Gus knew they'd seen him at his most vulnerable... his most intimate and he hated the person who'd exposed him.

'Where are they, Compo?'

Compo continued working, his eyes darting across his screen as he spoke. 'They're everywhere. Fucking everywhere. Soon as I get them down from one site, they pop up elsewhere.' Gus strode over until he could see Compo's work.

'They're on *Facebook*, *Twitter*, *Instagram*... they're being shared faster than I can stop them. Patti's school *Twitter* and *Facebook* accounts have been tagged. The Fort's been tagged and West Yorkshire Police and Visit Bradford.'

Gus' phone rang. Patti. He answered, aware that he was breathing heavily. 'You've seen them? Compo's on it, Patti. He'll get them down.'

Gus walked over to the corner which afforded a semblance of privacy and back to the room, fingers dragging through his dreads, he asked, 'Are you okay?'

Patti's words came out slow and precise. 'What do you think? The kids are sharing it. My *pupils* have seen this, Gus... how can I run a school when the pupils have seen me having sex? My career is shot to pieces.'

Her voice cracked and Gus could tell she was narrowly holding it together. This wasn't like Patti. He'd never heard her so defenceless before. 'I'm coming! Wait there. I'm coming.'

Her reply was colder than a glacier. 'Don't you dare come anywhere near *my* school. You've done enough damage. Stay *away* from me... just stay away.'

'Patti... wait...'

But she'd hung up and as Gus slipped his phone back into his pocket, he became aware of the silence in the room. Everyone was looking at him. And as his heart collapsed, he looked back, unable to speak until Compo said, '*Facebook's* trying their best. They're trying to remove them.'

Inhaling deeply, he tossed his phone on his desk and shoved his hands in his pockets. Maybe that would stop the shaking. He strode over and positioned himself behind Compo, watching in fascination as, before his eyes, the images of him and Patti were liked and shared. One hundred shares... one hundred and twenty, one hundred and fifty...

Ping!

Ping!

Ping!

> LMAO, Ms Copley screwing that hot copper :)

Got some tits on her has Ms Copley.

Wouldn't mind a bit of that!

So, *this* was the power of social media? Gus, unable to watch any more, turned and walked out.

CHAPTER 42

Zodiac

P issing myself laughing. It was better than I thought it would be. I deliberately waited until lunchtime so the kids in school would have their phones on and see it. It was all scheduled ready to go at the press of a button. Can't believe how many shares on *Facebook*. Over eight hundred. It's brilliant.

> Patti Copley's racked, in't she?
>
> Watch the tits on her, eh?:-)
>
> Wouldn't mind a go with Mr Hot... Well
>
> fit for an old geezer!
>
> He's dad fit, he is. Bit of a DILF
>
> Wonder if he cuffs her up.

All afternoon the images were posted on *FB* and *Twitter* and *Snapchat*. They might have brought the photos down but loads of kids screenshot them and they're still doing the rounds.

Just a nice little distraction for DI McGuire, before things hot up even more.

I hang about outside school until home time. Should've seen her face as she came out to her car. All the kids were sniggering, and she couldn't do a damn thing. She's got herself a policeman following her. Doesn't matter to me. I couldn't care less... who says it's her I'm after?

Time to head home for a bit of distraction. All that stuff's made me well horny.

CHAPTER 43

By the time it got to seven o'clock, Gus knew he could put it off no longer. He'd told Katie he'd turn up for tea and, with no more leads on the case, there were no excuses left. The fact that they hadn't wanted Patti around pissed him off big time. Although, with the images of the pair of them having sex all over social media, she wouldn't have come, anyway. He fleetingly wondered if Katie and Gabriella would have seen it... or his dad... or mum? He reckoned not. It wasn't like any of them would be following Patti's school *Facebook* or *Twitter* accounts and anyway, his dad could barely use *WhatsApp*, never mind anything else.

The *Facebook* shares had come to well over eight hundred by the time the company had managed to shut them down and Patti was still not answering his calls. He wondered if she ever would, or if his stalker had driven too wide a wedge between them.

He'd been subject to some juvenile grins and smart-ass comments from colleagues, but Patti was the head teacher of a secondary school. Where Gus could brush it off and ignore it, Patti was in a very different position. Her ability to command respect from her pupils was paramount... who knows if she could get that back? Who knows how the parents would react? Who knew how the kids would be with her? It was crap. It was especially crap because, he suspected, that had it been a male head teacher, reactions would be very different.

Obviously, that smarmy arse Jez Hopkins had tried to get in on the act, phoning up for a comment. *Tosser*! It had taken all Gus' self-control to drop the receiver without giving him a comment. What with the *Snapchat Killer* and now this, that little turd would be creaming his pants. He was surprised the idiot wasn't stationed outside The Fort when he left. Of course, Patti was prettier than he was.

As he crossed the road from The Fort to Lister Mills, where his sister and Gabriella lived, he felt at a disadvantage. Two against one – typical Gabriella bullying tactics. While Katie could be manipulative, Gabriella was normally brutally blunt to the point of cruel. This was not an evening to look forward to. On the plus side, his parents would be pleased that he'd at least made the effort to smooth over their differences. It was that 'we've got something to ask you' of Katie's that niggled him though.

He got into the elevator wishing with every fibre in his body that he could just go home and share a drink with Alice, but no, he had to suffer Gabriella's half-hearted attempts at a reconciliation because his sister felt bad. As the elevator pinged open, Gus realised he hadn't brought wine. *Tough shit*! He was investigating a murder, if they wanted wine then they'd have to open one of their own bottles.

Straightening his spine, he reached out a hand, and pressed the doorbell. From inside he could hear voices and, wishing he was anywhere but here, he pasted on a smile as Katie opened the door. She stepped back, revealing Gabriella standing just behind her… his smile faded. 'Hi.' He nodded at his sister and then, keeping his gaze slightly to the right of his ex-wife's shoulder, he repeated the nod.

'No wine, I see?' Gabriella's voice was like cut glass and Gus' head jerked up his gaze spearing her.

Before Katie could respond he said, 'No. Didn't think it was a priority in light of the dead boy who's murder I'm investigating.'

Gabriella's chin lifted and she opened her mouth. Before she could speak, Katie ushered Gus past the shelving unit in the hallway that housed a cloying lit scented candle and led him into the kitchen where a small table was set for three people.

Gus sat down without being asked and waited while Katie pottered about pouring wine and bringing the pasta bake onto the table. Her body seemed tense, and her face looked strained, like she was barely holding it together. She was on water, so things must be serious. Seemingly aware of his scrutiny, she smiled at him and handed him a full plate, before doling out one for herself and Gabriella.

Well this was nice! With conversation at a minimum, Gus wished he could just eat and go. This was going to be a disaster. What had Katie been thinking? Gabriella could barely look at him and he could think of nothing to say. Gabriella, not for the first time, had behaved appallingly, blaming him for her brother's death, although in fact, it was her brother who had been responsible for the deaths of many people. Though Gus wasn't one to bear grudges, he had no desire to have her in his life. Of course, there was the tricky fact that Gabriella was living with his sister… that made the idea of never having to interact with her again impossible. With that in mind, he raised his wine glass.

'Here's to the future, leaving the past behind us and moving on.'

With a nervous smile at her partner, Katie raised her glass, water he noticed, while Gabriella hesitated. 'Gaby,' Katie's tone was pleading, and Gus had the desire to tip his wine over his ex-wife's head. How dare she make Katie feel like this, especially when he was trying so hard? Finally, Gaby lifted her glass a few inches off the table and tipped it in Gus' direction.

Katie shook her head and glared at Gaby, who lifted her glass higher and said, 'Moving on.' In a tone that left no doubt of her sincerity.

They ate in near silence, Katie trying to keep the conversation going, but failing to hold a conversational ball between the three of them.

At last, Gus placed his fork over his half-eaten food. 'Look, I really need to get back – you know, active investigation and all that?'

Katie wiped her mouth with a napkin. 'Before you go, Gabriella and I want to speak to you. About something very important to us.'

A flicker of a smile passed over her lips as she linked her fingers through Gaby's. Gus swallowed his sigh. He'd suspected this was coming and he could just about stand to go to their wedding. Might be a bit odd – his ex-wife marrying his sister, but he'd cope. It would only be one day after all, and he wouldn't have to do much. He began to smile, congratulations forming on the tip of his tongue...

'We've decided we want to start a family.'

For a moment, Gus was stunned. Kids? Gaby and Katie? This was the last thing he'd expected. A wedding, yes. Kids, no. Gaby had never wanted kids when she was with him but judging by the indulgent smile as she looked at his sister that had changed big time. He wasn't quite sure how he felt about that. Still, he kept the smile on his lips. Katie was his sister after all, and she deserved to be happy. 'Great. That's brill... you adopting? Fostering?'

The couple again exchanged glances and Gus began to wonder what all of this had to do with him.

'The thing is, Gus, I have...' She glanced at Gaby a nervous smile flitting across her lips, '...fibroids and so it's very unlikely I'd be able to carry a baby, so Gaby's going to carry the child.'

Okaaaay, that was unexpected, but reasonable. He risked a quick smile at Gaby and found her staring at him. He frowned. What the hell was going on? This was odd.

Katie reached over and grasped his hand, squeezing tightly, her words coming out on a rush. 'We want you to be the father. That way our baby would be as genetically close to both of us as possible.'

What the...? Gus opened his mouth to speak and closed it again. He must have misheard. Katie was asking him to father a child with his ex-wife, who just happened to be her lover. He must have got that wrong. He looked between the two of them. Katie's eyes glistened and Gabriella stared right at him as if willing him to agree.

He laughed, hollow and cracked. 'Nice one... Nice joke.'

'No joke, Gus.' That was the first time, all evening that Gaby had addressed him with anything other than disdain in her voice.

He glanced at Katie. Her face was pale, and she was shredding a napkin, her fingers shaking as they worked, her eyes trained on him.

And *that's* when it sunk in. They really wanted him to father a child with his ex-wife. They wanted him to father the baby he'd always wanted with his ex-wife and then have to give it to her, so she and his sister could bring it up. They wanted him to donate his genes, his DNA, and then to play Uncle Gus to his own child? How fucked up is that?

He scraped his chair back, flung his napkin down, and strode out of the flat, ignoring his sister's tearful calls and Gaby's accusing, 'Told you he wouldn't. He's just selfish, Katie. Totally selfish.'

Liz Mistry

CHAPTER 44

Pisces

L east that stuff with Ms Copley and the policeman who spoke to us in school is a distraction from the other shit I have to think about. Dirty cow, getting all down and mucky with that copper. Wouldn't have thought old Copley had it in her. Just goes to show. She didn't look so stern in the sack, did she?

Fucking Zodiac's at it though… and Leo. 'Got to keep up the momentum.' 'Can't stop now.'

I've about had it though. Feel like ditching the phone… they can't do owt if I ditch it, can they? What can they say? They won't turn up at the door, will they? I walk into Undercliffe Cemetery. Reckon that's as good a place as any to dump it. Could bury it under one of the stones. They'd never find it.

Ping!

Fuck, Zodiac! It's like I'm being watched. I glance round. Nobody there but that old git with the dog. Disrespectful that is, letting the dog shit on the graves and not even picking it up. Wish I had the guts to go over and say summat, but he's big… way bigger than me.

I plonk myself down on one of the raised stones and stare at my phone. If I dump it now, I don't have to see what Zodiac's saying… I practice shrugging and saying, 'I must've lost it.' Even to me that dun't sound convincing.

Ping!

Fuck, I nearly drop it. I glance round again. Wish I'd stayed at home. I'm safe at home, they can't get me there. I wipe my fingers on my shorts and leave a streak of red there. Shit, I'm a twat… picking my spots again and not even noticing.

Ping!

Ping!

The knobhead with the dog's gone. My leg's shaking and I want to scream. I never signed up for any of this... not really... did I? Zodiac says I did. Leo says I did... I must've.

I press the button to view the texts:

> Zodiac: Next one tonight. That's what you said. We still on?
>
> Zodiac: You did say tonight? This one's your choice.

Now it's ringing! *Zodiac*!

'Yeah.' Even to my ears my voice is wobbling.

'You okay, Pisces? Been worried about you. Not replying. Thought you'd lost the phone.'

'No, no... course not. I've not lost it.' Shit, now I can't say I've lost it. Would be too obvious. Why am I such a twat?

'So... we're on? Leo and I were wondering.'

'Yeah, yeah. We're on.' There I go again, agreeing with them. Get a grip... get a fucking grip. I don't want to be Pisces anymore. I just want to be me.

I hang up. The graveyard's right peaceful... quiet like. Maybe I could stay here forever. Maybe I don't have to answer that phone ever again. I pull the knife out of my rucksack and press the blade against my wrists... I can't do it.

I'm such a coward, I can't even do that. Can't say no and can't fucking end it either... useless twat, that's what I am. And as I sit, the sky darkens... it's going to thunder.

Maybe if I just sit here, I'll get struck by lightning. Then I won't have to be Pisces anymore.

CHAPTER 45

Gus didn't wait for the swish elevator to make its way back up, but instead, dashed down the stairs, his feet pounding in time with his heartbeat. This was crap... total crap. When he burst out into the heat and realised the evening sky had become overcast, dark clouds gathering on the horizon, the air close and stagnant, he paused. Should he go back to work where his team would soon suss out that something was wrong, or... what...? or what? Home to an empty house? The distant rumble of thunder echoed his mood as he shoved his hands in his pockets and, head down, began to walk down Oak Lane. A quick power walk round the block would ease his tension and then he could return to work.

The sky got darker, with ominous gun metal grey clouds, bearing down on the layers of heat, stealing every gasp of air. And then, in an electrical explosion, the sky erupted. Thunder and lightning clashed, and great drops of rain bounced onto the pavement staccato-like. Gus held his face up to the rain and as it soaked his T-shirt, he experienced the slow release of his initial pent-up anger and frustration leave his body... the relief was palpable. If it had continued, he was sure he would have snapped, and it had been a long time since he'd thought like that... been like that.

As he walked, torrents of rain gushed down the road, desperately seeking drainage grates. The heat was still unbearable, but the heavy pre-storm threat had all but dissipated. Soon, his clothes were sodden and, with relief, he saw his best friend standing in the window of Mo's SaMosa shop looking out at the deluge. Mo glanced up and

Gus raised his hand. He wanted nothing more right now than to spend some uncomplicated time with his best mate.

Before he reached the door, Mo had yanked it open and ushered him in. The familiar smell of spicy chai and warm samosas was like coming home. In silence Mo handed Gus a towel and then disappeared through the beaded curtain that led to the kitchen. Within seconds he returned with a pair of jogging bottoms and an old T-shirt.

'Get changed... then we'll talk.'

Gus met Mo's eyes and hoped that his didn't reflect the same pain he identified in his friend's. As well as being a crap godfather, he'd been a crap friend too. He hadn't seen Mo for over a fortnight and one glance was enough to tell him how much things had deteriorated in the Siddique household.

He took the clothes and slipped into the small toilet cubicle to get changed. When he exited, Mo was sitting at one of the tables, looking out the window watching the downpour. Although still heavy, the rain had lost its earlier ferocity. On the table was a plate with samosas and raita and two cans of Rubicon Mango, bubbles of condensation dribbling down the sides.

Mo turned and pointed to a plastic bag on the counter, 'Put your wet things in there, you div.'

'Div?'

'Yeah, only a div would decide to go walking in that damn downpour.'

Gus shrugged, accepting the observation, and shoved his dripping clothes into the bag, before joining Mo at the table. Realising he'd barely touched the meal at Katie's, he dived into the samosas with relish. Mo's business was doing a roaring trade. So much so that he'd expanded into all sort of ranges from vegan spicy spring rolls, to paneer and pea samosas. Gus' favourite were the bite sized samosas with spicy lentils. Lifting his can and rolling it across his forehead and cheeks to cool himself down, Gus observed his friend. Mo had lost a bit of weight and, unusually, a scowl scarred his forehead.

'Alice is back.'

A smile flashed across Mo's face. 'Yeah? That's brilliant. Tell her to pop down. Can't wait to catch-up. How's her parents?' Alice's parents had stayed at Mo's for a short time during the winter and Mo had grown fond of the eccentric couple.

They talked about Alice and her recovery and her parents for a while until Gus said, 'You're working late.'

'Yeah, well. Thought I'd give Zarqa the chance to tell her mum about her exam before I went home. Soon as I walk through the door, she either walks out or locks herself in her room.'

'Things no better?'

Mo opened his can and took a long drink. 'Nah. She won't talk to either of us properly, but she completely ignores me unless she deigns to swear at me and storm out.'

'That bad?' Gus wondered whether to mention to Mo about Jerry and Dave seeing Zarqa pelting down Oak Lane on Sunday night. Last thing he wanted to do was worry his friend, but on the other hand, didn't Mo deserve to know that his sixteen-year-old kid was out on her own after dark? Who was he kidding? Course Mo knew she'd been out… the thing was, did he know where she'd been or that she'd been on her own and obviously frightened? But Mo was speaking again.

'Sunday night, for example. She stormed out and was gone for hours. Naila and I were frantic. She wouldn't answer her phone and Naila refused point blank to access the tracker we have on it.' He made bunny ears with his fingers and spoke in a near perfect imitation of his wife's tone. ''No, Mo, that would be an infringement of her privacy. She'd never trust us again if we did that.' Like I was going to *broadcast* the fact we'd spied on her. But no, Naila got all indignant the way she does and then the two of us are fighting.'

Despite his friend's obvious distress, Gus found himself smiling. Mo was only concerned about Zarqa and, in his eyes, that trumped minor considerations of privacy. After all this time with his wife, you'd think he'd have known she wouldn't go with that. 'So, what happened?'

Mo's frown deepened as he drained his can and crushed it with one hand. 'I was just about to go out trawling the streets looking for her, when I decided to look along towards Oak Lane through the staircase window. You know, one last time to see if she was walking along the road.'

Glad that *he'd* not betrayed Zarqa's privacy, Gus said, 'And was she?'

'Nah, she wasn't…'

Gus hadn't been expecting that and he could tell from the vibrato in his friend's voice that what he was about to say was upsetting.

Eyes focussed on the rain trickling down the window making visibility poor, Mo sniffed and rubbed his hand over his face '… she'd clearly sneaked in through the hedge, like they used to do when they were little. Probably to stop the security light from going on…' He turned, and eyes fixed on Gus said, 'and you know what she was doing… my beautiful, wonderful daughter…?'

Dreading his friend's next words, Gus shook his head.

'She was sitting on a patch of grass, her knees pulled up to her chin and she was rocking back and forth sobbing like I've never seen her do before.'

Mo stopped to wipe his own eyes. 'My baby crying, and I couldn't go and comfort her because she hates me…

because *I'm* the cause of her pain… because it's my fault she's suffering on her own…'

Gus reached over and squeezed Mo's hand. 'She doesn't hate you, Mo. You know deep down inside she doesn't. She just doesn't know how to cope with the adjustments to her life, that's all.'

'It's more than that though, Gus. I've fucked up. Well and truly fucked up. Naila blames me for not listening to her. She's right; we should have told Zarqa the truth years ago… then it wouldn't have been such a big thing… *then* we might have survived it. You should be glad you don't have kids, Gus – it's a minefield.'

Seemingly seeing something in his friend's reaction, Mo stopped and studied Gus' face. 'What have I said… you and Patti arguing about kids?'

Gus snorted. 'If it was me and Patti talking about kids, I'd be over the moon… but it's not…' his voice died away at the last word. Shit, where had that come from? He and Patti having kids? Christ, they didn't even live together, what the hell was he thinking? She wasn't even returning his calls. He didn't even know if there was any more 'he and Patti'. Now it was his turn to look out the window to avoid meeting his friend's gaze.

'Okaaay. I'm confused – if it's not you and Patti talking about kids then *who* is it?'

With difficulty, Gus tried for a neutral tone as he waved one hand dismissively. 'Aw, it's just Katie and Gabriella.'

When after a few minutes Mo hadn't responded, Gus turned his head away from the window. Mo was biting his lip, clearly not sure how to respond to Gus' words. Finally, he said, 'Thought Gabby didn't want kids.'

Head to one side, lips in a tight line, Gus forced his next words out. 'Apparently, she's changed her mind, and, with Katie's fertility issues, she'll be the one carrying the baby.'

'Weeeeell, I suppose, it's a good thing, if they want kids. Katie'll make a great mum... and *you're* great with kids... you'll make a great uncle.' Mo's tone was that of a mother coaxing a child to eat broccoli.

Staring straight at Mo, the words catapulted out of his mouth. 'That's just it, mate... they don't want me to be just the kid's uncle... they want me to be its dad.'

If it hadn't been so upsetting, Gus would have laughed outright at Mo's expression. Mouth hanging open, Mo gawped at Gus, taking him right back to Year Seven, when Gus had told him that not everyone shaved their pubes.

Mo wiggled his index finger back and forth. 'You telling me... you and Gaby... yeuk... that's just yeuk.... and Katie's okay with that?'

Gus reached over and slapped Mo lightly over the head. 'Idiot. It'd be done through artificial insemination.'

Rubbing his head, Mo exhaled. 'Oh... that's okay... Ah no, it's not... that's just yeuk – a bloody glass bottle? Yeuk.'

The friends sat in silence and then Mo asked, 'So, what you gonna do?'

Gus shook his head.

'You spoken to Patti about it?'

Again, he shook his head and explained about the anonymous letters and the uploaded images. 'You're the only one I've spoken to. This is crap, Mo, just crap. How can they even ask me to create a child with my ex-wife and then just pretend to be its uncle for the rest of its life?' He squished his mango juice can and tossed it on top of his empty plate.

'That's well fucked up... but then I've always though Gaby was fucked up. Why can't they just do it through a damn clinic, like other folk do?'

'Katie wants the kid to be as close genetically as possible to the pair of them.'

'Well, that's just stupid.' Mo looked out the window again, his thoughts clearly not only with Gus' predicament. 'Genetics don't make a family… love does that.'

Gus stood up to go, wondering if he'd just added even more of a burden to his friend's shoulders. 'Rain's stopped; I better slope back up to The Fort. You any samosa's left I can take as a peace offering to Compo for disappearing for so long? You know the lad needs his sustenance.'

Mo laughed, his face lighting up, as he jumped to his feet. 'Yep, give me a sec.'

Gus watched his friend pack samosas into a box. 'They find the people that graffitied your mosque yet, Mo?'

Cursing under his breath, Mo added more samosas to the already bulging box before replying. 'Not a bloody dickie bird. Bloody travesty, what they sprayed over the walls.'

'LIARS! SINNERS! RAPISTS! in foot-high letters. Makes me sick. Who'd deface a mosque like that?'

'Some right-wing idiot, more than likely. But I thought you had cameras and CCTV all over.'

Mo's voice was grim. 'We do. That's the point – we do. Fuckers used some sort of drone or other to deactivate it before they climbed the fence. Caught it flying towards the camera and then the signals just went off. Your lot reckon they must be right techie experts to be able to do that. Maybe you could ask Compo what he thinks.'

More drones…

CHAPTER 46

Leo

I don't want to let them down. We've come so far and all that, but it's gonna be hard for me to get away. This one is one of Pisces' choices, but still, I should be there... that was the deal... all three of us together... a team.

Ping!

> Zodiac: You still on for tonight? That chicken shit Pisces is going all wobbly. Am relying on you. You know that, right?

I knew it. Knew that bell end Pisces would cause a stir, make it hard for everyone. I push my specs back up my nose. I could do with a cig. I've only got a few minutes to reply. I need to think. Can I manage it? Should I ask to delay by a few days? It's not what we agreed; I know that. What an arse. I sigh. There's nowt else I can say.

> Me: Sorted. I'm in. Laters!

CHAPTER 47

Wednesday

Gus peered through the darkness, squinting to see the time on his phone as it vibrated on his bedside table. *Fuck's sake! After two o'clock.* He didn't recognise the number, so it wasn't a work call. That was strange as the only calls he got in the middle of the night were usually work related. His thoughts immediately went to his parents. Had something happened to them? Was one of their neighbours phoning with bad news? A familiar tension gripped his stomach like a vice and squeezed, pushing the tension upwards into his chest.

Ignoring the discomfort, he slid his legs round until he was sitting on the edge of the bed and tried to keep his voice down so as not to wake Alice in the next room. 'Yeah, Gus McGuire, what can I do for you?'

The voice on the other end of the phone was garbled and for a moment Gus didn't recognise it, then it came to him. It was Jerry, one of the two homeless men he saw regularly at Lister Park. Breathing a little easier now he knew his parents were okay, he suspected something had happened to Dave, Jerry's friend. He resigned himself to jogging over to the park to help out when he thought of something else. What if Jerry had seen Zarqa again? What if something had happened to *her*? Gus ran his fingers through his dreads and stood up, speaking quietly into the phone, as he paced the room. 'Calm down there, Jerry, I can't hear you properly. You need to hold the phone closer to your mouth.'

Two small taps on his bedroom door and the door opened. Alice poked her head through, and he shrugged in response to her, 'Who's that?' and flicked the phone to speaker.

'Jerry, slow down. Take a deep breath and tell me what's happened… is Dave okay?'

A different voice came on the phone and Gus recognised it as belonging to Dave. 'I'm okay, Gus.'

Gus raised an eyebrow. This Dave sounded comparatively calm, which was unusual as Jerry was normally the leader of the two of them. 'You okay, Dave? Jerry okay?'

Not one to mince his words, Dave got straight to the point before hanging up. 'Get yourself over here. Botanic Gardens. Dead kid.'

Gus stared at the silent phone for a few seconds and then blinked. Shit. Dead kid! Fuck, could it be Zarqa?

Alice prodded his arm. 'Dead kid, Gus, Botanic Gardens, chop chop. I'll phone it in, you phone the team.'

'What if it's Zarqa?' He hadn't meant to speak, hadn't wanted to put voice to his greatest fear, but the words wouldn't remain unsaid.

Alice looked at him, her expression puzzled. 'Why would you think it might be Zarqa? Why would it be?'

Shrugging, Gus shook his head as if to clear his mind and began to pull on a pair of jogging bottoms. 'Just me being daft. Not proper awake yet.'

Alice's eyes narrowed and he suspected she wasn't wholly convinced by his response. Her next words confirmed that. 'Seems like I've missed a lot in the last six months. Now we better get a wriggle on.'

Gus pulled a T-shirt on as his friend walked towards the bedroom door and as his head popped out the top, he said, 'But what if it is, Al?'

She paused and stood with her hand resting on the door handle for a brief moment before turning around to meet his eye. 'Then, we'll deal with it… and we'll be there for

Mo and Naila.' Her voice hardened, became brisker as she added, 'But what the hell's got into you? You need to get a grip, Gus. Move it!'

Walking through Lister Park, mere minutes later, the air was filled with the warm mulchy smell of vegetation after the earlier rainstorm. As they approached the Botanical Gardens with their decorative bridges, Gus saw two figures crouched on the ground. 'Dave, Jerry, that you?'

One of the two figures stood and turned towards them. Gus recognised Dave. Jerry remained crouched. As he and Alice neared the two men, Gus could hear the sounds of sirens approaching. Just in case, they'd alerted emergency services and requested an ambulance as well as police units to come. In the distance, to the right of the gardens, he heard voices and called out, 'Who's that over there?'

A disembodied voice floated through the air. 'Police. Identify yourself.'

Gus shone his torch towards the voice and saw two uniformed officers approaching down the hill from the North Park Road entrance. 'Stop where you are. I'm DI Gus McGuire with DS Alice Cooper. Wait there until I've established what's happened. Make sure no other units come any closer okay?'

Hearing a 'Yes, sir,' followed by the mumble and crackle of police radios, Gus was reassured that his instructions were being taken care of. Approaching the two men, Alice following in his tracks, he said, 'You said there was a dead kid, Dave?'

Gus' heart was hammering and the feeling of foreboding hanging over him seemed to get heavier with each step he took. Directing his torch light at an angle so as not to blind the two men, Gus studied them. Why was Jerry not standing up? Why was Dave doing all the speaking?

'Yep, a girl.' Dave's eyes remained on his friend's hunched-up figure as he spoke.

Gus' step faltered and then, pulling himself together, he moved closer. Dave was pointing to an area of shrubbery to the right and Gus, deliberately slowing his breathing, moved over, casting his torch light on the body of a young girl. Almost sagging with relief, he closed his eyes when he realised it wasn't Zarqa lying there. This was followed almost immediately by guilt, because whoever this girl was, she was someone's daughter, sister, friend. He edged closer to the girl, registering the similarities between this and Pratab's crime scene. Hoping for a miracle, but expecting none, he extended two fingers and felt for a pulse. Nothing.

Alice had waited on the path so as not to disturb the area any more than was necessary. Gus retraced his steps back onto the path and was already on the phone directing his team and giving directions for the CSIs as well as the pathologist. For once, he hoped his dad was the pathologist on call. It would be better to have the same pathologist do both post mortems, since the two crime scenes indicated the same perpetrator.

Between them, he and Alice established an inner cordon around themselves and Jerry and Dave. All they could do now was wait for the crime scene investigators. He was glad that the two older men had had the presence of mind to move away from the body. This would minimise cross contamination. As he walked over to them, Dave spoke, his voice a little higher, a little more agitated, than it had been on the phone earlier. 'Soon as we saw her like, Gus, we backed off and phoned you. Jerry's not right good. Got a shock like… daughter that age himself. Fainted… cracked his head on summat… bleeding… bleeding. Needs help, he does.'

Shit. He hadn't stopped to question Jerry's huddled position on the ground. Had been too keen to make sure the dead girl wasn't Zarqa. Gus hadn't known Jerry had a daughter, never mind one so young. Truth was, he'd put him at being in his late seventies and hadn't given much of a thought to the two men's backgrounds. Now, he was angry with himself for being an idiot. Of course, these two men had had a life other than the one they lived now.

He kneeled down beside Jerry, cursing himself for not realising sooner that Dave wouldn't have been so vocal had Jerry been well. 'Don't worry, Dave, I called for an ambulance.' As the sirens got louder, he continued, 'You can hear it now, yeah?'

Ignoring the overpowering smell of unwashed clothes, Gus concentrated on the Jerry. A trail of blood smeared across his forehead, coming from a gash just beneath his hairline. He must have cracked his head on a rock or something when he fell. The bleeding had slowed to a trickle and Gus suspected that it was shock rather than his injury that was affecting Jerry. Behind him, Dave fidgeted, moving from one foot to the other in a sort of nervous shuffle. Jerry was pale, but conscious. 'In my pocket, Gus. Dave's meds. Was gonna give them him.'

Overcoming his distaste, Gus rummaged in the man's pockets until he found a box with blister packs of Clozaril in.

'Just one. Give him one.' Jerry's voice was a whisper and Gus had to lean in to hear it.

With a nod, Gus turned to Dave. 'Here, Dave, Jerry's fine. Just needs a couple of stitches. He says you've to take this.' And he held out the blister pack. Obediently, Dave held out a hand, and when Gus popped a pill onto his palm, Dave threw it into his mouth and dry swallowed, opening his mouth immediately to let Gus see it had gone.

Ignoring the wave of halitosis that wafted out, Gus smiled. 'Great. That's great. Now here's the ambulance. You need to go with Jerry, okay? He needs you to look after him. I'll come and find you at BRI later on.'

Gus yelled up to the uniformed officers at the top of the hill. 'I need one of you to accompany my friends to the hospital.' When an older officer approached, Gus moved to meet him and spoke in a low voice. 'Go with them. See what you can find out. If they saw anyone hanging about or anything. But don't frighten them. Dave in particular is a bit fragile.'

The officer nodded, switched on a smile, began to help Jerry to his feet and said, 'Looks like we're getting a ride in an ambulance. Come on. I could do with a cup of tea and last time I was at the BRI they had some hot chocolate in one of the vending machines too... Galaxy hot chocolate, no less.'

CHAPTER 48

Zodiac

Really wanted to stay. Couldn't have planned it better if I'd tried. Just as well we'd finished though. Those two smelly old dumbasses turning up was bloody brilliant. Pisces and Leo – shit! Should've seen their faces. Nearly shat themselves. Then we were off, running... running like the wind. I nearly yelled at the top of my voice, 'Run, Pisces, Run! Run, Leo, Run!' Like in that stupid film my mum made me watch the other week, *Forest Gump* or something... box of chocolates indeed... life's more like a pile of crap than a box of chocolates... unless of course you make your own box of chocolates. Maybe that's what Gump did. Maybe he made his own box of chocolates and maybe that's exactly what the Zodiac Club are doing... creating our own chocolate fillings... blood and murder and revenge.

We'd no idea the tramps were about. By the time Leo had convinced her to meet us and she'd downed the drugged booze and smoked half a spliff, we were at the point of no return. It'd been easy to convince her to skip out. Leo was very persuasive. I'd listened in on the conversation.

'Please, you got to come. With everything that's happened recently, I need a friend... someone who understands the sort of shit I'm going through.'

Pure genius. Leo went well up in my estimations... played a blinder there. Pisces, not so much. Wittering on, moaning. Wanted to slam a punch into that pock-marked face... only the thought of pus splattering all over my fist stopped me in the end. That and the fact that I knew the best way to get Pisces onside was to be sympathetic. If there's one thing I've learned over the years, it's that keeping them off-balance is the best control there is... sympathise one minute, then admonish them, a little bit of guilt tripping, a few hours of ghosting... A fine art, polished over years of practicing with equally gullible idiots.

Betsy was an easy target. A bit rushed in the end, but enjoyable, nonetheless. Just got to dump the phone and it's done.

It never ceases to amaze me what you can make people do... with the correct nurturing that is.

As we skipped, I heard the old guys whispering. One of the minging idiots fell over trying to get away from the body. Weeping like a fucking wuss. Then they're whispering like an old couple,

'What should we do?'

'It's that *Snapchat Killer* innit? Bet that's who's done this.'

'Yeah, but should we phone Gus?'

'Maybe just leave it. Someone else'll find her soon enough. They'll think we done it if we phone.'

'Gus won't. He won't. I'm phoning him. Help me phone him, Dave. That's someone's wee girl there.'

Idiots! I'd have loved to have stayed. Seen Gus' reaction first-hand. That'd have been cool as crap. Too risky though. Never mind, I've other things to do... important things. It's all part of the plan. I'll be in touch with DI McGuire again before too much longer. I can hardly wait.

CHAPTER 49

By the time Dr McGuire arrived, an outer cordon had been established surrounding the Botanic Gardens as far as the Emm Lane park boundary and swooping around the park as far as Cartwright Hall. Hissing Sid had set up a crime scene tent and his CSIs were combing the immediate vicinity. Despite their disagreement at the previous crime scene and the fact he'd been called out in the middle of the night, Sid seemed in good spirits.

Dr McGuire, dressed in shorts from which two sturdy, hairy legs protruded, tackled the hill from the boating lake up to the Botanical Gardens. A mega sized T-shirt, under which his man boobs wobbled distractingly, finished off his ensemble. Gus watched his dad struggle up the slight incline with a frown. The doc's red face and heaving chest told Gus just how out of condition his dad had become in recent months. His hair, sticking up like two demon horns at either side of his skull, indicated how quickly he'd responded to Alice's call.

Gasping to catch his breath, Dr McGuire stopped and when he recognised Alice, now suited and booted up, his eyes widened. 'Aw, yer back, Alice. It's grand to see you and looking so fit too.'

Alice grinned as Dr McGuire shimmied into his XXXL crime scene suit and pulled the hood over his errant hair. 'You're looking grand yourself, Doc.'

And, when he was fully suited, she went over and was enveloped in a bear hug.

Gus tapped his toe in an exaggerated fashion. 'Time's a ticking, you two.'

The whole greeting had taken two minutes, but prior experience told him that if he didn't nip it in the bud pronto, his dad would start a full investigation into the last six months of Alice's life. Time for that later.

Opening the tent door, Gus ushered his dad through, with Sid following.

Sid was the first to speak, 'You notice?'

Gus nodded. 'The phone?'

'Exactly.' The CSI moved closer. 'No phone anywhere, but mark my…'

At that moment Gus's mobile rang and seeing it was work, Gus held up a gloved finger and answered. 'Yep, Hardeep?'

'Just texting you a photo, boss. A Ms Reavley just come in saying her daughter's missing and… well, you know?'

Gus did know. No such thing as coincidence. 'Good thinking.' His phone pinged. 'It's arrived… I'll let you kn—'

'That's not all… the boss came in five minutes ago and…' Hardeep paused.

Keen to get him off the phone so he could crack on with things here at the crime scene, Gus interrupted. 'Nancy? Did you tell her what's gone off?'

'Eh, no. Not Nancy…… it was the big boss.'

'Bashir?' Gus was puzzled. What the hell was the DCS doing at this time of the night in The Fort?

'She's with her daughter. The girl's in bits. Says she got a *Snapchat*…'

Fuck! Gus had been expecting that. He just hadn't expected his boss' daughter to be the recipient.

'…she says, the boss's daughter, Mehmoona that is, that it's from her friend Betsy Reavley.' He paused a moment and Gus heard him inhale sharply before continuing. 'She's a smart girl that Mehmoona. When she saw the Snap the first time, she realised what it was and so managed to screenshot it when she viewed it the second time. Lucky for us. It's the same girl, boss. Ms Reavley's a single mum – she came in on her own.'

Gus' heart sank. He understood what Hardeep was telling him. The victim's mum had no one to support her and she was going to be given the worst possible news any parent could ever receive. 'Right. Okay. Keep both parties in separate rooms. Brief Taffy and get him to sit with Ms Reavley. Tell Bashir I'll be up as soon as I can, but in the meantime ask for Mehmoona's phone and get Compo working on that.'

'Should Taffy tell the mum?'

'Look, let me see for myself if the photo matches. I'll be as quick as I can.'

Gus accessed the photo quickly and sighed. Turning it round he showed it to the other three. 'Looks like we've just ID'd the victim. Alice…'

'I'm on it. I'll head up now and inform the mum and get what I can from her.'

Gus spoke onto his phone. 'You get that, Hardeep? Alice is on her way. Tell Taffy to just stay there. Alice will help him with the death notice.'

If there was anybody best suited to breaking the news to a mother that their teenage daughter was dead, it was Alice. Gus just hoped it wouldn't put too much strain on her. Although she'd put on a brave face, Gus had heard her pacing the house in the early hours of the morning for the past two nights. He wasn't surprised she chose to roam the entire house. After her spell in prison, the confined space of a bedroom probably conjured up too many bad memories for her. Maybe what she needed was a distraction. Maybe this investigation would take her mind off her own demons.

As Alice left the tent, Gus looked at Sid. 'So, if a *Snapchat* photo was sent, that begs the question... where's the damn phone?'

Sid spoke into the walkie talkie. 'We suspect a phone may have been ditched nearby, extend the initial bag and grab area keeping a special lookout for a dumped phone.' He turned to Gus. 'We may need to consider trawling the lake in case it's been dumped there. Wonder why it was taken this time?'

Dr McGuire looked up from his kneeling position next to the teenage victim. 'Well, that may be a change in MO, but my initial examination says that most other things are consistent with the previous murder. Again, the jugular has been stabbed, although this time it looks like they took a couple of attempts to get it just right. The hands are positioned in the same way and there's evidence of cable ties.'

'Yep, we found those thrown in a bush,' Sid confirmed.

'A bit of bruising to the head, again as if someone yanked it in position and held it steady. I'll confirm at the PM.'

As his dad struggled to his feet, Gus stepped forward and lent his arm. 'Will you be able to prioritise this?'

Doc McGuire nodded. 'Yes. I've got a non-suspicious death – probably a heart attack which I'll do first thing and then get cracking on this one by ten. That suit you?'

Mind back on the crime scene and the conundrum of the missing phone, Gus nodded absentmindedly. 'Thanks, that's great.'

Dr McGuire began to edge his way past CSIs to get out of the tent and as if he'd only just remembered, he turned back and leaned right over Gus, his morning breath sour as he said, 'Whatever you decide is fine with me and your mum, Angus.'

Gus frowned, momentarily confused and then, as realisation came, his shoulders stiffened, and blood rushed to his face. 'You knew? You bloody knew... the both of you... Mum too? And you didn't think to warn me?'

Shrugging off his dad's huge hand, he pushed past him. 'Get away from me. Like always, you've no sense of professionalism. This is not something for now. Just go away and leave me to do my job.'

He moved off, paused, and swung back round to face his dad. 'And...' his voice sounding strangled as he spat the words out, '...you've always taken her side...'

CHAPTER 50

Leo

Still boiling, even at this time. I'm sweating like a pig after running. Need to stop smoking… really do. My chest's gonna explode in a minute… phlegm crackling right across it and up to my throat. I stop, cough a couple of times, wishing it wasn't so loud in the dark, and hoik up a gob of gunge. Disgusting or what?

Zodiac said not to take a taxi, not to draw attention to ourselves… but what the heck? It's late and I need to get home. If anyone notices I'm not there, things could go badly wrong. What excuse could I possibly give for being out at this time of the morning?

Anyway, I'm smart. Didn't take the taxi all the way home. Just from Oak Lane to a few streets away. Driver never even looked at me and I used the burner… no trace. Anyway, it's not like I've got *Snapchat Killer* tattooed on my face, is it? Nobody's looking at kids for this… we're in the clear.

Won't tell Zodiac though. Nobody needs the wrath of Zodiac when they're in top form, even less when they are under the weather and right now, I feel like crap. Just hope Pisces holds it together. Think Zodiac has a plan though… we need one… a contingency… just in case.

CHAPTER 51

This situation was one of the strangest professional ones Gus had found himself in. Interviewing a distraught witness was always fraught. Interviewing a distraught witness in the presence of their parent was worse and interviewing said witness in the presence of their mother, when that parent was also your big boss, was like walking on thin ice and expecting it to crack under your feet at any moment. Alice had arranged for Ms Reavley to be escorted back home with a Family Liaison Officer and had come in to sit with Mehmoona while they waited for Gus to arrive.

Alice had wanted to keep Mehmoona Bashir and the DCS in the comfortable interview room downstairs. With its soft couches and pastel coloured walls, it was custom built for sensitive interviews. However, the DCS had had other ideas and had insisted she take her daughter up to her office.

This was yet another thing that put Gus at a disadvantage. Walking into the room, he'd smiled at Alice and judged, by the strained smile she offered back, that the previous hour or so had been uncomfortable to say the least. Mehmoona was sprawled over the couch in the corner, head resting on a cushion, her long dark hair with its bleached tips spread out behind her. She held a strand of it and was twirling it round and round between her thumb and index finger as she stared at the ceiling. DCS Bashir was behind her desk sifting through paperwork. The remains of a vending machine sandwich and a squashed Pepsi Max can were on the coffee table.

As Gus strode into the room, Mehmoona swung her legs off the couch and stood up, smiling, hand extended. 'Hello, DI McGuire. Nice to see you again.' As if the girl realised how trite her words sounded under the circumstances, she grimaced, withdrew her hand, and sank back onto the couch. Immediately, she was transformed from a self-confident teen who'd had manners instilled in her from a young age, to a hesitant, awkward girl, who didn't know what to do with herself.

Her mum, DCS Bashir, stood up gracefully and moved round her desk. 'At last.'

Gus glanced at her but got no indication that her words were accusing.

She moved over, sat down beside her daughter, put her arm around her, and squeezed the girl's shoulder. This left Gus to sit beside Alice at the other side of the coffee table. Gus studied Mehmoona and his boss. He'd already ascertained from the phone conversation he'd overheard the other day that there was some friction between mother and daughter, but right now all he saw was a shocked girl, pleased to have her mother beside her.

'You've already seen the *Snapchat*?' The DCS' tone was brusque and business-like.

Gus nodded. It had been almost a carbon copy of the one sent to Haider, except the victim was Betsy Reavley. Mehmoona's quick thinking had preserved the image for their perusal. She was clearly her mother's daughter. Maybe she'd have a career in the police in the future. At the point the image had been taken, the knife was still inserted in the wound. It looked similar to the previous weapon. A bog-standard kitchen knife that, until they found the weapon and matched it to the wounds, added little to their case.

'Was Betsy a particular friend of yours, Moona, or do you prefer Mehmoona?'

The girl exhaled and glanced at her mother before replying. 'Either's fine. Didn't really know Betsy. From school, of course, but we didn't hang out. She was in a couple of my classes. Haven't seen her for ages, because it's exam time. We have study days.'

Ah, this was different. Haider had been Pratab Patel's best friend at one point, but Mehmoona claimed hardly to know their newest victim. That would need verifying. He glanced at Alice and was pleased when her slight nod told him she'd get it checked out.

'Can you remember when you last saw her?'

Mehmoona frowned, tapped her leg with her fingers, 'Well, I saw her on Monday. In the hall for our Maths GCSE. But to speak to...' She pursed her lips and began twirling her hair again. 'Can't be sure, but not for weeks, I'd say.'

'What can you tell us about Betsy? Who were her friends? Do you know where she hung out, outside school? Anything you can tell us, no matter how unimportant it may seem to you, might help.'

'Well the thing is...' she glanced at her mum, gave a small shrug and said, 'Betsy didn't really have many friends.' She wrinkled up her nose in an apologetic gesture and continued, 'Nobody liked her that much. She was a bit of a telltale... you know? Got that Pratab's sister in trouble a couple of times, that sort of thing. Other than that, I don't know.' She looked down at her hands and then glanced up again. 'Why don't you ask Ms Copley, she'll be happy to help you.'

Gus froze. Was that a smirk that slid across her lips or did he imagine it? He glanced at Alice and saw she was looking at the girl, her forehead creased. So, not his imagination. Well, it was to be expected. Probably every kid at the Academy had seen it.

DCS Bashir glared at her daughter. 'Moona, I spoke to you about this.'

Mehmoona rolled her eyes, 'Yeah well. It's not like I can pretend not to have seen them, is it? Every kid in school's seen him having it off with Ms Copley. Can't pretend it never happened, can I?'

She turned to Gus. 'Not that I'm judging or anything. Think it's pretty cool really that old folk still like...' She grimaced in a sort of '*it's gross*' gesture. 'You know, like, get it on?'

Conscious of both Bashir glaring at her daughter and Alice's snort of laughter disguised as a cough, Gus wanted to throw his arms up in the air and say, 'For God's sake, I'm not old, you cheeky cow,' in the same tone he would have used with Zarqa. Instead, he grinned, adopting a self-effacing manner and said, 'Well, you know that was an infringement of both mine and Ms Copley's privacy, yeah?'

Mehmoona nodded.

'So, maybe now you've fessed up to seeing it, we can move on from that childish rubbish and get on with the thing that's really important here... the murder of your school friend.'

He was pleased to see the girl bite her lip, a flicker of confusion in her eyes, but then it was gone, and she exhaled. 'Yes, you're right. Sorry. That was tight of me. Poor Betsy... poor Betsy.' And she turned, flinging herself into her mother's arms, sobbing as if she'd never stop.

For a moment, Gus felt like a dick. He'd been firm with the girl and hadn't really taken into account how traumatic it must have been for her to see that *Snapchat* and to realise its significance. She'd done well to screenshot it and he could have been a little less brutal with her. He raised his head to meet his superior officers gaze, expecting to see condemnation in her eyes. Instead she gave a curt nod, her lips scrunched up in sardonic approval, and continued to soothe her daughter.

'Al, maybe we need some drinks, yes?'

Alice tore her gaze away from the mother and daughter and nodded. 'I'm on it. Back in a moment.'

By the time Alice returned, Mehmoona had stopped crying and, face tear-stained, was leaning against her mother. Gus studied the tableau for a moment. Bashir looked embarrassed to be in the vulnerable position of comforting her daughter... but there was something else. She looked uncomfortable, uncertain of herself. That little insight into his boss's frailty made Gus like her just a little bit more. Good to know she was human too.

As Alice deposited a range of soft drinks and bottles of chilled water on the table, Gus smiled at Mehmoona. 'Can you tell us anything about Pratab Patel? Were Betsy and Pratab friendly?'

Mehmoona lifted a strand of hair and began twisting it round her finger, looking thoughtful. 'I wouldn't have said so... not really. Though I heard she left a mushy message on his *Facebook* page.'

Although Compo was monitoring the outpourings of grief that had made it to Pratab's timeline, he hadn't come up with anything that seemed dodgy or suspicious, but Gus was the first to admit that the best judges of 'dodgy and suspicious' were undoubtedly Pratab's peers. He made a note to get Compo to cross reference the two *Facebook* pages. No doubt Betsy Reavley's would soon be filled with just as many outpourings of grief. 'What sort of message?'

The girl shrugged. 'Dunno. Never saw it. I'm not friends with either of them on *Facebook*. Just heard someone on the bus on the way home from school laughing at her. Don't think Pratab thought much of Betsy, by all accounts.'

'You pick up anything else? Hear anything else?'

Mehmoona scrunched up her nose. 'No... I'm not really in the loop. Not been here long enough to be in the *in crowd*.'

That's right. Mehmoona had only moved from Birmingham with her mother just over a year ago. Was it strange then, that the killer had sent the *Snapchat* to Mehmoona or was it just a random thing?

'When will I get my phone back? I got to have it. How else can I keep in contact with my mates?'

Before Gus could reply, the DCS, voice harsh said, 'For God's sake, Moona. A girl is dead. A girl you knew. You can do without your phone for a few days, until DI McGuire is done with it.'

If it hadn't been in such dire circumstances, Gus would have laughed out loud at the outraged look on the girl's face. Only a teen could open their eyes so wide, raise their eyebrows so high, and twist their mouth into a silent snarl of derision, while their entire body radiated annoyance.

'Okay, I was only asking. Yeah?'

Exhaling loudly, Gazala Bashir stood and stretched. 'You can have my old one if it really bothers you that much. Come on. Let's get home. Maybe we'll be able to catch a couple of hours' kip.'

Gus looked out the window and saw that the sky was getting lighter. How he wished he too could grab a few hours kip, but alas there was work to be done and the next. day was forecast to be the hottest day yet. Oh joy.

CHAPTER 52

Right, the first thing we need to do is find Betsy Reavley's damn phone.' Gus had had no sleep and it was now eight in the morning at the start of another scorching Wednesday. Already, he was sticky and irritable, and the day wasn't going to get any cooler. Compo had made a trip to The Lunch Monkey café and the air was filled with the smell of bacon butties, reminding Gus that he hadn't eaten yet. His stomach growled and he grabbed the last one, before Compo, the human hoover, could devour it as quickly as he had the other three. He was sure the lad had worms.

As he watched Gus bite into his roll, Compo looked crestfallen. 'I've initiated a trace on the phone. If it's switched on, we should be able to locate its whereabouts. If it's still with the bastard who did this, then he's toast.'

Gus didn't hold out a lot of hope. He suspected the perpetrator had been disturbed by Jerry and Dave and taken off with the phone. No doubt, by now it would have been dumped in the boating lake or in a bin somewhere. He turned to Sebastian Carlton, who was picking his teeth with a paperclip. 'Any thoughts on these new developments, Sebastian?'

The man's sigh would have been annoying, had Gus not recognised it for what it was; frustration at having nothing much more to add.

'At this stage, Gus, I can't say much. Two victims aren't much to go on. The killers haven't been going long enough to make many mistakes... to leave many clues.' He nodded at Compo. 'Unless we get lucky with the phone of course. At this stage, I can only advise that you work on victimology. Everything you can find out about the victims… there must be a link between the victims and the killers. Alice tells me both victims attend the same school… I'd start there.'

Inwardly Gus groaned. He hadn't spoken to Patti since, what he now referred to as 'SexTapeGate', and he didn't fancy braving the school. Asking questions of teenagers was never easy, but the knowledge that they'd each probably giggled over his bare butt, made it even less appealing. Maybe he'd send Alice. She was good with kids.

He re-ran Carlton's words through his mind. 'That's twice you've said killers… plural. You agree there's more than one perpetrator?'

'Yes, definitely.' Carlton dug a bit deeper with the paper clip, making Gus cringe. 'I've got a bit of a thought spinning in my head, but nothing concrete to back it up… it's to do with this *Snapchat* thing.'

'Yeah, I was wondering about that… it seems to be a kid's thing, doesn't it? I know Mo's eldest three use it, but I don't know any adults who do.' Gus took another bite of his sandwich, ignoring Compo's plaintive gaze. 'Of course, that could just be a smokescreen?'

'Yeah.' Carlton dropped the clip on the desk and ran his tongue around his mouth. 'Although, the way this is going, we could be looking at serial killings, and you know there are not too many serial killer teams around – strange dynamics if it's a team.'

'You mean a team like Rosemary and Fred West or Hindley and Brady?' Compo was always keen to get brownie points from his mentor and was positively bouncing in his chair. Carlton smiled at his protégée, again reminding Gus of how incongruous *that* partnership was. Maybe Carlton should write a paper on *those* dynamics.

'Exactly, Compo, prime examples. Makes me wonder if it's just a pair or perhaps more than two. It could be a spree. Sprees normally occur within a short time span, often resulting in the death of the perp… either by suicide or suicide by cop. We can't rule that out, either. Despite the posing, the seeming lack of a sexual motive makes me question the serial killer idea. Although knifings often have a sexual element, they're usually more frenzied and not normally directed at the jugular in such a clinical way. I wonder if our perpetrator or perpetrators is or are playing games with us… taunting us. Throwing down the gauntlet. They're definitely after attention. It remains to be seen whether general attention will do or if they're focussing on a particular person.'

Gus rolled his eyes; *here we go again with the Americanisms*. He'd almost forgotten Carlton's tendency to Americanise everything. The other man said it was as a result of his time with the Behavioural Unit. Gus suspected it was an affectation.

Carlton's eyes lit up as if he was discussing a tricky political topic. 'Fascinating… lots to think about.' And he leaned back, folded his arms across his chest and closed his eyes.

Gus blinked. Apparently, that was all they were getting for now! He turned to Compo. 'Can you get a list of contacts on Betsy's phone, and cross match them with Pratab's?'

'Yep, I can… hey, Gus. The tracking's come in for Betsy Reavley's phone. Let me download it.'

They waited, ignoring the small snores coming from Sebastian Carlton as they watched the map appear on the large screen. For a moment there was a stunned silence. The phone was switched on, which was surprising in itself. Gus took a step closer…

On the screen a green light flashed. 'What the…?'

Compo jumped up. 'Shit, Gus, that's…'

But Gus was already heading out the door, yelling after him, 'Get patrol cars, Alice and Taffy there, right now…'

CHAPTER 53

Zodiac

The waiting is killing me. How long does it take them to hack into a phone, for God's sake? I switched it on and dropped it off over an hour ago so, for now, it's a waiting game. Can hardly contain myself. Can't wait to see what they'll do. This plan was sheer genius. He'd never in a million years expect this... how could he? He was still in the dark. But now the *Snapchat Killer's* in control.

I sip my water. It's already getting lukewarm and my T-shirt's sticking to me. Hope I don't have to kick my heels here for much longer. Don't want to catch anyone's attention, especially with the pigs all over the shop. Crime scene tape's still up. It'll be there for days still. The pigs are mixing with folk, talking and asking questions. Like that'll do them any good. How many of this lot would've been around last night? No wonder they're no further forward. Two kids dead and they're kicking their heels wasting time. *Snapchat Killer* Two: Bradford Police Zilch.

I'll head off for a walk. Only so long you can sit on a bench with headphones in and pretend to be engrossed in your phone. They're still at it on *Facebook*, posting photos of Betsy, and posting on her timeline.

There's one more angel in heaven, love

Jess xxx

Miss you Betsy Boo xxx

> How can I go on without my best
> friend? Love Sadie

It's gross. Half of them don't know her or even like her. Fucking Sadie, only last week she was mouthing off in the canteen about Betsy being a two-faced bitch and now she's her best friend. Serves them right. Serves them all right. Maybe now they'll sit up and take notice.

I reach the end of the path near the play area before I see him. *Knew it*! Just knew he'd come tanking down through the park as soon as they got into the phone and tracked where I'd dropped it. He almost looks like a superhero or something, with his dreads all splayed out behind him.

Oh, this is good. So bloody good. Jo Jo came up trumps this time. Amazing what you can do with a bit of technology.

I step behind a tree, but McGuire's focus is only on his destination. He doesn't even glance to the side… doesn't notice me. This is brilliant. Fucking brilliant!

CHAPTER 54

The image of the phone tracker bleeping from the interactive screen pushed Gus to move. In that split second, he made the decision to run, reckoning that by the time he'd accessed a pool car, got it out the barrier, and drove down Oak Lane in rush hour, he'd be too late. Putting on the fastest spurt he could, he ran full out and by the time he was exiting Lister Park opposite the now empty Turf pub, the sirens were only just making their way along Bradford Road. His throat was parched, and his heart boomed against his chest, his gasps racking up his dry throat. Ignoring the way his shirt stuck to his chest he pushed himself to run faster. And all the while he was cursing in his head. *Fucking bastards taunting me like that, fucking bastards. If anything's happened to him, I'll kill them!*

Dodging the traffic, ignoring the beeping horns and the squeal of brakes behind him, he skidded into Marriners Drive and, despite the pain in his thighs and calves, he pushed himself even more for the last twenty metres. When he reached his home, he ran up the drive, skirted the front of the house and, pausing only to unlock the six-foot side gate leading to his garden, he thrust it open. Leaving it juddering on its hinges, he entered his garden.

Bingo, who'd only come home the previous evening after Gus' new security system had been installed, clearly heard him, and was already dancing at his feet, yapping excitedly, to see his master. Gus collapsed to his knees, and breath hitching in his chest, allowed the dog to lick the sweat from his face. 'Thank God, Bingo, Thank God.' He hugged the squirming dog close to his chest and glanced

round his garden for signs of an intruder. He saw none...
except for a small square item in the middle of the garden.

Minutes later, two police cars, sirens blazing pulled up
in the street outside. Taffy and Alice spilled from the first
one and ran up to where Gus was sitting sprawled on the
path, just inside the garden gate.

'We'll need Sid's crew here, Alice. Look.' And he
pointed to the small patch of grass, he called Bingo's
'pooey grass'.

Alice, pulling her phone out of her pocket, started to
dial while Taffy silently offered Gus an open bottle of
water.

With a brief grin, Gus grabbed the bottle and glugged.
Although his heartbeat was returning to normal, his legs
still shook, and he doubted he'd be able to get to his feet
without falling over. Best just to sit and cuddle Bingo for a
bit longer. He leaned his head back against the wooden
fence and, face lifted to the sun, thanked God that his pet
was okay.

Scratching Bingo's head, he realised that security
system or not, Bingo would have to go back to his parents
for now. Gus didn't believe in coincidences and while
having one stalker delivering letters to his house was
conceivable, having a separate person, a possible killer,
dump a victim's phone in his garden was stretching the
boundaries. Somehow, the deaths of these two teenagers,
must be linked to his anonymous letter writer... and that
made it personal.

Despite his wobbly legs, Gus handed Bingo to Alice and
using the gate and wall for support, got to his feet. 'Let's
see if our *visitor* managed to get inside, then.'

Flanked by Alice, still carting a wriggling Bingo, and
Taffy with two uniformed officers taking up the rear, Gus
unlocked the front door to be greeted by the warning beep
of his new security system. Reassured, Gus thought it was

unlikely the intruder had made it indoors. Still, best check. Switching off his new alarm system, he made his way into the hallway. 'I'll check downstairs with you two.' He gestured to the two officers. 'Alice, Taffy, you go upstairs.'

Houses had a way of telling you if they were deserted or not and Gus had the sense that, apart from the police officers currently checking his home, it had not been violated. His pumping adrenalin had heightened his senses and he was aware of the faint scent from Patti's perfume lingering in the air, reminding him that his relationship very nearly lay in tatters. Forcing himself to focus, he swallowed the surge of anger that exploded in his chest and concentrated on the task in hand as he edged his way from room to room downstairs.

Five minutes later, they congregated in Gus' kitchen, having found the house empty and Gus said a mental thank you to Patti for hounding him about getting an alarm and better locks. Who knew what these killers would have done if they'd been able to gain easy access?

The uniformed officers wedged themselves around his kitchen table, as they waited for the crime scene team to arrive. Taffy busied himself making them all coffee while Alice, still holding Bingo, stood by the sink, looking out into Gus' back garden. 'How do you think they got in?'

Gus moved to the small dog flap and locked it so Alice could release Bingo, and filling a glass with water said, 'Let's find out, shall we? No point in having my snazzy security and not using it.'

He led them through to the small home office that he hardly used and started up his PC. 'My new security system's all linked up, so I'll be able to access the different cameras. The guys showed me how yesterday.'

After a couple of wrong passwords, a lot of impatience, and some cursing, Gus accessed his security system, but stared blankly at the menu, unsure of where to go next. Alice nudged him out of the way. 'For God's sake, let me. We don't have all day.'

Within seconds they were looking at footage of the back garden where Betsy Reavley's phone still lay, next to a pile of dog turd on Bingo's pooey grass.

'Rewind it. The phone wasn't there when I let Bingo out at half six, so rewind it until then.'

Alice glared at him as if to say, 'you think?' Gus grinned as her nimble fingers moved over the keyboard. Soon they were watching fast forwarded footage of Bingo tearing round the garden like a blue arsed fly, chasing butterflies, flinging himself under a bush for a doze, slurping at his water bowl and having a dump. It was strange to see what his dog got up to in his absence and Gus was pleased to see that he seemed happy. Bingo had access to the house whenever he wanted but seemed content to be outside. 'Wait, what the hell's that?' Alice rewound the tape and they watched as Bingo jumped to his feet and began barking furiously at something in the air that looked at first glance like a crow.

'Zoom in, Al.'

'Fucking hell, Gus,' said Taffy as they watched Bingo, ears back, tail down flee into the safety of the house. The black shape seemed to hover, and Alice zoomed in more. It was like a miniature spacecraft. And then they saw it… It dropped something that landed just next to Bingo's still steaming turd.

'A drone… a bloody drone.' Taffy was all but pissing his pants as he pointed.

Alice hit replay and they watched the footage again,

'Compo's been telling me all about them… since you know… the photos and all. You can make them yourself.'

But Gus was thinking he'd heard someone else mention drones before… something separate from this case. He just couldn't quite remember when. Then, there was the fact that Compo suspected the images of him and Patti had been captured by a drone. Now this. All in all, the coincidences were racking up just a little too smoothly for his liking. And then there was Carlton's most recent suggestion that they'd thrown down the gauntlet.

Well, now they knew who was expected to pick the damn   thing   up.

CHAPTER 55

Gus showered and changed before taking his car and dropping Bingo off at his parents' house. He hated the cloud that passed over his mum's face when he told her to be extra vigilant. It wasn't so long ago that she'd been targeted by a killer right outside her home and although he wished he didn't have to remind her of that, he wanted her safe. He was tempted to confront her about his sister's little bombshell but decided that then wasn't the time. The fact that his mum had known what Katie was going to ask him sat heavy with him. She'd always been scrupulously fair in her interactions with her children. The fact that she'd kept this secret from him smacked of favouritism and Gus found it unsettling. He wasn't sure he wanted to push it with his mum… wasn't sure what the outcome would be… or, more to the point, if it would wound him. The real stumbling block for him was the fact that his mum had welcomed Patti into the family so easily. Didn't she realise that this whole mad paternity crap would put a strain on his fledgling relationship with Patti? How could she side with Katie on this one… how could she?

Despite his need to hurry back to The Fort, Gus forced himself to wait patiently while his mum packaged up the remains of an inedible coffee cake for him 'To share with your team'. Glancing out the kitchen window, he was sure the sparrow sitting on the bird feeder was laughing at him. The bird was probably relieved to avoid yet more burnt offerings heading in its direction. Accepting the cling-filmed package, he'd hugged his mum close to his chest. 'Mum. When you let the dogs out the back, you need to keep an eye out. Whoever dropped that phone in my garden using the drone could've just as easily dropped poisoned meat… or a bomb. You see anything like that, and you lock yourself in and phone me.'

Her lips had tightened, and her chin lifted. 'I've no truck with bullies, Angus. I won't change my routines.' Her expression softened and laying a hand on his arm she relented. 'But I *will* keep an eye out. I'm not a fool you know?'

'That's just it, Mum. You've *got* to change your routines. Just juggle them around a bit. Don't do everything exactly like you always do. The person who sent that phone to me, he or she knows where I live… so, by extension they may well know where you live. I want you to be safe.'

She flapped her hands at him. 'Och, Angus, let's stop all this depressing talk. I'm more interested in hearing about Alice. Your dad says she's back. I'm so pleased. He says she's a bit skinny. But then Alice, bless her, was never on the heavy side, was she? You'll have to bring her for lunch on Sunday.' She rubbed her hands together. 'We'll get her fattened up, no bother. Oh, and tell Patti, I've got a new recipe I'm going to try.'

Gus grunted a non-committal reply and got into his car. The last thing he'd be doing would be coming to Sunday lunch for a while. At least not until he'd processed the bombshell Katie and Gabriella had dropped. Nor, did it seem at all likely that he'd be bringing Patti round for lunch either. Not if her complete silence in response to his calls and texts was anything to go by. At the back of his mind he could hear Alice's mocking tone telling him to make a point of going to see his girlfriend… to 'get it sorted, Gus.' He suspected the word 'wuss' would pass her lips, along with a few other choice phrases. How the hell had he got himself into this mess?

By the time Gus got back to The Fort, the phone had been confirmed as belonging to Betsy and, as expected, the only discernible fingerprints belonged to her too. Compo by-passing the fingerprint access, had hooked it up to his system and was downloading as much information from it as he could. At the same time, on the interactive screen, he was zooming in and out, replaying the CCTV footage of the drone from two different camera angles.

Preparing to be baffled by most of Compo's answer, Gus asked anyway, 'What can you tell us about the drone?'

Compo shoved a half-eaten Mars Bar next to his keyboard, seemingly oblivious of the toffee, dribbling down onto the surface and grunted, 'Not a lot yet. It looks like a bog-standard do-it-yourself drone you can buy off *Amazon* or *eBay* or a Robot shop. However, it's been adapted.' He zoomed in until the drone seemed to hang in mid-air in Gus' garden. Up close it looked like an alien spaceship taken directly from *Star Wars*, with its multiple legs, acute angles and glossy metallic body.

'In what way?'

'Well…' Compo looked ready to go into techie mode, so Gus interrupted.

'Simple, yeah… keep it simple.'

The enthusiasm on Compo's round face faded a little. With an exaggerated sigh, that said clearer than any words, 'bloody simpletons', he homed in even closer to the image of the drone just before it dropped Betsy's phone in Gus' garden. A claw that looked remarkably like the ones at the 'grab a toy' machines at the seaside amusement arcades, held the rectangular item. 'It's like the ones Amazon uses to drop off parcels, but it's been adapted so that it can hold a smaller package safely… like the phone, without any packaging or owt. Also.' He pointed to the screen. 'If you look closely, you can see the camera here. Whoever is controlling the drone is able to view exactly what's in your garden in real time. The camera will transmit the recording to a phone or tablet. That way they can choose exactly where they'll drop their package.'

Whirling his chair over to another keyboard, Compo pressed some more keys. 'I've chopped the footage up a bit and slowed it down. You can see here that the drone hovers over the decking for a couple of seconds, then veers over to the grass, then... look...'

Compo elbowed Gus' arm and pointed, as if Gus could miss it, considering the size of the damn screen.

'It swoops closer as if considering exactly where to drop it. It's hovering again, now, look. Right above Bingo's poo poo...'

Poo poo? For fuck's sake.

'...and then, as if the controller reconsiders, it edges to the right just a touch. This joker chose precisely where he wanted to drop that phone and we should be thankful it chose there, next to it, not actually right on top of the p...'

'Yeah, the poo poo. I get it.' Despite the overpowering heat in the room, a shiver rattled up Gus' spine. This was creepy as hell... creepier even than the damn letters. The drone itself, like a miniature spacecraft was chilling enough, but the realisation of just how easily they could be used to infringe on a person's privacy made it ten times worse.

'But...' Compo wasn't finished. 'Look at this...'

As Gus watched, the drone, after making its drop, circled round, swooping and diving like an aerial dance routine, before hovering right in front of one of the two security cameras covering the back garden, before swiftly redirecting over to the other camera. It flew right up to it, as close as it could get. Gus could almost believe the drone winked at him. Whoever was controlling it was taunting him.

Gus exhaled, then turned to look at his team. Alice, Taffy, and Sebastian Carlton had all watched the sloweddown action and now each sported a slightly stunned expression.

'There's no way in hell you can convince me that the murders and…' Gus waved his hands at the now still image on the screen, 'that aren't connected to my anonymous letters.' As he uttered the words, Gus wanted nothing more than for one of the team to form a coherent argument against his hypothesis.

No one uttered a word.

Carlton nodded twice, his lips in a tight line, telling Gus that the psychologist shared Gus' own belief that the *Snapchat* Murders, as the press had dubbed them, and Gus' stalker were linked. Taffy, Alice, and Compo all exhaled at the same time like a synchronised swimming team, their eyes still fixed on the drone.

Biting the inside of his lip, Gus tried to control the surge of anger that made his head pound. If he'd acted more quickly on those letters, made identifying the sender a priority, then perhaps two kids would still be alive, sitting their GCSEs, smoking weed, and exploring relationships… just being kids.

This had just got very personal.

CHAPTER 56

Pisces

D idn't really want her dead… not really. Just hated her, but that doesn't mean she had to die, does it? She was a bitch though… a real bitch. Got all the other kids chanting, 'Smelly! Smelly! Smelly!' on the bus to school. Even the younger kids were doing it. All I wanted was to be left alone. Not our fault we have no money, is it? Not our fault the house is damp, and the landlord won't sort it. And our old washing machine is broken more often than not. Fucking damp makes my clothes smell. If she'd just let me be, none of this would've happened.

They kept telling me to do it: *Leo did it, now it's your turn.* And just like that, I'm caught. No escape.

Wonder what Zodiac's done with her phone? Can't get caught with that. But Zodiac's too smart to get caught. I almost want to get caught. That's why I'm down here at the park again. Half waiting for somebody to shout *Stop! You did it*!

I'd hold my hands up. Let them cuff me, take me away, lock me up… maybe then I'd be able to sleep. Be able to rest. I don't want to do it again. Can't bear it. Can't bear seeing all the posts on *Facebook*.

CHAPTER 57

I didn't know Betsy Reavley very well... not really... but I didn't like her. She could be a bully, so I don't know why I'm making Jo Jo come down here to Lister Park with me. It just seemed the right thing to do. Two people out of our year group are dead and we've got plans to make. Know he thinks we should stop while we're ahead, but I'm not done yet... not by a long shot. Where the hell is he? He must have dropped Jessie off by now. Wish he'd hurry up.

I push my foot against the ground and my swing moves back and forth. The movement doesn't even make a breeze and I can't be arsed. Too hot! The park's nearly empty. Partly because it's a weekday and partly because the crime scene tape around the top part of the park must be off-putting. There are a few mothers with their kids toddling around, some with pushchairs, some gripping plastic bags containing bread to feed he ducks. Don't they know that could kill them? It's not heaving like it is on a weekend, though. The traffic's died down a bit on the main road. Rush hour's over. I could go back to the house. It'll be empty. Mo and Mum at work, the kids at school, but it's nice to be outside.

'Hi, Zarqa.'

I glance up scowling. It's Claire and my heart sinks down to my boots. Can't I have a little personal space? I don't want to talk to anybody except Jo Jo, but then when I see how pale she looks, I relent. No point in being a bitch for the sake of it, besides, I think she was friends with Betsy. Maybe she'll know what's going on. 'Hi. You okay?''

She sits on the swing next to me, her hands tight round the chains like she thinks she might fall off as she rocks herself to and fro. She looks distraught, poor cow. Must be hard for her. There's a sheen all over her face and I'm not sure if it's sweat or oil. I'm just about to ask her if she's heard owt when Mehmoona Bashir saunters over.

Mehmoona's funny. I don't know her very well, but she cracks me up. She doesn't say much but when she does, it's usually sarcastic and to the point. She leans against the metal pole, her phone in her hand, scrolling through *Facebook* no doubt.

'Do you know there are one hundred and fifty-two messages on Betsy Reavley's timeline?' She angles her head to the side and pushes her sun specs onto her head. Her dip-dyed hair's got a nicer colour than mine and I consider asking her where she got it done, but it's too much effort.

Claire's stopped swinging now. From the corner of my eye, I notice she's staring up the park to where the crime scene tape is spread around the trees. I glance at Mehmoona and shrug. She nods and moves in front of Claire, blocking her view. 'You left a message yet, Claire? She's a friend of yours, isn't she?'

Claire flinches like Mehmoona's asked her to soak her face in acid and shakes her head. When she speaks, her voice trembles, 'No. wouldn't know what to say.'

And on the last word her voice sort of hitches and I think she's gonna burst into tears. Fuck's sake Jo Jo. If you'd just be on time, I wouldn't have to deal with this shit. 'Tell you what, we could help you. Me and Mehmoona. We could help you write something.'

Biting her lip, Claire shakes her head. 'No, no… I'll just leave it.'

But Mehmoona's having none of it. 'Get your phone out, girl. You'll feel better after you've left a message. I know I did.'

Claire looks at Mehmoona. 'You left one?'

Mehmoona shrugs. 'Course.' She turns to me, 'You did too, didn't you, Zarqa?'

'Eh, well, actually no. I didn't. Didn't know what to say.' Not into that sort of stuff. It's all a load of bullshit.

Hands on hip, Mehmoona looks at each of us in turn. 'Phones out, girls.' Her tone leaves no room for dissent, so rather than have to summon up an argument, I take my phone out and Claire does too.

'Right, all you need to do is say RIP or Miss you or Taken too soon or some such shit. Whap on a couple of emojis and you've done your bit. It'll help her family feel better.'

Claire gulps and a tear rolls down her cheek. 'Don't think an emoji's going do that, Mehmoona.'

I can't help thinking she's probably right, but still… better to do something than do nothing. I scroll through *Facebook* until I find Betsy's timeline.

> RIP Betsy, love Zarqa :(

'There done.'

As Claire writes hers, I scroll down the few that are there.

> Another angel in heaven. The stars will shine brighter, love Mehmoona

Bit poetic.

> Gone but not forgotten, love Ben xxx
>
> Will miss you, Jo Jo xx

Ping!

> I'm sorry you're gone, Claire :(

I look at her. 'There. That wasn't so hard was it?'

She shakes her head, but it's like she's been tortured and all I want to do is to get away from her misery. Jo Jo jumps the fence at the side. He's clearly climbed the wall from the main road and run up to the park.

'You all right?' His greeting takes in all of us and I notice Mehmoona straightening up, sticking her tits out. Almost makes me laugh. Likes she's got a chance. Then, I notice Razor and Goyley entering the enclosed park area through the small swing gate. Bloody hate those two. Why the fuck have they shown up? Thought I'd seen the back of them when they got expelled from school. They shouldn't be in Manningham – that's a riot just waiting to happen. Goyley throws himself down on the green ground covering.

'Heard the bitch was stabbed… blood everywhere…'

Jo Jo opens his mouth to say something, but I jump in first. They're less likely to be violent to me… dicks yeah… actually violent…? probably not. 'Show a bit of respect, eh? We don't know who's gonna be next.' As if in an afterthought, I smile my sweetest smile and bat my eyelashes. 'Would be a shame if it were you, though, wouldn't it?'

'Ooooooooh!' Razor says wiggling his fingers like a tosser in front of my face. 'The paki's threatening you, Goyle. You scared?'

Goyley jumps to his feet, pulls a knife from his back pocket, and gets in my face. The knife right at my throat. *Shit! That escalated quick*! I feel the point dig into my neck and instead of backing off like I know I should, I jut my chin out and say, 'Piss off, tosser!'

Next to me I hear Jo Jo's near silent groan and then Mehmoona's speaking. 'Smile, Goyle.' She's got her phone up taking a photo. 'Might just send this to my mum if you don't piss off. You do know she's a copper, don't you?'

Just to add to the circus, I hear barking from behind me and someone else is speaking. 'Fucking drop the knife, Goyley, or I'll set the dog on you.'

And for the first time in… forever… I'm happy to hear Karim's voice. The dog's straining at its lead now and snarling right at Goyley's legs. For long seconds, the knife nips my skin. Then Razor does a slow hand clap. 'Come on, Goyle. We'll split.'

He turns to Mehmoona. 'Delete it, sweetheart, or I'll find out where you live… you get me?'

Smiling widely, Mehmoona inclines her head to Goyle. 'I'm waiting.'

When Goyle steps back and pockets his knife, she holds her phone out so Razor can see the image of Goyle looking right at her, his knife pressing into my neck. Razor nods and she presses delete. 'All gone.'

Razor studies her for a long moment. 'I see you,' he says and raises two fingers to his eyes and then swipes them towards Mehmoona. 'You're on my radar, bitch.'

Shoving his hands in his jean's pocket, Razor turns to Karim, who juts his chin out in a fair imitation of a 'fuck you' stance. 'You better watch out, paki boy. You won't always have your dog with you.'

And he backs off, retracing his steps out of the kiddies' playground and towards the boating lake, Goyley following.

In silence, we watch them go. My throat's dry as owt. I swallow and accept the bottle of water Karim offers me. 'Thanks. For the water and… well.' I gesture towards the two retreating figures. And he nods.

Claire's shaking, like it was her who was on the receiving end of Goyley's charm. Silly cow looks like she's gonna puke. Mehmoona's face is unreadable and Jo Jo's avoids looking at anyone.

Karim's the first to speak. 'D'ya think they did it? D'ya think they killed Betsy and Pratab?'

'They got knives… I'd say it's worth mentioning to the police,' I say returning Karim's water bottle to him. 'You could tell your mum, Mehmoona.'

'Sure. I'll do that. Got to share any information we have. Don't know which of us will be next, do we?'

With that sobering thought hanging between us, she turns to Claire. 'Come on, girl. I'll walk you home.'

Claire shakes her head, but we can all tell it's half-hearted. As they leave, I turn to the boys. 'So, anything exciting going down?'

CHAPTER 58

Sebastian Carlton had taken over the back wall of the incident room. He'd had Gus' anonymous letters enlarged and, willfully ignoring the large printed sign saying,

Our newly painted walls

thank you for not using Blutak!

he had stuck them up in chronological order across the paintwork.

He'd also had printed copies of the images taken of Gus and Patti as well as the uploaded ones of both victims. Gus groaned. He'd get it in the neck if Bashir caught sight of that, but deep down he really couldn't care less. He'd told her they needed an extra board across the back wall, but she'd insisted that Compo's new-fangled interactive swipe board would suffice. Gus had argued his corner, but she'd been stubbornly insistent. Like Carlton, Gus liked to see things spread out. He liked to see as much of the information around him on walls, so he could dip in and out. It was the way he worked. He didn't compartmentalise into handy little folders. He liked to see the whole picture.

It was strange seeing the anonymous letters all in a line like that. Usually the stuff they pinned on the walls were details about a victim or suspect, not anything personal to him or his team. In isolation he'd been able to downplay the seriousness of them. Now, all together like this, even he could see how sinister they were. There were six in total. Carlton had scribbled on multicoloured Post-it pads and dotted his observations and thoughts around the letters and now he had reclined his chair as far back as it would go, positioned another chair in front to elevate his legs and was studying his collage with his hands clasped around his middle and a half-eaten doughnut balanced on top of his belly. No wonder Carlton and Compo got on so well!

A pulse throbbed in Gus' right temple reminding him of how charged he was. Every time he touched something, he expected it to burst into flames or, at the very least, give him an electric shock. He was desperate for action... yet there was little he could do right now. Two dead kids, a few anonymous letters, and no damn witnesses. The investigation was stalling. It was as if the heat was suffocating every clue he had. They could find no unusual links between Betsy and Pratab. And neither could they link the victims to Gus himself. The only common denominator was City Academy. Gus and Patti were both closely linked to it, and Betsy and Pratab had both attended the school... as did upwards of a thousand other kids and over a hundred staff. He was impatient for a breakthrough, and with City Academy the only link, Gus had set Taffy and Compo the task of trawling through Gus' past cases.

Two recent cases had involved him with City Academy. The first was when a serial killing tattooist had targeted a parent from the school and the second was more recent when a house party had gone wrong resulting in the deaths of two children and with the perpetrator having links to the school. More recently, since he and Patti had begun their relationship, Gus had supported Patti through the suicide of one of her students and the arrest and imprisonment of a staff member for grooming one of the students. These may well be unrelated incidents, but Gus wanted Compo to use his skills to scratch beneath the surface on this one.

Gus moved closer and studied the display. Each letter had used the same form of address: *My Dearest Detective Inspector Angus McGuire*. Carlton had commented on this in his sloppy handwriting with a series of questions circling the greeting on a variety of neon sheets:

Deliberately formal?

Contrived?

Use of language?

My dearest – from a book/Internet?

Use of 'Angus'?

Use of full title? – Knowledge of Gus as DI?

He'd commented on the use of the perfume Obsession to scent the letters.

Adult fragrance?

Significance of fragrance name?

Each letter had been signed off in exactly the same way:

Watch this space!

Around these Carlton had repeated the process with the Post-its: Language – youthful? Implied threat? Warning? Link to Snapchat – usually a teen app? – distraction or clue?

Gus thought it was clear that the last two observations were pretty near the mark. Especially when combined with phrases like:

> 'Your girlfriend's pretty... very pretty!'

> '...and your dog's so sweet. Soooo tiny! I could squeeze and squeeze and squeeze him.'

> 'You must tell Patti that I love that blue dress...'

> 'Do you and Patti use social media much?'

Carlton lifted the doughnut off his wobbling belly and took a bite. Gus took it as a sign that the profiler was ready to impart some insight into the mind of the anonymous letter writer. 'What you got, Prof?'

'Well, you've certainly piqued someone's interest, Gus. The question is whose.'

Give me strength. Gus struggled for calm rather than the 'for fuck's sake you've been staring at these for ages and that's all you can come up with?' Finally, he managed a nod. 'You're not wrong there.'

Carlton pushed his specs back up his nose and swung his feet off the chair sending a flurry of chocolate sprinkles from his doughnut onto the floor. Inconsequentially, Gus noticed that the Barbie plaster around the profiler's specs was unravelling and had left a sticky black mark across the bridge of his nose. Carlton stood up and began pacing in front of the letters. Realising he'd just have to bide his time, Gus pulled a chair up, sat down, and waited. Carlton, as usual, would speak when he was ready.

'I don't need to tell you there's been a bit of an escalation…'

Gus bit the inside of his lip. *A bit of an escalation*? Two dead kids, threatening letters, dumping the victim's phone in his garden and a stalker was 'a bit of an escalation?' No, you got that right. You don't need to tell me that. Trying to bite back the cutting response, Gus folded his arms across his chest and with an effort stopped his foot from tapping impatiently on the floor.

Carlton, hands linked behind his back, rocked back and forth on his heels and studied his display. 'The language is contrived. It's a disguise of sorts, an attempt to deflect our understanding of who the writer is. However, some of the vocabulary that's slipped through makes me think, we're talking about a relatively young person. The *watch this space*, the *loved-up couple, all that*… Say under twenty-five?

'Of course, I'm combining that with the assumption which I think is sound, that the use of drone technology overlapping the teen murders and your being stalked points to a very definite link. If we take the drone technology. Compo tells me that these drones appear to have been 'build it yourself' sets, easily bought via the Internet, that have been adapted. He says a lot of skill would be needed for that. He's already checking supply sites to see if we can find the supplier. Long shot and time consuming, in my opinion, but there can't be that many drone experts in Bradford. However, with the Internet, they could have bought their parts from almost anywhere. If anyone can find this information, Compo's your man.'

'Although I agree with you that my stalker and these deaths must be linked, I'm going to need more than that. You got anything else? Surely anyone of any age could learn how to do the drone technology stuff?'

'Yes, of course, you're perfectly right. But it is a combination of things. The fact that the victims are teens themselves, the use of *Snapchat* to taunt their friends, the ease with which they uploaded the images of you and your delightful girlfriend to social media, but…' He turned and looked at Gus. 'Perhaps the most telling indicator is the fact that you, an observant and skilled police officer, have been observed for months and yet you've not noticed anything. That tells me your stalker was someone you didn't view as a threat… a kid, a woman, someone you're used to seeing hanging around.'

Gus thought back over the past few weeks. Had he seen anyone hanging around? He couldn't say. Carlton was right, he hadn't paid a lot of attention to people he didn't perceive as possible threats. The only people he'd seen regularly hanging around were Jerry and Dave and they could be discounted – neither the money, the ability, or the know how to devise something as complicated as this. Carlton was still speaking.

'Another thing points towards the perp being younger… the fact that the two victims attend the same school and also the fact that the murder scenes are quite close together and took place quite late in the evening. Kids sneak out of their houses all the time, but they're more likely to stay close to their homes when they do. Less chance of being noticed wandering around the city. Also, they showed a familiarity with the CCTV coverage.'

'So, you think, they're definitely linked, my stalker and the dead kids.' Gus' heart contracted. No matter how much logic told him that it was the killer that was responsible for Pratab's and Betsy's deaths, he couldn't dodge the guilt that landed squarely on his shoulders. If he'd taken the anonymous letters more seriously earlier on, he might have been able to prevent two kids' deaths.

Whipping his spectacles off his nose and sticking one leg in his mouth, Carlton frowned. 'Yes. They're linked...' He made a strange sucking sound as he chewed the spectacle leg. '... but you can't forget the forensic evidence and that's what makes this case so fascinating.' He turned and looked at Gus, his eyes shining as he did the strange rocking motion he did when excited. 'There's more than one killer, Gus. We're looking for a team.'

Gus let the words sink in. He'd been well aware that the forensics pointed to two killers. He just hadn't expected them to be teens. It made him feel queasy. What could prompt two kids to work together to kill another youngster? A thought struck him.

'You think they're both teens?'

Carlton grinned. 'That's what makes it so fascinating. I just don't know. We haven't enough victims to make any sort of real decision on that. The dynamics of the duo, to date are unconfirmed. I'll keep working on it.'

Gus wanted to shake him. This wasn't an academic question. This was real. Real people with families and friends now bereaved.

'It could be that the teen is working with an adult and doing all the social media, technical stuff at the behest of a grown up. That doesn't sit comfortably with me. There seems too much evidence indicating a youthful mind. However, their keen attention to forensics points to a very savvy person, whether a teen or not. So… the big question is… which teen have you pissed off big time? Preferably one with other stuff going on that could act as a catalyst… get your thinking cap on.'

Gus' stomach lurched. He hated the places his thoughts were heading. 'I'll send some officers over to City Academy to re-interview students and staff with this profile in mind.'

CHAPTER 59

Zodiac

This afternoon's pyjama time. Lounging about, scoffing what I like, drinking voddy, watching *YouTube* videos, and planning. That's the best thing about having exams… the study time. That's one of the reasons I chose this part of the term for my adventure. It gives me the time to do all the – what I call, finishing touches, without anyone catching me. Everything has been so exciting. Last night was the best… don't know if we'll be able to top it, the excitement, the adrenalin.

The others let me down a bit. Pisces in particular… talk about being a baby about stuff. You'd think we hadn't talked about it all… planned it. Never mind, they both came around in the end. How could they not? The important thing now though is to keep the pressure on; keep them on side.

The press conference earlier was brilliant. That stupid DCI Chalmers all pouting and flirting at the cameras, full of her own self-importance. Thinking she was all that. But the best bit was McGuire standing just behind her. He'd ditched the bandana and his cargo shorts and T-shirt in favour of a shirt and tie. Boy, did he look hot… and I don't mean in a sexy way… Boom! Boom!

He's well pissed off, I can tell. The way he scowled the whole time, glaring at the journalists when they asked questions.

'DI McGuire, do you think there is a link between The *Snapchat Killer* and the intimate images of you and head teacher Patti Copley leaked through various social media channels?'

'Is the *Snapchat Killer* calling all the shots right now?'

'Is it fair to say that the police investigation into these teen killings has been less than effective?'

'What measures are Bradford police taking to ensure the swift arrest of The *Snapchat Killer*?'

With every question his face got more and more sour. Poor old Gussy boy. You could almost feel sorry for him. Bet he can't wait to get his hands on me. Trouble is he'll be waiting a long time, for I've no intention of getting caught. By the end of the summer, it'll all be over. I've got it planned down to a T.

The one sure thing about my plan is that McGuire will start to relax, start to ease up... he'll get careless with his security... think it's all wrapped up and then BAM! My last act will wipe him out... wipe him out completely.

But for now, I click a few keys and send my baby off into the ether. Leaning back, I spin the computer chair round for a bit, then tip some more voddy into my glass. Who says you can't drink in the afternoon? My burner phone buzzes and, frowning, I retrieve it from where I've stuck it under my desk. Should have had it on vibrate. Last thing I need is anyone else hearing it... good thing I'm home alone again. It's Pisces. Fuck's sake! That name's so apt. Wet as a bloody fish, that one.

'Yep?'

'I'm scared. I feel sick. Can't believe we did that. It's wrong. Can't do it again.'

Irritation seeps from my pores. Can't be doing with this stupid self-pitying carry-on. Why does Pisces have to be such a dumbass? What's done is done. Deliberately, I hold the phone close to my mouth and exaggerate my breathing... just a little. Just enough to show I'm pissed off. I take my time to respond. I want to smash the phone down on my desk. What the fuck? Phoning me up, bursting my bubble… spoiling things for me. 'You're. Being. A. Dick.'

I can hear Pisces' breath catching and I hate that wobbling whingy voice. and I want to smash the phone into Pisces' stupid face. I'll make sure the idiot will suffer for this. I take another swig of my drink as I listen to the stuttered words over the line. 'I can't do this again. It's not right. Didn't think we were going to…'

I cut the words off right there. 'RUBBISH! You knew *exactly* what we were doing. YOU agreed. You and Leo both agreed. You were all full of swag… well up for it. It's too late to back down now. You need to keep your shit together. Got it?'

The sniffling on the other end of the phone irritates the hell out of me, but I know I have to change tack. 'Look, everything's all good. We're doing the right thing. We're in this together. The Zodiac Club. The *Snapchat Killer*s. Besides, last thing you want is any little secrets getting out, isn't it? You've got a lot to lose if those get out… won't just affect you either, will it? It'll affect your family too. Look we'll meet up later. The three of us. You'll feel better then.'

'I saw them on the news. They say they're closing in on us. It were that copper. The one who's shagging Ms Copley.'

I laugh out loud, genuinely amused at such naivety. 'Idiot,' I say, my tone full of indulgence. 'They've got nothing – not a fucking thing on us if we all just stick to the plan.'

My computer screen flickers in front of me and then, there it is, on the screen. Large as life. The product of our hard work. *Twitter* and *Facebook* and *Instagram* – all through the Dark Web. 'Check *Facebook*, Pisces. We're famous again.' And I hang up.

Somehow, the thought of McGuire's team scurrying about trying to get it taken down amuses me. As I watch, I see the shares and retweets escalate. Everyone likes a bit of drama and… grinning, my hand drifts down to my crotch.

CHAPTER 60

Gus was walking through the Smith Lane entrance to Bradford Royal Infirmary on his way to visit Jerry and Dave, when Compo rang. The recent renovations were a vast improvement to the hospital environment with a food court, shops creating a nice vibe for out-patients and visitors. The only downside was the abysmal lack of parking in the vicinity. Aware of the parking difficulties, Gus had parked on Toller Lane and jogged down rather than spend ages driving round looking for a spot closer.

The fact that he'd been expecting the photo of Betsy Reavley to be posted to the Internet, didn't make it any more palatable. There was nothing he could do about it other than curse, which he did, rather more loudly than he'd intended, causing a few visitors to scowl in his direction. He'd probably just confirmed any racial stereotypes they already held. Raising a hand and shrugging in apology, Gus moved swiftly on. No point in dwelling on it. His team were on the case and they'd get the offending images down as quickly as they could. Still, Gus trusted that Ms Reavley's FLO had managed to keep her away from the Internet. When he'd seen the woman briefly that morning, she'd looked ready to slump into a heap and just give up. Her mother had been with her smelling heavily of smoke and BO and blaming the police in strident tones at every opportunity. The FLO was in the process of trying to convince the mother to go and leave her daughter in the more capable hands of two neighbours who'd turned up with a bagful of groceries and a pragmatic attitude. Gus hoped she'd succeeded.

According to the officer who had accompanied the two old men after Jerry had fallen, the hospital had taken the opportunity to do a barrage of tests, which had thrown up various inconsistencies and they were keeping him in for now. The officer had been pro-active and arranged for temporary space at a hostel for Dave and had deposited the old man there earlier on and picked him up to bring him back to see his friend a short time ago. Gus made a mental note to get the officer a commendation. This was the sort of community policing they should be praising, and he'd make sure the officer got credit for it.

Gus walked into the small side room where he'd been told Jerry was and nearly turned and walked out again. Jerry wasn't there. But a, 'Hey, Gus, nice of you to drop in,' had him spinning round and looking at the man lying in the bed in an incongruous floral hospital gown. Gone were the layers of dirt that had been ingrained in Jerry's wrinkled face and instead of the mop of matted hair Gus had grown used to, his hair was cut and shampooed and now sat tamed on his head. Next to him sat Dave, looking much the same as he had earlier. He had a newspaper open at the crossword page and leaning on Jerry's table, he was filling it in with a biro. His only acknowledgement of Gus' presence was a distracted grunt.

'You're looking well, Jerry. They looking after you?' Gus' smile was genuine. The old boy had had a shock. Almost immediately Gus rethought his words. 'Old boy' was definitely not an appropriate description. Looking at Jerry, all spruced up, with his beard shaved off, he could tell the man was much younger than he'd previously thought, mid-forties, perhaps.

'Can't complain, can't complain. Though they say I've got to stay in today. Dave's okay with that. He's going to stay at the hostel until I'm up and about again.' Jerry's eyes had lost some of the spark they'd held earlier. 'That poor lass. Dave says she's definitely a gonner.'

'Yes, I'm afraid so, Jerry. That's why I'm here. I need you and Dave to tell me about how you found her.'

Jerry's fingers kneaded his sheets and he glanced at Dave, who'd folded the newspaper and placed the pen on top. It was strange to see the role reversal with Dave being the protective one for a change. But Gus suspected it would do Dave good to realise he could be strong for his friend.

'It's okay, Jerry. We've done nowt wrong. Gus just needs to know, that's all. So he can find the bugger that done this.'

Gus nearly smiled. A few months ago, Dave would have been the uneasy one. Clearly his meds were working for him and Gus was glad. It was hard to be homeless without having to cope with untreated mental health problems too. He filled a glass of water and placed it on the cupboard close to Jerry. 'Here, have a drink. Don't be getting all flustered. It's just routine.'

'Aye, I know that, Gus. It's just I got me a bit of a shock when I saw that lass lying there. I got a daughter that age meself and that just threw me.' He sighed and lifted the glass as Dave patted his leg.

For a second Gus wondered if he was going to cry. He wondered about the circumstances that had made Jerry homeless but wasn't sure if he had the right to ask him. 'How old is your daughter?'

Focussing on something just over Gus' shoulder, Jerry held onto the glass with both hands. A play of emotions drifted over his face, making Gus wish he'd not asked, then Jerry began to speak in a quiet voice, a slight smile on his lips. 'She'll be sixteen will Gemma... Gemmy we used to call her, because she was our gem... our precious stone. The most wonderful thing in the world...'

The pause lasted so long, Gus wondered if Jerry had finished and was about to speak when the older man continued. 'Down's Syndrome... she has Down's Syndrome, but it never mattered a whit to me and Natalie, not one whit. She was the light of our lives. But when Natalie died... the big C, I fell to pieces. Lost my job, couldn't keep up with payments, couldn't keep up with... life.' He looked right at Gus, tears filling his eyes. 'That's it. I couldn't keep up with life... not even for Gemma.'

Gus tried to swallow the lump that was in his own throat, but couldn't dislodge it, so he nodded, hoping that his inadequate response hadn't come across as uncaring or judgemental. Jerry was in a fragile way and Gus didn't want to distress him any more than was necessary. It seemed the man had suffered enough anguish in his life already.

Dave plucked a tissue from the bedside cabinet and handed it to his friend. 'They took Gemma away from Jerry. Said he wasn't looking after her properly.'

Jerry blew his nose before responding, 'And they were right, Dave. I wasn't looking after her. My Gemmy deserved more than I had to give. She deserved me there full-time. She deserved a dad... not an empty vessel.'

'Yes, you're right, she did... but they should've looked after you too. Helped you get better. Helped you get over your grief.'

Jerry's smile was sad. 'Aye, maybe you're right, but that's water under the bridge. She'll have forgotten me now. She'll be a young woman.' He turned to me. 'I saw her once, at her school. She must have been ten. She came running out into the playground, her hair was in pigtails... flying out behind her, she ran, and this man crouched down, arms opened right wide and she screamed with laughter and launched herself right into them. He whipped her off the ground and spun her round. Gave her a big kiss on the top of her head and then passed her to the woman standing beside him. They were all smiles. The three of them walked out of the playground, with them swinging her between their arms, just like Natalie and I used to do. As she passed, I heard her say, "Mummy, Daddy, guess what I painted in school today?"'

Tears streamed down his face and yet he was smiling. 'Gemma, my precious Gemma had a new family and she was happy. That's enough for me.'

His last words about family reminded Gus of Mo's words about genetics not making a parent and Katie's face as she looked at him so pleadingly. Why did things have to be so damn complicated?

But Dave was speaking. 'Gus needs to know about the girl last night, Jerry. You tell him.' And he settled back into his chair and folded his arms across his chest.

Gus nodded and smiled and, his tone conversational, asked, 'How did you come across her?'

Jerry glanced at Dave before speaking. 'We were looking for somewhere to bed down for the night. We like the Botanical Gardens. Always a nice breeze there and the birds come in the morning, it's nice and comfy. But soon as we got near, we could see her lying there. Dave went over, but he said she were dead, and I just lost it a bit. I went a bit faint. The moonlight played a trick on my mind and I thought for a moment it was Gem. We didn't touch owt. I fell over and cracked me head.' He touched his forehead which had a couple of stitches in. 'We just stayed where you found us and phoned you.'

'Did you see anyone else in the park? Hear anything?'

'Well, we'd only just got to there. We'd been up in the Heaton Allotments. Had a bit of a picnic there and waited until it got quieter outside in the village. Sometimes, there're lads that'll hassle us. So, we'd only just got to the park five minutes before we found the poor lassie.'

'So, you never saw anyone?'

'Oh, yes we did. Some youngsters ran past us laughing and jeering they were. They jumped over the wall into North Park Road. Too far away for us to see them properly, mind. But they were just kids. Wouldn't have been them that done this... they were only kids.'

CHAPTER 61

'So, you going to tell me?' Alice perched herself on the edge of Gus's desk. He'd been aware of her casting glances in his direction for the past half hour. The room had quietened off a bit. Compo was in his own little world with his headphones on, Taffy was at the post mortem with one of the uniformed officers, and Carlton had decided to go for a walk. After his earlier chat with the profiler, Gus had come away feeling unsettled and he didn't like where his thoughts were going. Carlton had asked him if he knew any teens with a lot going on that could act as a catalyst and although, he'd shrugged it off, he couldn't rest easy. After Jerry and Dave's statements saying they witnessed a group of teens in the vicinity of Betsy Reavley's murder, he'd sent the police artist to see if they could tease out a more detailed likeness. Unfortunately, their descriptions had been too generic, leaving Gus frustrated that, once again, they'd missed out on a lead. They hadn't even been able to agree on how many kids they'd seen.

Now Alice was staring at him, her head to one side, her black T-shirt just a little too big, falling off her shoulder, revealing a clavicle that protruded more than it should. Despite her obvious improvements, it made him all too aware that his DS wasn't completely back to full health. He rolled his shoulders, trying to get rid of the persistent tension that had settled in his upper body. 'Tell you what?'

She pulled up a chair in front of his desk and rested her elbows on it, propping up her chin and looking just like a little elf with her short black hair and pointed chin. Gus settled back, knowing that whatever Alice wanted to discuss with him was going to be discussed... she had that stubborn look in her eye and, to be honest, Gus was glad she was up to pinning him down, although he wished it was about something a little less sensitive.

'Why you immediately thought that dead girl would be Zarqa?'

Ah! He should've known better than to think that momentary panic of his, when Dave had told him about the dead body in the park, had escaped Alice. But how to answer? Since his chat with Carlton, things had become even more complicated. From terror at the thought of Mo's eldest daughter as a victim, to worry that she might be the killer, he was going round in circles and he didn't know how much to share with Alice.

Hell, he didn't know what he thought himself. Could the trauma of finding out, not only that Mo wasn't her biological dad, but that Mo had actually killed her real dad be a trigger for Zarqa to commit murder? Gus just didn't know. Did he tell Alice about Zarqa being out and about the night Pratab was killed? About her running away from the vicinity of the crime scene? Did he tell her about the girl's increasingly troublesome behaviour? About the way she was with her dad? About the guilt he'd seen in her eyes when he questioned her at school?

What was he thinking? This was Zarqa. He was her godfather. The person who was supposed to have her back... guide her through life... help her be the best version of herself she could be... and still that little worm of uncertainty ate through his heart like it was a rotten apple.

Alice frowned. 'Gus? What are you not telling me?'

Gus studied his friend for a moment. Her eyes were troubled, and he knew it was because she thought he was holding out on her. It wasn't that he didn't trust her. He trusted her with his life. It was quite simply that he was concerned this would knock her off kilter. And, if he was being honest, the lingering guilt he harboured about doubting Alice's innocence when she was in prison, made him loathe to verbalise the possibility of Zarqa's guilt. Once it was out there, it couldn't be unsaid.

She raised her chin, her eyes sparking. 'Don't you dare patronise me with some shit like, 'oh it's nothing' or 'I was being a dick' – which of course you actually are being right now.'

Lifting his hands in mock surrender, Gus tutted. 'Okay, okay… but I'm going to need coffee.'

Scalding coffee in one hand and a cereal bar in the other, Gus wished he'd ordered a pizza earlier when Compo had headed down to Raja's. Truth was, he'd been too nauseous to eat and the mere thought of even his favourite keema achar pizza was too much. Now his stomach growled, causing Alice to head over to the mini fridge where she fiddled about readjusting the contents, before retrieving a bag of samosas she'd hidden earlier.

Minutes later, when the stale incident room smells had been replaced by spicy pastry smells, Gus was ready to fill Alice in.

When he'd finished, Alice exhaled. 'Fuck. I didn't realise I'd missed so much when I was gone. I thought I was the only one with shit happening. Selfish cow that I am.'

She played with the samosa crumbs on her plate and then raised her head and stared right at him. 'Look, the way I see it is this. You never once faltered in your belief in my innocence… so why would you falter in your belief in Zarqa? You need to keep the faith in her, just like you did in me.'

And there it was!

The guilt flooded Gus' body. He couldn't look at her, couldn't risk her seeing the truth in his eyes… that when she needed him most, he had failed her. Alice had the utmost faith in him yet, when she needed his unquestioning support, he'd wavered. He was a shit friend and, much to his undying shame, it had taken Compo to make him face it.

But Alice had moved on. 'You need to talk to her. You need to talk to her tomorrow and get this sorted out. She's a teenage girl. Course she's got secrets, just not the ones you think. Unsuitable boyfriend or girlfriend, hormones, anger, worry over failing her exams, grief, guilt... all sorts of crap.' She looked at Gus, her eyes all serious. 'There's no end to the shit teenagers put themselves through.' She bit into another samosa, then waving the remains in the air sending flakes of pastry flying over his desk, she added, 'Last thing she needs is you being an arse. Be her friend, Gus. Yeah?'

Still avoiding her gaze, he nodded. The thing was, he wasn't so sure Alice was right. She'd not seen first-hand the changes in Zarqa. The way she'd been unable to look at him. The guilt and anger and hate that flashed from her eyes when he challenged her at school. Alice was basing her belief on her knowledge of the girl she'd been last summer. This Zarqa was an entirely different ball game. This Zarqa was filled with turmoil... he was sure of it.

However, one thing was certain. Gus needed to confront her and that's what he'd do first thing in the morning, without Mo or Naila about to make things worse for all of them. Quelling the niggling worry that his delay might prove too late for some other poor kid, he threw his half-eaten samosa back on his plate and looked at the images of Pratab Patel and Betsy Reavley on the wall. No way could the Zarqa he knew, the one underneath the snarling, wounded girl she was now, be responsible for this... no way!

CHAPTER 62

Leo

I could lie here for hours with the fan drowning out all the chatter from downstairs. Can still hear the kids outside yelling and giggling, getting in my head. Feel like all I want to do is escape. Need something to take the edge of everything that's going on here. It's all crap. I'm dying for a smoke, but soon as I move everyone's on my case.

Clauuuus troooo effing phobiiic, or what?

He cornered me again earlier, going on and on and effing on about smoking and all sorts. Bell end! Like he's such a goodie two shoes.

Really pissed off with those two dirty old scumbags from last night. Scared us shitless for a minute, then we realised it was just the old mingers. Fuck! My heart hammered like shit. They fucked it up for us though. Spoilt it. I hardly got the chance to look… to savour it.

Should've knifed them too… that would've made everyone sit up and take note. Mind you, I can't afford to get messy again… not like the first time. They could have caught me all covered in blood. Only just got away with that. Good job they were too distracted. Zodiac was right though. It does get easier… so much easier.

Can't wait to see it. Hope it's up soon. Come on, Zodiac! Come on!

Ping!

At last!

> Zodiac: It's up… enjoy!
>
> Me: Brill! Laters!

I sit up, my hands are shaking as I scroll. Fucking yeah! There it is. Good old Zodiac!

Not as good as seeing it for real, but good all the same. Betsy fucking Reavley with a knife stuck in her stupid little neck... Sorted! I look at it for a long time, trying to remember the smell. That's one thing I didn't know before... how it would smell. The blood that is. The coppery, animal stink. Gets right up your nose.

I'm so engrossed in Zodiac's post that I nearly don't hear him at my bedroom door. He's got the door half open before I hear him. Fuck! I slip the phone under the duvet and glare at him. 'What do you want?'

He shrugs, his eyes all over the place, like he's checking for something. 'Nothing, just checking on you, that's all.'

He thinks I don't see him sniffing the air. Well bully for you, matey, you won't smell owt. I've swiped Mum's expensive perfume to cover-up the ciggie smell. I smile, pretending to be nice, but what I really want to do is stick a knife in his neck too. Still grinning like an idiot, I jump up off the bed. 'Come on. Let's go downstairs.'

CHAPTER 63

'Somebody's popular tonight.'

Gus had been on his way home when his desk phone rang. Cursing, he lifted the receiver to Hardeep's voice. 'What you on about, Hardeep? I'm knackered. If it's not urgent, put whoever it is off please.'

Hardeep was clearly in a playful mood. 'Well, I don't know if it's urgent or not, but the looks the two of them are flinging at each other tells me that if they don't get to see you pronto World War Three might erupt... and I'm not insured for that.'

'For God's sake! Who is it?'

'As I said, you're Mr Popular. Both your girlfriend and your ex-wife are demanding an audience with you.'

If the wall had been closer, Gus would have banged his head against it. He'd had a shitty day and now this. Patti and Gaby didn't get along at the best of times, but right now when he had bridges to build with Patti and a tunnel to dig to escape from Gaby, the last thing he wanted was the two of them in the same square footage.

'Well, what shall I tell them?' The humour in Hardeep's tone was inescapable.

'Stop fucking gloating. Send Patti up first and tell my ex-wife she'll have to wait.'

That seemed to be the best solution – keep them separate. Last thing he wanted was Gaby to realise there was any rancour between him and Patti. She was such a bitch she'd just stir things up even more than they already were. He'd been hoping to phone Patti from the comfort and quiet of his home when he got home, but she'd pre-empted that. As he waited for her to arrive, Gus wondered what she would say. Quite rightly she was angry about private moments being shared on the Internet, but equally, he was beginning to be a bit irked at her response. It wasn't his fault a stalker had targeted him, and it certainly wasn't his fault the images had been uploaded. He'd hoped giving her some space would make it easier for them to discuss it, so after trying to phone a couple of times, he'd left her alone. Now, he wondered what the purpose of her visit was. Was she going to give him the big heave ho? Many homicide detectives found it near impossible to hold down a relationship because of pressures from the job... but this had gone beyond that. Their private lives had been aired in the most public of forums and he wasn't sure Patti would be able to forget that.

He was aware that he'd got off lightly. His colleagues, after a few light-hearted and borderline sexist 'Jack the lad' type jibes which had resulted in Alice giving them a piece of her mind, had let it go. But God knows how Patti had fared. Her staff would probably have sympathised. He'd met most of them and it wasn't like she'd embarked on a *50 Shades of Grey* fling with a stranger. However, he could only hope that the governors and parents would realise that Patti was the victim in all of this. As for her pupils? Gus had an almost pathological fear of dealing with large groups of kids, so he couldn't begin to understand how Patti would cope. He could imagine their cruel snickers and sly looks... their pointed remarks. Hell, even Bashir's daughter had had a dig at him, hadn't she? On the one hand he was desperate to see Patti, to set things right. On the other he was petrified of what she would say. He didn't know if he'd cope with a repeat of the conversation he'd had with Sadia a couple of years ago when she dumped him.

A peremptory knock at the door signalled Patti's arrival. Gus got to his feet as she walked in, smiling tentatively.

Then, when he saw she was followed by Gaby, his smile morphed into a frown. Patti's mouth was in a stern line and there wasn't a single iota of warmth in her face as she strode over to him. His heart plummeted. What had the bitch said to Patti?

He looked over Patti's shoulder and addressed his ex-wife, not bothering to hide his anger. 'I told *you* to wait. I need to speak to Patti first.'

But before Gaby could respond, Patti spoke, her eyes flashing, her colour heightened. 'Oh, no need for that Gus. I came here to apologise for overreacting and blaming you for that fiasco with the photos. But now I've found out about your cosy little happy family plans with her,' she jerked her head towards Gaby, her accusing eyes never leaving his face, 'I've changed my mind.' Her shoulders slumped and she shook her head.

An immeasurable sadness engulfed Gus, immobilising him, stabbing him, as she uttered the words he'd been dreading.

'It's over... we're over.'

And spinning on her heel, she left the room slamming the door behind her.

Gus took a step towards the door but was halted by Gaby's amused drawl. 'Well, well, well, someone's got a temper.'

Gus had never hated her as much as he did right then. Her obvious glee made him wonder how he could ever have loved someone so shallow... so unnecessarily cruel. How could Katie not see her harshness? With difficulty he kept his tone flat as he pushed past her.

'I'll have someone escort you from the building. We're done.'

He strode out of the room shouting, 'Patti!' The lift doors closed, cutting off his view of her anguished face, her chin tilted defiantly. *I can't lose her. I just can't*!

Cursing Gaby, cursing Katie, and cursing the damn lift, he took to the stairs, taking them two at a time, using the banisters to swing round each floor and arrived at the main entrance to see Patti exiting the building. Exerting himself he sped up, wrenched the doors open and pushing a couple of uniformed officers out of the way, he jumped the four steps, landing on the pavement.

Sweat pouring down his face he yelled the only thing he could.

'I love you. *You're* the only person I want to have kids with.'

For a second, he thought his words had fallen on deaf ears as she continued walking, her body rigid. Then, she stopped and for long seconds stood with her back to Gus.

He faltered and held his breath, waiting, hoping. Should he run to her or wait? Before he'd made up his mind, she turned around. Ignoring the cheers from the two uniformed officers and Hardeep who'd congregated on the steps, Gus ran to her. When he reached her he put his arms round her and pulled her to him, breathing in the coconut fragrance in her hair, savouring the weight of her body moulded to his as all his doubts faded away until grinning, she pulled slightly away from him...

'If that's a proposal, McGuire, then you really need to work on it.'

CHAPTER 64

Getting away from them even for a minute is hard. I tried to check out Mita's room – see if she had anything, but it's hard. Everyone's acting all weird. I suppose that's what happens when your brother gets killed. Never thought something like that would happen to us. All I want is a bit of privacy... just some time to myself... time to breathe, to do something normal, for once. I collected the business phone from the field earlier... so I've got it, just in case.

Instead of all this intense shit... prayers and tears. Can't use the Xbox, can't stay in my room, can't go out, can't do anything but suffocate. It's like they think I'm not grieving if I'm not with them twenty-four seven. Course I am... but I just need some space. Don't need the whole family there all the time. Pratab'll be laughing his arse off up there. I can't stay away from *Facebook* either. All the shitty messages:

> Fly with the angels, Pratab. I'll never forget you, love Priyanka xx :(
>
> I look at the stars and see you twinkling there, always in my heart, Iqrah xx

Who the fuck are these people? I wanted to change the settings on his page, but Mum and Dad like to scroll through it. They don't get that half these people hated Pratab or, worse still, didn't even know him. None of this is about my brother… none of this is him, not how he really was. He could be a right knobhead. Getting lasses to sext him and then he'd upload it so everyone could see their tits and fannies. Stealing and shit. Winding the other kids up. He was a tosser.

The tears come again. Wish they'd fucking stop as well. No way I can go down now, not until I've got it together. Not that I want to go down. Fuck that, I've got stuff to do and if I don't do it, all hell's gonna break loose. It's not like I have much choice in the matter. Can't even have a phone conversation – too many ears around for that, too many nosy aunties and cousins.

I lock my bathroom door and look at myself in the mirror. Shit are those eyes mine? Big fucking bags and all red too. Look like a real stoner, I do. That's mad… fucking well mad. It wouldn't be so bad if I was stoned. Could do with some bud right now. Anything to just let me drift off for a while… forget all this crap. I sit down on the toilet lid. Glad of the privacy. Before long though, someone will be hammering on the door, demanding I tell them I'm okay, demanding I step up to the mark and take my responsibilities seriously. Fucking annoying. It's okay for my dad to fall apart, but me? No, I've got to be brave, got to be strong… hold things together for everyone else.

Like I don't have my own crap going on. The smell of incense drifts up the stairs and mingles with lemon bleach and Adidas Shower Gel, it's almost overpowering. The window's open and I can hear some of the kids in the back garden. They're playing with a football. To them it's just one big party. They play outside while the grown-ups pray inside.

I pull myself together. I've got a job to do and I only have a short time to do it. I get out my phone and text.

> Me: Need to dump the shit. Too busy here. Need to shift it quick. Not safe.

Come on! Come on! Reply! I stare at the phone willing a response to miraculously appear on the screen. In the distance someone's calling my name, getting louder as they come up the stairs. Fuck's sake, can't I have a minute to myself?

'Kiran, do you want some chai?'

Fucking chai. If I have to drink another cup of fucking chai, I'll explode. It's like there's some unwritten rule somewhere that says, if you lose a family member you must drink your bodyweight in chai.

I'm on the point of screaming, *Leave Me A Fucking Lone* when I get a notification. Shit, now they're knocking on the door. Fuck's sake I could be having a crap or anything. Can't they just leave me in peace.

'Are you okay, Kiran, beta?'

No, I've got a dose of the shits that'll keep me confined in here until a week on Tuesday. Just leave me the fuck alone. I huddle over, my stomach's clenching and I want to throw up. 'I'm fine, Auntie. I'll be down in a bit.'

'I've made some chai. Come and sit with us and have your tea. It's not good to be on your own. Your parents need you.'

Fuck's sake, chai, chai, and more fucking chai. Bet you're up there fucking pissing yourself, Pratab. Looking down at us, drinking ourselves to death on chai while you're lying cold in a fucking morgue. Trust you to get yourself fucking killed. Silly little fucking knob. Selfish little bastard.

I look at my phone.

Razor: Whassup dude? You owe us money. Need to sell the stuff.

Me: Summat's come up. Need time

Razor: No time. Money by tomorrow or else

Me: Shit dude, my bruv got killed. You see it on the news?

Razor: Not my prob. Deal's a deal. It's pay day!

CHAPTER 65

Zodiac

It's good to be outside now it's cooler. I like being outside in the dark. Makes me feel invisible. I get out easy enough, but Leo? Must be hard for Leo.

> Me: Am here. Usual spot.
>
> Leo: On my way. Pisces?
>
> Me: No, just us. We need to talk.

Leo's street is always heaving, so I stick to the shadows. Stay invisible, that's my motto. All of a sudden, speccy four eyes is there looking at me and I grin. *Funny*!

'That was quick.'

Leo starts to walk further away from the house. 'Yeah. But I can't be long. Pisces grounded or summat?'

I shrug. 'No idea. Pisces has become a liability, I think. Might need to deal with that. Stress the importance of holding it together. Can you sort it? Tomorrow, eh?'

Leo shrugs, lights up a cig and inhales deeply.

I hate the smoke in my face and start wafting it away, but Leo just grins. And starts blowing smoke bubbles like a pro.

'Fuck's sake, don't be a div.'

Taking a last drag, Leo shrugs and flicks the cig in an arc until it lands on the road. 'You're such a square sometimes, you know that?'

'Whatever. So?' I pause and study my friend. 'You're okay?'

Leo kicks the kerb, then laughs. 'Course I am. No worries. I'm sorted.' Then as if it only now occurs that it's the first time we've met here, Leo looks at me. 'What you up to tonight?'

'Nothing. Just needed fresh air.'

'You're not doing something without me, are you?'

'No, course not.' I punch Leo's arm and then say, 'But you'll never guess what happened in Lister Park today...'

CHAPTER 66

Pisces

Don't think I can do this anymore. I'm shitting it. I never meant for all this to happen. Zodiac's arranged a meeting, but it's only me and Leo so far. I'm sitting on the ground and my whole body's shaking. I've not stopped shaking since the other night. People are beginning to notice. It's crap. They all think it's because of my exams, but fuck. If they knew.

It's like I'm shell shocked or summat. Thought Leo would look as bad as me, but no. Steady as a die, that one. Digging into the wooden floorboards with the tip of the knife. Every time I look at it, I see the blood on the tip. Dun't matter how clean it looks now, that's all I can see… inside my head, like. To be honest, I'm surprised Leo's here. Thought maybe it'd just be me and Zodiac. Not that I want Zodiac here either. Wish I hadn't come.

I look round the room. All the bits of paper. All our plans. Photos with darts in them, lists and lists of the things they'd done to us. It all seemed so trivial then… a game. *Shit, wish my leg would stop jittering!* Didn't expect everything to get so serious. Not now though. It all started as a prank. A way to get our own back on some of the idiots at school. Never meant it to get to this. Never thought we'd really kill somebody. Thought Zodiac was chatting shit. Thought Leo was just acting up too, full of swag, acting big in front of Zodiac.

I shake my head. I've been asking myself the same question again and again. How did it all get so out of hand? Even right up to the moment I pushed the knife in, I kept thinking we'd stop… that *I'd* stop, but I didn't. Why the fuck didn't I stop? Not even sure I regret that Betsy's dead.

I hated her. Getting me in trouble, telling tales, spying on me, and reporting back to the teachers. I just wish one of the others had done it. Zodiac has all the photos… all of them and that worries me. It's like I'm out of control.

'What are we going to do?' My voice sounds shaky… weak and Leo smirks, mouth curling up… pure evil. I flinch. That one look holds so much venom and an image of Leo pushing the knife into Pratab's neck hits me. Bile fills my throat, acid stinging and then there it is. An image of Leo taking that knife and sticking it right into my neck. I swallow it down and instead of the bile, it's blood I taste… my own blood. Shit, I'm losing it big time now. Then it hits me. *This* is why I'm here. This is what it's all about. They've decided *I'm* next.

Leo's standing up now, tapping the blade on one hand. It's then I notice the glove. My gaze flicks to the list on the wall. My name's on it… in pencil at the bottom… and then, like an afterthought, Leo's scrawled next to it 'For Being A Bell End.'

I jump up, stumble a little. *Fucking leg!* Now that it's going to happen, I realise I don't want to die. I'm dizzy, sweat's dripping down my face, the salt stinging where I've scratched my spots and I realise the weird rasping sound is coming from me.

Leo's between me and the door now. I'm bigger, but I still don't reckon much to my chances. I try to edge closer to the door, but Leo matches every move I make, like we're dancing or summat and all the time that evil grin leers at me. I'm bricking it big time now. This is the end. I'm going to end up dead in a dingy squat. Tears pour down my face, but I barely notice them.

Then, what the fuck? Leo's laughing… and handing me the knife handle first.

I just look at it. What's going on? I can smell my own fear through the mildew.

'Take it, go on take it!' Leo's thrusting it at me. Grinning.

I want to slap the grin off that stupid face, but I'm too scared.

'Your face were a right picture then, tosser. What? Did you really think I were going to do you? It's not in the rules, is it? You know that. We can bring a name to add to the list, but we each need to agree that the person deserves it, yeah?'

Leo plops down onto one of the cushions and chucks the knife on to one of the boxes we use as a table. 'Tosser!'

Then, with no warning the laughing sneer is gone and Leo's eyes all sparky and dark bore into me. I've edged closer to the door, but now I stop and listen as the words drop like ice through the heat.

'This was just a message from Zodiac. You need to keep on side. Got it?' Leo's hand darts towards the box and I freeze. Leo grabs something and throws it at me. I catch. Leo waves a hand towards the list with my name at the bottom. 'Rub it off, then, you bell end. You're back on track now, yeah?'

My knees wobble, but I make it to the list and as I rub my name off the bottom, Leo strikes a match and the smell of smoke fills my nostrils. By the time I turn around, Leo's talking to Zodiac on the phone. 'Lesson delivered. Pisces back on track. I'm heading home before they miss me.'

Alone in the headquarters, I wish I was back in the park, on my own and none of this had happened.

CHAPTER 67

Gus hadn't slept well and even an overload of caffeine and the walk through the park to Zarqa's house wasn't improving his mood. Unsociably, he kept his head down as he walked and pondered the events of the previous evening. If Patti had been surprised by Gus' rather public declaration of love, he'd been doubly so. Yes, he'd been thinking about their relationship for the last few months and was well aware his feelings for Patti ran deep. Deeper than those he'd had for either Gaby or Sadia. Still, there was that momentary flutter of panic as the words left his lips, that second of wanting to suck them back in. Now, it was too late.

What was worse was that, what he'd meant as a declaration of love, Patti had taken to be a proposal of marriage and knowing how close he'd come to losing her, made it hard for him to backtrack. Yes, he loved her. Course he did. But settling down? Making a family scared the shit out of him and he didn't know why. Maybe the whole Katie–Gaby debacle had upset him. His track record so far had been pretty dire, yet if he was to have kids, Patti would be his only choice. That was why he'd said it. He could see how she'd misunderstood, but he'd been talking in relation to Gaby's bombshell.

Patti and Alice had spent the previous evening drinking wine and gushing about wedding venues, engagement rings, and bridesmaids. He'd spent the evening with a rigor grin on his face, that thankfully neither of the two women noticed. Things were moving too fast, that was all. He just needed time to process it. Trouble was, with a double murder to solve, time was one commodity he had little of.

This morning's visit to Zarqa was, he hoped, more to reassure him that his goddaughter had done nothing wrong, than anything else. Yet, he wasn't looking forward to the meeting. Zarqa was not pleasant to be around at the moment

He knocked on the front door and stood with his back to it as he waited. Mo's story about Zarqa crying her eyes out on the grass stuck in his mind and he looked at the corner of the garden, imagining his goddaughter crying there. Hearing footsteps approach from inside the house, he turned. When Zarqa saw him, her eyes flitted away, her annoyance barely concealed as she licked her lips.

Not giving her the chance to close the door in his face, Gus pushed past her. 'Glad I caught you. You on your own?'

Slamming it shut, Zarqa slipped past him and stood blocking his way into the house. 'You know now's not a great time for me. Exams.' She shrugged. 'Gotta study.'

Gus smiled and took a step closer, forcing her to move to the side as he walked past her and into the kitchen. 'Pop the kettle on, squirt, we need to talk.'

Standing in the doorway, Zarqa glowered at him as he took a seat at the table. Mo and Naila's kitchen was as familiar to him as his own. He could smell the lingering spicy chai aroma from breakfast time and as if to confirm this, he saw the upended chai pot on the draining board. There were some new paintings and drawings pinned to the walls and he tilted his head to one side trying to decipher the content of one in a particularly virulent shade of purple. It took him a moment to realise it was a painting of Alice's Mini. He spotted the family organiser that Naila had stuck by the fridge in the hope that she could bring some order to their somewhat chaotic lifestyles. And a smile tugged his lips as he remembered Mo moaning about his wife getting uppity when he forgot to fill in his section. The windowsill behind the sink had an army of potted plants and all the normal domesticity of his friend's kitchen brought a pang of guilt at what he was about to do. He swallowed it down and smiled. 'Go on then. I'm gasping. Kettle on. Any biscuits?'

With an exaggerated sigh, Zarqa moved over to the kettle, checked it for water, and then flicked the switch. 'Look, I can do without the pep talk, Gus. Dad, I mean Mo's put you up to this, I know. But there's nowt you can do. I've had it with him.'

Keeping the smile on his lips, Gus let her wind down before saying, 'I'm not here to talk about your dad.' He met her eyes. 'It's more serious than that and I think you know what it is.'

He didn't imagine her shaking hands or the slight quiver of her lips before she turned away and began getting mugs out of the cupboard and his heart plummeted. The disquiet he'd felt the other day when he spoke to her at school had returned. She was hiding something, and he wasn't leaving this house until he'd found out what. If she was implicated in any of these deaths, then she'd be punished, but he needed to find out from her unofficially first. He suspected Bashir would have his badge for this, but sometimes what was right had to supersede what was legal. Remembering Alice's defence of Zarqa, Gus' heart flipped. Maybe Zarqa had nothing to do with any of this… but what was she hiding, then?

She plonked a mug of coffee in front of him, deliberately making it slop onto the table and followed that with a packet of digestives that landed with similar force. Gus kept his smile intact. This was going to be bad enough without him losing his temper and by forcing himself to smile, he was able to keep his anger at her stubbornness simmering just beneath the surface. Why did she have to be such a little cow bag?

She tossed her phone on the table and slouched into a chair opposite him. Despite her bravado, fear lurked in her eyes. Gus wanted to pick her up and cuddle her. Tell her everything would be all right, like he used to when she was a kid. She was in pain. Every tense muscle in her body, every tight-lipped smile, every shadow in her eyes, told him that.

Pulling one foot onto the chair, the bent leg tucked into her chest, she put her arms round her shin and rested her chin on her knee. Gus had interviewed enough people to know that she was erecting a barrier between them. Her phone vibrated and bounced across the table. Its screen lit and the name Jo Jo danced across it. She snatched it up, her face flushed as she dismissed the call. Gus wondered why that phone call had warranted such a flustered reaction… boyfriend? Partner in crime?

Not sure where to start, he decided to jump right in. 'You know shit's been happening in the city, Zarqa, and I'm not going to mess you about. You've been seen in the vicinity of a crime scene and, as a favour to you and your parents, I'm here asking you about it in private instead of dragging you up to The Fort. I need to know who you were with and what you were doing on Sunday night.'

Blinking rapidly, Zarqa's eyes flitted round the kitchen as if she was looking for an escape route. There was none. Gus lifted his cup and sipped the coffee. It was only lukewarm. Little bitch had only half boiled the kettle. Pretending not to notice, he took a sip, his eyes focussed on her face the entire time and then, still staring at her, he opened the biscuit packet, took one out, dunked it, and put it in his mouth. These were the sort of intimidatory techniques he used on hardened criminals and, here he was, using them on his goddaughter. Sometimes life was shit. 'I'm waiting, Zarq. I'm not leaving until I've had a reply.'

She shrugged. 'Was out walking. Couldn't stand being in this shit here any longer.'

Her eyes were still all over the place. Her knuckles, clasped round her leg, were almost white, she was clasping them so tightly.

'On your own?'

'Yeah.'

Now her knee was shaking. Gus took a punt. 'Not with Jo Jo, were you?'

Immediately her entire body stilled. Her eyes widened, and she swallowed noisily. 'No. Course not. Why would I be with that loser? I were on my own. Walking like I told you.'

Fuck! Zarqa was a crap liar. But the fact that she was lying told him that a chance phone call had given him a name and that name had caused a reaction. Whoever this Jo Jo was, he, or she, he supposed, was a person of interest.

He narrowed his eyes, pushed his mug to the side and leaned on the table before spitting his next words right into her face. 'You were seen, Zarqa. You and this Jo Jo.'

The words made her recoil, and she unclasped her hands, her leg fell back to the floor, and she scraped her chair away from the table. Her chest heaved and her darting eyes filled with tears. 'He'd nowt to do with it. It were all my idea. He wasn't even there.'

Gus wanted to exhale, but he knew he had to keep the pressure up. He had to find out everything. His shoulders ached with the strain of keeping them relaxed. What the hell was he going to tell Mo? And Naila? This would break her heart. As he looked at Zarqa, the angry teenager was stripped away, replaced by a frightened vulnerable girl…

but still he had to know it all. It was the only way he could help her… Then his phone rang. Shit!

He snatched it up and growled down the line. 'I'm busy, be quick.'

Compo hesitated before responding. 'Got a couple of hits on those drone part orders, Gus. One's a man in his seventies so he's probably discounted on account of the fact he's on oxygen for emphysema and housebound. Another one is a technology teacher at a school in Leeds, and the third is a lad from Belle Hill Estate… a lad called…'

Eyes still on Zarqa, Gus, sensing the inevitability of it all, said, 'Jo Jo?'

'How'd you know that? Psychic or summat?'

'Yeah, something like that. Get Alice ready, we'll go together to bring him in. I've got another suspect here. We'll need responsible adults in place. Two child interview rooms and get Carlton there. I want his input.'

Zarqa was visibly shaking and Gus strode over to her and put his arms round her. This was the shittiest situation he'd ever been in. He and Mo had been through a lot, but never had he experienced something like this before. How the hell would Mo and Naila ever get over this? And what would the rest of Zarqa's life be like?

'We tracked the drones, Zarqa. You need to come down to the station. I'll phone your parents. When we get there, you need to tell the whole truth. You understand me? Everything! It's the only way forward for you.'

CHAPTER 68

Razor: Expecting my dosh today, brown boy. No excuses.

> Me: FFS Razor. My brother's been killed. Give me a break. I don't have the money. You can have the goods back.
>
> Razor: Deal's a deal, tosser. Money, Money, Money... you know the score. 2 p.m. No excuses.

Fuck! What am I going to do? What the hell am I going to do? There's one thing I could do, but that'd take a bit of planning and I'm not sure I can. Not with the house as busy as it is. I lean against the wall, glad to be on my own for once. It's so claustrophobic indoors. Maybe I should just ignore Razor. What's he gonna do? I mean, would he really carry out his threats? Who am I kidding? Course he would, guy's a bloody psycho, in't he? Why the hell did I let Pratab get me involved in all this crap. Another notification and, heart hammering I look at the screen. Razor's sent an image. I open it and nearly vomit. The sick fuck's sent a screenshot of one of those images of Pratab with the knife in his neck.

I jump a mile when Mita speaks. Why does she always creep about like that?

'Who's that, Kiran? One of your homies?'

'Piss off, Mita. None of your business. Where have you been? Mum's been looking for you. The Brahmin's coming soon, and she wants you here.'

'Aw, poor little Kiran, all upset… got yourself in too deep, have you?'

I really want to slap her, but now's not the time. If she goes in and distracts Mum for a bit, I might be able to access Pratab's stash of money. It's the only chance I have. Just hope dad's downstairs too. I wait a few minutes until Mita's indoors, then I follow her, slipping past the living room, where I can hear her talking to Mum and I head straight upstairs. When I first found Pratab hiding his drug money in the gap at the bottom of Mum's wardrobe, I thought it was a great hiding place. Mum would never think to look there. We all knew she did checks in our rooms for drugs and stuff and we'd all got wise. I kept mine in the field opposite, don't know where Mita keeps hers, and Pratab used his en suite cistern for drugs and Mum's room for the cash.

I hesitate outside their room. The aunties have been going in and out as if they own the joint, putting their saris on in front of the big mirrors. I'll need to be quick. Pushing the door open, I listen. The coast's clear and there's no one in the hallway either. I nip in, shutting the door behind me, straight over to the wardrobe. The one on the right, under all her boxes of shoes. How many shoes does she need? And I prise it up with my nails and look in the gap. Nothing! The entire stash has gone. Three hundred quid… disappeared, just like that! It can't be. I stretch my hand back, but no… nothing! Then behind me I hear the door open and I fling the boxes back in and am closing the door when I hear Mita's smarmy voice.

'Looking for something, Kiran?'

Fucking little bitch beat me to it! What am I gonna do now?

Unseen Evil

CHAPTER 69

Of course, Jo Jo tried to run. Gus was expecting it and took off after him, elbowing aside the bruiser who'd been loitering outside Jo Jo's home. The lad had gangster written all over him and it gave Gus pleasure to have an excuse to land one in his belly. Who knew why he was staking out Jo Jo's home, but it would, no doubt, be for some gang related reason or other.

Jo Jo was faster than Gus had expected, as he took off down the street and further into the estate. Aware of the two uniformed officers pounding the concrete after him, Gus focussed on the lad in front. The officers, with their kit, carried an extra twenty pounds, which although it offered them protection, close up, it definitely slowed them down. Gus' stab vest was heavy, but he hadn't bothered with all the other paraphernalia and he wondered how the hell they managed, particularly in this heat.

Out of the corner of his eye, Gus had spotted a red-haired freckled face peering out from behind the lad before he'd taken off. Gus presumed Alice had remained with the little girl and now her plaintive cries followed him, getting fainter as he gained on her brother. He was just wondering if he could summon a final spurt to get within tackling distance of the lad, when Jo Jo ground to a halt, bent over, hands on knees wheezing like a fifty-a-day man. Droplets of sweat dripped from the lad's fringe onto the pavement as he dragged air in through his mouth.

Drawing level, Gus, remained alert, ready to dart after him, if he decided to take off again, but Jo Jo glanced up and scowled. 'You can take me in. I've had enough.'

Gus studied him. The lad oozed discomfort. His face contorted in anguish, his lower lip trembling just a fraction and Gus, seeing in his face someone who had given up, raised a hand to stay the officers who had just arrived. Bending over again, still gasping but not quite as laboured, Jo Jo spoke, 'Anything'll be better than having to sell my soul to Goyley and his boss.' He lifted his chin in an infinitesimal gesture towards the thug who Gus had elbowed earlier. Gus realised quickly that Jo Jo was using his lowered head to impart this information without being seen. 'Got you. One of Razor McCarthy's thugs or Hammerhead's?'

Still bent over, Jo Jo said, 'Razor's.'

Gus considered this for a moment. Jo Jo seemed more concerned about McCarthy than about being arrested and Gus wasn't entirely sure what that implied. 'Reckon we can do without the cuffs, eh?' Gus linked his arm through the boy's and led him back towards his house, the officers trailing behind.

A bit of a crowd had gathered in the street. Nothing like a police presence to bring folk crawling outside. McCarthy's thug stood at the back, keeping a watchful eye on proceedings. His phone was glued to his ear and as they got closer, Gus saw that his lips were moving. More than likely keeping his boss in the loop. Gus focussed on Jo Jo but directed his next words to the two officers. 'Go over and hassle that thug, will you? See if he's carrying anything. I don't like the look of him, and he tried to obstruct me when I was chasing Jo Jo. That's a good enough excuse to hold him for a bit.'

Leaving the officers to it, Gus guided Jo Jo through his front door. After closing it behind them, they made their way through to the kitchen where Gus could hear Alice talking. As soon as they walked through the door, the little girl jumped to her feet, her face tear streaked, and ran to her brother. 'Jo Jo, what's going on. Why did you run off? I was scared.'

Jo Jo lifted her up and hugged her close. 'It's fine, Jessie, everything's fine. Just got to help these people for a while, that's all. Someone will look after you.'

Gus frowned. The lad's ready acceptance that he would be taken away seemed to confirm his guilt. Watching the brother and sister together, Gus was reminded of his relationship with his own sister. The only difference being that Katie was the older sibling. Glancing round the kitchen, Gus could see that although it was basic with little in the way of homely touches, it was clean. Similar to Mo's kitchen, the walls were covered with bold artwork, still brown damp stains escaped from beneath the paintings and peeling wallpaper. The fridge made a peculiar sound that told Gus it was on its way out and the back of one of the oddly matched kitchen chairs was held together with string and gaffer tape.

Voice gentle, Alice smiled at the little girl. 'Where's your parents, Jessie?'

Jo Jo ruffled his sister's hair and made an admirable attempt at keeping his tone level. 'It's just me mam. She's not right well. Please don't tell her what I've been doing. It'll kill her.'

As if on cue, a faint voice drifted downstairs. 'Jo Jo. What's happening? What's all the noise?'

Immediately the lad glanced up at the ceiling, his eyes blinking rapidly as his gaze settled on Gus.

Voice gentle, Gus asked, 'Your mum?'

Jo Jo repeated his earlier words. 'She's not well. She won't be able to cope with this. What's gonna happen to her… and Jessie?'

Exchanging a quick look, Alice left the room and went upstairs. Jessie, thumb in her mouth gazed up at her brother, her eyes filled with unshed tears. Jo Jo smiled at her. 'It'll be all right, Jess, you'll see.'

But the tears began to roll down Jessie's cheeks. This was so unfair. Gus had seen it before, and it didn't take a genius to realise what the outcome of all of this would be. Social services would become involved and this little family would be obliterated. Sometimes, Gus wasn't sure what the best course of action was, but looking at the siblings together, he was certain that the repercussions for both of these kids would be far reaching. When Alice returned, she switched the kettle on and with a forced smile said, 'I think we could all do with some tea. Pop for you, Jessie?'

The little girl looked up at her brother for permission before nodding and hiding her face in her brother's shoulder once more. Alice made the pop and placed it on the table. With a smile at the boy, Alice took her phone out of her pocket. 'Need to make a phone call. I'll do it outside.'

Jo Jo, eyes downcast, nodded. He'd no fight left in him and Gus could see the guilt in his eyes. Before following Alice into the hallway, he squeezed the lad's shoulder. There was a backdoor in the kitchen, but Gus knew the lad wouldn't try to use it.

Once out of earshot, the door closed behind them, Alice ran her hand over her face and exhaled. Her eyes had darkened, and her entire body bristled. 'This is fucking shit, Gus. Fucking shit. That kid's been looking after his invalid mum and his sister for months now. The mum says the carer who's supposed to come daily, blobs most of the time and they're too scared to complain in case they take Jo Jo and Jessie away. Now, I'm going to have to phone social services and try to be civil. This shouldn't be happening. Not in this day and age.'

Closing his eyes, Gus swallowed. He'd seen the look in Jo Jo's eyes. When he'd been a kid, his friend Greg had often carried the same haunted expression – despair and fear and hatred all rolled into one. It wasn't until adulthood that Gus had realised how bad things had been for his friend. Society had let Greg down and now, thirty years later, it was still letting families like this down. Although Gus wanted nothing more than to rant and rave and possibly punch a wall, he took a deep breath instead. 'We need to do our job, Alice. Jessie will be taken into foster care and the mum will be taken to hospital. You *know* that's what has to happen. Neither of them is safe here. At least now they'll be looked after.'

'But they'll be split up.' She spat the words at him, her eyes blazing.

'Yes, they will. But they'll be safe. Now if you can't hold it together, leave. Go for a walk, calm yourself. This family needs us to be professional.' When her eyes still blazed, her body still tense, he added 'Perhaps you came back too soon, Al. Perhaps you need more time.'

For a moment he thought she might turn on her heel and walk out or punch him. Either was a distinct possibility, but she did neither. She straightened her back and gave a curt nod. 'I'll be back once I've made the call.'

He watched her walk down the hallway, rigid and fragile all at once. She stopped when she reached the door and without looking back said, 'You need to ask him for the key to the padlocked bedroom before they take him away.'

CHAPTER 70

C an't bear this. Can't bear to see Mum and Mo, their faces all worried and underneath all of that they'll hate me. I know they will. How could they not? Anyway, I made Uncle Gus promise not to let them in. He wasn't happy about it, but I insisted. Now I've got a stuck-up smiley social worker, who probably knows my mum and is more than likely laughing up her sleeve at this turn of events; Middle class kid goes wrong... middle class *Pakistani* kid goes wrong. Shit! Everything's got scary all of a sudden. I don't know what to do with myself, don't know what to say... so I'll just say nothing.

I've really landed Jo Jo in it and that's the last thing I wanted to do. Jo Jo's had my back for so long. He doesn't deserve any of this. He's got responsibilities... he's not like me. Jo Jo's got his mum and Jessie to think of, so why the hell did I drag him into all of this shit? That's where Gus has gone... to bring Jo Jo in. I've really messed up.

I pull my knees up to my chest, my heels balancing on the edge of the soft chair and catch the frown from the social worker. Sod her! Ms Bloody Perfect. If I'm gonna end up in the nick, then I'll sit how the hell I like. I glare at her, daring her to say something, but her frown goes and a slight smile tugs at her lips. Why the hell is she just sitting there, arms crossed and knees together. Bet that dress she's wearing isn't Armani... what's it Jo Jo calls it...? ah, yeah Primani. Yes, the stuck-up cow's probably all cheap clothes and attitude.

The door bursts open and my mum, followed by Mo, are there in the room. Mum pulls me up and into her arms, her perfume embracing me like invisible armour. For a moment, I want to give in and let them stay, share my pain with them. But then I jerk out of her arms, pushing her away and look at the social worker who has jumped to her feet, glancing between the three of us and the officer who's just rushed into the room.

Stepping between the officer and my mum, she puts her arm round her. 'Naila!'

So, she does know my mum!

'You can't be here. You know that.'

Mum looks at me, her tear-stained face scrunched up, her eyes pleading, and I want nothing more than to say, 'Stay, Mum, please stay.' But I can't. I flick a quick glance at Mo. He's so skinny looking, his chin is quivering, and I know he wants to hug me.

I straighten up and although I'm bleeding inside, I pull a scowl on my face and make my voice cold as ice. 'Get them out of here. I never want to see them again.'

The social worker leads my mum from the room. Something inside my stomach squirms as Mum's sobs cut through me, but it's Mo who breaks my heart. As the officer guides him from the room, Mo turns back, not bothering to hide his tears. 'No matter what you've done, Zarqa, I'll always love you. You're my daughter… now and forever. I love you.'

As the door slams behind them, I keep breathing. How can I keep breathing when I'm dead inside?

'I love you too, Dad,' I mumble, but it's too little, too late. I turn and sit down again, keeping my feet on the floor this time.

CHAPTER 71

G us found the key on the top ledge of the door where Jo Jo had told them it would be.

He'd walked up the worn stair carpet after Sid and his team with Alice trailing behind. They were already suited and booted. The house, although not spotless, wasn't filthy, like some of the houses they'd had the pleasure of searching. The wallpaper was shabby and marked. There was a faint damp smell, mostly overlaid by lemon disinfectant. Jo Jo had tried his best to keep on top of things.

A quick glance into a single room saw a made bed, with a pink, princess duvet on top and a bundle of soft toys spilling all over the pillow. Jessie had chosen two toys to take with her and, crying her eyes out, she allowed the social worker to lead her by the hand to the waiting car. Alice had turned abruptly and returned to the house, her anguish at the desperate situation resonating with Gus. When Jo Jo had been escorted to the police car, Jessie had clung to him like a limpet, until he said, 'You gotta be a big girl, Jess. You gotta keep an eye on mam. I'll come see you soon as I can.'

Her lower lip had wobbled, but she'd done as her brother asked, which only made the separation of mother and child worse. Jo Jo's mum, almost too weak to speak, tried her best to reassure her daughter, but Gus could see that she was resigned to losing both her children. When the paramedics arrived, they'd lifted her emaciated frame onto the gurney with little effort. Standing aside to let them wheel her down the path, a drip attached, feeding her fluids, Gus cringed at the sight of her skeletal frame.

'She going to be okay?' Even as the words left his lips, he realised how stupid they were. Even with the right care, it was clear that the children's mum was in for a long and possibly painful recuperation, if she made it all. He hoped that worry over Jo Jo wouldn't impact negatively on her recovery, but deep down he knew it would. If there was one thing he was sure of, it was that this little family loved each other very much.

Sid unlocked the padlock, bagged both the lock and the key, and pushed the door open while Gus stood aside to allow a lanky CSI, who was carrying the evidence storage box, to enter.

Jo Jo's room was unlike any other teenage boy's room Gus had ever seen. It was divided into two distinct areas. The wall behind his bed was painted black and his bedding was a deep purple. To the right of the bed was a long pasting table that the lad was clearly using as a worktable. And behind it was a shelving unit containing eight drones of different sizes and shapes. Laid out along the bench were Jo Jo's tools; electrical screwdrivers, pliers, spanners, and the like. Battery casings and a selection of different parts and controllers took up the rest of the space, with an extendable spotlight positioned at one end.

If Gus had needed evidence that Jo Jo was in some way involved in the murders, it was here, laid out on a platter for him. So, why did the knowledge deflate him? They were on the cusp of closing this case and yet his overriding feeling was one of regret. How the hell did the lad afford all this stuff?

On a dresser at the foot of the bed was a large screen, hooked up to a smaller laptop, with a webcam attached to the top. Gus' gaze drifted to the two spotlights directed towards the bed. It was then he noticed the handcuffs attached to the bedpost and as his gaze moved round the room, he saw another surface with an array of sex toys ranging from butt plugs to dildos and cock-rings of every imaginable design, and some Gus hadn't ever imagined. Large bottles of oil and lubricant stood among tissue boxes, wet wipes, and antibacterial wipes… Gus' stomach lurched… there was his answer. The lad was webcamming to make ends meet and to fund his DIY drone hobby.

Gus was overcome with a sense of futility. No matter how often he witnessed how other people lived, no matter how hard he tried to make things better, he would never get to the bottom of the cesspool. Heavy-limbed and equally heavy-hearted, Gus turned to leave the room. Jo Jo might well be a cold-blooded killer, but still, Gus couldn't help but feel sorry for the lad and desperately frustrated with the situation he found himself in. 'Get that PC and all the drone stuff to Compo as soon as you can. I'll take his phone with me.'

CHAPTER 72

This was the longest Thursday Gus had ever endured. Every passing minute added a further twist to the toxic coil in his gut. Speaking to Mo and Naila earlier had been torture. For the first time, he'd noticed streaks of grey running through his friend's hair, but what worried him most was Mo's glazed expression and the way he stood back, his body so tense that Gus thought it would snap and Mo would end up a rubble of bones at his feet. The last time Gus had seen an expression like that had been when Alice had been arrested and look how that ended up. He wanted to hug his mate and tell him everything was going to be all right and that he'd get Zarqa out of there no matter what, but he couldn't.

Naila had grudgingly given them permission to search Zarqa's room. Her eyes, like a laser, had pierced Gus' heart. Her tone was accusing. 'My daughter has done nothing wrong, Gus. You of all people should know that. I hope you're ashamed of yourself.'

Mo had tried to reason with her, saying, 'Gus is on our side, Naila. He's our friend. He's Zarqa's godfather.'

But Naila had turned on Mo, her teeth bared. 'If he was on our side, he wouldn't be accusing his goddaughter of being a murderer, would he?' She turned to Gus, eyes flashing, 'My daughter is not a murderer, so just you get the fuck out of my sight. You're a disgrace… an absolute disgrace.'

Her words stung, and Gus was ashamed… ashamed and angry and confused. He'd followed the evidence. Zarqa had admitted culpability, saying it had all been her idea… he didn't know what else he could've done, yet the guilt was threatening to strangle him. They'd found nothing of consequence in Zarqa's room, bar some weed and a few spray cans, but then Zarqa was an artist in the making, so that wasn't unusual. Sid had suggested she may have access to somewhere else that may hold incriminating evidence and Sebastian Carlton had backed that idea up, suggesting that if Jo Jo and Zarqa were working together, they may keep incriminating stuff like burner phones elsewhere.

Now, watching the interview from a screen in another room, Gus' heart hammered, his mouth was rancid, and his head throbbed. The smell of Sebastian Carlton's aftershave was forcing him to take shallow breaths through his mouth and he could feel his chest tighten. He hoped he'd be able to hold it together... at least for a while longer.

Alice entered the room and sat down opposite Zarqa who sat with her social worker.

Calmly, with a small smile, Alice introduced those present for the video and began the interview. 'Zarqa, you've not been charged yet and you have declined a solicitor, is that right?'

'Yes.' Zarqa glanced at the social worker who smiled reassuringly.

'You understand why you're here?'

Zarqa nodded and Alice gently reminded her she needed to speak.

'Yes, I did it.' The single word response was barely a whisper.

'What did you do, Zarqa?'

The girl looked down at her fingernails and then glanced up at Alice. 'I spray painted the mosque.'

Alice's mouth fell open and she took a quick sideways glance at the camera. 'You spray painted the mosque?'

Gus looked at Carlton who was frowning. 'I thought you said the girl had admitted to the murders, Gus?'

Gus shook his head trying to clear his thoughts. 'I thought she had... she did.' *Didn't she*? He cast his mind back. He'd seen Jo Jo's name flash on her phone and taken a punt. She'd immediately admitted doing 'it', saying that Jo Jo hadn't been there.

'Okay, you spray painted the mosque. Who was with you?'

'Nobody. Did it on my own.'

Alice nodded. 'You want to tell us anything else, Zarqa? It'll be better for you if you tell us everything at once. You know anything else the police might be interested in.'

Sniffing, Zarqa's eyes flicked up and to the left. Then, wiping the back of her hand over her nose she nodded. 'I've got some weed.'

Weed... weed and spray-painting a mosque. Was that all she'd done? Okay it had been a pretty vile slogan, but if that's all she'd done, things might still be okay. Then he remembered Jo Jo and the drones, and he knew that things were never that easy. Zarqa could still be a barefaced liar. He'd seen it before, kids looking them straight in the eye and lying. They were masters of the art of deceiving adults. He placed a hand on the mirror, wishing he could see right into Zarqa's mind.

Then from nowhere, the image of Alice and Zarqa began to shimmer, black dots punctuated his vision and Gus began to blink. He grabbed the back of a chair and cursed. Why did this have to happen now? Sweat dappled his brow and then his chest shrivelled into a tight knot and his breath came in heaving pants. Staggering, as dizziness overcame him, he tried to make for the door, banging into furniture, knocking past Carlton. Fuck! Sick! Vomit rose, stinging his nostrils and the back of his throat. Blindly he tried to locate a bin... anything...

Then, a hand was on his back, firm and soothing, and a bin was thrust under his chin. 'I've got you, Gus. I've got you. Slow breaths now… slow and easy.'

Vomit splattered into the bin and Gus was, at once, embarrassed and grateful for Sebastian Carlton's calming presence. He owed him big time.

CHAPTER 73

Compo was in his element doing all things techie and was excited to get cracking, dissecting every aspect of Jo Jo's computer and phone. He settled down, headphones on, The Kink's 'Waterloo Sunset' blaring on repeat and a supply of snacks and drinks within reach.

He started with the phone because that was the easiest thing to do. It was a battered old Nokia with a cracked screen and limited data. Jo Jo had given permission for it to be accessed and Compo sifted through his social media accounts. *Instagram* and *Facebook* were Jo Jo's favourites although on *Facebook* he was a bit of a lurker rather than an active *Facebooker*. He had a modest number of *Instagram* followers, which surprised Compo. He was used to seeing thousands on a youngster's account, but Jo Jo, it seemed, wasn't your typical selfie king. On *Instagram*, more of Jo Jo's interests became apparent. He followed some drone enthusiasts and occasionally he posted photos of a drone he'd modified.

Going through the lad's texts, Compo took note of one anonymous sender. The texts were infrequent, yet the most recent had been received earlier this week. Opening the texts, Compo soon realised that Jo Jo was being blackmailed. This matched what the lad had already told Gus, and judging by the contents of Jo Jo's bedroom, it wasn't much of a leap to conclude that it was his webcamming he was being blackmailed for.

There didn't seem to be much more he could learn here, so Compo printed off the threatening texts and set up a triangulation request to find out where the sender was when they sent the text and almost immediately the information that the phone was unregistered bounced back. Still, if he could narrow down the location of the phone when it sent those specific texts, it may come in useful further down the line.

The next step was Jo Jo's hard drive. Compo had seen the photos of the lad's room and was aware that some of what he might find would be disturbing. An hour into it and Compo was feeling thoroughly sick. Jo Jo had a Bitcoin account, which probably allowed the lad to finance his drone interest but, as Compo went deeper, he discovered the full extent of Jo Jo's exploitation. Images of the boy performing various sex acts using a variety of sex toys had gone viral on the Dark Web.

As he delved farther into the depths of the Dark Web, Compo turned and flung his half-eaten sandwich in the bin. Standing up abruptly, he switched his music – sunsets had no place in this abyss, to 'People are Strange' by The Doors. Somehow, in Compo's mind, Jo Jo had become the tortured soul of Jim Morrison and the discord of the song suited his mood. As he delved further beneath the surface, the enormous extent of the tangled network of people accessing Jo Jo's web services was made apparent. What was worse, was that the lad's Dark Web controller was using remote access technology to record *all* the boy's activities, not only the ones he was being paid for.

Watching Jo Jo fling himself onto his bed and punch his pillow before covering his face with it as he sobbed, made Compo's skin crawl and this was compounded by the insidious comments from the voyeuristic bottom feeders in the depths of the web.

> Buttcomber: A tub of Vaseline and I'll give the lad something to cry over…

> hell never mind the Vaseline. I'd go bareback on him.
>
> Freshbaiter: Don'tcha love it when they cry? Bet he's ready for the big boys.

The comments during Jo Jo's 'shows' were equally offensive, and Compo was relieved the lad wouldn't see those. His only regret was that in order to monitor the low lives that skulked beneath the surface, Compo would have to leave these forums live until they could be monitored by the Vice Department. The worst bit came when Compo found a clip of Jo Jo's little sister, in her pyjamas, her hair all mussed and innocence written all over her little face, as she stood looking at someone just out of shot, holding a butt plug and nipple clamps in her hands. The five second image had gone viral. Users with names like *Cumraider* and *Vio-hate-her* were bidding for a longer clip of Jessie, the equivalent of tens of thousands of pounds.

It wasn't so long ago that he'd been Jo Jo's age and in similar circumstances. He knew only too well how hard it was to survive when you were always the kid on the outside looking in. Jo Jo hardly had a chance, yet here he was doing whatever he had to, to keep afloat… to hold his little family together. If there was even the smallest possibility of finding evidence that would exonerate Jo Jo in the lad's devices, Compo made a silent promise that he'd find it.

Gus came in and Compo got to his feet, glad to be away from his computer. His skin was itchy and despite realising it was a reaction to the filth he'd had to sift through, Compo couldn't shake the unclean feeling. He'd have a shower in a bit. 'I've found loads of stuff, Gus, but nothing to implicate the lad in any of those deaths. He wasn't friends or in contact with either of the victims on social media. There's nothing at all, unless he had another device. I can't find anything to link him to any of this other than the fact that he bought drones and drone parts.'

'That's circumstantial unless we find the actual drones in Jo Jo's possession and unfortunately, that's not looking likely. We don't have anywhere else he could be keeping them. You said the drones he had in his room are the same as the one caught in the CCTV image at the mosque, but the one that dropped the phone in my garden wasn't found at Jo Jo's. He admits to making two drones for an anonymous blackmailer and accepts that his fingerprints will be all over them. Maybe he's being set up as the fall guy. We don't have anything concrete yet.'

Compo nodded. 'Ah, but what I *do* have is text evidence from a burner phone, of someone blackmailing Jo Jo into making a specific drone. When I pinpoint where the phone was when the text was sent, it might give us some more information. At the very least, the fact that a third party is anonymously requesting a drone casts doubt on Jo Jo's guilt for the killings.'

Compo had heard from Carlton about Gus' panic attack and he was pleased to see his boss smile, however briefly. 'You're brill, Comps, you know that?'

Trying to hide his pleasure at Gus' words, Compo turned to his workstation with a shrug.

'Dun't look like Jo Jo posted the images online either. S'ppose he could've used another device, but... well...it's inconclusive.'

'So, we're no further forward with that?'

Compo shook his head. 'I'm getting closer, it just takes time. It's inching through the layers, little by little that's so time consuming, but we'll get there.'

'Yeah, I only hope we're not too late. What if we're wasting time on this pair of idiots when the real killers are still out there? Who knows what they could be planning next?'

'No idea… but.' He pressed a few keys bringing up his earlier findings on the screen 'This isn't pleasant, Gus, but you need to see it, before I forward it on to Vice. Jo Jo's webcamming has gone viral and it's attracting all sorts of vermin from under the floorboards.'

CHAPTER 74

I'd never been in the Belle Hill Estate before and I'm fucking shitting it. It wasn't that there aren't any Asians here. It's just that none of them are like me. Everybody I pass has a look about them – a 'don't fuck with me' look. I thought I was tough at school and that, but this is some other level. Even the little kids on their bikes and skateboards stare at me with attitude, their grubby faces snarl at me in silence. My heart starts to thunder, and I wonder if I'm having a heart attack. The way some of these kids are looking at me, I almost wish I was.

I deepen my voice and approach one of the bigger kids. He's passing a football from hand to hand and staring right at me, his eyes like acid against my skin. Inside I'm saying, 'Show no fear, Kiran,' outside I'm barely managing to stare the kid out.

'I'm after Razor, you know where he is?' I think I've made a reasonable attempt at not looking like bricks are about to fly out of my arse, but the other kid's smirk tells me I'm mistaken. He doesn't even make an effort to intimidate me. Just keeps passing the ball back and forth, back and forth. The slap of the leather on palms taunts me and I feel like grabbing him by the scruff of the neck and marching him into the nearest flushable toilet. But even I know that's just in my dreams.

'Who wants to know?'

I bulk myself up. I'm double the kid's size but feel like a pygmy beside his attitude. He snorts at my efforts and I take a step towards him. Before I can take another, six guys fall in behind the lad with the ball. I hadn't noticed them approach, I was so focussed on the kid.

'You really want to try that, eh? Come on then, let's see what you got.'

Things are getting out of control and I don't know what to do to stop it. All I want is to see Razor… to explain to him about my brother, to ask him to take the stuff back. I've got some of the money. Maybe that'll be enough to get him off my back for now. I was already sweating when I arrived, but now it's dribbling down the inside of my cargo shorts. For a second, I wonder if I've pissed myself. The kid moves closer, his mates keeping pace behind him. He tosses the ball backwards and one of the littlest kids catches it, while one of the others passes him a baseball bat.

He takes another step towards me and it's then I see glints of metal in his mate's hand and hear the thud of wood hitting the pavement, in a trial swing. I drop to my knees and curl into a ball, hands over my head, ready to take the beating that's coming.

The laughter is incongruous, and I tense… waiting… nothing happens… then I feel something splattering on my back. The stench of ammonia rises in the air making my eyes smart and then there's more laughter followed by a staccato…

'Enough!' And I hear a zip being pulled up.

I lie where I am, soaked with piss, scared to move, nearly shitting myself. Their taunting voices begin to fade, and I can hear that familiar slap, slap, slap of the fucking football… but it too is growing fainter. When it's nearly out of earshot, I uncurl, roll onto my back and open my eyes and immediately wish I'd stayed where I was… or better still, never left my cushty little street in Clayton.

The sun haloes the person standing over me, casting sparks of light that almost blind me, making it hard to recognise him. He steps forward, raises one foot, and whams it into my stomach and I'm curling up again, the acidic remnants of spicy tea burning my throat as it spews onto the pavement.

'That's for being a prick. You don't go down without a fight… ever. That right, lad? And you never, ever let kids piss on you!'

It's only then I realise Razor's got two mates beside him; Goyley and HP. For one stupid delirious moment I actually think about asking HP where his scar is, but I stop myself just in time. Razor nods to his thugs and they each hook an arm under mine and yank me to my feet. My knees wobble and I nearly topple over, but Goyley, yanks me up again, with a laugh. 'Fucking know this one, eh, Raze?'

Razor doesn't answer, just looks at me, his hand extended. 'Money!'

I shake my head and wish my legs would stop shaking. 'I told you, my brother died… got murdered, like. You must've seen it in the papers.'

Razor shrugs. 'Not my problem. Just want my dosh.'

I glance round, desperate now. 'I've got your stuff. It's all there… every last bit of it.' I fumble down the front of my pants where I'd hidden it and offer the padded envelope to Razor.

He takes it and I think I'm free. I sigh and risk a half smile, but Razor's not done with me. 'You owe me interest. Give me what I'm owed.'

The colour drains from my face and it's at that point that I realise that I truly am a knob. What was I doing, thinking I could play with the big lads? I swallow. 'How much?'

'Two grand… and we're quits.'

'*Two grand*…? But I…' I bend down and fumble in my trainers and bring out the folded notes I'd withdrawn on the way. Surely, he'd take that, and we'd be quits? He'd got his stash back after all. 'Two hundred, that's all I've got.'

Razor signalled. HP stepped forward, took the notes, and licked his index finger before flicking through them quickly. 'Yep, two tons.'

Razor turns and begins walking away and I swallow my relief. 'You messed me around... but... we're all square now.'

He raises a finger and drags it across his throat. I barely have time to understand what it means when Goyley grabs me and stabs my stomach. A warm trickle of blood oozes through my fingers. As their footsteps retreat, my last thought is, *How are my parents going to cope with two dead sons*?

CHAPTER 75

Still wobbly after his panic attack, Gus sat opposite Jo Jo in one of the interview rooms dedicated to minors. Soft chairs, cushions, and coffee tables were supposed to make it less stressful for the kids. Gus didn't know about Jo Jo, but right now his stress levels were through the roof. It was hard to focus, and he was glad that the chill from the cold bottled water between his hands grounded him a little.

Jo Jo's solicitor was a short, bulky man with a receding hairline, and beside him, Jo Jo tall and gangly, looked like an overgrown puppet with invisible strings that jerked his angles out every time he moved. The lad's feet tapped a rhythm on the tiled floor and his lips were flaky and raw where he'd been gnawing at them. Despite Zarqa's denials that she had anything to do with the murders, denials that Alice told him were convincing, Gus was too much of a professional to believe them without hard evidence to back them up. So, Zarqa, at least for the time being, was being kept in one of the family rooms.

Taking his time, Gus studied the boy. His spotty face was streaked with dried up tears and despite the lingering aroma of 'teen boy spray', Gus could smell the boy's fear filling the room. Despite his suspicions, Gus liked the teenager. How could you not like a lad who tried his damndest to keep his family together? Who was prepared to do unpalatable things in order to protect his much younger sister and his invalid mum? Gus doubted he'd have been able to take on such a responsibility at sixteen and he wanted to rage against the self-satisfied adults who so blithely disparaged an entire group of people purely on merit of their age; 'Teenagers this, teenagers that'. He and Patti frequently talked about how easy some people found it to spout vitriol about the flaws of teen behaviour without once considering the problems and temptations they had to face. On the other hand, despite appearances, there was a strong possibility that Gus was looking at a lad who'd killed, or was instrumental in killing, two of his contemporaries.

Aware of Carlton and Alice watching proceedings from the other room, Gus was simultaneously nervous and relieved. At least if he lost it again, one or both of them would come to his rescue. Alice had offered to conduct the interview, but Gus had refused. Interviewing Zarqa had taken it out of Alice. Questioning suspects was draining at the best of times, but interviewing a kid was worse and interviewing one you knew – on suspicion of murder nonetheless – was almost unbearable. Still, Zarqa had consistently denied any involvement and that was a bonus. With a sigh, Gus set up the equipment, did the necessary protocols, and looked at the boy. 'You okay, Jo Jo?'

Foot tapping momentarily paused, Jo Jo looked right at Gus. 'How's me mam… and Jessie? How's Jessie? She okay?'

Gus' heart contracted. He'd been dreading these questions. 'Jessie's fine, Jo Jo. She's with a foster family in Bradford and she's okay. Your mum…' He hesitated, feeling like a coward for allowing the meaningful pause to do half of his work for him.

Jo Jo frowned, waited, colour blanched from his face and he gripped the edge of the table. 'Mam… What about me mam?'

Wishing he was anywhere but here in this room, Gus got on with it. 'I'm afraid your mother's taken a turn for the worse, Jo Jo. She's on a ventilator in the BRI. She's got an infection. They're doing everything they can for her.'

Jo Jo slumped back in his chair and closed his eyes. The sound of the lad's rasping breaths as he tried to process the information was almost too much for Gus to bear. Instead of looking sixteen, Jo Jo now looked like a lost twelve-year-old. Finally, he spoke.

'I did this. It's all my fault. I should've got the doctor in sooner, but I was scared... scared they'd take Jessie away... split us up. Now look what's happened.' Jo Jo fell to the floor, gasping for breath, hyperventilating.

Shit, Gus had been prepared for a panic attack... just not Jo Jo's.

'Interview terminated. Medics, right now!'

He kneeled beside the boy and schooled him through the panic attack. There was no way they'd be interviewing Jo Jo in the foreseeable future, but what they could do in the interim was collate as much evidence as they could to either corroborate Zarqa and Jo Jo's innocence or prove their guilt.

Surely Compo would come up with the goods soon. If anyone could pinpoint Zarqa and Jo Jo's whereabouts at the time of the two murders it was Compo. Officers were still trawling through CCTV in the vicinity of both murder locations and now also in the vicinity of the mosque. The problem was that although Bradford had a proliferation of CCTV, the two areas around Smith Lane and in the middle of Lister Park were 'dead' areas.

Never mind, Gus had faith in his team. They'd keep going.

CHAPTER 76

'Call's come in, Gus. Kid knifed in Belle Hill!' Taffy's face was flushed, and Gus suspected it wasn't just the heat that was making it so. He'd spotted the shy smiles exchanged between Taffy and the police officer who was just leaving the room as Taffy entered.

Gus had set up an alert so he would be notified immediately of any knifings in Bradford. That discounted the frequent machete attacks that were becoming more common throughout the city. He'd narrowed the parameters to knife attacks as that seemed to be his killer's preferred murder weapon.

'Same MO as ours?' Gus was on his feet and heading out of the room, exchanging the uncomfortably hot and humid environment of the office for the blanket heat surrounding the city. This could be what they needed to exonerate Zarqa and Jo Jo. Both were still in custody, so if this was another *Snapchat* attack that would mean their killer or, if Carlton was right, killers were still out there.

Chasing after Gus, Taffy filled him in. 'They reckon it might be a drug related attack. A neighbour phoned it in, anonymous like, and the boy was lucky, because there was an ambulance two streets down called out on a prank call. They were able to stop the bleeding and the kid's on his way to hospital right now.'

'Right, we'll head to the BRI then and see what the lad's got to say for himself. If this is our killers, it could be a breakthrough. Maybe they're decompensating. Carlton said that might happen. Kid got a name?'

Taffy flicked through the notes he'd taken and slowed to a halt. 'Fuck, Gus you'll never guess who it is.'

Frowning Gus glanced round at his officer, startled by his use of the 'F' word. Taffy wasn't a swearer. 'Spit it out.'

'It's only bloody Kiran Patel.'

Gus took a moment, his brow furrowed as he tried to work out why the name was so familiar to him. 'You mean Pratab's brother… Kiran.'

Taffy frowned, 'Unless it's someone else with the same name. Says he's from Clayton though. And it's too much…'

'…of a coincidence. Yeah, you got that right. Wonder what Kiran was doing over in Belle Hill. Not like it's anywhere near his neck of the woods, is it?' Gus bit his lip. 'Right, you get over to BRI and I'll head to the crime scene. See if we have any similarities.'

The knowledge that Belle Hill was Jo Jo's estate combined with the victim's link to their ongoing case, worried Gus. There had to be some connection. What was the likelihood of a murder victim's sibling being attacked within a week of his death, never mind on the same estate as one of their main suspects; it was all beginning to feel very incestuous and Gus was sure he was missing a key element.

The CSIs had erected a tent and the police had cordoned off the area. Gus greeted the officers in charge of maintaining the integrity of the outer cordon. He signed himself in, and under cover of chatting to the officers, Gus surreptitiously observed the lookie-loos who lined the tape, bantering with the uniforms, moaning about their civil liberties and demanding information they knew they were never going to get.

'You got someone photographing the crowd?'

The younger officer nodded. 'Yep, we're doing a photo trawl every ten minutes or so. Chances are the scrote that did this is hanging around. They like their moment of fame, don't they?'

That was true. In the distance Gus could see Jez Hopkins chatting to some of the spectators, his photographer trailing behind. Catching his eye, Jez raised an eyebrow and grinned. Gus scowled and turned away. Hopkins wasn't one of his favourite journalists, yet Alice, for some reason, seemed to like him. He wondered if Jez knew Al was back. Gus wasn't going to share anything about Alice. If she wanted him to know anything, she'd tell him herself.

Loitering toward the back of the crowd, Gus saw the lad they'd taken in earlier… Goyley or something, if he remembered correctly. He was with another big lad and a skinny lad, who Gus recognised as Razor McCarthy. From their body language it was clear that despite his lack of bulk or inches, it was McCarthy who called the shots. 'Get a photo of those three lads over there, will you? That's Razor McCarthy and his goons. Leader of one of the two gangs on this estate and keep an eye out for Hammerhead. If I were you, I'd be questioning them. Not much happens on Belle Hill without the say so of either Hammerhead or Razor.'

Approaching the inner cordon, Gus could see Sid and a bulky DS deep in discussion. As Gus approached, Sid raised an arm in greeting. 'Didn't expect to see you here. This doesn't look like your case. No phone, no positioning of the body, stab wound to the gut not the neck, broad daylight… feels more gang than anything else.'

Shaking hands with the female officer, a DS Iftikhar, Gus introduced himself before addressing Sid. 'You're probably right, but I'm interested in the victim. He's my first victim's brother and you know what they say? No smoke without a gallon of petrol and an arsonist.'

Laughing, Sid waved him through. 'There's not much to see, and we're done here, so have a look.' The three of them walked towards the tent, and Sid swept the flap open. 'All there is to see is that.' He pointed to a pool of blood on the floor, before raising his voice to the crime scene photographer. 'Here, Jen. Let DI McGuire have a look at the crime scene photos, will you?' He turned back to Gus. 'There was no evidence of cable ties or anything. He'd been beaten up and some arse had pissed on him, but no real similarities to your kids… though, it is strange, isn't it? Two brothers attacked within a week of each other. It's the parents I feel sorry for.'

Gus flicked through the photos and had to agree with Sid. Apart from the two victims being brothers there was nothing to link the two attacks and that worried Gus.

What the hell was happening in Bradford?

CHAPTER 77

If there was one thing Gus hated doing, it was packing the damn dishwasher but, fair was fair. Alice had cooked a curry, so cleaning up the kitchen was his job. He'd opened the kitchen window as far as he could and the back door too, but even with the desk fan in the corner of the room, the air barely moved. To be honest, he welcomed the break away from Alice and Patti. It didn't sit well with him that Zarqa and Jo Jo were still in custody. Mo and Naila had blanked him, refusing to answer any of his calls... he couldn't blame them, but it still hurt. DCS Bashir had given him permission to take Jo Jo to see his mum at the BRI and she'd shot right up in his estimation for that. The kid had looked petrified at the machines and suchlike that his mum was hooked up to, but he'd held it together, chatting on cheerfully to her, pretending he'd been at school all day and that Jessie was at a friend's. It broke Gus' heart to drag the lad away. As the machines wheezed and beeped, Gus worried that this might be the last time Jo Jo would see his mum.

Alice and Patti were in the living room and the murmur of their voices punctuated with the odd burst of laughter kept him company, although the thought that they might well be making ever increasingly lavish plans for their wedding put him on edge. Truth was he thought Patti was using it as a distraction from all the pressure at school with the press camped outside and the avalanche of emails from parents regarding her 'indiscretion'. Some people didn't seem to get that none of this was her fault. Someone invaded her privacy and yet she was the one getting the flak. She often lapsed into silence, a faraway look in her eye, deep in thought and Gus wasn't sure her thoughts included him… or certainly not in a good way. After this case, he told himself, he'd speak to Patti. Explain that he loved her, but that he wasn't in a desperate rush to settle down. After all that had happened, they could probably both do with slowing things down. Marriage wasn't an essential for him and he'd done the all singing all dancing crap with Gaby and look how that had turned out. All he wanted was to share a commitment without the formality of a wedding. The whole wedding thing was too much too soon, and he couldn't get his head round it. It felt more like a reaction to their private life being made public and less about a commitment to each other.

So engrossed in his thoughts was he, that he only noticed the high-pitched humming noise when it was right outside the window. He glanced up and recoiled. His first instinct was that the drone was taking photos of him and he wanted to smash it to bits. He dived out the back door and ran towards it, but just as he reached it, it swung upwards abruptly just out of reach of his flailing arms. Bloody bastard was taking the piss… taunting him.

'Al! Patt! Drone!'

It hovered for a moment and then swooped down to release the item it was holding in its custom-made grabber. The familiar blue envelope drifted to the decking, but Gus wasn't interested in that. No, he was determined to get the drone. It turned and began to fly out of the garden towards the woods. Gus had two options, follow it and hopefully catch the drone's operator or catch the damn thing. Although the first idea appealed, the inbuilt camera would alert the pilot if he was getting close to them. Instead, he sprinted towards the fence at the back of his garden, scrambled up on top of his compost bin and stretched towards the drone. His fingers caught one of the legs, but they couldn't gain purchase. He lost his grip. The bloody machine was going to escape. He had only one option left, so he put one foot onto the top of the fence, balancing with his arms, he stood in a crouch steadying himself for a mere second before he jumped toward the drone arms stretched ahead like Superman.

He fell hard onto the hard mud path in the woods below, yet still managed to twist and roll so as not to damage the drone. Winded, he lay there, doing a mental inventory of his body. Feet... working, arms... working... neck... working. As he tried to get his breath back, he heard Alice and Patti yelling his name.

'I'm here.' He wished his voice sounded less tremulous. The voices grew closer, then the gate rattled, but, with the padlock on, they couldn't open it. Within seconds, Alice's face popped over the top of the fence, her worried expression replaced almost immediately by a mischievous one. 'Good dive, Gus... Didn't know you could fly.'

'Ha bloody ha. It appears I can't but...' He raised his hands outstretched before him... 'I can catch things that do. Now go get the key for the gate from the kitchen drawer and let me in. Doubt I'll be able to climb that fence again.'

As Alice's head disappeared again, he held the drone in front of him, and staring straight into the camera said, 'Whoever you are... you murdering perv. I'm on to you! You'd better watch out!'

He switched it off, placed it on the ground and struggled to his feet, acknowledging that a hot bath might be in order to deal with some of his bruises. His shoulder protested as he bent down to pick up the drone. Carrying it carefully, in the hope that he might be able to get some prints from it, he waited until Alice opened the gate and hobbled back into the garden, wishing his back and legs didn't feel like jelly and trying to ignore the twinge that accompanied each movement. 'What do you make of this?'

Alice inhaled. 'Well, if we reckon the stalker and the killers are linked, then maybe Zarqa and Jo Jo are telling the truth... maybe they did only do the mosque spraying. This confirms Jo Jo's story and the texts Compo retrieved. On the other hand, maybe one or both of them are in it with the person who sent this monstrosity flying over here. Maybe it's an elaborate plan to obfuscate things. Bottom line is, we can't let them go yet, Gus.'

They joined Patti who was on the decking staring down at the blue envelope. 'You've really got to get this bastard, Gus.' She glanced around as if expecting a swarm of drones to appear over the horizon and despite the heat, wrapping her arms round her body, she shuddered. 'Everywhere I go, I feel like someone's watching me.'

Carefully placing the drone in the plastic bag produced by Alice, he nodded. Patti was right. This was too personal. The only endgame he could imagine was one involving him... and, more than likely, violence. His earlier adrenalin rush faded, leaving a trail of anger that throbbed through his body slow and painful. Suspecting that his motives weren't entirely those of a police officer seeking justice, but of an injured individual wanting to inflict payback, he allowed the feeling to grow instead of swallowing it down like he usually did. Whoever was out there killing kids and toying with him, threatening the people he loved and invading his space, had overstepped the mark. He wanted to inflict hurt and, as he accepted that thought, his fists clenched. When the time came, he'd have difficulty controlling himself, for the person with the drone, he was sure, was the driving force behind everything and everything was somehow directed personally at him. Gus moved over and put an arm round Patti's shoulders, pulling her to him, savouring the coconut fragrance of her shampoo. He loved her... desperately... but bad things happened to the people he loved... his thoughts flicked from Greg, the best friend he'd killed, to Alice whom he'd doubted, to Sampson, a colleague who'd died in the line of fire. Perhaps he didn't deserve her... maybe he needed to let her go in order for her to be safe? He held her tight, eyes closed for a moment longer. 'You need to distance yourself from me for now. Go and stay at a friend's house.'

Her head jerked up; her cute nose crinkled like it did when she was annoyed with something. 'No bloody chance. We're in this together... and...' She pulled out from his embrace. 'I'm not running from anyone... especially not a damn psycho who's killing my students and threatening my... fiancé.' Her lips quirked briefly as the last word and Gus felt like a tosser.

'Well, when you two lovebirds are finished with all the soppy doo dahs, can we crack on with some *actual* police work?' Alice had donned gloves and popped the letter in an evidence bag. 'Come on, let's get going.'

Gus cupped Patti's face with his hands and dropped a quick kiss on her lips. 'This is about me being able to focus, yeah? If you're at Chrissy's, I'll know you're safe and I'll be able to focus. I need you to do this for me.'

For a moment he thought she was going to argue, but at the last minute, she seemed to reconsider. 'Okay. I'll give Chrissy a ring.'

'But you'll wait here until I have an officer to escort you.'

Patti smiled. 'You do realise that if this stalker is savvy enough to orchestrate two murders and infringe your privacy with their infernal drones, then chances are they'll be able to follow me wherever I go.'

She was right, but Gus wanted her away from him in the hope that whoever was stalking them would focus on him and he wanted her with someone else at all times. But he could feel the frustration rolling off her. 'There is something you could do. We're going through the interviews we did with your kids as quickly as we can, but maybe you could narrow it down a bit for us? Ask your staff if they know of any pupils, past or present, who demonstrated some sort of technical expertise. My guess is that whoever customised these drones, wouldn't have gone unnoticed.'

Patti frowned. 'You really do suspect one of my kids, don't you?'

'We're still narrowing things down, but we'd be fools to ignore such big coincidences. You being the head teacher, me being the detective, two victims – both from your school, both of a similar age, and *Snapchat*s sent to other kids from your school,' he paused for breath. 'And that's even without Sebastian Carlton's profile.'

CHAPTER 78

Zodiac

Aaaaah. Who the hell does he think he is? I play the scene again on my phone. His face right up to the screen, those unusual blue eyes of his with their dark rim round the iris, sparking – ice flames sparking from them. Who knew blue could be so hot? His dreads bounce round his face, like a mane. That's what he's like… a lion… a lion with a mane bouncing about.

'Whoever you are… you murdering perv. I'm on to you! You'd better watch out!'

Who does he think he is? Perv? He's angry. Spitting the words out at the screen.

Shit! Shit! Shit! He's got my drone. I pace the living room, glad that I'm on my own. I slop some vodka into a glass, top it up with Pepsi and take a long swig… Aah! Better! – Not much… but it'll do. Don't care if she finds the bottle. Not like she's a proper Muslim anyways.

I scrape my fingers through my hair, not caring when my scalp starts to bleed. What to do? What to do? If I could, I'd do another one tonight… no probs. But after all that family stuff with Leo, that's impossible… best to let Pisces have a bit of time to recover too. Pace them out. Why's all this stuff happening at once? It's getting near the end now, anyway. But no. I'm not going to let them push me. I'm setting the agenda, not them.

I pick my phone up and play it again. Torturing myself… yes, I know, but, so what? I've got to see him!

'Whoever you are… you creepy perv. I'm on to you! You'd better watch out!'

Repeat!

'Whoever you are... you creepy perv. I'm on to you! You'd better watch out!'

Repeat!

'Whoever you are... you creepy perv. I'm on to you! You'd better watch out!'

Aaaaaaaaah!

I throw the phone against the wall. Maybe those tramps of his need to get it! Yeah. Maybe that's what I'll do. Kill the fucking tramps and I fall onto the couch, laughing.

That'll teach him. That'll teach *My Dearest Detective Inspector Angus McGuire*.

CHAPTER 79

You'd think by the look on Compo's face that Gus had presented him with a million pounds rather than a chunk of plastic that looked like some sort of miniature alien spaceship. Compo was bouncing around, desperate to get his hands on the drone, wittering on about, 'battery life' and 'distance waves' and the like. All things that Gus was sure were very enlightening, but not anything he wanted to have to get to grips with. All he wanted were some decent fingerprints, and then some of Compo's magic to tell him who had been flying the damn thing.

On the plus side, Compo did have some good news. The spray cans found in Zarqa's room chemically matched the paint on the mosque and the style of writing matched with graffiti work Zarqa had done at school. Alongside that, Compo had managed to obtain CCTV footage of Jo Jo buying the cans. So that part of their story held up. And according to the time recorded on the mosque cameras, they were in the process of doing their artwork, around half an hour before Karim found Pratab's body, which was around the time of death.

Gus initially considered taking Zarqa back home to her parents, but then reconsidered. Mo and Naila wouldn't forgive him for a while, if ever, and Zarqa and her parents had a lot of things to discuss, so he delegated Taffy to take her back home, before dropping Jo Jo at his mother's bedside. News from the BRI was that she was unlikely to make it through the night and Jo Jo wanted to be with his mum. Jo Jo's social worker had reluctantly agreed after Taffy had volunteered to stay with Jo Jo. Gus had never been prouder of Taffy, who had cancelled a date to be there for Jo Jo, saying, 'That poor kid's gonna miss his mum every day for the rest of his life, so I can surely miss one date.'

They were in Sid's lab who'd come in as a special favour to Gus. Gus had already mentally chalked up a bottle of the finest malt for Sid, but that could wait.

'Any prints, Sid?'

The CSI shook his head. 'Tut tut tut. I've told you before about your impatience. This is going to have to be a joint venture between me and my man Compo here, if we're to get anything.'

'Eh?'

Sid's sigh was exaggerated, and Gus wanted to hurry him along, but he knew it would do no good.

'This creature is a basic drone with adaptations according to Comp. This means that it's not only the outer casing that needs printing; it's all the added extras too. I suggest that I print the outer casing and then Compo, bit by bit, can dissemble the creature and I continue printing as we go along. That way you'll get my forensic input and Compo will be able to work out what information he can glean from the drone.'

Despite finding it a little creepy that Sid referred to the inanimate object as 'the creature', Gus realised that what the CSI proposed made sense. If only he could shake off the *Dr Who* vibe that Hissing Sid's words had evoked. Last thing he wanted was the damn drone coming to life and floating about Sid's lab saying 'exterminate' in a squeaky robotic voice.

Three hours later, by which time Gus' muscles had stiffened and his body was protesting, Compo and Sid had finished. Many of the prints Sid had isolated looked promising and had been sent to the Integrated Automated Fingerprint Identification System to look for matches. With

Sebastian Carlton's suspicion that their killers were youngsters, Gus suspected that they'd be lucky to find a match, however, when they found the killer, the prints might be the difference between a successful prosecution and a failed one… and you never knew, maybe their perpetrator had got in bother before.

Compo was as excited as Barbie at a sleep-over and had been mumbling under his breath the entire time he'd been working. He now turned to Gus, without his usual beanie on his hair was strangely flat, making him look even younger and more childlike than usual. It was as if his mum had patted his hair straight down from crown to brow. The thing was, Compo hadn't had a mum. He'd been brought up in a series of foster homes, where his eccentricities had left him a target. Gus felt a flutter of appreciation for his friend and smiled.

'Go on then, Compo, hit me with it… but go easy on me, eh? Techie whizz kid, I'm not.'

Compo waved a hand, indicating that Gus should join him at the counter where all the components of the drone had been laid out in an orderly line. This was so different from Compo's usual seemingly chaotic way of working, that Gus was impressed.

'This is a budget drone, a Yuneec Typhoon H – one of the cheapest on the market at around two hundred and fifty quid. It's got a flight time of less than half an hour and the distance it can be controlled from is no more than a mile.'

How the hell could kids afford that sort of money – from a paper round? Drugs? Compo continued, 'This isn't the same base as the other drone, the one that dropped the phone. From the CCTV it looked more like a Phantom Obsidian… costs a lot more. You'd be lucky to get change out of a grand for that. I'd guess both have been adapted though, so whoever's doing that has some real knowledge of how these things work.'

Gus was glad he'd set Patti on the case. Surely one of her staff members would be aware if any of their students possessed such specialist skills. Bone tired, stiff, and bruised after his dive to catch the drone, Gus wanted to go home, but before he did, he needed to see what the letter had revealed.

Sebastian Carlton made it back to the lab just in time to witness the envelope being opened releasing the unmistakeable smell of Obsession into the room. The font, envelope, and tone were similar to the previous ones and, as expected, there were no fingerprints on the envelope. The CSI opened it and slid the contents onto a sterile tray. As usual there was an A4 sheet folded in half and Gus could tell from the bulk that there was also something else. He braced himself for it to be another photo of him and Patti in some compromising position. Relief washed over him when the letter was unfolded to reveal a photo of him talking to Jerry and Dave in Lister Park. According to the forensic expert, the previous photo had been printed on a home computer with bog-standard printer ink. Gus suspected the same would be true for this one.

'This perp is definitely taking pleasure in getting up close and personal to you.'

Gus could have forgiven Carlton's enthusiastic tone, if the other man hadn't been rocking back and forth on his heels when he stated the damn obvious.

'Can you remember when this was taken? Did you notice anyone in the vicinity?'

Gosh, never thought to think about that, Prof! Gus bit back a sarcastic comment. He was tetchy because he was tired and there was no need to take it out on the professor. He remembered chatting to Jerry and Dave on… Monday. Had it been Monday? Or maybe Tuesday? It was so frustrating to think that while he'd been engrossed in conversation, his stalker, the killer had been right there. Hell, he'd probably passed them and not given them a second glance.

Carlton looked at Gus for a moment. 'You want to try a cognitive interview?'

Gus glanced from Carlton to Compo. The short answer was no! The last thing he wanted to do was put himself under Carlton's influence, then he remembered how kind the man had been during his panic attack and, with a sign to the CSI to wait for them, he nodded.

Carlton guided him over to a chair and made him sit before he dragged another one over and positioned it in front of Gus. With Compo hovering by his shoulder and Carlton's knees brushing his, Gus couldn't have been any more uncomfortable.

Exhaling, he relaxed his shoulders as per the professor's instructions, closed his eyes and waited.

'What are you talking to the two men about?'

That was easy. 'Their phones. How the sunny weather meant they liked sleeping out. How worried they were about Zarqa being out on her own after dark.'

'The park was busy, then?' Carlton's voice was low, conversational.

'Yeah, I passed loads of people; the power-walkers, the joggers, kids on their way to school.'

'Just turn your head in the direction the photo was taken from. What can you see?'

Gus frowned. In his mind, he twisted his body to the left and looked across the pond towards the boating pavilion. 'The path's nearly empty… a couple of old Muslim men with walking sticks. I've seen them before. They always say hello. There's someone getting up from the bench, swinging a bag onto their shoulders. A rucksack? They're walking towards the kids' play area. Hold on… They stop, glance round, and then they're off again.' Gus' heart pounded. He didn't know where that memory came from. Couldn't remember seeing that person earlier. He screwed his eyes closed, focussing, willing them to turn around so he can see their face. 'Shit! They're too far away. Can't see who it is... not sure if it's a boy or a girl. They've got a cap on. Shorts and a blue T-shirt!' Gus' eyes sprang open and meet Carton's smiling gaze. 'Can't see their face! I couldn't see their damn face!'

'You did well, Gus.'

'Not really... how does that help? Might not even have been them who took the photo.'

'Oh, I think it was. That's why you noticed them. Your subconscious made you. Now, this gives us someone to cross reference with your friends and with the staff at the café and boating pavilion. Any of them may remember the same person, but with more details.'

Gus shrugged. Despite his earlier doubts, he was disappointed. So near and yet so far away.

'Did you get a sense of this person's age?'

'A kid... late teens... early twenties, I'd say – but who knows?'

Sebastian stood up, smiling at Gus. 'Well that's consistent with my existing profile, isn't it?'

Yeah, but who knows if your profile is right? Gus narrowly stopped himself from saying the words. Instead, he moved over to where the CSI had been watching the cognitive interview with interest. 'Let's see what my stalker's got to say for themselves this time.'

The CSI unfolded the letter and laid it flat so they could all see.

My Dearest Detective Inspector Angus McGuire,

> It's becoming more and more of a delight to watch you. Are you enjoying the show so far? I must admit it's been a fascinating project for me. How are your tramp friends? Pity they didn't turn up just a little earlier the other night, isn't it? Who knows what might have happened?
>
> Anyway, just wanted to keep in touch... let you know I'm thinking of you.
>
> This is not the end... not by a long chalk!
>
> Watch this space!

'This person knows you know Jerry and Dave well. They've also confirmed that they are aware of Jerry and Dave's role in finding Betsy. I think this is a definite indication that your stalker is involved in these murders.'

Confirmation of something they already suspected, but nothing fresh. 'How does that sit with your profile, that there are more than one of them involved?'

Carlton studied the letter for a bit longer. 'I think this letter is personal to you, Gus. I think your stalker knows you personally and you know them. They may have only ever come across you in passing, but in their mind, they've magnified a connection to you. The letter is their baby... it's separate to the killings. *You* are their obsession.'

None of this was helpful... not now. Not to help catch the killer and meanwhile, who knew who the next target would be?

Carlton was talking again. 'If there are two of them, then this one is the leader... the manipulator. The other is just their pawn. But the fact that the stalking incidents have increased, intimates that the killings may increase too. I think we need to be prepared for another attack very soon. I think it's time to get your lovely Nancy and the indomitable DCS Bashir in front of the camera. You need to issue a warning. This could all accelerate very quickly. With these sort of spree killings over a short period, the endings are usually violent, unpredictable, and sudden. You need to issue a warning. We don't want any more dead kids in Bradford this summer, do we?'

CHAPTER 80

Leo

> Me: You see this crap on the telly? You
> know what it's about?

I'm hunked down in a chair, minding my own business, ignoring the drama… the crying and shit that's going on around me. Rather be anywhere else but here, but I'm not allowed. It's like they're glued to me. Can't breathe without them being all over me. I'd rather be at home than in this hellhole. Really want a cig!

Can't believe *Look North*. Mehmoona's mum on the telly telling us to keep safe. Not to let the teenagers go out alone. Keep them indoors.

We have reason to suspect that there is a danger on the streets of Bradford and while the police are working to…

I tune out for a moment, wondering if I can make my escape… but no. She's back, sitting next to me, crowding me.

…anything to report at all, please contact us immediately on 0…

My phone vibrates and I stand up. 'Need the loo.' Surely, they won't follow me there too? But no. She's distracted and so I sneak away.

Can't stand the stink of these places… all bleach and stuff. Catches in my throat. I lock myself in a cubicle and relax. First space I've had all day, but I know it won't last for long. Have to be quick. I look at my phone. Pisces! Aw crap!

> Pisces: You see the news? I'm scared. We gotta stop.

Should I wait for Zodiac? I look at my phone willing Zodiac to reply. Nothing!

> Me: Don't be a div. We're okay. Stop worrying! Laters!
>
> Pisces: What if they know? Mehmoona's mum said they were closing in.
>
> Me: Rubbish. Go to bed. We'll talk tomorrow. Laters!

Despite my words to Pisces, I'm a bit nervous too. Unsettled. Wish Zodiac would reply.

CHAPTER 81

Gus hadn't expected to see Katie for a while. He'd hoped she'd give him some space and not hassle him, but he was wrong. He came downstairs when the doorbell rang and glanced at the CCTV. His new home security had been great so far... as long as he remembered to switch it on, that was. Katie stood looking all wan and waiflike, and Gus' stomach contracted. She was clearly in 'I'm a victim' mode. She looked like a ten-year-old in her knee-length shorts and strappy top. When she looked up at the camera, he was shocked to see huge black bags under her eyes. Her cheeks were hollowed out and her arms looked skinny and pale. The deterioration in her physical appearance since the last time he saw her only a few days ago was what prompted him to open the door. He felt a right dick for his earlier thoughts.

'Shit, Katie. What's wrong?'

Katie, a slight smile teasing her lips, stepped into the hallway. 'You're not saying you care, are you?'

For some reason, her words seemed hollow as opposed to the jovial way he thought she'd intended. Her eyes filled up and Gus stepped forward sweeping her against his chest. 'You've got to tell me what's wrong,' he whispered, scared of her reply, yet trying defiantly to keep upbeat. Whatever was troubling Katie was serious... very serious. 'I can't help you if you don't.'

Katie pushed away from him, took a scruffy tissue from her pocket, blew her nose, and stepped towards the kitchen. 'You know me. I'm not doing owt without a cup of Yorkshire Tea in my hand.'

Thanks to Alice he had milk that wasn't completely out of date and ginger nut biscuits. As he made the tea, he observed his sister from the corner of his eye. Close up she looked even more gaunt that she had on the camera. Her hair was the only thing that seemed radiant and healthy. If Gabby had taken out his refusal to father their child on his sister, he'd kill her. He'd bloody kill her. Dropping the used tea bags into the bin, leaving a trail of dark droplets on the worksurface, he worked himself into even more of a fury. Gabriella was a problem. She was selfish, manipulative, and a pain in the backside. He couldn't work out what Katie saw in her. He'd long since learned the truth about his ex-wife. It seemed, though, that his sister was as in love with Gabby today as she'd been the day Gabby left him and moved into Katie's flat.

He sat opposite Katie and, for want of anything better to do, opened the ginger nuts and grabbed a couple before pushing the packet towards Katie. 'So, you gonna tell me what's up? Gabby taking it out on you that I said no?'

Katie blew on her tea but placed the cup on the table without drinking. Sounding tired, her eyes flitting to a point beyond Gus' shoulder, she said, 'I wish you and Gabby would just get on you know? Put your differences behind you.'

Gus wanted to rage about the way Gabriella had treated him on numerous occasions, but something in his sister's expression stopped him. Instead he hunched over the table and, with an inexplicable dread weighing down on him, dunked another biscuit he didn't want into his mug.

'I'm not very well, Gus.'

His heart faltered. He heard the words, but he wanted to thrust them away. Bundle them up and throw them into the garbage. Something about Katie's calm expression told him it wasn't just a sore throat she had. He tried swallow, but somehow, a chunk of broken glass had got into his throat and he couldn't. His heart sped up, and his breath came in pants. Still not looking at her, he forced himself to slow his breathing slooooooow, slooooow.

When he looked at Katie, she met his gaze, her dark eyes full of shadows and doubt and right then it clicked that this was serious… really serious and he had to step up to the mark. He opened his mouth to speak, realised his throat was too dry and took a quick gulp of his drink… he tried again. 'What's wrong?'

Katie smiled and raised her hand and whipping off her wig, she threw it on the kitchen table. 'Big C. Ovarian.'

Gus stared at the wig, a riot of dark curls lying like a discarded poodle on his table, then lifted his eyes to Katie. 'You've started treatment? You've started treatment and you didn't tell me.'

Her voice was sharp. 'This isn't about *you*.'

That was true. It wasn't about him, still, he was wounded that she hadn't confided in him… asked for his support, shared her anguish with him. As if she read his mind, Katie continued, 'I was so angry with you for not letting me in when Greg died, you know? So angry and frustrated and let down. I wanted to help you, but you shut me out and I couldn't understand why. Now I do. It's hard enough coping with it myself without sharing it with the world. All I want is to curl up with Gaby and let the rest of the world pass by outside without me having to interact with any of it.'

That was exactly how it had been for Gus. He nodded, understanding, yet hurt that he hadn't been there to help her. 'I would…'

She reached over the table and squeezed his hand. 'I know you would. But I wasn't ready.'

'Mum and Dad know?'

'Last week. I told them last week.'

Again, he was the last to know.

'I wanted to… well, we wanted to ask you about the baby, before we told you. Didn't want it to look like we were guilt tripping you… but, you said no.'

Yes, he had said no… not surprising really, was it? Yet now, looking at his sister, it all seemed different. The words stumbled out of his mouth, 'What's your prognosis?'

Grinning, Katie again lifted her cup, this time taking a minuscule sip. 'Well, I'm not planning my funeral yet…' She pursed her lips. 'We don't know. I've just completed my third lot of chemo… but we just don't know.' She fidgeted on her chair. 'What you're really asking is, why now, when I might not make it, do I want to start a family with Gaby?'

Gus shrugged. It was what he'd been thinking but couldn't put into words.

'She's my soul mate, Gus. We want to have a baby… a family. I'm going to get through this, but Gaby will have to be the one to carry the baby. Just in case, I don't make it long-term, I want the child to be linked to me. I always have. I've always wanted to carry a baby… more than one, if I'm honest, but Gaby's doing it for me. She's making that sacrifice.'

Was there a slight inflection on the word she? Gus couldn't be certain, yet here she was, and he knew she was playing her last card. That was how Katie worked. He played his own trump card, yet it was accompanied by an inevitability he hated. Katie always won at cards. 'DNA doesn't make a family, Katie. Love does that. You don't need me for that.'

'No, you're right, DNA doesn't. But this way, it won't be so bad when they whip out my womb. It'll be almost as good as carrying my own baby. Please do it for me, Gus. Please.'

And there it was. The double trump!

CHAPTER 82

With Katie's visit still foremost in his mind, Gus had gone into work. He'd not slept well the previous night, half expecting to be called out to a third murder. When none had come, he'd determined to make the day count. He'd gone back into Patti's school, taking Sebastian Carlton with him in the hope that someone would have something for him. But they came up with nothing. He'd spent hours looking at CCTV in the streets around the park… again zilch. Compo had got a hit on one of the fingerprints from the drone, but it had been in a sealed record and Nancy had yet to get back to him with any information. He had hinted to Compo that he'd be happy to turn a blind eye if Compo could access the information in other ways. They needed a name. True, the fingerprint might belong to a factory worker, but it was another avenue that Gus wanted to eliminate.

He'd found the time to go to the hospital where the Patels were visiting with Kiran, who looked like he'd make a full recovery. It seemed so unfair that one family could have so much to contend with all at once. It looked to Gus as if Mr Patel was withering away before his eyes and his wife seemed older, quieter. Her face bore wrinkles that Gus was sure hadn't been there when he'd first met her. When he'd arrived, Mita had been talking to another girl in the smokers' shelter. The girl looked a little older than Mita, and Gus recognised her from Patti's school. She was one of those spotty, nervous girls who couldn't quite meet your eye. He'd smiled at her and been pleased to see her habitual scowl. At least Mita hadn't lost all of her personality. Kiran, predictably, had refused to implicate anyone in his attack and claimed he couldn't remember how he got to the estate. The attack had all the hall marks of a drug gang warning and Gus only hoped Kiran had learned his lesson – for his parents' sakes if nothing else.

The incident room had been unnaturally quiet for the rest of the day with Alice, Taffy, and Compo focussed on their tasks. The atmosphere was heavy, like a thunderstorm in the making, and Gus, constrained by his lack of leads, wanted to scream. Instead, he sent Alice off for supplies and he'd just about decided to go for a jog to help him think things through, when Compo slammed his hand down on his desk.

'This doesn't make sense, Gus.' Compo had pushed his headphones back, so they were dangling round his neck. 'I've managed to trace the server that uploaded the images... the ones of Pratab and Betsy as well as the ones of you and Patti, but...' His frown was tight across his forehead and combined with the little flick of fringe that flopped there, he looked like a confused four-year-old. 'I've checked it three times now and I'm coming up with the same result every time.'

'I trust you, Compo. If you've found something, I'd bet anything that it's correct. So, what is it?' Gus, reluctant to leave the faint breeze generated by his desk fan, got to his feet, and sidled over.

A map showing row upon row of domestic residences was on Compo's screen and a flashing light indicated that he'd found the one where the computer was that had uploaded the images of Pratab Patel and Betsy Reavley's dead bodies. He smiled. 'You located the computer?'

Compo blew upwards, sending his fringe wafting. 'It's proper weird. I just don't get it.'

'Okaaay.' Gus wasn't sure what to say. Compo's shoulders were hunched, and he was frantically tapping more keys, and staring at the screen after each flurry of keyboard activity. Whatever the lad had found it had thrown him and Gus hoped it had nothing to do with Zarqa. Not when they'd only just sent her home.

Exhaling again. Compo propelled himself backwards on his chair to make room for Gus. 'It's the address. I've checked it, but it stays the same.'

Compo was glaring at the screen as if he expected it to alter independently.

'Look, Comps, I've no idea what you're going on about... you need to make it clear for me.'

'It's Fieldgate Road!' He looked up at Gus, his face stricken as if Gus would hold him personally responsible. 'Number eighteen.'

For a second Gus couldn't work out what Compo was telling him. This information was truly bizarre. He opened his mouth to ask Compo if he was sure and then closed it again without uttering the words. He'd seen how distraught the lad was and had witnessed him trying again and again. 'You mean...?'

'Yep. Whoever uploaded those images and the ones of you and Patti, did it from her house... *that* house.' Compo jabbed the screen with his finger. 'Our killer has access to a PC in that house.'

Gus slapped his hand on the table, making Compo jump. 'Fuck, fuck, fuck, fuck!' Then, he was spinning on his heel and heading for the door, just as Alice came in carrying an aromatic bag of burgers. 'You're with me, *now*!'

Alice thrust the bag onto the nearest table, and he turned to Compo. 'Get a team there, pronto. Taffy get a pool car and a couple of officers and Carlton. Bring him too.'

CHAPTER 83

Zodiac

It's only a matter of time now. I always knew it would come to this. Now they've got the drone, they'll get my prints and all that stuff in Birmingham will come out. That sidekick of Gus' will unseal my juvie record and they'll know. *She* won't be able to cover it up this time. No calling in favours from her colleagues. No burying her head in the sand. No more pretending last time was a mistake. She'll always wonder if she was to blame… if she could've done something different and that's good. Let her wonder! Let her suffer! She deserves it for not appreciating me… not seeing my specialness as something to be proud of, something unique *She* covered it up for the sake of her glorious career, what now though? I thought Gus would have been a worthy opponent, but even he has been slow to figure it out… even he can't stop me, no one can! They can keep their kids in all they like, no one is going to stop me until I'm good and ready. And then, I'll still prove how clever I am.

Still, I'll get off lightly… just like last time. After all, I didn't kill anyone and sending a few letters, uploading a few pics to the Internet, is nothing. Well… I was coerced, wasn't I? That's the beauty of it… I'll be able to convince them that Pisces and Leo led little old me astray. Anyway, it's time for the endgame. Time to draw things to their natural conclusion.

It has to be today… tonight… NOW!

> Me: *Lister Park! You bring the stuff!*
>
> Leo: *On it. Will slip away. Laters*

> Now to see if everyone's on side.
>
> Me: *Tonight, bring the girl. Last one...*
> *then it'll all be over!*
>
> Pisces: *Can't! No more. Just can't!*
>
> Me: *Yes, you can. You know you can.*
> *You've done it before and this one was*
> *your choice. Remember? You chose*
> *her.*
>
> Pisces: *Changed my mind. Let's not do*
> *this anymore!*
>
> Me: *You know the rules. Just do it.*

If anyone was going to mess it all up, it was Pisces. I wait for the reply. It takes a while and then I punch the air when I see it.

> Pisces: Okay. Last one... no more.

I laugh and punch the air. Course there's going to be no more. That's the plan. No more after tonight. Shame Pisces and Leo don't know what I've got in mind. I grab my rucksack, pop my cap on, and leave the house.

Tonight's gonna be a good night!

CHAPTER 84

A s Alice drove, Gus phoned Nancy to bring her up to speed. 'We think we've identified the killer, Nance. I really need you on this one. It's sensitive.'

He could hear clothes rustling, followed by the flush of a toilet. *Please don't have just answered the phone when you're sitting on the loo*! Then he immediately dismissed the thought and continued, 'Thing is, we think the killer or one of them, if Carlton's profile is right, is Mehmoona Bashir... the boss' daughter.'

He braced himself, expecting some sort of argument, instead Nancy came through for him. 'Okay, I'm on my way. You need to secure the girl. Who knows what's going on in her head or what she's got planned. We need to keep the boss safe.'

He flicked a grin at Alice and hung up, but immediately his phone started to ring. *Compo*!

'You're on speaker, Comps, what you got?'

'She's on the move, Gus. Soon as you left, I started to track her phone and the DCS' too. The boss is still at home, but Mehmoona is on the move. Looks like she's heading in this direction.'

Alice pulled into the Co-op carpark, did a U-turn, and parked up illegally on the side of the road, engine still running.

'We're on Duckworth Lane, facing towards the roundabout. Can you tell how she's travelling?'

'At the minute, she looks to be on foot, nearing the BRI now.'

'Right, I need to keep my phone open. Phone back on the radio and patch Taffy, Carlton, and the back-up team into this. We need you to co-ordinate all of this. We can't afford to lose her... not now. I need to speak with Nancy. She's heading up to Bashir's house as we speak, and I think that's the best place for her. She can prepare Bashir for the worst.'

Gus hung up and almost immediately it stared to ring again. Mo! Shit! Not now! Much as he wanted to build bridges, now wasn't the time. He pressed decline, hoping that his friend would understand when he explained later. But it started to ring again almost immediately.

Meanwhile, Compo was on the radio, tracking Mehmoona's movements.

'She's cut up towards Smith Lane.' Alice did a quick U-turn and headed back towards the BRI and narrowly skirting through an amber light, drove up Little Lane. 'If she continues this way, we'll be able to nab her on Toller Lane.'

Alice's phone started to ring on the hand's free. Naila! And Gus' phone vibrated in his hand. Mo again! Shit! Mo and Naila both trying to contact them. This couldn't be good.

'Yep, Mo. What's up?'

'Zarqa's gone. She took a phone call a while back and then left. Snuck out the back door. Thing is, her phone's switched off and I can't track her.'

Aw no! Zarqa what are you playing at?

'I'm busy right now, Mo, but as soon as I can, I'll call back in. In the meantime, I'll see if Compo can find out where Jo Jo is. He gave him one of his old phones to be going on with. Zarqa will probably be with him.'

Well, that's what he hoped, anyway. Last thing he needed was Zarqa getting in the middle of this thing with Mehmoona.

'Shit boss!' Compo's frustration sizzled over the line. 'Mehmoona's switched off her phone. Last position was on Smith Lane. She could have gone in any direction from there. There're loads of sideroads.'

'Never mind, Comp's, you've done your best. Put out a BOLO for her and direct the back-up to scour the streets in the vicinity. Alice and I will drive round… we might be lucky and spot her.' Gus slammed his fist on the dashboard. 'Shit, where do you think she's heading?'

But Alice was already turning off onto Scotchman Road. 'Carlton thought she was threatening Jerry and Dave, yeah? We know she hangs about the park and we know they do too. What do you reckon? Lister Park, worth a try?'

'Definitely. Go for it.'

As they drove down Scotchman Road, past two primary schools and the Manningham Sports Centre, Gus kept a keen lookout. Trouble was, it was dark now and, in this area, there was a fair share of teens, not all of them instantly recognisable by gender. What if they were wrong? What if she wasn't heading to Lister Park? What if she had her eye on a victim elsewhere? No way could there be another teen killing on his watch.

On North Park Road, Alice parked up and they got out of the car. Gus radioed in his position to Compo and asked for back-up to be directed to both the Oak Lane and the Emm Lane park entrances. Fastening her stab vests, Alice grinned. 'Lot of good these'll do us… this one aims for the throat.'

But Gus had noticed her fingers fumbling with the Velcro and registered the telltale tremor in her voice. Alice was as nervous as he was. Mehmoona's unpredictability, plus the dark and the possibility of at least one accomplice was worrying. A surge of adrenalin pistoned through his body, increasing his heartbeat and he knew he was as prepared as he could be.

At night, Lister Park had a different, more malevolent feel to it. Gone were the family groups and in their place were looming shadows and hidden unlit areas. Gus and Alice climbed the knee-high wall and entered the park, keeping to the shadows themselves.

'Can you see anyone?' Alice's voice was a whisper breaking through the evening heat.

'No. We'll split up. You go towards the Botanical Gardens and I'll head towards Cartwright Hall.'

As they moved off, Gus hesitated and then turned back. 'Hey, Al.'

She glanced towards him.

'Be safe… yeah.'

CHAPTER 85

Zodiac

Couldn't have planned it better if I tried. They're all there. I take a moment to watch them in the band stand. They're in high spirits… none of them has any idea what's going to happen tonight. As I climb the steps, I see that they've done as I asked. All their phones are piled in a little heap in the middle of the circle and Leo has lit a candle, just like I asked.

Most of them think we're here to think about Pratab and Betsy… but I have other plans and even Leo and Pisces don't know them yet. Talking of Pisces – there she is, all miserable and wan, like someone stole her favourite toy. She's edged closer to Jo Jo, but he's not interested. He looks distracted, like he's got something else on his mind. Dozy cow can't even tell he's gay! Story of her life. But, hey, at least she did as she was told and brought Zarqa with her. Leo's come up trumps… she always does. Two bottles of voddie and some weed. Just enough to get the party started. I start to climb the steps, when someone bumps into me from behind.

My heart starts to hammer for a second, I think I've been caught. I know it won't be long. But it's just that tosser Karim, with his stupid bloody dog. *Who invited him*? He barrels past me laughing and joking, the dog whimpering, and he settles down next to Zarqa.

It's nearly time. I plonk my rucksack down and sit next to it. Leo's passing round the voddie and Jo Jo's rolling a joint. The bitter smell of bud fills the air as he lights it, inhales, and then blows out a smoke ring. Leo's getting giddy quickly. Bet she started drinking before she even left home. Not surprising really. When this goes down, she's going to pay for what she did. I sort of admire her – in a way – it takes guts to kill your own brother. Right until the last minute I thought little Mita Patel would back down, but it seemed she'd been on the receiving end of her brother's cruel taunts and tricks too many times. I mean, what sort of brother sets up a recorder in his sister's bathroom and then uploads the clips to *Facebook*? Bet the Patels didn't tell Gus what a prick their son really was. It didn't take too much encouragement on my part to push her in that direction. Hell, even she thinks it was her idea.

Pisces is hanging onto Jo Jo's every word. Desperate to impress. Stupid cow can't even inhale properly. I lean over and prod her. 'Stop fucking coughing. You're going to get us caught.'

She looks at me like she's only just noticed I'm here. I lean in close. 'You got the knife. You know your job.'

Her eyes are wide, pupils dilated already. She shakes her head, and I pinch her arm. 'You have to. It's your rules.'

I sneak the knife out of my rucksack and slide it across the floor to her. She doesn't notice my glove. Nobody does.

I nod to Leo, giving her the sign, and she jumps to her feet, light as a feather. 'Let's play a game, guys. Hide and seek.'

Everyone moans. They all want to just chillax and get stoned and blasted. But it won't work then. I need to split them up. Need to direct them.

'Yeah, let's play.' I make a quick assessment and then speak. 'Karim, you're it…' and with a slight nod towards Jo Jo, I give Leo her instructions – Keep Jo Jo occupied.

Pisces is paler than ever, but she's got the knife in her hand, I can see it outlined through her pocket. She'll do as she's told. I grab Zarqa' and Pisces' hands and drag them to their feet, running down the steps and off towards the Mogul Gardens. 'Start counting, Karim.'

Behind me, Jo Jo and Leo head in the opposite direction towards the Botanical Gardens. I keep hold of Zarqa and Pisces, dragging them behind. Zarqa pulls against my grip but Pisces is compliant. 'Down to the fountains. Quick. He'll never find us there.'

We're nearly at the steps, just out of sight of Cartwright Hall CCTV when it happens. 'Police. Stop where you are.'

I hesitate, only for a second. Gus' voice, I'd recognise it anywhere. A quick glance at Zarqa tells me she's recognised it too.

I scream, 'Knife, knife. She's got a knife!' Pisces looks at me, glances around, and then looks down at her hand only then realising that it's her I'm yelling about.

Zarqa looks at her. 'Shit, not you? Surely not you?'

It's better than I could have imagined. I can hear footsteps running towards us and I push Zarqa. She falls sideways, stumbling for a moment before righting herself. I grab Pisces' arm and wrap it round me, positioning her hand with the knife at my throat. 'Help, help!'

Then Zarqa's on her feet and she's got her hands out in front of her. 'Take it easy, Claire. You don't have to do this. Let Mehmoona go!'

But Pisces can't let me go. I'm holding her arm tight to my neck. I press a little more, letting the knife nick me and the pain when it goes in feels good and as the blood trickles down my neck, I allow my voice to quiver. 'Help me, Zarqa. Make her stop.'

Zarqa's looking beyond my shoulder and I know Gus is there. 'She's got a knife. She's already drawn blood.'

'Okay, okay.' His voice is low, calming. 'Let's just slow down. Put the knife on the ground. Nice and easy.'

I can feel Pisces start to comply. And I can't let that happen. Zarqa takes a step closer and that seems to waken something in Pisces, and she tries to push me away, but I'm bigger than her. I twist her and propel her towards Zarqa, throwing myself on the ground. It's like it's happening in slow motion. Pisces, hand still raised, blade pointing right at Zarqa moves closer and at the same time, Zarqa's moving to meet her. I smile. It's going to happen. Right there in front of Gus, Pisces is going to stab Zarqa.

A few things happen at once then and it's a bit blurry. Thundering footsteps from behind me and a strangled. 'Nooooo, Zarqa!'

From nowhere, another figure dives towards Zarqa and all three of them are on the floor, blood spurting everywhere, and that bloody dog growling at me.

What an end game. I just hope Leo's doing her job!

CHAPTER 86

Shadowy shapes combined with unfamiliar night-time noises set Gus on edge. Mehmoona could be behind any of those trees and knowing how personal things had got meant that every rustle was a possible threat. Sticking to the darker areas, Gus made his way down the side of the tennis courts, his eyes darting from side to side, straining through the dark, looking for movement, his ears tuned to distinguish human sound against the inevitable animal activity. He jumped as a fox leapt out of one of the metal bins, dragging a fish and chip wrapper in its teeth and as it ran off, Gus took a moment to still his thudding heart and steady his breathing, before continuing with his search.

He reached the top of the hill past the bowling green before he heard the first indication of human activity; a low laugh, voices. *But is it her?* He paused, trying to decipher where the sound was coming from. The band stand or farther away? The quiet of the night made sound travel over a longer distance. He crept forward, peering ahead, willing himself to see human figures. But all he could see was the bandstand at the bottom of the slope. He scanned the surrounding area, shapes forming into trees and bushes as his eyes became accustomed to the environment.

As he listened, the voices ebbed and flowed in the night air, punctuated by the odd high-pitched giggle, low male rumblings, and the occasional yelp of a dog, still he wasn't sure where these sounds were coming from. *Was it beyond the bushes towards the boating lake?* He repeated the scan, forcing himself to hone in on the darker areas... no movement! Then, from the corner of his eye, he spotted a mass of activity accompanied by voices, louder now… excited. He jerked his head back. A group of amorphous figures stumbled down the steps of the bandstand. They must have been sitting down, out of view. Two of the figures ran towards the Botanical Gardens and Gus hoped Alice would hear them coming. The other three seemed to be heading towards the museum building. Gus ran soundlessly after them.

And as the moon slid from behind a cloud, he saw them clearly silhouetted at the top of the steps leading down to the Mogul Garden. *Zarqa! Mehmoona and another girl*! His heart hammered. There could only be one reason that they were gathered here in the park and, not bothering anymore to be stealthy, he ran after them, wishing he wasn't carrying the added weight of the stab vest.

'Police. Stop where you are!'

One of them yelled, 'Take it easy, Claire. You don't have to do this. Let Mehmoona go!'

Not Zarqa! Gus sped up and stopped abruptly. Claire had grabbed Mehmoona and had a knife at her neck. *Shit! Have I been wrong? It isn't Mehmoona*?

Mehmoona was in tears. 'Help me, Zarqa! Make her stop.'

Zarqa looked petrified, her eyes wide and staring straight at Gus, yet she took a step closer. 'She's got a knife. She's already drawn blood.'

There's nothing he could do. It was too risky, and he lowered his voice, schooled it to be calm, conversational, 'Okay, okay, let's just slow down. Put the knife on the ground. Nice and easy.'

Zarqa starts to move closer. *What the hell is she doing*? Claire threw Mehmoona to the ground and, knife pointing straight at Zarqa, she dived towards her, arm extended and there was blood everywhere.

'Nooooo, Zarqa!'

Gus lunged forward but before he could reach them, another figure dived into the chaos, pushing knife girl to the ground. A familiar dog pranced around the group, barking. *Trixie-Belle*?

Desperate to get to Zarqa, Gus dragged the boy off. The two girls lay on the concrete. Zarqa's hand still wrapped round both the other girl's and the knife shaft. The blade protruded from Claire's stomach.

Gus pressed two fingers to her neck and felt a pulse. He glared at Karim. 'Give me your T-shirt. Now! Somebody phone for an ambulance.'

Zarqa struggled to her feet, her face pale. 'We left our phones in the bandstand. That was the rule – No phones.'

Relieved that Zarqa was talking and brushing herself down, Gus wanted to gather her up and hug her, but he was too busy bundling up Karim's T-shirt and wrapping it around the knife. 'Press down on this.'

As he phoned for an ambulance, uniformed officers appeared, shining their torches on the scene. Trixie-Belle seemingly distraught by the activity, began yelping loudly. Karim, hands covered in blood, bare-chested, and smelling faintly of vodka, called the dog to him with a nervous glance at the officers. 'Shit! I'll be in trouble big time!'

Mehmoona jumped to her feet and ran over to Zarqa. 'Thank you. Thank you. Thank you. You saved my life.'

Gus studied the two girls for a moment. Zarqa shuddered and pulled away from the other girl. *Was she being too effusive*?

It was then that a scream rent the air. Alice! Gus jumped to his feet and started to run towards the Botanical Gardens, yelling over his shoulder. 'I need the injured girl accompanied to hospital and the others taken to The Fort. You two with me.'

Raised voices, yelling… *but where was it coming from*? Swinging his gaze from side to side, welcoming the torchlight of the two officers, Gus searched for movement. Then, another yell. This time from the near side of the boating lake. He increased his pace, running down the hill until he saw two figures standing behind one of the park benches with another two sitting on the bench. Closer now, Gus, by the torchlight, recognised both of the standing figures; Mita and Jo Jo! *What the hell! Mita*! And as he got closer, he recognised Jerry and Dave on the bench.

Mita had yanked Jerry's head back and now held a kitchen knife at his throat. *Not another fucking knife*! Jerry, eyes wide, mouth silently opening and shutting like a stranded fish, hands flailing by his sides, was choking, she was holding him so tightly. Dave, began to turn around but was stilled by her harsh, 'Stop right there or I'll do it. You know I will, you smelly old tramp.'

Close enough now, Gus could see that she'd nicked Jerry's neck. 'You don't need to do that, Mita.' He kept his voice low, almost intimate. 'You tell me how we can sort this out and I'll see what I can do.'

He glanced at Jo Jo, who stood slightly behind Mita. The lad's mouth was slack, his fists clenching and unclenching by his side. 'Step back, Jo Jo. You need to move away.'

Mita, eyes flashing, flung her head back and released a high-pitched laugh. Gus' heart sank. Whatever her plan was, negotiation didn't seem to be part of it. But negotiation wasn't necessary, for Dave without notice, flung himself to the side and was on his feet. Mita jerked towards him, the knife leaving Jerry's throat and that was all it took. Dave jumped towards her and with the heel of his palm whacked her under her chin, jerking her head backwards.

Screaming, her hands began to flay, until Jo Jo sprang to action and grabbed her from behind. Gus jumped forward, grabbed her wrist, and twisted until she dropped the knife.

Struggling and squealing, Mita fought as the officers cuffed her and as Gus wondered how the hell they were going to get to the bottom of all of this, Alice arrived from the opposite direction, panting. Gus shook his head. 'Good job I didn't need the cavalry.'

CHAPTER 87

Saturday
Leo

Still feeling a little bit stoned. Can't believe it went down like that... not really. Pigs weren't supposed to be there. Just as well, really. Pisces was getting on my nerves, moaning on all the time... was never sure if she'd be reliable or not... and she stinks. Can't stand that! Dying for a cig, but they've taken them.

The sofa is lumpy. S'pposed to be all child friendly, but in reality, it's hard and it smells a bit, like someone'd spilled milk on it or something. The walls are covered with photos of big bright animals, grinning at me... no, not grinning... leering. Bastards are taunting me, laughing at me for getting caught. Sooo tired, head's starting to hurt now too, voddie's made me dehydrated, and I need to sleep. Could do with a chokkie bar. I giggle. Got the munchies... Maltesers, that's what I fancy... or a Dairy Milk. Wonder if they still sell Creme Eggs. 'Can I have some water?'

The pig stares at me, one eyebrow raised... waiting for something else.

I sigh and smile sweetly, fluttering my lashes at her and say in an exaggerated tone, 'Puleeese.'

I wait until she hefts herself off her immense ass and add, '...and a Creme Egg.'

She looks at me like I'm something she's brought in on her shoe and ignores me. Snooty cow! I glare at her as she waddles to the door and says something to the guard outside. Hope it's my water she's asking for and my chocolate. When she turns around, the fat cow leans on the wall beside the door, arms folded under her boobs. What sort of police officer is she? Would like to see her trying to run after a suspect... Thud! Thud! Thud! The dinosaurs are coming! I giggle and stretch my legs out on the couch, resting my head on the arm. Head's really sore now... I close my eyes. And then...

'Ahem. Feet!'

Bitch! I ignore her. Keep my eyes shut. I hear her thumping over... Thump! Thump! Thump! Here come the dinosaurs again, still I keep my eyes shut. I can feel her peering over me, some manly perfume hanging in the air, making me feel sick.

'Feet.'

I want to open my eyes cause I'm feeling a bit giddy now, but I don't. 'Yeah, got two of them.'

She inhales, loud and rattley. 'Take. Them. Off. The. Couch.'

Oooh, Temper! Temper!

Before I have a chance to move, the door opens. *Thank God! Gasping for a drink*!

'Mita! Mita! What are they saying about you? Tell us they got it wrong.'

Crap, crap, and crap! Why did they have to bring her here?

I slide my legs round and look up at my mum. She's all hands fluttering and tears. Looks a mess. Bags under her eyes, stain on her sari. Her face is all scrunched.

I look up at her and smile, deliberately making it reassuring and soft.

Her face smooths over, relief flooding into her eyes and I blurt it out...

'Pratab was a knob and I killed him.'

A flutter of confusion flits over her face, she takes a step towards me, stops. Her hand drifts up and covers her mouth. 'Mita! Why would you say that? That's horrid.'

I stand up, move towards her, and bare my teeth in a snarl. 'Because it's true and I would've killed the dirty tramp too if I'd had the chance. Truth is, I'd like to kill you too.' And I lunge for her, but fatty's there, dragging me back, pinning my hands behind my back, yelling, 'Help!'

And as I strain against her grip, snarling and spitting at my mum, another officer storms in and drags my mum from the room.

I relax my body, stop fighting. 'Can I have my Creme Egg now?'

CHAPTER 88

It had been a long night and an equally long day. Five teenagers at The Fort, one teenager in the BRI, anxious parents, lawyers, a boss who had fallen to pieces and who had become a witness; and Gus was no further in making sense of things. The only thing he could be reasonably sure of was that there would be no more dead teens and no more macabre *Snapchats*.

Zarqa, Karim, and Jo Jo had provided straightforward accounts of the previous evening and then in the early hours of the morning, Gus had had to break the news to Jo Jo that his mother had died. Jo Jo had nodded once and looked down at the floor. Gus hadn't known what to do, but Alice spoke to Naila and between them they'd managed to get Jo Jo some breathing space, before any final decisions were made about his future and for now, at least until after his mum's funeral, he could stay with Mo and Naila. Mo had come clean to the Imam at the mosque and he was prepared to overlook the spray-painting incident, after a sizeable donation from Mo and with only circumstantial evidence linking Zarqa to the offence, no prosecution would be pursued.

The atmosphere was heavy. No one, by the looks of it, had slept well and the reality of the events of the previous night were still sinking in. Gus looked round at his team, which included DCI Nancy Chalmers and Sebastian Carlton. 'DCS Bashir has taken a leave of absence in the aftermath of last night's events. She has been cooperative and her statement, while illuminating in some respects, also casts doubts about the finer aspects of the killings. Compo has applied for a court order into the specifics of

Mehmoona Bashir's juvenile record, but in the meantime, DCS Bashir has furnished us with various facts.'

Gus cleared his throat. The interview by himself and Nancy of their superior officer was heart-rending. He respected the quiet dignity with which Bashir conducted herself throughout, while being incredulous that an experienced officer like herself could be so blind to the truth. He nodded at Taffy to write up the facts. 'Extrapolating from the interview – the full transcription is in the files – the details are as follows:

'Mehmoona, in Birmingham, was implicated in instigating a campaign of bullying by a group of her peers which resulted in one girl attempting suicide on three separate occasions and another girl succeeding. The group of girls who perpetrated the bullying all cited Mehmoona as the ringleader, however no direct evidence was found linking her to any of the actual bullying.'

Alice tutted. 'Hence the sealed juvie file.'

'Exactly.' Gus sighed. 'It seems DCS Bashir pulled in some favours on her daughter's behalf and relocated to Bradford. She believes that her marriage breakdown and the subsequent estrangement of Mehmoona from her father were contributing factors in the girl's behaviour.'

Compo spluttered and sent crisps flying across his desk. 'Loads of kids have bad experiences. They don't bully other kids to commit suicide and they don't progress to killing people.'

'That's true, but let's try to focus. This investigation is a minefield. We have hearsay, we have contradictory eyewitness statements and we have no proof of Mehmoona's guilt. She could get off with little more than a warning, unless we step up to the mark. So, Professor, what do you suggest?'

Blinking myopically at Gus, Carlton shrugged. 'For now, the same approach you'd use for any other investigation. You need to target the weakest link, exploit it, get all the information you can and then regroup to come up with a strategy to coax Mehmoona to confess.'

'Yeah, like that'll be easy.' Taffy's tone was despondent and Alice, who was sitting next to him, punched him on the arm. 'Don't be a wuss, Taff. We'll start with Claire. The doctors at the BRI say she's up to being interviewed. Then, if Mita hasn't lost all grasp on reality, we'll progress to her. We'll do this.'

Gus smiled. Alice's optimism was just what they needed right now. 'Okay, Taffy, you're with me at the hospital. Let's see what Claire Stevens has to say.'

CHAPTER 89

Claire Stevens' mum looked as pitiful as her daughter. Her acne-scarred face told Gus that Claire's complexion was an inherited condition. She was emaciated and seemed to not quite have grasped the seriousness of the accusations against her daughter. Gus sent the duty officer off for a break and chatted idly to the mother while they waited for the duty solicitor to appear. Moments later a young, fresh-faced woman with a wide smile and optimism oozing from every pore, breezed in, introducing herself as Claire's representative and saying her client was happy to cooperate.

Gus turned his attention to the young woman who was nearly as pale as the sheets on which she lay. Her wound had missed all major organs and she had said it was an accident. Zarqa, on the other hand, had claimed self-defence. Claire's lips quivered, and tears seeped from her eyes and ran down her face. Her mother periodically mopped them up. Gus suspected Claire was barely aware of them.

Despite the fact that he'd seen her holding the knife to Mehmoona's neck, Gus pitied the girl and had a hard job believing that she could have planned any of this. He gestured to Taffy to pull up a chair and set up the recording equipment. Introducing those present, Gus hoped he'd judged the weakest link correctly. 'Claire, can you tell me what happened last night?'

Claire glanced as if for reassurance, not to her mum, but to the solicitor who nodded. 'I didn't try to kill Mehmoona. She was the one holding my hand to her neck. She gave me the knife. She wanted me to kill Zarqa like I killed Betsy. I told her and Mita I wanted to stop. It were bad enough before when we weren't killing anyone, but then Billy sodding Clark-Tosser killed hisself. I wanted to stop, but they said no. Said they'd hurt me… hurt me mam.'

'Who killed Pratab, Claire?'

'That were Leo. I mean Mita. We all have code names. Mehmoona is Zodiac, Mita is Leo, and I'm Pisces. Mehmoona found a place we could have a headquarters. It was all a game… that's all it was supposed to be… a game.'

'Who was the leader?'

'Zodiac… Mehmoona. She made us do everything, though I think Mita liked it. She was happy to see Pratab dead.'

'How did you communicate? We have no evidence of the three of you being in contact.'

'Mehmoona gave us burner phones. We only used them to text or phone each other.'

That was more like it. Something concrete they could use. 'Where is your phone now?'

'Mehmoona made us chuck them all in the lake last night. Said she was destroying evidence.'

Shit! Wonder what the chances of retrieving info from waterlogged phones is? He turned to Taffy. 'Get the divers on it. We need those phones.'

Then Gus turned back to Claire. 'What sort of evidence was on the phones, Claire?'

The girl shrugged. 'Dunno, texts and stuff. Mehmoona recorded what we did to Pratab and Betsy. She recorded stuff in the headquarters too. She were always filming.'

'Why did you kill Betsy, Claire? You must have known that was wrong.'

Claire sniffed, her bottom lip quivering. 'I hated her. Betsy made everyone hate me because of my spots, because my mam's a druggie, because I smell… not my fault the house stinks. Didn't want to kill her though. Thought we'd just frighten her.'

Gus had his doubts about that. Mita had already killed Pratab, so no jury would believe Claire's claim that she didn't think she'd be expected to kill Betsy. He had no doubt she'd been bullied. No doubt she was heavily influenced by the other two, but at the end of the day, she *had* taken a life.

The doctor came in, frowned at Gus, and said, 'You need to wind this up. She needs to rest.'

'Just one more question then. Where is this headquarters of yours?'

The address she gave wasn't far from Lister Park. A series of small shops fallen into disrepair. No different form the sort of places he, Mo, and Greg had used as dens when they were young. Only difference was they weren't planning murders.

CHAPTER 90

Sipping a coffee in the observation suite, Gus reflected that that had been the easy bit. Straightening out the stories from the three girls would take a lot more work.

Sebastian Carlton walked in and pulled up a seat next to Gus. 'Ready?'

Gus was far from ready. He'd spent the last ten minutes wondering if this would work. Mehmoona was in the interview room with her solicitor and this was her second interview, the first had been led by Alice, and if they didn't break her soon, she could get away with everything. 'Just waiting for the others.'

And as if on cue, the door opened and in trooped the rest of the team and Nancy. Gus waited until they'd settled in front of the one-way mirror before nodding to Alice and Nancy. They'd agreed that, bearing in mind they had evidence linking Mehmoona to Gus' stalking, he should not be on the interview team and Carlton had suggested that two female officers might provoke her more as she seemed to enjoy the male attention.

When Alice and Nancy entered the interview room, Gus studied Mehmoona. *Why had she focussed her attention so firmly on him*? He barely remembered the few conversations he'd had with her. Yet, if Carlton was right, the girl sitting opposite Nancy and Alice, with her dip-dyed hair and insolent expression, was the ringleader. *How could someone so young be capable of manipulating her friends into killing*? As Alice completed the formalities and switched on audio and video recording, Gus could see that Carlton was equally focussed on Mehmoona. When the door opened, her head jerked up, immediately a smile on her face, eagerness written all over it. However, that faded when she saw Nancy and Alice and she slumped in her chair.

Carlton gripped Gus' arm. 'You see that? She's pissed off. Let's keep her that way, eh?'

Nancy, looking as different from Mehmoona's mother as it was possible to be, made a big show of smoothing down her floral dress and patting her hair. Her bracelets jangled as she rested her hands, loosely clasped, on the table. She looked like anyone's grandmother and that was exactly what Carlton had suggested, in order to subvert the girl's expectations at every turn.

Nancy sighed. 'Well, my dear. What sort of bother have you been getting yourself into?'

Beside her, Alice glowered and Mehmoona cast a quick glance between the two of them and a sly smile flitted across her lips. Gus relaxed a little. So far so good. She was falling for their trick.

Lip trembling a little, Mehmoona, looked down. 'This is all a huge mistake. I've not done anything wrong. Zarqa saw Claire attacking me. I don't understand why I'm still here.'

Alice snorted and rolled her eyes, but Nancy angled herself away from Alice and reached across the table, resting her hand on the girl's arm. 'We've had Zarqa's statement and we know you're an innocent party in all of this. Gosh, even Gus saw the girl attack you.'

Alice shuffled a bit in her chair and cleared her throat. 'With respect, DCI Chalmers, there is evidence that…'

Nancy turned towards Alice, straightened her shoulders, and stuck her chest out. 'Excuse *me*, DS Cooper. When I want your input on this, then I'll ask for it. Please don't interrupt again or I'll ask you to leave.'

Mehmoona's solicitor glanced between the two officers. 'I'd like a word with my client please, in private.'

Gus held his breath. This was the point when everything could go wrong. They relied on Mehmoona's narcissism to continue. The solicitor suspected what they were doing, but if his client refused to accept his advice there was nothing he could do.

Nancy rolled her eyes and shared a smile with the girl. 'Really?'

She made to stand up, but Mehmoona jumped in. 'We're fine here. I don't need you telling me what to do.'

'But…' The solicitor didn't get his sentence out before she cut him dead.

'Enough. You're being paid to do what I want, and I want *you* to shut up.'

Under his breath Carlton muttered, 'Classic narcissist.'

Blinking rapidly, the solicitor glanced from Nancy back to his client and then shrugged.

Nancy pulled her chair closer and, elbows on the table, chin resting on her steepled hands she nodded her approval. 'So, all this stuff with Gus… I get it. He's hot, isn't he? And it all got a bit out of hand. We might be able to make that go away. You just need to tell us all about the other stuff, you know, with Mita and Claire?'

Again, with the trembling lip. Nancy kept her smile in place and passed a tissue across the table.

'I was lonely. No friends.' She paused and blew her nose. 'Mum dragged me here, didn't let me see my dad. It was all too much. I thought it was all a game and then Mita started saying we should do stuff for real. I refused.' She looked right at Nancy, 'I should've told someone, but I was scared they'd kill me. That's what they said… that they'd kill me.'

Nancy smiled. 'Don't you worry yourself, dear. We already know that Mita and Claire are the ringleaders. You just got caught up in all.' She gave a little giggle that made Gus's estimation of her as an actress increase. 'There's no way a simple girl like you could've masterminded all this. No. It's quite clear to us… and she's confirmed it, Claire was the mastermind. All of it, Pratab Patel's death, Betsy Reavley's death, it was all her idea.'

Gus was on the edge of his chair. Mehmoona had gone completely still, a frown fluttered across her forehead, then her lips pursed. She glanced at her solicitor, drummed her fingers on the table. The atmosphere in the observation room was stagnant, waiting for the knife to fall whichever way it would. Carlton's leg was bouncing up and down, Gus' heart was hammering. *Bring it home, Nance, Bring it home!*

'A nice normal girl like you could never in a million years dream up such a plan…' Nancy patted Mehmoona's arm again. 'No, dear. This took brains and deviousness and daring to execute.'

Gus held his breath. Come on, come on, go for it!

The silence in the interview room went on for too long. Carlton's leg stopped thrumming, Gus' chest tightened, then… Mehmoona laughed a shrill high-pitched laugh not dissimilar to the one Mita had produced the previous night.

'Idiots. All of you, idiots. That fucking Claire couldn't plan a shag in a brothel. Course it wasn't her. It was me. I planned it all… I set them up…'

She jumped to her feet, her eyes wide, fists clenched and, as Alice and Nancy smiled at each other, she roared, 'Bitches!'

Gus collapsed onto his chair, exhaustion overtaking him while Carlton, Taffy, and Compo did a dance which involved a lot of high fives and whoops.

They'd rattled her… and the rest was easy as the whole story spewed out in all its sordid glory.

Liz Mistry

CHAPTER 91

Hissing Sid motioned Gus and Alice into the gang's headquarters. Both suited up, Gus stood by the entrance as Alice moved into the small room and turned in a complete circle. He wanted to absorb the entirety of this room where so much planning had been done. Once Mehmoona started to talk, she wouldn't shut up and by now Gus had a good sense of the three girls escaping here, getting drunk, smoking weed, and Mehmoona ultimately leading the other two on a destructive journey, culminating in the deaths of two teenagers and the destruction of their families.

Mildew hung in the air, heavy and oppressive, making the atmosphere even more cloying. Was it the stench of evil? It was the sort of smell he'd easily dismissed in the dens of his childhood with his friends. Now though, it clogged up his throat and made his eyes itch.

The space was full of contrasts. Brightly coloured cushions scattered on the floor. Small makeshift tables fashioned from old boxes with tealights on top, stood beside each cushion. A larger one in the centre was covered with a sheet of stained plywood and an empty bottle lay on its side in the middle, its neck pointing accusingly at Gus, making Gus remember the girls' description of the game they chose to select their victims. The floor was littered with cigarette stubs and spent spliffs, sweet wrappers, empty cans, bottles, and dirt. However, what was most interesting, were the walls.

Here Gus could track the girls' progress from malicious bullying, to the more sinister acts of character assassination. The list of names, the newspaper articles…

all of it spoke of organisation and planning. What had these girls been thinking? Carlton, after intense scrutiny and analysis of their interviews, suggested they each had their own distinct triggers and Mehmoona had developed the knack, even before her arrival in Bradford, of preying on her contemporaries' vulnerabilities. At great length she'd described how she saw each of the two girls, talking of them in disparaging ways. Gus of course had used this to drive a wedge between the girls to get to the truth.

They were all scheduled for in-depth psychiatric assessments and, with the amount of evidence, plus each girl's confession, Carlton had told him they would serve time in a juvenile detention centre, followed by psychiatric rehabilitation and, depending how they responded, they may be released with new identities in the future.

Gus took a last look round the room and had a desperate urge to escape the malevolence that seemed to seep from the walls. He was being fanciful, he knew, yet his skin prickled. His head buzzed and the laughter of three young girls plotting and planning various revenges against people who had slighted them, seemed to echo back at him. At what point had they decided to take the step to commit murder? To take the lives of those they sought revenge against? Had it all been, as Mehmoona insisted, a game led by her to prove that she was superior to the other girls? And if so, what had flipped in Mita's and Claire's brains to make them susceptible to this degree of violence?

Images retrieved from their dumped burner phones by Compo were damning. Three girls, drunk and egging each other on to commit murder and laughing and joking and taking selfies as they did so, was sickening. Gus pitied any jury that had to see that. He tried to balance the outpourings of support for Betsy and Pratab's families online, with the images of the murdered bodies that had gone viral and the filth that lay just under the surface of the

Internet. They kept popping up, despite Compo and the IT specialists' attempts to block them and what was more disheartening, were the sheer number of views and shares they gained. Were there really so many sick, heartless people out there who took gratification from the snuffing out of a human life? What sort of society was this if dead kids were amusement fodder?

Pratab's mum, in particular, had taken great comfort from the online support. Yet, Pratab himself hadn't been completely innocent. Comps had found an image that Pratab had posted outing Jo Jo and there were others; bullying texts, malicious *Facebook* posts, cruel *Instagrams*, all among normal, jolly everyday posts. Mr Patel had been admitted to Lynfield Mount hospital when the enormity of nearly losing one son, losing the other, and then discovering that his daughter had been the one to kill him, prompted him to attempt suicide. Betsy Reavley's mum was a wreck and was drowning her grief in alcohol combined with pills. Gus suspected it wouldn't be too long before she would join her daughter.

Then there was Jo Jo's abuse. *Poor kid*! Not only were there images of him all over the Dark Web, but he'd lost his entire family, his home… his innocence. They'd found a hidden camera in Jo Jo's room and initially, Jo Jo blamed Razor McCarthy for that, saying he'd had access to his room. In interview though, Mehmoona had admitted to planting it, after finding out Jo Jo was a drone expert through some of his *Facebook* posts. The delight on her face when she'd described breaking into Jo Jo's home, looking down at his mother as she slept, stealing one of Jessie's beloved stuffed animals, before finally finding the key and breaking into his room was creepy. It was as if she expected to be congratulated on her ingenuity. Her plan had been to steal a drone, but when she'd seen Jo Jo's equipment, she formulated another plan.

Her glee, when she described the things she saw Jo Jo doing, had made Gus want to vomit. He still didn't know how Nancy and Alice had sat through those interviews so calmly. But when they came out, they seemed to shrink, their control during questioning stripped right back the moment they left the room. Gus had applied for mental health support for both of them. No way was he allowing either of them to internalise any of this. Mehmoona Bashir's warped mind was baggage they didn't need to carry. Later, he, Carlton, Alice, and Nancy had got very drunk and although it didn't make them forget, it at least gave them a temporary reprieve from exposure to the malevolence of Mehmoona's twisted mind. Unfortunately, catching evil didn't make it go away.

Gus and Compo had taken to talking about the unseen evil of social media... the persuasive and abusive stuff that was unmonitorable and the sick minds that exploited that weakness. Compo admitted he had an online friendship group which kept him sane when he was investigating this sort of shit and Gus was glad the lad had that support system. The more he found out, the more Gus wanted to punch walls. If he could crawl into the Dark Web and physically catch these child abusers, he wouldn't be able to hold himself back. Gus' anger was ever present; roiling and snarling inside him, making him jumpy and snappy at everyone. He jogged every spare moment he had now, trying to banish the tension, trying to evict the tightness in his chest that had taken up permanent residence. Nothing worked. He was a stick of dynamite just waiting to explode.

Compo was working to pinpoint the john who'd lured Jo Jo in, but he reckoned that the most they'd be able to do, would be some 'under the radar' fishing to hit the bastard where it hurt... his wallet. Gus was happy to turn a blind eye to that if Compo and his online friends were able to make this pervert's bank accounts inaccessible. It wasn't a solution though... just a temporary band-aid... but it would have to do... for now.

Alongside all of that, the violation of his own and Patti's privacy was making him a little paranoid. He'd seen how quickly the images of himself and Patti had gone viral and it made him wonder how they could ever stop the flow of unseen evil now that the world had become so small. He'd got Compo to reinforce his home PC security, had deleted all his own social media accounts, not that he actively used any except *WhatsApp*. However, it was Patti who was suffering the most in the aftermath of the posts of their sex life going viral. The media was on her case the whole time. Jez Hopkins had had the audacity to ask for an exclusive interview for his rag. *Little creep*! Her position at the school was becoming more and more untenable. Initially they'd thought the story would all die down, but when news of the arrests had hit the press, it had been resurrected. She was blanking him, and Gus could understand it. As ever, he, the male, was getting off lightly and she was on the receiving end.

Only a few days ago he'd been thinking of the 'L' word, now he thought their relationship could be better described by the phrase 'it's over, don't contact me.' He wasn't even sure how he felt about that. Too many other things to think about and therein lay one of the problems; as much as he cared about Patti, maybe even loved her... it just wasn't enough to make him prioritise their relationship.

Overwhelmed by everything the room symbolised, Gus walked out into the heat, stepped out of his overalls and yelled, 'See you back at The Fort, Al.'

Then he was off, jogging as fast as he could, hoping that he'd be able to exorcise some of the demons chasing him, but knowing that no matter how many runs he did, the demons would catch-up with him at night.

EPILOGUE

Six weeks later

Gus looked at the screen and smiled. Carlton hadn't bothered to dress up for the occasion. His specs were held together by masking tape and his yellow T-shirt vied with the *BBC News* studio lighting for dominance.

…and today we have Professor Sebastian Carlton from the Forensic Psychology Department at Leeds Trinity University. Professor Carlton has worked with the FBI's behavioural analysis department and more recently was a consultant on Bradford's The Snapchat Killers case.

Professor Carlton, isn't it unheard of for three girls to work together to perpetrate the acts of murder we witnessed earlier in the month? Could you give us some insight into these unnamed girls' psyches?

… what interests me most about this case is the dynamic between the three girls. The alpha teen is a fascinating study. She exerted an unparalleled influence over the other two. However, what I found particularly interesting is that the Beta teen absorbed some of the Alpha's qualities… her desire to dominate… to lead… to be in control. This is…

Gus switched the TV off and grabbed Bingo's lead. 'Come on, boy. Let's go see Zarqa and Jo Jo.'

Bum wriggling in excitement, Bingo's tongue lolled from his mouth and he emitted a round of overexcited yelps. Gus ruffled his head. 'You love playing with Mo's kids don't you, Bingo? And your mate will be there too.

Karim's bringing Trixie-Belle, someone for you to play with.'

Gus called the trio *The Survivors Gang*. They'd been through a lot, Jo Jo and Zarqa more than Karim. Jo Jo was still grieving, but Naila had worked wonders and got him and Jessie a foster home together. Jo Jo was a regular visitor with Zarqa at Gus' house, and he had a good feeling about Jo Jo's future. Taffy had been there for him during his mum's death and since then he'd spent long hours discussing all things techie with Compo. All of it did the officers as much good as it did Jo Jo.

It was Karim who lifted them out of the darkness when they thought too much about everything that had gone down. Karim, whose humour and sensitivity forced them to engage with life. Even Mo was all right with the lad dating Zarqa... how could he not be? Karim had done exactly what Mo himself had done at around the same age; put his own life at risk to save the girl he loved.

It pleased Gus to see Mo and Zarqa interacting again. Mo was beginning to lose that haunted look and although they still had some sticky moments, the future for Mo's family looked a lot better. Naila and Gus had smoothed over their differences too, although she'd made him promise to talk about his 'trust' issues with his psychiatrist and, over the weeks she'd held him to his promise to do just that. To the point as ever, Naila had told him, 'You can't keep erecting these barriers or you'll end up a lonely old man.'

That was a direct reference to the demise of his relationship with Patti. Unable to take the ongoing media circus and the endless snide comments from students, not to mention some less than supportive emails sent by parents who questioned her authority now their Jane, Jaffer, or Jasdeep had seen her boobs, Patti had resigned from her post at the school and decided to travel to Jamaica to reconnect with her mother's side of the family. Their parting had been amicable, yet neither of them felt able to consider the possibility of a future together. In his less depressed moments, Gus was able to accept that if they couldn't withstand the first real crisis they faced as a couple, then they probably wouldn't have been able to hack it long-term.

In the dead of night though, when neither he nor Alice could sleep, he admitted that he questioned his ability to connect with people, to commit himself fully. In many ways that was exactly the point Naila and Compo had made; he was damaged. He knew it all stemmed from killing Greg. That was when the blanket of despondency had first descended and the time he stopped trusting or believing in himself. He'd thought Patti would be the one to help him exorcise that once and for all, but he'd been mistaken.

The single bonus from all of this was that he and Alice had grown even closer. They'd both learned the hard way that evil wasn't always right there in your face, that it was a shapeshifter with no set form; malignant and remorseless. Alice living with him was his salvation and, he suspected, it was hers too. She'd put her house in Saltaire on the market saying it held too much negative energy and Gus was in no hurry to evict her, for despite their pain, Alice brought life to the house.

With Bingo dancing at his feet, Gus yelled up the stairs to his lodger. 'Come on, Al, or we'll be late.'

As he waited for Alice to appear, his phone rang. *Katie*!

Why couldn't she just leave him be for a while? Typical Katie, wanted everything her own way, right there and then. He dismissed the call, which was almost immediately followed up by a text:

> Katie: You're not being fair keeping us hanging on like this, Gus. You need to let us know your decision!

Fair? Fair? Nothing that had happened in the last month was fair.

Filled with the desire to run out of the house and throw the phone into the boating lake so he never had to hear from his sister again, Gus' chest tightened. Then, inhaling slowly, he counted to ten, before walking through to the kitchen where, with controlled deliberation, he placed his phone on the kitchen table. For a while he wasn't going to engage with anyone other than his friends. He'd make his decision when he was good and ready, and Katie and Gaby could like it or lump it. He was fed up with being expected to do what everyone else wanted. For once, he was going to be sure that whatever he decided, it was right for him.

Seconds later, Alice bounced down the stairs, thrust her arm through Gus' and together they walked to the park, Alice's good-natured chatter a contrast to the tears he'd heard from her room the previous night. *Two broken souls together, that's what we are.*

Halfway round the boating lake, a frantic, 'Gus, Alice' boomed from their right. Glancing round, Gus saw Mo and three of his daughters in one of the pedaloes with Naila, Jo Jo, Zarqa, and Sabah in another. They appeared to be having some sort of race with Karim who was running along the edge of the lake with Trixie-Belle beside him. Bingo began straining at his lead when he saw his friend.

'DI McGuire, DI McGuire.' Karim skidded to a halt in front of them. 'Got some news for you. Mrs Brown's moving into sheltered housing and they don't allow pets, so I'm getting to keep Trixie-Belle. That's great innit?'

The lad's beaming face made Gus smile. Maybe they could bottle Karim and prescribe him on the NHS. The lad was a real tonic. He reminded Gus of Mo. 'Great news, Karim, but remember you can call me Gus, you know.'

The two dogs fussed and sniffed each other, and Karim tugged on Trixie-Belle's lead. 'Aw shi... I mean, yeah. Forgot like. Gus it is.'

'Talking of names. What you gonna do about her name?' Gus inclined his head towards the Rottweiler with the unlikely name.

Karim grinned. 'Got that sorted. Gonna call her TB, you get it?' He raised his hand for a fist bump and Gus obliged.

'Great choice.' He turned and yelled to the kids on the boats. 'Ice cream?'

Judging by the excited yells, that would be a yes.

This was one of those times he needed to savour. So, Gus allowed the happiness to wash over him like a balm and tried to enjoy the moment. After all, he knew only too well how short-lived it could be.

ACKNOWLEDGEMENTS

Unseen Evil is the novel I've written as part of my PhD in Creative Writing at Leeds Trinity University and, as such, has had many incarnations. Leeds Trinity University has given me the confidence and space to realise my dream: that of being a writer. In particular the support, encouragement and critical engagement of my PhD tutors Oz Hardwick and Martyn Bedford has been invaluable, so a huge shout out to them. Alongside that, my PhD colleagues are a constant source of knowledge, advice, laughter, and support. Thanks guys!

I have been lucky to have benefitted from the tireless advice that Toria Forsyth-Moser brings to my first draft. She challenges me to better my writing and I think she knows my characters nearly as well as I do. Huge thanks to my editor, Emma Mitchell, from Creating Perfection. She has been professional and efficient, and I am so glad she gets my Bradford setting and characters.

Betsy Reavley won the MIND charity raffle She requested a particularly brutal demise – don't know if I managed that, but a huge thanks for both your donation and lending me your name. The cover design is down to CherieFox.com – many thanks.

As ever any mistakes are my own and some artistic license has been used also.

I dedicated this book to my family because they are the best. They catch me when I'm down and support me when I'm up. I probably don't say this enough, but I wouldn't be able to do this without their support, particularly Nilesh who knows how hard I struggle with the 'events' side of things and so accompanies me to many of them.

Thanks, also to my ARC group, who are so supportive they often have me in tears –sometimes of joy, sometimes of laughter, but always of happiness. You are brilliant.

Last of all, but definitely not least, a heartfelt thanks to all you readers and bloggers who have got behind Gus and the gang and who have so generously left reviews, tweeted, shared and liked posts about Gus and Co. You are amazing… truly amazing!

If you liked *Unseen Evil,* I'd love it if you could leave a review. Reviews are an author's lifeblood and I read every one (even the bad ones).

Here's till next time
Best Wishes

Liz Mistry

If you want to connect with Liz, you can do so on:

Twitter: @LizMistryAuthor
Facebook: LizMistryBooks
Amazon: https://amzn.to/2xhdOgG
Website : https://www.lizmistry.com/

Made in the USA
Coppell, TX
01 December 2020